Bloodstock was a labor of love, and, in some ways, a family history. My DNA says I hail from the Hungarian/Romanian part of the world. Family anecdotes say one of my ancestors raised horses for the Hungarian Army. The vampire part could be the fact I did have fangs, subsequently removed by enduring several years of braces.

For those of you who are wine connoisseurs, Egri Bikaver, or Bull's Blood, is a red wine so dark it's almost black. It is Hungary's national wine, and comes from one of the oldest vineyards in the world. As Prince Rackoszi would tell you, it packs a considerable wallop, so refrain from guzzling, and enjoy reading about the most unusual Viceroy of Transylvania.

Tricked into giving his word by a dishonorable man's maneuvering, Prince Szigismond Emre Janos Rackoszi, Viceroy of Transylvania, is honor-bound to marry a woman he doesn't love. He's also required to gather to the bosom of his family the man's widow, and mother of his intended, who despises him. The silly creature believes he's a revenant, a vampire bent on making her daughter one as well, and she vows to see him staked and in his grave before she gives her daughter to him. But the prince isn't soulless or undead, nor does he drain humans of blood. No, Prince Szigismond Emre Janos Rackoszi is a very different creature altogether.

As he paces the corridors of his dark castle, awaiting the arrival of the artist hired to paint miniatures of himself and his bride-to-be, he prays to the ancient gods to help him figure a way to break his promise without losing his honor.

Bloodstock

Copyright 2020 by C.L. Hadyn

ISBN: 978-1-68361-406-7

Print ISBN: 978-1-68361-452-4

Cover art by Fantasia Frog Designs

Published by Decadent Publishing Company, LLC

Look for us online at:

www.decadentpublishing.com

Dedication

To Beatrix Elizabeth Early: This one's for you, *kincsem*.

Also by C.L. Hadyn

Off Track

The Danegeld

Guarded Hearts

Bloodstock

By
C. L. Hadyn

Chapter One

Akos, Prince Rackoszi's valet, shuddered in his bed when awakened by a wolf's anguished howl. He didn't bother lighting a candle but dressed in the dark in his hurry to render what assistance he could, because no other being, man or wolf, would answer the lament of a wolf with no pack of his own to offer sympathy or support.

His steps dragged as he climbed from his room below the stairs to the prince's suite, not from tiredness but more from distress over the need to offer consolation to a proud man. The news of Baron Szechenyi's suicide this afternoon spread through the staff faster than a plague, and he and everyone who served the prince understood their master had no recourse but to accept the duty the suicide thrust upon him. Keeping the pledge made to Baron Szechenyi would change the order of things in the prince's domain, and not for the better.

The valet stopped before the closed door of the royal bedroom and crossed himself. He hoped his hasty prayer would be interpreted by the ancient ones as one seeking assistance solely for Prince Rackoszi and not as a selfish appeal to preserve the lives of everyone else who called this dark castle home.

***

Viscount Horthy opened the first letter by mistake. He had assumed it to be another commission for his services as a painter of miniatures and hadn't read the front of the vellum envelope. As he discovered, the commission was for his daughter, Beatrix.

Fatherly pride in Bibi's accomplishments, and a surge of relief, washed over him as he read the response to his reply of the letter he received over a month ago. It confirmed his belief this was an excellent chance for Beatrix to resume her life amidst the quick. Married and widowed on the same day made his formerly cheerful, inquisitive, self-assured daughter vanish into the sequestered gloom of mourning. Well, today the somber-hued dresses, and abstinence from anything smacking of frivolity or joy, was over. He wanted his daughter back, even if it meant sending her to Transylvania to paint portraits for a prince.

Too excited to keep the news to himself a moment longer, Viscount Horthy mounted his horse and rode to the practice field to find his daughter. As part owner of the Horthy horse concern, the viscount comprehended any interruption of the maneuver in progress would not be well received, so he resigned himself to be patient and observe quietly as riders formed themselves into a cavalry wedge. It was a final test of the Horthy-trained mounts to determine how well suited they would be for serving in the Emperor's cavalry.

With a surge of anticipation, he watched as the formation of horsemen moved fluidly from a trot to a canter. Although too far away to hear the command clearly, he saw sabers drawn from scabbards and the flash of sunlight on the steel of

2

their blades. He had to rein in his own horse, who pawed the ground in demonstration of its wish to join the action.

He held his breath as, in one synchronous motion, the entire formation galloped forward to close with an imaginary enemy. The only way he could distinguish his daughter from the rest of the *Csikos*, the Hungarian cowboys who broke and trained the horses, was by her unusually large, charcoal-gray gelding, and the fact she was the point of the wedge. He waited until his daughter slowed the formation to a cool-down walk before he spurred his horse toward them.

As he approached Beatrix, he waved the letter in his hand and immediately wanted to recall the action when her horse shied violently. He waited until his daughter brought the gray under control to apologize. "I am sorry, my dear, I should know better than to wave things around."

"No apology needed, Father, but do hold out whatever it is so I can show Shadow he's being a silly boy to be frightened of such a harmless thing."

His daughter dismounted with the grace of long practice and led the gelding, whose eyes were rolling, toward the letter. Despite his dancing and obvious reluctance to approach, Shadow was firmly guided close enough to nuzzle the paper and put his lips on it.

"See, you silly goose, it won't hurt you," she crooned as she patted Shadow's neck and spoke nonsense to calm him.

"What brings you to the practice field, Father?"

"I wanted to surprise you with this news, but I got tired of waiting for you to come back to the house. You have a commission, and this one for a prince."

"But, Father, you know I'm still—"

"No, you are not still in mourning. As of today, your year of mourning is over and you will stop sequestering yourself on the farm. And before you try to dismiss the prince's request, I will confess to accepting the commission on your behalf. You'll leave next week with your uncle Andris. He'll be delivering the latest batch of trained horses to the Hungarian Army's remount depot, and the prince's domain is relatively near."

His daughter's deep frown broadcast the fact she was unhappy with his acceptance of the offer.

"Why would this prince want my services? You are the artist, not me. I'm merely your assistant, Father."

Viscount Horthy laughed at the disclaimer. "You are no longer a mere assistant. Quite honestly, your talent surpasses mine with the technique you learned while studying in Russia. The prince admired the miniature you did for Countess Krisztina and specifically requested you."

"And this prince wants me to paint his miniature?"

"He wants you to paint two miniatures. One of himself, and one of a woman he is interested in. They will be the first token exchange for what, I presume, might lead to a marriage proposal."

With flattened lips, Bibi huffed, "I hope he knows I paint true likenesses. I won't make either the prince or his intended more pleasing to the eye, even at the risk of losing the commission."

The viscount smiled at her determination to find a reason to decline the offer. "I so informed him, and he wrote back and agreed to true representations in the portraits."

He waited for her reply and was surprised when he didn't receive one. His daughter simply vaulted back into the saddle, and turned Shadow toward the barn for a well-deserved rubdown.

Her ramrod posture and the absence of a warm smile left him with a familiar sadness and guilt for what had befallen his sole offspring. It was he who'd pushed for the marriage to her childhood friend. Had he not done so, she might still be the carefree girl he gave away at the altar. But only a true gypsy *dukerin* could've foreseen the bloodbath her wedding night turned into. He shivered at the memory of how closely he'd come to losing Beatrix. She refused to speak of it, and he refused to force her to relive such a horrific event in the telling. As a father, he sensed his daughter was still not free of the burden, despite her attempts to mask her sadness with vigorous activity.

Viscount Horthy gave himself a moment to recall how his daughter used her mourning period to involve herself in her deceased husband's failing horse-breeding farm. And though restricted by what was proper behavior for a widow, his clever offspring managed to make the Baranyi stables profitable by merging it with their own.

The viscount sighed softly at the thought it was probably his daughter's business acumen, and her talent with the four-legged creatures, that convinced the haughty mother of Baron Baranyi to champion her son's offer of marriage in the first place. The old baroness possessed a keen eye for good bloodlines, and perceived the decline of the Baranyi line due to her son's lack of interest in anything but partying. She wanted Beatrix Horthy to give her strong grandchildren to ensure the continuation of the Baranyi line.

Straightening his shoulders for the oncoming battle to overcome his daughter's objections, the viscount resolved to remain firm in his conviction this commission was an excellent opportunity for her to begin a new life. The prince's offer would reintroduce her to a world outside the great plains of Hungary, and, hopefully, give her an interest in things other than breeding and training cavalry horses for the Hungarian Army. Indeed, every parental fiber in his body realized the time had come for his daughter, Beatrix Celine Baranyi, *nee* Horthy, to concentrate on people instead of horses.

***

With a final clap on the back, Andris sealed the contract, and the Army bursar handed over the payment for the horses. Her uncle's broad grin told Bibi the exchange added an impressive amount to the Horthy-Baranyi coffers. It was a matter of family pride no one delivered better horse flesh, or better horses broken to saddle, than those of the conjoined farms, and the owners demanded to be paid accordingly.

The idea she might, with her share of today's profits, use a small amount for personal enjoyment, entered her mind. Perhaps, after she completed the commission her father accepted for her, she'd travel to Paris to study new painting techniques, or she could cast caution to the wind and take a world tour to visit the Seven Wonders, but one glance at her well-worn riding boots chagrined her. No, she needed to spend the first monies on her wardrobe. She couldn't travel to the capitals of the world dressed as a *Csiko*. However, the black memory returned and quashed her anticipation before she fleshed out a travel itinerary.

She wouldn't be traveling in style throughout Europe because she was a fraud, an imposter. She didn't deserve the attention a new wardrobe or attendance at a painting school would garner her.

"Why are you frowning, Niece? We've made a tidy profit this day."

Inventing a hurried excuse, she answered, "Ah, just thinking ahead and wondering what the prince who hired me will be like." Her uncle's familiar booming laugh lifted her spirits.

"There's no need to guess, my darling Bibi. For all he's a prince, he'll eat, drink, and make love the same as the rest of us men do."

She hoped her uncle spoke true. After the horror of her wedding night, she needed Prince Szigismond Rackoszi to be nothing more than a normal man.

Chapter Two

Bibi wryly surmised her little band of *Csikos* was probably as tired as she was from wrangling horses to the remount depot and eating unrelieved goulash for a week as they traveled on to the prince's domain. But as the hot, dusty plains gave way to the fresh scent of pine, and the deep shade of mountain forests, she perked up. Not one to announce any weakness, she kept her desire for a bath, a featherbed, and a decent meal served in courses rather than an iron pot, to herself.

As they rode down a broad avenue lined by ancient oak trees, the only sounds they made were the clop of hooves and the snores coming from Bernat, her uncle's herd dog. With no horses to herd, Bernat sat next to her uncle in the wagon and caught up on his sleep.

Noting how much space still remained on either side of their small formation, she called out to the rest of the *Csikos* they could easily fit a troop of hussars on the avenue and still have room to maneuver.

Honest to a fault, she admitted to cracking jokes to cover her nervousness after she'd caught a brief glimpse of the castle through a gap in the oaks. For the construction loomed like a nightmare, with its towers, crenellations, and deep, water-filled moat. It lacked for nothing in the way of Transylvanian castle accoutrements, including an appearance of being dark and forbidding in broad daylight. As any such nightmare would, it raised the hair at the back of her neck. Even the *Csikos'* loud joking and ribald comments diminished the closer they got.

Although the ride through the mountains and shady forests was a pleasant change from the flat plains of the horse farms, she was not altogether sure she wanted to be so isolated from family.

Able to judge her moods as well as her father, her uncle Andris gave voice to reassure her. "Say the word, and we'll leave before anyone knows we've been here."

Though grateful for the offer of rescue, she squared her shoulders and dismounted from Shadow. "Thank you, but no. We're Horthys, and no mammoth pile of stones can scare us." Before her bravado deserted her, she stepped forward and lifted the huge wolf's-head knocker on the oversized door and slammed it down with a satisfying thump.

She resisted the impulse to jump back when the door swung open, having expected it to take some time for anyone to answer her summons. She also hadn't expected to encounter such a diminutive woman. Lowering her eyes to the approximate level of her own waist, she started to introduce herself.

The servant rudely held up a hand to forestall further speech. "Cowboys? Why are you knocking at the front entrance? Go around to the stables and speak to the stable master if you have horse issues. If you are seeking work, there isn't any at present, but some sustenance will be provided you before you leave."

Bernat's bark cut off further instruction by the ill-mannered servant, and Bibi couldn't fault him for taking offense at the woman's harsh voice.

As she leaned to the side to observe who was behind the castle's unexpected caller, the diminutive gate-keeper gasped when she spotted Bernat for the first time and immediately tried to shut the door, but she couldn't out muscle a Horthy, and the door remained open.

"Why are you traveling with a bear? If it isn't chained, please do so immediately."

Andris defended his faithful companion. "Bernat isn't a bear. He's a *Puli*, a herding dog. But he can be as ferocious as a bear when he's defending our horses and foals against wolves."

The mention of wolves increased the servant's agitation, and she made shooing motions. "Leave. Go around to the stables and state your business."

Offended by such rudeness, Beatrix Baranyi narrowed her eyes and repaid the servant's brusqueness by using the same tone of voice. "I'm the artist the prince commissioned to paint his miniature, and my uncle accompanied me to see me safely here."

"Yes, the prince mentioned he'd engaged someone. Please go around to the kitchen entrance and wait there until a room is arranged for you."

The *Csikos*, familiar with the Horthy response to being treated in such a manner, backed their mounts away.

Bibi, fists clenched at the servant's uncouth reaction to her introduction, turned brusquely away and called, "Uncle Andris, please deliver my trunk to the kitchen entrance."

Bloodstock

Without waiting for her uncle to reply to the request, she picked the tiny servant up by the waist and carried her into the castle.

As her spurred boot kicked the heavy door closed, she issued instructions of her own. "Whoever you are, madame, you will inform Prince Rackoszi, Baroness Baranyi has arrived."

Chapter Three

The instant he awoke, the scent stunned him. Tuber rose, musk, and...horse? If the previous two fragrances had been sweat and leather, he'd bet the stable master was flirting, yet again, with the cook in the kitchen. He remained silent when his valet slipped quietly into the bedroom and opened the heavy drapes around the bed.

"The painter has arrived, Your Grace." Akos proffered the prince's usual breakfast beverage and continued, "Erzsebet assigned her the green bedroom in the south wing."

With raised eyebrows, Prince Rackoszi inquired of his valet, "Green bedroom, south wing? Erzsebet does not approve of the painter?"

"I think the sentiment may be mutual, Your Grace."

"Really? What contretemps could have occurred so soon?"

"The, er, baroness arrived accompanied by *Csikos*, and Erzsebet assumed they were all seeking work in the stables, so she refused the main entrance."

"Surely Erzsebet can tell a baroness from a cowboy," the prince scoffed. He plumped his pillows behind his back, eager to learn the rest of the story.

"No, Your Grace, not when the baroness herself was also dressed as one. In all fairness, the baroness did not immediately reveal her status until Erzsebet refused her *entre'*."

The unusual sound of his valet's mirth startled him. "And how much outraged shrieking occurred after she did so, Akos?"

"None, Your Grace. The baroness simply lifted Erzsebet off her feet and carried her inside then kicked the door shut behind herself. I think, for once, Erzsebet was incapable of speech."

"By the ancient gods, I would've enjoyed witnessing such a scene. The baroness sounds like a veritable Valkyrie."

"Indeed, sir, strong and tall, and most unusual. She insisted on grooming her horse herself before settling into her room. The stable master was quite taken with her knowledge of horses."

"Well then, I best complete my ablutions and arrange to meet the baroness. Come, Akos, choose something for me to wear. Oh, and tell Cook I'll be joining the baroness for dinner so she's to prepare something interesting to the palate."

The valet froze in mid-reach for the empty goblet. "You..." A distinct croak came from Akos's throat as he continued, "You'll be joining the baroness for dinner?"

Flinging the linens away, Prince Szigismond Emre Janos Rackoszi, prepared to meet the day with unaccustomed eagerness. "Yes, I will. I think my appetite is returning. Perhaps some fruit to tide me until dinner, what do you think, Akos?"

The valet snapped to attention when a royal finger closed his gaping mouth. "At once, Your Grace. I'll have a maid bring you an assortment after I draw your bath."

***

The dusty ride to the prince's castle, the argument with the small dragon masquerading as a housekeeper, and seeing to Shadow's stabling, equated to a very wearying day. Bibi stretched the kinks from her body in anticipation of a soothing soak in the bathtub she insisted be sent to her room.

She frowned in displeasure at her assigned accommodations. They smacked of a set down. The window was small, the furnishings spare, and the bed, by the sight of it, lumpy. But damn if she would complain and give the housekeeper, who'd grudgingly introduced herself as Erzsebet, the satisfaction of knowing she was discommoded.

An unexpected knock on the door made her falter and slosh water on the floor as she hastily aborted her climb into the fragrant water. Before she could so much as think the word, *enter,* the door flew open and the housekeeper stood in a halo of light from the hallway.

Annoyed to be found in such a state of undress, she robed herself and bit back her temper before saying, "I don't believe I gave permission to enter."

"Your pardon, Baroness, the viceroy requests your presence at dinner this evening."

"This evening? But it is already past eight o'clock. I was about to bathe and retire for the night."

"The viceroy keeps his own hours. It is most unusual for him to invite anyone to dine with him, as he usually prefers to dine alone. I would not disappoint him. I've taken the liberty of assigning a maid to help you dress. Did someone, a maid, perhaps, pack suitable attire for you?"

Ah, here was the crux of the matter. She eschewed the services of a maid at home and had no idea what her aunt Margareta had packed for her; therefore, she had no idea what items of clothing her aunt had chosen for her to wear. The contents of the wardrobe were bound to be dismal because, for the last year, her wardrobe had consisted of nothing but black mourning dresses or *Csiko* boots and trousers. Well, if fusty black dresses were all she had, they would have to do. To say the least, it would be in keeping with the dark atmosphere of the prince's castle.

She squared her shoulders and used the crisp diction befitting a baroness to reply, "Yes, of course. I thank you for the offer of a maid to assist me." It was a small victory to observe her cordial thank you appeared to fluster Erzsebet.

"The prince dines at ten. I'll send the maid to you in an hour. Do you require anything else?"

"Yes, a glass of wine to sip while I relax in the tub."

The housekeeper gave a grudging nod. "I'll send it to you. Enjoy your bath."

Bibi dipped her finger into her bath water before climbing in to gage whether or not Erzsebet's frost-rimed farewell hadn't cooled it.

The surprisingly excellent wine and hot bath did wonders for her fatigue and aching muscles, and welcoming the return of her energy, Beatrix Baranyi bade the maid enter one hour later.

"Good evening, Baroness. My name is Cata, and I'm to be your dresser this evening. Do you have a preference in

16

gowns?"

She gave a mental slap to her forehead for forgetting to check on the state of her wardrobe. Still unwilling to face what was sure to be a disappointing selection, she answered the eager maid. "Why don't you choose? I'm not sure what dresses were packed for me."

Expecting a sigh of dismay over the shabby state of her apparel, she goggled in surprise when the maid called out in admiration after opening the massive armoire doors.

"Oooh, my lady, such wonderful gowns."

The multitude of jewel-hued dresses hanging neatly in the armoire lent considerable color to the dreary room. Her aunt had packed the unworn dresses of her bridal trousseau. The very sight of the dresses she'd selected before her marriage made her dread dining with the viceroy. After the trauma of her wedding night, she never wanted to wear a single item of the designer clothes she purchased in Paris. Indeed, she explicitly ordered them burned, but her father, who in all fairness had paid for them, must have countermanded her order.

Turning her back on the unwelcome memory, she sighed in defeat. "Choose whichever one you want, Cata, I don't have a preference."

"Then I choose this one, my lady. The color will suit you well. If you will please raise your arms, I will help you into it."

Bibi was slightly breathless by the time Cata finished with her. She stood before her mirror corseted, gowned, and bejeweled, and awed by the efficiency of an excellent lady's maid. Tilting her head to the left and right, she smiled at how well Cata followed her instructions on no crimping or frivolous curls.

Her compliments to Cata were interrupted by a knock on the door, and Cata hastened to open it for her.

"Good evening, Baroness. My name is Akos. I am the prince's valet. He's sent me to show you the way to dinner. It takes a while to memorize the castle's many rooms."

"Thank you, Akos, His Grace is most kind." Spying her sketch pad, she swept it up. No time like the present to begin making sketches. If the prince didn't stand on ceremony, there would be time between courses to sketch him in more natural poses. She wanted to get a sense of the real Viceroy of Transylvania.

Chapter Four

Akos insisted on carrying the sketch pad for her as they walked through rooms and a series of confusing corridors, and she remarked on her loss of direction.

"Don't worry, Baroness, someone will always escort you until you are familiar with the layout of the castle. Ah, here we are, My Lady."

As the door was held open for her, she hesitated a moment before entering. It surprised her to find it led to a private suite with a small table set for two in front of the fireplace rather than a formal dining room. She blushed at the reminder she stood balking in the corridor when the prince's valet tilted his head at the delay.

"May I serve you a glass of wine or sherry, Baroness?"

"Yes, sherry, please." She hoped the liquor would quell her misgivings. She couldn't remember the protocol but didn't think it proper to be dining so familiarly, never having met the man. She crossed her fingers the prince would not turn out to be an aged letch with less than honorable plans for the evening. Squaring her shoulders for battle, she turned at the sound of the suite's inner door opening.

***

All previous expectations Baroness Baranyi would lack pleasing attributes vanished upon first sight. He was stunned into boorish gawping.

Gilded by firelight, the vision before him was of a ruby, no, a single drop of life's most precious elixir. The blood-red velvet gown did, indeed, drape a Valkyrie. A Valkyrie whose lush features would make a Renaissance Master beg for the privilege of painting her. His artist had an oval face with large, luminous eyes. She was graced with a nose neither too large nor too small, but arrow straight, and centered between rose-tinted cheekbones. But her hair, the pale blonde of a ripe wheat field, made him want to weep at his inability to paint.

The dress, obviously expensive, was worth every forint paid, for it showcased a magnificent body of rounded breasts and creamy white skin, which deepened to a rosy blush at his prolonged scrutiny.

Akos, whom he'd forgotten was even in the room, made him cease his ill-mannered scrutiny of the baroness with an unusually loud clearing of his throat.

"Would you care to be seated, Your Grace?"

Shaken out of his stupor, Janos cleared his own throat twice before a word, not sounding like it came from a frog, left his throat. "Thank you, Akos, I'll seat the baroness. You may serve the first course."

As he held the chair for his artist, he gave in to his desire and leaned down to surreptitiously inhale her scent of tuber rose, musk, and lavender soap, which took the place of the previous scent of horse. He couldn't recall smelling a more wonderful combination, and his manhood twitched in agreement, making him fumble in the act of seating her.

"Forgive me, Baroness Baranyi, but I must be honest. You are not what I expected."

"Please call me Bibi, Your Grace. I'm uncomfortable with titles. Would it be impertinent to ask whom you were expecting? I was given to understand you'd requested me by name."

Seating himself, he stared into the artist's sapphire eyes before breaking away to cover his lap, and his willful appendage, with a linen napkin. When his gaze returned to her lovely face, she wore a slight frown, and he hurried to explain.

"Forgive me, I'm not usually this *gauche*. My outspoken valet is correct, I need to step out more in society before I lose all my social skills. I didn't mean any criticism, only you are quite lovely. I'd expected a much older person commensurate with the skill you display in your work. And if we are to drop the titles, you must call me Janos."

"But isn't your name..."

"Yes, yes, Szigismond. Emre. Janos. Rackoszi," he intoned with mocking solemnity. The previous two are old family names. Janos is original to me. My family called me Jancsi when I was a child, but at this particular moment I am extremely grateful to have reached my majority." His reward was a beautiful smile and hearing his name on her lips.

"I am honored to make your acquaintance, Janos."

***

While she couldn't exactly say his smile dazzled her, the prince's wide grin did disarm her, and her hand twitched with the need to pick up her sketching pencil. Her itch to draw loosened her usual guard on her tongue, and thus she blurted, "And you are not as I expected."

No, she expected ordinary and been surprised by compelling. Her artist's eye immediately reduced the prince to the oval and triangle of the basic figure-drawing class, and it would be her extreme pleasure to fill in the details.

The prince possessed luxuriant, dark hair, long enough to be worn in a queue. There was a small cleft in his clean-shaven chin, and a regally straight nose, and very nicely shaped lips balanced the perfect oval of his face. She also noted the prince's lower lip was just full enough to suggest kissing him would be a wonderful experience.

Broad shoulders tapering to narrow waist defined the triangle. His long legs were encased in well-tailored trousers, and, studying the hand resting on the arm of his chair, his supple musician's fingers, made for an artist's dream subject. Her standard of painting the truth of what she saw was in no danger of displeasing the prince.

Her rush to cover the lapse of conversation caused by her perusal of the prince made her blurt, "I expected a much older man. No, excuse me, not older, um, more mature, er, not more mature as in aged, but..." She couldn't continue. Her gaffe was monumental, and she closed her eyes, hoping to disappear completely. At the sound of rich laughter, she raised her eyes to ascertain whether or not she was the subject of ridicule.

"Here, my dear, let us enjoy a glass of wine. This is from my own vineyard, and quite good, if I do say so. I believe we are even in *faux pas*. I, too, expected someone of advanced years and without your beauty."

Accepting the proffered wine, she responded, "Then we both erred in our assumptions." Her response elicited an actual blush from her host.

"Which puts us on equal footing. Please, let us dine. Akos, you may serve."

Bibi dutifully lifted her fork in between listening and responding to the prince's excellent dinner conversation, but when their server inquired if she cared for dessert, she had to shake her head in bemusement. The prince's skilled conversation swept her initial unease away, and to be totally honest with herself, so enraptured was she over his sable, ridiculously long eyelashes, she couldn't bring to mind whether the main course consisted of fish or fowl.

"Thank you, no. I'm afraid I've eaten far too much."

Janos scoffed. "You hardly touched the food. Please join me for dessert. *Dobos torte* is a particular favorite of mine. I can't remember the last time the cook honored me with one."

Bibi could've sworn Akos muttered, "Not in this century," but the late hour and the potent red wine at dinner made everything a little fuzzy-edged, but she changed her mind when the prince used his compelling eyes to counter her refusal.

"Please, you must at least try a small sample. Shall we share a slice? I don't want to come across as boorish for gobbling in front of you."

She shook her head at such blatant wheedling before giving in. "I will accept a small bite on one condition. You will allow me to do a preliminary sketch while you enjoy your treat."

23

"What, you want to sketch me while I'm stuffing myself with seven layers of chocolate?"

Her witty retort of, "I promise not to make it a study of gluttony," made the prince and Akos roar with amusement.

"*Touché* madame, but you must take the first bite." And Janos placed a generous portion on his fork and offered it to her.

When she attempted to take the utensil from his hand, the prince stopped her with a soft request as he raised the sweet morsel to her lips.

"Please, my dear, allow me a small liberty this memorable evening."

***

He held his breath as he waited for Bibi to refuse such an intimacy. When a blush stained a faint rouge over her porcelain skin, and her lips parted in invitation, he leaned forward in anticipation.

His hand trembled, infinitesimally, as he lifted the fork and regarded the unexpectedly beautiful woman as she accepted his offering. When her lips closed delicately around the rich chocolate, he swore he perceived the gentle slide of them directly on his shaft rather than the tines of the fork.

"Your chef is to be commended, Your Grace. The cake is exquisite."

Janos clamped his hand firmly down on the napkin in his lap and responded with a hoarse rasp. "Indeed, I must raise her salary. I wouldn't want to lose such culinary prowess."

He didn't know which he enjoyed more, having her eyes on him as she sketched, or the sweetness of the seven-layer cake on his tongue. However, remembering himself to be in the beginning stages of a marriage proposal to his deceased neighbor's daughter, served to deter him from formulating any plan to savor the richness of the artist the same way he did his favorite treat.

The dessert and the sketching ended simultaneously when a huge yawn made his artist blush furiously.

"Oh, do forgive me, Your Grace. How rude of me. I'm afraid I'm tired beyond good manners. It has been a long day for me. What time may I begin sketching you tomorrow?"

"Ah, yes, tomorrow. I suppose this is a good time to explain my, er, condition."

Caught off guard at his mention of an infirmity, she parroted, "Condition?"

"Yes, an inherited weakness, I'm afraid. Everyone in my family line is sensitive to direct sunlight. The Rakoszy castle was designed with few windows for that very reason. We can go abroad on cloudy days, and we can be exposed to direct sunlight for a few moments, but any more and we suffer extreme burning. We are forced to live in indirect light or shadows and darkness, which is why any foray outside the castle isn't attempted before knowing the setting and what the weather will be. I hope this doesn't present too much of a problem in painting me?"

"I am sorry to hear of your affliction, Your Grace. No, it won't be difficult to sketch you in less than full sunlight, but I'll need to move closer than I normally would."

At last, a positive experience as a result of my affliction, he wryly congratulated himself.

"Of course, when I start the actual miniatures, I'll need strong sunlight, but you won't need to pose by then."

"You may use the solar as your work space. It is seldom used during daylight hours. You must tell Erzsebet what you'll need to accommodate it to your needs.

"Akos will escort you back to your room. I hope it won't inconvenience you too much, but I'll instruct Erzsebet to select a room with better light than the one you presently occupy. I apologize for not remembering to inform her of an artist's need for strong lighting. I bid you sweet dreams, Bibi."

"And the same to you, Janos. Despite our initial reservations, I think we will work well together."

He stood and gripped the back of his chair as Baroness Baranyi exited his rooms with a soft swish of ruby velvet, before giving soft voice to an unexpected desire. "If I am fortunate enough to dream this night, Beatrix Baranyi, it will be of the two of us lying very naked in my bed. Which will be a welcome dream, indeed."

Chapter Five

Her back spasmed in complaint when her feet hit the floor, and she winced. It was no surprise to find herself the possessor of aches and pains. The bed was, as she expected, lumpy, but the heavy evening meal, and glasses of dark-red wine, mercifully delayed all sense of discomfort until this morning. Her usual cheerfulness reasserted itself with the rueful realization the uncomfortable mattress facilitated an early start on her preliminary sketches.

She was eager to discover what her artist's eye and discerning mind would create for the prince's portrait. Staid portrait poses didn't interest her at all. She preferred the illustrated Russian folk tales with their vibrant jewel tones and so modeled her miniatures after them.

Her aches were quickly replaced by satisfaction when she surprised Erzsebet by being fully awake and out of bed when the housekeeper, once again, flung open the door with a knock too brief, and too quiet, to be considered knocking.

"Ah, an early riser, how unusual."

Unable to restrain her inner imp, she glanced pointedly at the lumpy mattress before replying, "Yes, I am not one to linger abed."

"The prince requested you be transferred to a room with more light. Cata will help you dress and then show you the way to the breakfast room. Your things will be transferred while you breakfast."

"I'll be sure to thank the prince for his courtesy, when next I see him, but Cata's dressing services will not be necessary. I plan on riding this morning, and it won't take me long to dress. Tell Cata to knock on my door in fifteen minutes to show me the way to the breakfast room."

Erzsebet's silence and raised eyebrows spoke volumes. She'd shocked the housekeeper with her refusal of Cata's services, but donning trousers, tunic, and boots did not require two people, and Shadow didn't care what she wore, as long as he got his daily exercise and his measure of oats.

She made a mental note to compliment the prince on his stables. She meant to do so last night, but meeting Janos for the first time discombobulated her. No one who loved horses could deny his stables were anything but magnificent, or be able to say his stable master didn't take pride in his job. The stalls were made of mahogany, the floors red brick and spotless. The individual stalls all had fresh hay, and several stable boys ran to and fro, tending the carriage and work horses or cleaning tack. As she approached his stall, Shadow nickered and jutted his nose over the stall door for petting.

"Did you rest well, boy? I spy no lumpy straw in your room," Bibi teased. "Are you ready for your morning ride? I could use some company."

Breaking her fast in a large room with herself as the sole diner made her uncomfortable. She was accustomed to dining with her father and aunt and uncle. Despite having servants, her family dispensed with the fuss and served themselves at the day's first meal. Being waited on by one of the prince's footmen, who seemed disappointed she hadn't eaten every

28

scrap in the large chafing dishes, dampened her usual hearty appetite. She looked forward to a long ride to banish her dysphoria.

"You have a beautiful horse, Baroness."

She ceased stroking Shadow's ears and smiled at the stable master's compliment. "Yes, he is. I'm very pleased with him. I bred him from the finest of our stock, but he is a gentle lad and not at all high-strung."

As if to mock the praise of her horse, a shrill whinny sounded from the stall at the very end of the row. It was followed by the loud bang of hooves hitting the wall for emphasis.

"Well, the horse making all the noise is as high-strung as yours isn't." The stable master's shoulders jerked upward in dismay, and he winced, when yet again, hooves drummed on the stable wall. "Excuse me, I'd best find out what the demon wants."

Always deferring to curiosity, she followed the man to the largest stall and whistled in surprise at the horse prancing agitatedly back and forth, and side to side. "What a magnificent creature. I've encountered Arabian stallions before, but this one is a cut above."

"Yes, he is, and probably worth every forint the prince paid for him, but he's the devil incarnate to care for. A long, hard run calms him, but his grace can only ride him on cloudy days."

It was apparent having an audience was to the stallion's liking, for he approached the door and jutted his nose for petting. She reached out to comply, but the stable master stopped her hand.

"Please be careful, Baroness, Anubis relishes his pound of flesh."

When she withdrew her hand, the inky-black stallion twitched his ears back in annoyance. She instantly resolved to trust him. "Well, Anubis, guide and friend of departed souls, will you bite me, or will you let me scratch behind those flattened ears?"

She chuckled at the stable master's involuntary exclamation when Anubis once again proffered his regal head for scratching.

Bibi crooned to him as she scratched behind his ears and stroked his neck. "Here you go, you handsome boy. I'm sure Shadow won't mind sharing one of his apples with you. Ah, how daintily you accepted your treat. I think you could probably teach Shadow some table manners, but I must make my excuses, Shadow needs his exercise."

As if he understood her every word, Anubis withdrew his head from the door and whickered softly.

"Baroness, I'm standing right here, and I still don't believe it. No one but the prince can approach this temperamental horse without a healthy dose of fear. And certainly no one but the prince has ever fed him by hand."

"Perhaps the prince will let me exercise his horse for him on sunny days. It might put Anubis in a better mood."

"I will most heartedly champion your cause, should you need me to. A calmer stallion will mean a calmer stable all around."

As one of the stable boys led a fully saddled Shadow to

her, the stable master inquired, "May I give you a leg up, or do you prefer to use the mounting block?"

Grinning saucily, she replied, "Neither are necessary, but thank you for the courtesy," and vaulted smoothly into the saddle. The exclamations of approval she received from the stable boys made her giggle as she guided Shadow out of the stable and broke into a gallop.

The stable master allowed his lads to gawk for a few minutes. "Remark it well, boys, for that is how a true *Csikos* rides."

Beatrix knocked on the heavy oak door to the prince's suite of rooms, and the valet opened the door.

"I'm sorry, Baroness, the prince is still abed."

"I don't intend to disturb him, Akos. The prince said I could visit his chambers during the day to study the objects familiar to him. I need to get a sense of what things interest him, and of his color preferences, before I paint his portrait. I promise I'll be very quiet as I browse through his sitting room."

The valet stepped back to permit her entrance to the prince's private suite, and she moved quietly about the room, pausing to lift an object, or make a note as to the color of the draperies and carpeting. But, as she skirted a massive wing chair, she froze and quietly called over her shoulder to the valet, "Does he bite?"

The valet hurried to her side, carrying a pile of freshly laundered shirts in his arms. "Oh, I do beg your pardon,

Baroness. I had no idea Lucifer was in the room."

"Lucifer?" Beatrix repeated, as she studied the enormous black-tipped gray wolf. "Hopefully, Lucifer is not aptly named, but I would appreciate knowing if the prince bites."

The valet's voice quavered as he asked, "The prince?"

She hurried to explain. "You know, prince, as in Lucifer, Prince of Darkness. Um, should I stand still to remain un-punctured by those enormous teeth, or can I move freely about?"

"Oh, I dare say the, er, prince does bite but never without good cause, Baroness."

The valet's answer was not reassuring, especially since the wolf, whose golden eyes were locked on hers, stalked her as she moved about the prince's anteroom.

"Please remain still for a moment, Baroness. I believe Lucifer wants to make your acquaintance."

Beatrix acceded to the valet's request and held her ground as the wolf circled and sniffed delicately at the hem of her gown. When he sat on his haunches and cocked his massive head at her, she dropped into her best curtsy.

"I am sorry, Your Grace, Prince of Darkness, but I left my calling cards in my room. My name is Baroness Beatrix Baranyi. You may call me Bibi."

The wolf, who stared intently at her lips through the entire introduction, chose to sidle close enough for her to reach out and touch him. He was even larger close up, and she had to raise her hand to give him a tentative pat on the head. Noticing Lucifer enjoyed the attention, she stroked his head and ears with careful, slow movements. She stopped when a low rumbling sound emerged from the animal.

"It would appear Lucifer accepts your presence, Baroness. I don't recall him letting anyone pet him before."

"Then why is he growling at me, Akos?"

"Oh, he's not, My Lady. He's just expressing pleasure at being petted."

She tentatively resumed the stroking and was almost knocked off-balance when the wolf leaned his entire body into her caress. The wolf's enthusiasm emboldened her to run her hands along his flanks and sides of his face.

"Well, Lucifer, if a person really knew how friendly you were, they would call you Lucy instead," she teased, but stopped when a most definite growl emerged. "Okay then, Lucifer it is."

Under the observant eyes of the wolf and the valet, she resumed her walk through the prince's study and made several quick sketches of various objects catching her eye. As she turned to leave, she stopped at the door to thank Akos and then stooped to address the wolf. "Thank you for showing me your master's chambers, Lucifer. I'm glad to have made your acquaintance."

When the valet held open the door for her, the wolf looked directly into her eyes and slowly nodded his head before backing away. She comprehended a regal dismissal when she saw one and retraced the route to her north tower room.

***

The signature scent of tuber rose and horse awakened him before the knock on the door. Janos chose to remain still for a moment and ignore his valet's knock, but he couldn't ignore the ache in his groin, and the tent he made in the bed linens. It was obvious his body, as well as his mind, wanted to know what Bibi was about this day, and so he gave permission to enter but not before rearranging the duvet to hide his arousal.

He finished his breakfast drink as he strolled from his bedroom to hand the empty goblet to his visibly ruffled valet. "I'm ravenous this morning and fancy inviting the baroness to join me for breakfast."

Accepting the empty glass, Akos replied, "You'll need to rise much earlier than this to join the baroness at breakfast. She's already eaten, had a morning ride, and wants to know if she can exercise Anubis for you on sunny days.

"Erzsebet already transferred her possessions to the north tower. You can probably find your artist there doing some preliminary sketching."

His valet's next pronouncement made him start the day by losing his temper.

"Your Grace, won't you please reconsider your wedding plans? It's obvious to me, the baroness, even though she just arrived, has attracted your notice. I've never seen you so interested and entertained by a woman before. Here it is still morning, and you're awake and looking forward to her company. Indeed, the return of your appetite, and I'm not talking just about food, is a very good sign."

Janos glowered with the pent-up fury of an approaching

thunderstorm as he turned to chastise his valet. "Cease your prattling, Akos. How do you know the return of my interest and appetite isn't due to my arrangement with Margyth? Indeed, I visited her just before Baroness Baranyi's arrival.

"Finish tying my cravat. I want to see if the light in the north tower room is acceptable to my artist for her drawing."

He headed for the north tower to the staccato sound of his leather heels hitting the stone floor. Once he realized he was almost marching, he slowed to consider the unfamiliar emotion. He was upset, no not upset, he was hurt.

As the newly discovered emotion revealed itself, he stopped in the middle of the passageway. He was actually hurt. What a curious emotion and a totally new experience for him. He couldn't remember the last time he and Akos quarreled, and to have his valet question his plans, especially when they were to ensure all who depended on him could continue to live in peace and prosperity, caused quite an ache in his soul.

Shaking his head to rid it of the buzzing, he continued on his way, all the while castigating himself. What did you expect, effusive praise, public huzzahs, groveling loyalty? No, nothing so fawning, just a small acknowledgement for the sacrifice of having to do what you promised to do even if it meant swallowing your personal desires to accomplish it.

His ruminations took him right to Bibi's door, and he intended to knock politely, until he overheard her startled exclamation.

"Ow! Son of a diseased cow!"

He bolted into the room, only to be painfully assaulted by

bright sunlight and the disturbing sight of his artist holding a handkerchief to her bleeding hand.

"May I ask you to draw the drapes so I can see?" he called from behind the hands he used to shield his face from the sun's rays.

"Yes, immediately, Your Grace." And Bibi drew the drapes with her uninjured hand.

With the sunlight managed, he approached the artist. "Are you all right?"

"I'm terribly sorry you had to hear my indelicate language, Janos. I spend most of my days with horses and *Csikos*, and the refinement my mother tried to instill in me has suffered. Please, forgive me."

"There's no need. I'm not a prude, and Akos possesses an even more descriptive vocabulary than yours. But what did you do to your hand?" She reluctantly allowed him to unwind her hasty dressing.

"I cut my finger while sharpening one of my drawing pencils. It's rather an occupational hazard. Just let me get a fresh handkerchief to bind it."

Before she could pull away, he lifted her hand and placed his lips on the cut. The sweetness of her blood almost overwhelmed him, and he made a herculean effort to rein in the urge to sweep her into his arms and bond with her on the spot. As much as he wanted to shout his desire loud enough to crack the mortar in the great stones of his castle, he proffered only a mild explanation to keep Bibi from thinking him mad.

"Permit me the honor of kissing it better. My mother always did so for my cuts, and it took the sting away. See, the bleeding stopped."

Cognizant his guest failed to miss the lust-induced shudder he gave as he kissed the small wound, he denigrated his actions. "Forgive me, it upsets me when a guest in my house suffers an unfortunate accident. Shall I send someone to clean and bandage your hand?"

Relieved by her assurance the wound was minor but more relieved to note no change in her voice due to his odd behavior, he changed the subject. "I came here because I wanted to see if this room is more suitable than the other."

"Oh yes, much, better. The northern light is perfect, and there is more than enough room for my easel. I was about to go to the solar and judge the quality of light there. Would you care to show me the way, or will it be too sunny for you?"

Acutely aware Bibi's eyes were still upon him, he remained with his back to her as he fought desperately to get himself under control. His brain was screaming two words over and over: *This one. This one. This one*, so loudly he wanted to cover his ears and run from the room, but he managed to answer her question.

"Ah, the solar. Yes, it will be much too bright for me. I'll send Cata to attend you." And without turning around, he effected a hasty departure. He was well aware it was a breach of social etiquette, but he was incapable of correcting his actions without exposing his inappropriate emotions.

His footfalls were in syncopation with his mind, as the words *I want her, I want her, I want her*, called cadence as he retreated with un-princely agitation.

***

Akos waited until he could no longer hear the prince's footsteps, before swearing long and descriptively over His Grace's refusal to comprehend what was in front of his aristocratic nose. Baroness Baranyi was his chance for true love, while Margyth Szechenyi was strictly a matter of business. It was not what Janos's long duty for the good of his people merited at all.

The prince's recent outburst aptly demonstrated going head-to-head with his employer would be counterproductive. He needed an ally to help him convince the stubborn viceroy to reassess his plans. Erzsebet had been part of the Rackoszi household since the prince's birth, and would possibly be amenable to helping, but she and the baroness had not started off on a promising note. The valet quailed inwardly at having to sweet-talk the austere chatelaine of the castle, but he loved the prince fiercely and would gladly beard a dragon in its lair if it meant the prince could find happiness.

His hope Margyth Szechenyi would love the prince the way he deserved to be was now no more than a pile of ashes. For though the woman held great love within her, it was solely for herself. He resolved to approach Erzsebet over midmorning tea, a particularly calming event in the housekeeper's long day, to enlist her aid in somehow rescuing the prince from his own honor.

When the prince in question slammed open the door to his suite, he was startled into dropping the jacket he'd been brushing.

"Your Grace, what has happened? Why, you are deathly pale and shaking. If my earlier impertinence upset you, I most humbly apologize."

Waving his valet back, he rasped, "Leave me. No, wait, I need a drink. Pour me a drink and then leave."

Akos was staring at the prince's closed bedroom door before he even had a chance to respond. He was alarmed when the door opened just wide enough for the prince to grasp the requested drink and slammed closed again. Not daring to open the door between them, he called out, "Your Grace, may I be of some assistance?"

"No. Yes, you can take the rest of the day off, but first tell Cata to show Bibi to the solar. And will you please stop hovering outside my door and leave me in peace."

Whatever the cause, the prince didn't sound angry, he sounded frightened, and Akos suspected Baroness Baranyi was at the root of it. Since his morning was his own to do with as he wished, he intended to be the one to escort the baroness to the solar. Whether she fathomed it or not, the baroness was breathing new life and excitement into the gloomy pile of rocks the prince called home, and he, for one, did not want it to stop.

Chapter Six

He spent the morning pacing his room and mentally kicking himself for his less than manly performance in front of Bibi. While the drink calmed him, somewhat, he couldn't escape recalling his odd actions with absolute clarity, and he wanted to smack his head into the nearest wall.

She probably thinks you are some sort of milquetoast who can't stand the sight of blood, his evil alternate ego told him. *Stay hiding in your room and you'll give credence to her estimation of you,* the imp gloated.

Fortunately, his good angel took over and settled the matter. *All men can be overwhelmed by their baser desires, but you need not be. Leave your room and go find her and ask her to ride with you. Today is cloudy enough, and Anubis needs exercise.*

With a calming breath, he opened his door and sought out his artist in residence.

***

The sun dropped behind the clouds and told the artist in her this would be an excellent chance to sketch the prince in light suitable to his allergy, and so she grabbed the drawing she'd completed of Lucifer, and ran from the solar, and into the prince's arms, literally.

"Oh, I beg your pardon, Your Grace. I wasn't remarking

where I was going. I was…" Observing the prince this close, and being still held in his embrace, words failed her. He was devastatingly handsome. Her artist's eye made a note to remember candlelight and shade appeared to be the mediums best suited to him.

When a grin quirked his cheek, Bibi warmed with the heat of an immediate blush and was surprised and flustered by the fine shiver of goose bumps the sensation of Janos's arms around her elicited. She also discovered she didn't want to break the embrace, as propriety demanded.

"Er, I was going to ask if this might be a convenient time to sketch you? The solar is not sunny at all this morning."

At his pointed glance at the paper she still clutched to her breast, she remembered her other mission and offered, "Oh, I finished a sketch of Lucifer. Would you like it?"

"Bibi, this is wonderful. Such detail. I can almost feel his breath. I think you captured Lucifer in all his magnificence."

"Yes, I am rather proud of the pose. He's sporting an almost-devilish grin, like he knows a secret and won't tell."

The prince glanced up from his study of the sketch to find her studying him with great intensity, and she commented without thinking.

"As a matter of fact, I discern the same insouciant expression on your face. Perhaps Lucifer is merely aping his master."

"Indeed. Would you care to go riding with me this cloudy day? Heaven knows both Anubis and I need the exercise, and I want to test how well you handle him before I agree to let you exercise him. He can be willful if he gets his head."

At her slight pout, he softened the disappointment.

"I promise to sit for you after the ride and after dinner. I'm sure a long ride will engender hearty appetites in us both."

Giving in with good grace, she conceded. "I'd be delighted to ride with you, Your Grace."

"Your Grace? How formal. I loathe such formality from someone I consider to be a friend. Please use my name, Bibi."

"As you wish, Janos. Permit me a moment to change. I believe I spotted Erzsebet in the kitchen, and I need to ask her if I can borrow Cata to assist me."

***

Erzsebet finished pouring him a cup of tea and called *Enter* when the knock sounded at the door to her private sitting room. If the housekeeper was surprised at Baroness Baranyi's seeking her out, he couldn't tell. Akos marveled at her *sangfroid* as he stood to greet the baroness.

"Oh, please remain seated. I hate to interrupt, but I wanted to ask for Cata's service for a moment. His Grace asked me to accompany him on a ride this morning, and I need help with my riding habit, um, the nice one, not my usual *Csikos* attire."

Ever the consummate valet, Akos ignored the blush her admission occasioned.

Erzsebet fielded the request. "Of course, Baroness, I'll send Cata to your room immediately."

When the door swung shut on Bibi's retreating form, Erzsebet lifted her tea cup, and before sipping the fragrant oolong, cast a piercing look his way and broke her silence.

"I will help you with what you want to do."

Akos could not believe his ears. He'd sought the housekeeper out prepared to cajole, wheedle, and argue. Her unexpected capitulation left him openmouthed with amazement.

"Oh, do close your mouth, it's most unbecoming. I know you came here convinced I would oppose your plan."

"If I might ask, Erzsebet, why such a *volte-face*?"

"Two reasons. First, I've kept vigil as a lonely little boy turned into a lonely man. His Grace takes care of everyone's needs but his own, and this must stop. Second, my ears aren't deaf to the talk coming from the Szechenyi servants. Our prince, who is wont to look for the good in others, will find none in Margyth.

"As we both witnessed, Baroness Baranyi is blessed with a solid, inner core of good breeding. Her parents are to be commended for raising a daughter with excellent manners. She asked for, not demanded, Cata's help, and unlike others of her class, she deprives herself rather than make the servants work harder. I believe she'll be a good match for the prince.

"Let us put our heads together, shall we, Akos, and strategize how to divert the good man we know from a path of onerous duty to one of love."

Akos resumed his seat and grinned at the housekeeper. Erzsebet did not return the friendly gesture, but when she launched into her ideas for getting the prince and the baroness together, he didn't object. The woman was either a brilliant strategist or a witch, and he didn't have a preference, as long as her plan worked.

Chapter Seven

At the sound of booted feet on the cobbled courtyard, Janos broke off his perusal of the skies and was momentarily struck dumb. Bibi stood quietly while his eyes feasted on her emerald-green wool riding habit trimmed with black, military-style frogging. Her hat was a jaunty archer's cap with a long pheasant feather rising softly in the slight breeze.

"Do you approve?" she asked.

The baroness's failure to keep the blush from staining her cheeks at such an outrageous compliment, pleased him.

"You are too kind, Janos," she shyly replied.

To alleviate her discomfort, he changed the subject. "I think I will ride Anubis first and let him expend some of his pent-up energy. We can switch mounts for the ride back."

"Perfect, but I must warn you, Shadow is trained as a cavalry horse and responds to leg and hand commands."

"As is Anubis. May I give you a leg up?"

***

Bibi accepted the prince's offer of assistance and waited for him to mount his high-strung stallion. His black riding coat, fawn breeches, and black knee-high boots were a perfect foil for the inky Arabian, and his eager anticipation and joy to be outside would've dimmed the sun, had the fiery orb chosen to show itself.

Now there's a look I will attempt to capture to dazzle his intended bride and assure a positive response to his proposal. The prince interrupted her contemplation.

"Having heard of your riding prowess from my stablemaster, I'm going to give Anubis his head. I'm sure you'll be able to keep up."

Bibi controlled Shadow as the prince leaned forward in the saddle while Anubis gathered himself on his haunches, and, without any urging, leapt forward to imitate a cannonball being shot from a cannon.

Shaking her head in pure awe, she patted Shadow's neck and murmured to the gray as he pawed the ground, awaiting her command. "I think the prince misnamed his horse. He should've named him Comet, for he truly runs like a blazing streak of light. All right, Shadow my dear, let's show him you are aptly named to shadow a comet."

For the next several hours Anubis and Shadow engaged in nothing short of an English steeplechase. Jumping ditches, startling game in the fields, splashing through shallow streams, until, finally, the prince called a halt at the edge of a small pond to allow the horses a brief rest and a cool-down drink.

***

"My God, what a ride." His expostulation ceased abruptly as he dismounted and turned to help Bibi.

Alerted by his expression, her hand rose to touch her face, and he winked as she flicked a piece of mud from her cheek.

"You won't need a mirror to discover if your face is dirty as well, Your Grace. You only need to study mine, we're a matched pair," she chortled. "I agree, this afternoon was wonderful. I can't remember when I allowed Shadow the liberty of deciding when and how to take the obstacles. I thank you on Shadow's behalf."

His attention returned to Anubis when the willful stallion almost tugged the reins from his hand as he jerked his head and attempted to rear. His admonition for Anubis to behave himself was interrupted when Bibi asked, "Since Anubis appears to have regained his wind, let us switch mounts."

Janos looped the reins over his wrist, moved to Bibi's side, and held his hands up to help her dismount. He was surprised his offer of assistance flustered her. How odd such a beautiful woman was not accustomed to having a man's help to dismount.

But when he removed his hands from around her waist and stepped beck, Anubis gave him a forceful nudge between his shoulder blades and propelled him right into her arms, and she had to cling to him to keep from falling. Not knowing exactly why he did so, he wet his thumb and slowly removed another steak of dirt from her cheek.

His willful steed broke the spell when he rested his head on his shoulder and blew through his lips to cover both riders in horse spittle.

His uncensored oath as to his mount's dubious bloodlines sent his riding companion into a fit of giggles.

"Don't try to deny it, Your Grace, your red face tells me Anubis succeeded in shocking you."

"Alas, words fail me. I am compelled to apologize for my horse, but I don't think standard etiquette covers such a situation. Here, you may use my handkerchief, and then I'll help you mount this four-legged cad."

Anxious to be away, Anubis sidestepped and pawed the ground. He would've had a difficult time adjusting the stirrups for Bibi if she hadn't had firm hands. His devil of a horse made it all too obvious he did not care for standing idle.

Bibi had no trouble at all keeping Anubis under control until he adjusted Shadow's stirrups to suit his longer legs and mounted. Curious as to what she was about, he leaned forward in the saddle to hear what she was whispering into the Arabian's twitching ears.

"It's time to garner your master's admiration, Anubis. Come, let's show him how well you perform your cavalry skills."

He held his breath as she effortlessly put his stallion into a *piaffe* by asking him to engage his hindquarters, and then she led him smoothly into the *levade*. Anubis, with excellent control, balanced and raised his forehand off the ground and tucked his forelegs to carry all of his weight on his hindquarters in a forty-five-degree angle.

He was afraid to voice any comment as she worked with the headstrong Arabian and nibbled the corner of his lip in nervous anticipation as Anubis transitioned into the *capriole* by leaping horizontally in the air, the height of a man's head, and striking out with front and hind legs. While serving the emperor, he'd witnessed the success of the deadliest of the airs above ground. Invented to break the enemy lines, if done in simultaneous jumps, the maneuver succeeded admirably during a battle against the Italians, and the emperor's cavalry won the day.

"Excellent, Anubis, let's complete the quartet," Bibi encouraged, and gave his horse the rein and leg signals.

He could only gape with astonishment when the contrary stallion performed a strong *courbette*, the most strenuous of all the moves, for Anubis had to leap on his hindquarters and execute three or four jumps forward before touching down.

"Words fail me, Bibi. I was unaware Anubis had the training to do a fraction of those difficult movements. It makes me think he deserves a better rider than me."

"He is magnificent, isn't he? If you ever consider putting him to stud, my family would be happy to have him service our mares. An infusion of such royal bloodstock would be most welcome."

***

The prince made no comment as she led Shadow into his stall after their ride, and refused the stable master's offer of help. She preferred to groom her own horse, so the fault lay with no one other than herself if a small pebble remained undiscovered in a hoof or his mane became tangled.

She grinned when he demanded a curry comb from the flustered stable boy who materialized at his elbow. Apparently, the prince intended to follow her example.

She finished grooming Shadow before he finished with Anubis, and, without being asked, helped him brush the

Arabian in companionable silence. The noise of curry combs running through the silky coat of the Arabian was the only sound for quite a while, until she found him studying her over Anubis's back.

"I'm quite certain Anubis never experienced such a marvelous day as today. Come, my dear, let us return for dinner."

He was about to lead the way out of the stables but stopped and laughed sheepishly. "Perhaps I should rephrase my invitation. Would you dine with me after ridding yourself of dirt and horse spittle?"

The sun chose to break through the thick clouds as they reached the massive front door of the castle, and in his haste to escape the harmful rays, the prince flung the door wide and rushed inside. From her vantage behind him, she witnessed the collision with Akos, which almost sent the hapless valet careening arse-over-head.

She studiously refrained from commenting on the *contretemps*, despite suffering an almost overwhelming urge to lay her lips on the rose blooming on both of the prince's cheeks.

Akos, with unflappable domestic hauteur, righted his disarranged clothing and asked, "May I offer you both a glass of wine to mark a pleasant ride?"

When his proffered goblets were accepted, Akos added, "I'll send Cata to draw your bath, Baroness. There is heated water standing by for yours, Your Grace. Cook will serve dinner when you are ready."

***

One hour later, Bibi answered the knock on her tower room door.

"His Grace requested I accompany you to his rooms for lunch, if you are agreeable, Baroness?"

"Your company is always welcome, Akos." This time she handed over her sketch pad rather than argue with the determined valet over who would carry it.

Upon entering the prince's drawing room, she inquired, "Where is Lucifer? I looked forward to meeting him again."

Akos responded before Janos. "I dare say he's having his dinner, Baroness."

"Dare I ask what a wolf dines on?" She winked at the prince behind Akos's back.

Once again, the valet beat him to reply, "Oh, he's become quite domestic and eats whatever the cook chooses to serve him."

Not missing a beat, Akos continued, "May I seat you, Baroness? I'll begin serving the soup. Cook makes wonderful beef soup."

The prince smiled and winked back at her as she raised the first spoonful of soup to her lips, making her hand tremble. *How could I have overlooked such an adorable dimple?* Bibi chastised herself. With his pale-olive skin, black hair, and straight, white teeth, and an added fillip in dimple form, the Viceroy of Transylvania was a feast for the senses. Her fingers tingled in demand she put down the spoon and pick up her pencil.

"You are doing it again, Bibi, and I'm at a loss as to whether to freeze in place or blush at the scrutiny. Such close regard suddenly makes me want to do both.

"Have I missed a speck of mud on my face? Indeed, my bath water can attest to the peck of mud I carried into it when we splashed through every stream on my property.

"Today's ride was the most enjoyment I've had in quite some time, and you must promise me we can do so again. Anubis adores you. I can still picture you putting him through those difficult movements as if he performed them each morning. I lack the words to describe such a beautiful harmony between horse and rider.

"Do you know, I would pay a fortune for a painting of you astride him as he performed the *courbette*. Although how anyone would capture Anubis leaping forward on his hind quarters for three or four times, without ever touching all four hooves to the ground, is beyond my artistic imagining."

She dabbed her mouth with her napkin before answering, "I am sorry, Janos. I'm so used to painting, I sometimes forget the directness of my gaze. Please accept my apology for giving offense. I'll try to confine my gimlet stare to when you pose for me."

Reaching out, the prince captured her hand and laced his fingers through hers. "No, you must not. I admire your directness. I was but teasing you."

"Well then, let me say I admire the way you ride with such controlled abandon. I will be delighted to ride with you on the next cloudy day."

***

"I can but hope we suffer a profusion of them very soon," he muttered under his breath as Bibi sipped from her spoon. Horses weren't what he wanted to ride with abandon at the moment.

"Ahem."

The mild exclamation startled him, and he dribbled soup on his chin. It embarrassed him to discover Akos, from his position behind his chair, possessed a clear view of his arousal. He didn't comment as his valet dropped another snowy, white linen napkin into his lap and whisked away the one he was using to mop his chin. He kept his eyes on his soup bowl because he lacked the courage to note if there was a smirk on his valet's face.

"You may serve the next course, Akos," was the only rejoinder he dared make.

As he placed his knife and fork across his plate to signal he was finished, he was quite satisfied with the excellent meal, until Bibi dragged a wing chair from its traditional place in front of the fireplace and opened her sketch pad.

"For feeding me such a delicious luncheon, you earn the right to be subjected to my piercing stare. Will you sit in this chair and let me do a preliminary sketch?"

He tried, but despite squirming around for a more comfortable position, he remained ill at ease. His back was as rigid as a board, and the stiffness radiated through his shoulders and back. And his hands ached where they grasped his knees, as if his legs were trembling and he needed to exert

55

force to anchor them to the floor.

His intense discomfort amused his artist.

"I'm not going to hurt you, Janos. I promise this is a painless procedure, unless you try to hold such a rigid pose for longer than an hour. Akos will then need to carry you out of here, and it might take days before you regain the use of your limbs.

"Relax your posture and sit in the chair as if you are enjoying the fire. No, don't look at me. I want you to think of something happy or something amusing. Yes, much better."

He was content to sit and listen to the sound of the pencil moving across the paper, until the unwelcome voice of his evil angel intruded.

If she were to intuit you are thinking of licking your way up the inside of her milky, white thighs, she would throw down her pencil and bolt like all of the demons of hell were after her.

Bibi startled him back to the present when she lightly placed her hand on the side of his face.

"You changed your expression, and not for the better. I'm not sure, but you look guilty, or you are chagrinned about something."

"No, no, merely thinking of, er, estate business," he extemporized then searched his pockets for a handkerchief to blot the sweat from his forehead. His fumbling halted when Akos handed him one.

"Well, try and conjure up something pleasanter. We don't want to paint you with a grimace." Using both of her hands, she tilted his head a fraction to the left. "Okay, this is much better, but can you open your eyes a trifle wider?"

Bibi leaning over him made his pulse pound and his blood pool in a most uncomfortable place. In an unconscious act of self-defense, he sat farther back in the chair and crossed his legs.

"Ah, perfect," she murmured, and resumed sketching.

Perfect for whom? his evil imp screamed. Why don't you tear off your clothes and demand she sketch you nude? After all, she is yours, and after the sip you took from her, you understand why.

"Janos, you are fidgeting. Please stay still," Bibi ordered, as she frowned at him and then at her sketch pad. "Drat, the light is failing. I need to position myself closer to you."

He catapulted from the chair. "I think it would be best if we resumed in the morning. The light will be much better then. Thank you for accompanying me on the ride. Akos will show you to your room, as you must be fatigued from this morning's exercise."

Silently thanking her parents for teaching their daughter not to cavil when dismissed so rudely. "Until tomorrow, then."

"As you wish, Your Excellency," was the last thing he heard his artist say as he quit the room.

***

While his employer missed the baroness's reaction, Akos did not. Her use of the honorific was a subtle slap at the prince's high-handedness. Shooting a censorious glare at his master's closed bedroom door, he stepped forward and offered, "Allow me to escort you to your room, Baroness. If you desire anything at all this afternoon, please don't hesitate to ask."

Very aware of his master's abruptness, he tried to make amends. "I'm sure His Grace would be honored if you dined with him this evening."

"Thank you, Akos, but His Grace is correct. I am fatigued from this morning's exercise. I believe I shall have a tray sent to my room and retire early."

He admired the baroness's straight posture as she led the way from Janos's rooms and took the remaining light with her.

The walk back to her tower room was accomplished in silence, until he held the door open for her. "Would you forgive him for his rudeness if I said you make him nervous?"

Bibi halted mid-threshold and voiced her incredulity at his revelation.

"Me? I make him nervous? Whatever are you talking about? He is a prince, a viceroy of Transylvania. I am but a horse breeder and sometimes artist hired to paint miniatures for a possible marriage proposal."

Akos held up his hands in a placating gesture. "I'm quite sure His Grace would be most angry with me for divulging this, but the prince's affliction engenders a somewhat cloistered life. He is not at all comfortable or current on the social conventions pertaining to women."

The astonishment in her voice registered clearly in his ears.

"Surely he's managed to spend time with his intended?"

He turned away before answering the question. "Yes, Baroness, but as a member of the peerage, you must be aware most marriages are based on considerations of property or title rather than love. While the prince, and everyone in this castle who is devoted to him, would wish the union to be based on something involving, at very least, affection, the prince will wed, with or without it, to secure both estates, and to protect the people therein."

Her terse response to his revelation both surprised and dismayed him.

"And what of his intended? Is she aware she is but a pawn in a game of rents and mortgages?"

Stepping back from her door, he bowed. "It is not my place to say, Baroness. Mayhap you will be able to ascertain that for yourself when you visit the Szechenyi estate to sketch her. I hope the remainder of your evening is pleasant, Baroness."

Chapter Eight

Bibi's conscience kept her from falling asleep. Losing control over her undisciplined tongue, and all but calling the prince a mercenary cad in front of his valet, made her toss and turn for hours before falling into a fitful sleep. The sun was well up before she awakened to the sound of scratching at her door.

"Enter, Cata," she called, and frowned when the door failed to open. She grumbled under her breath as she left her bed to discover who sought her. If Erzsebet turned out to be the caller, this would be the first time the housekeeper stood upon ceremony to wait for her to open the door before entering. Annoyed at being roused so early, she flung the door wide to vent her spleen on her mysterious caller and found Lucifer standing outside her door.

Laughing away her peevishness, she put her arms around the wolf in an impromptu hug. "And to what do I owe this honor, my Prince of Darkness?"

She didn't expect a reply, but when the wolf brushed past her then used its nose to pop open her armoire door and select one of her riding boots, the purpose of his call became clear.

"Oh, so you want to go riding with me?"

The gray wolf bent on one knee and bowed as well as any courtier.

"Well, let me break my fast and I'll meet you in the stables."

Lucifer must've found the offer acceptable for he walked to the door and waited for her to open it.

Closing the door after her unexpected caller departed, she muttered *sotto voce*, "The wolf displays better manners than his master."

Since she would be accompanied by a wolf and not the prince, Bibi wore her *Csiko* trousers and boots. Today would not be a pleasure ride but a working day for Shadow.

How the stable master heard of her intention to ride, she couldn't fathom, but Shadow was saddled and waiting for her.

She addressed the wolf while strapping her Prussian saber to Shadow's saddle. "I intend to put Shadow through his paces this morning, but I will let you choose the path." At the last, she vaulted into the saddle and gathered the reins.

Bibi followed as Lucifer led them to the wide entrance drive of the castle grounds. It was a perfect place to begin. Using leg prompts, she directed Shadow from a slow walk, to a trot, and finally into a full gallop.

She dropped her reins and stood in her stirrups with drawn saber and practiced slashing and thrusting, and trusted Shadow to maintain the course. As the wide lane narrowed, she sheathed the saber and once again gathered the reins.

A flash of silver several yards ahead told her the wolf had kept pace, and she directed Shadow onto the same path when he swerved and headed into a heavily wooded and narrow trail. The wolf played tag with her by permitting fleeting glances of his lighter fur.

The path was difficult to negotiate, but she loved the challenge. A niggling worry surfaced when it dawned on her the path she followed took her out of viewing range of the castle, and she called out to Lucifer. "I do hope you intend to show us the way home and not play a diabolical trick by leaving Shadow and me lost in these woods."

It was a relief to ride up on the wolf a few moments later where he was stretched out upon the crest of a hill. From his obvious panting, Lucifer had received as good a workout as Shadow. The wolf did not stir as she worked her horse slowly up to the crest and followed his gaze to look down into a valley. What she observed was a manor house, nowhere near as large as the Rackoszi castle but in far sunnier surroundings.

She made her riding companion cock his head from side to side when she addressed him. "Ah, that must be Margyth's residence. Cata did say it was the only other dwelling within miles of the castle. This one is quite suitable for a baronial residence, don't you think?"

Shadow pranced nervously, and she checked to make sure the wolf would not be harmed. Before she could call out a warning to mind Shadow's hooves, Lucifer stood but did not remove his gaze from the mansion. She caught her breath when the wolf bared its fangs in a silent snarl, as if he found the sight of the Szechenyi mansion displeasing. She made no further comment as the wolf turned his back on the mansion and led her away from the valley.

As soon as the Rackoszi castle came into view, her companion stopped and once again bowed to take his leave. The last glimpse she had of him was a flash of silver through the underbrush. Probably hunting his lunch, she mused.

She returned to her room to find Cata making the bed and

putting her nightgown and robe away.

"Did you enjoy the ride, Baroness?"

"Yes, Cata, I did. Thank you for asking."

"Cook sent up a tray for you since it is past lunch hour. If you need anything at all, I shall be cleaning in the solar. Erzsebet said you might want to sketch there this afternoon. I took the liberty of laying out a dress for you and some hot water to wash with."

"You are ever so efficient, Cata. The water first, please. I will sketch in the solar this afternoon."

***

The wolf remained unnoticed beneath a bank of ferns, his silver fur blending with the dappled shadows of the solar. He flattened himself as Bibi peered around to make sure she was quite alone before propping her foot on the long bench she sat on, creating an improvised easel and a most unladylike pose.

When she stared in the direction of his hiding place, Lucifer froze but released the tension in his haunches when it was obvious her gaze was directed inward as she considered her next stroke. The sole motion he permitted himself was to prick his ears forward, the better to hear her soft murmurings.

"Yes, better, much better. I'm close, so close. Just a teensy more slant to the eyes. *Rohadt!*"

Lucifer drew his lips back in simulation of a grin, as the baroness searched the parameters of the solar to make certain no one heard her use of "damn" and ripped the sheet from the pad and tossed it away. Had she lifted her eyes from her sketching, she would've seen him stretch out one paw to, by infinitesimal degrees, drag the drawing to his hiding place.

Several more drawings were consigned to the floor before the artist stood in frustration and worked the kinks out of her back. His ears picked up her petulant complaint.

"Why can't I draw him? I captured the strong lines of his body, and the background he posed in, but his face eludes my skill."

The sun creeping toward sunset broke the artist's concentration, and Lucifer gave a soft growl of disappointment because it made her gather up her rejected sketches and leave the solar.

Not until his ears confirmed her steps headed to the north tower did he leave his hiding place to study the drawing he rescued from the artist's discards. This one showed Janos astride Anubis, and with an expression of fresh joy and enthusiasm wreathing his face. Slanting his head one way and the other, he could discern no error, no wrong proportions. Shaking out his fur, he picked up the drawing as delicately as he would a wolf cub and loped toward the prince's suite.

***

"You appear fatigued, Your Grace. May I offer you another glass of wine?"

Janos shook his head and finished the final sip of his special vintage, as a knock sounded at the door. Thinking it might be the very woman he hoped to see, he answered the door himself and chose to ignore his valet's chagrin for usurping his duties.

On the other side of the door stood a huge arrangement of flowers, incongruously held up by two, tiny, booted feet. Leaning to the side to peer around the floral monstrosity, he exclaimed, "Good heavens, it's Erzsebet. How on earth did you manage to find your way without running into things?"

"I am not without talent, My Lord," was the housekeeper's acerbic reply.

Standing aside, he gestured for her to enter. "The flowers are beautiful. Did the gardener strip every rose bush bare? To what do I owe this honor? I'm not celebrating another birthday, am I?"

"No, you are not. These flowers aren't for you, they are for the baroness."

"Well then, why bring them to my room?"

Erzsebet's cluck of annoyance came at the same time she shoved the enormous arrangement into his arms.

"Because you might elect to thank the baroness for being so accommodating as to ride with you, and dine with you, and agree to sketch you at your convenience."

Erzsebet gave the prince a glare, which did not neglect to include his valet, and left before either could comment.

The valet relieved the stunned prince of the bouquet and dared a wry observation. "That is, undoubtedly, the longest sentence Erzsebet ever uttered, but I second her suggestion. I believe the baroness is resting in her room before dinner. Will you deliver these, or shall I?"

Taking the arrangement back from Akos, he demurred, "No, I'll deliver them myself."

Feeling foolish and apprehensive by turns, he climbed the stairs to the tower room. As he reached forward to knock, he heard his artist's shouts of fear.

"No! Don't! Help us!"

He didn't know the cause of Bibi's alarm but didn't hesitate to burst through the door. Finding her still trapped by her dreams, he took her into his arms. "Bibi, *kincsem*, wake up. You are having a bad dream."

It took a few moments before she became aware he was holding her inappropriately close. So close he could feel her delightfully rounded breasts through the fabric of his shirt. His innate good manners forced him to let her go when she moved to disengage.

"I am so sorry, Janos. I had a bad dream."

"A very bad dream, *kincsem*. Some wine might help calm you. Yes? Let me pour it for you."

As he headed toward the small table, he had to step over a profusion of flowers, and he heard her gasp in dismay at the colorful disaster.

"What on earth?"

"Ah, the flowers. I was carrying them to you as a welcome to Castle Rackoszi gift when I heard you cry out. I entered hastily and didn't quite reach a table to place the arrangement. Do you want to talk about your dream?"

"No, I most definitely do not. I want to clean up this mess before Erzsebet lops off both our heads."

As Bibi threw back the covers and hopped from the bed to begin salvaging the blossoms, he caught his breath. She was clad exclusively in her chemise, thusly exposing her long legs and a length of thigh, both of which held him in thrall.

He didn't know whether to be mortified or resentful when she caught him staring and laughed until she had to sit down on the bed.

"I'm sorry, Janos. I know I should be shrieking in embarrassment rather than laughing, but I'm infamous in my family for having the most bizarre reaction to things. Perhaps you could turn around while I fetch my robe, Your Grace?"

If his artist were ever to discover how hard his good angel had to cudgel his bad one to silence his continued urgings to turn around and ogle her as she dressed, she would reward him with, at very least, a chaste kiss. Alas, it was somewhat of a pyrrhic victory for his decent side, as his good angel stood a snowball's chance in hell of erasing Bibi's long legs and perfectly shaped breasts from his memory.

Turning around, when he was bade to do so, he apologized, "I am sorry for the intrusion, but I opted for rescuing you from whatever troubled you rather than a display of good manners."

However much of a gentleman he was, not for life or limb, or the approbation of his good angel, would he inform Bibi her robe gaped open every time she stooped to retrieve a flower. When the last blossom was returned to the crystal vase, which had miraculously not shattered when tossed to the floor, he found himself kneeling on the carpet, face-to-face with the woman, and words failed him.

Covering his deplorable flirtation skills with action, he rose first and extended a hand to help her rise. "I always appear to start off on the wrong foot with you, and I am at a loss as to how to correct it. Will you dine with me again this evening? No sketch pad. I want this to be a dinner between friends and not a commission."

Bibi looked down at their joined hands. "I'd be delighted, Janos."

Not until he entered his own rooms was he clearheaded enough to remember he called Beatrix Baranyi, *kincsem*, his little treasure. He'd done so twice, and he couldn't make up his mind whether he wanted her to remember the endearment or not, but he definitely wanted to form a warmer, less stilted, relationship with her.

He counted the minutes and paced his suite until the appointed dinner hour, and eagerly opened the door when he heard her soft knock. "Welcome. Would you care for some sherry?"

Answering her unspoken question, he supplied, "I released Akos for the evening. I hope you don't mind receiving less than perfect service, but I think I can remember which course follows which.

"Shall we sit by the fire for a few moments? Despite being in each other's company nearly every day, I believe neither one of us knows much about the other. Why don't you go first, Bibi?"

She accepted the sherry and sat facing him as he took the other wing chair.

"Where shall I begin?"

"Well, tell me about your family. I know your father is a well-respected artist, but I know very little else of the Horthy family."

"The Horthys are horse people. We breed and train horses for the Hungarian cavalry. My father demonstrated his drawing talent at an early age and was sent to Paris to study. His brother, Andris, is the one who continues the horse business with my father's help in between commissions. My father and uncle swear I could ride before I could walk."

"When did they know you also possessed artistic ability?"

"Oh, I always sketched things, and I accompanied my father on many of his commissions. I learned to draw and mix paint at his knee, so to speak."

"Did you also travel to Paris to study?" He grinned when she snorted in a most unladylike fashion at his question.

"No, traveling far away from the family horse-breeding concern didn't appeal to me. But when I stumbled across my first Russian painting, I developed a penchant for painting with vibrant colors. The fact Russia also had Cossacks was an added impetus to study there. As you no doubt can tell, I divide my attention between horses and painting."

When she finished her sherry, he seated her at the table. With a good imitation of a footman, he whipped a napkin from its folded state, placed it in her lap, then set forth serving the dinner.

Janos lifted the lid of a white and gold tureen to inspect its contents and exclaimed, "Cold cherry soup, one of my favorites. I think you will enjoy this, it is most refreshing."

He tried to be discreet as his eyes followed each lift of spoon and fork to her ruby lips but had to cease staring at her tantalizing mouth to respond to her compliment.

"The meal was exquisite, Janos. As you predicted, I

thoroughly enjoyed the soup. I must ask your cook for the recipe for my aunt. I hereby resolve to continue to ride daily, or I shall become too heavy for Shadow to carry me."

"Ah, but the meal is not quite over. You must sample her apricot pastries." When his dinner guest groaned a refusal, he urged, "Cook would be absolutely devastated should I send any of this back. Indulge me, and try one."

He waited for her to reach for the flaky confection before asking, "How did you meet your husband?"

He had no idea why the question suddenly popped from his mouth, but it caused her to stammer a reply.

"I-I, um, Mihaly and I grew up together. We were the best of friends as children and often got into trouble together. In fact, if one was caught committing some transgression, they punished us both, as it was likely we were equally guilty."

"I'm sure you were thrilled when he asked for your hand." A brief veil of sorrow masked her face and made him want to recall the statement.

"More surprised than thrilled. While we were the best of friends as children, Mihaly chose to reside in Vienna as an adult. He preferred court life to the stodgy country scene. Only his mother's insistence he assume his responsibilities as head of the household made him stay after the sudden death of his father.

"I also think his mother's urging him to produce an heir, and take control of the family's horse breeding business, made him recall our childhood association and seek my company again."

"I'm sure he kept you in his heart while he was away," he

offered.

"While it would be nice to think so, I knew better. Mihaly was a true *bon vivant*. He delighted in partying, and playing pranks, and hunting. He did not find running an estate, or a business, or having to attend the season to find a pedigreed spouse, appealing. The easiest path was always the one he chose, and it's probably the reason he began to court me. I was close to home, had sufficient social status, and possessed a knowledge of horse breeding.

"Other points in my favor were he was comfortable being around me, and both our families offered no objections to the match. I can't lay all of the onus on Mihaly for such poor reasons in seeking a spouse. I didn't object to any of Mihaly's obvious stratagems, and truth be told, I believed the fairy tale where friendship grows into love."

"Judging by the sadness I see in your eyes, you did grow to love him, indeed." He reached across the table and squeezed her hand in sympathy.

Bibi tugged her hand from his grasp to rise and begin pacing.

"Looks can be deceiving, Janos. We were married for exactly one day."

"My God, what happened?"

"Mihaly's valet lost his reason and shot us as we lay in our marriage bed. I believe Mihaly did possess a certain *tendresse* for me, for he threw himself between me and the valet, and the shot took him in the neck before piercing my shoulder.

"Although I tried to staunch Mihaly's wound, it didn't help. Mihaly's mother, the first to respond to my cries for help, suffered a fatal heart attack after discovering her son dead amidst a truly horrifying amount of blood. I still suffer from nightmares."

"And with good reason. I am so sorry I ever began this conversation, *kincsem*." He rose and wrapped her in his arms and held her close. "I would take these memories from you if I could."

Her tone verged on cynical as she responded to his offer. "And I would let you, but I think it is my punishment for settling for a business arrangement rather than love. Like Mihaly, I took what was convenient and safe rather than waiting for someone who would complete me in things other than business.

"If you will excuse me, Your Grace, I wish to return to my room."

Amidst the evidence of a shared meal, he paced from the table, to the fireplace, to his bedroom, and back again, as he chided himself for being so gauche as to pry into her personal life.

Bloody hell, you didn't read her mind, so how were you to know? Maybe you should start doing so before you alienate her further, his evil angel offered.

Stay out of her mind and pay more attention to her good attributes, the good angel offered.

Yes, good advice, even if it comes from my adversary. Pay more attention to her luscious body. You won't need to read her mind if you are paying strict attention to those lovely physical attributes, Satan's advocate continued.

Bugger off, the both of you, he snarled. Suddenly, his

rooms were too oppressive to remain sequestered in. Grabbing his violin case, he headed for his favorite place to play. The solar in the evening, with the stars shining through the glass roof, was his sanctuary of choice to play and restore calm when he was upset.

***

Bibi's hope the heavy, late evening meal would make her drowsy was dashed after an hour of tossing and turning, until the bed linens were so twisted, she had to get out of bed and straighten them. It was then she became aware of the music. Someone was playing the most passionate, soulful violin piece ever to be heard outside of a gypsy performance. Not recognizing the piece, she opened one of the tower windows, the better to hear, and possibly learn, where it was coming from.

She spied the solar aglow with candlelight and grabbed her dressing gown to seek the musician who could imbue their music with such emotion.

Opening the solar door quietly, so as not to disturb the unknown violinist, she tiptoed through the lush foliage toward the center and seated herself on a padded leather bench. She remained unnoticed as Janos gave himself completely to the music. He was magnificent in his concentration, and his ability to wring notes from the violin touched something deep inside her. He played with his eyes closed, and the passion flowed across his face in unguarded waves.

With the last note still trembling in the air, she clapped

gently and whispered, "Bravo, Janos."

Her unexpected presence so startled the prince he almost dropped the instrument. "Forgive me for intruding, but your music called to me. It was a beautiful piece. I don't recognize it, who is the composer?"

The prince returned the violin to its protective case before answering. "I wrote it."

"I had no idea you were such a talented musician. You play with such passion, you could rival any gypsy violinist."

The Viceroy of Transylvania actually blushed at her effusive compliments.

"Indeed, I was taught by a gypsy. He would accept your praise as his due, for his pride equaled his skill as a violinist."

She attributed the release of her tension, caused by her employer's inquiry into her personal life, to the music. She had no desire to return to her room as he stood before her in the moonlight without his coat, and tie, and cuff links, and, she noted, his forearms were bare where he'd rolled his sleeves to play. Before she could stifle the impulse, she extended a hand and drew him down to the bench.

"I want to confess something, Janos. You are an enigma to me. Each time I sketch you, your essence escapes me. Not so with my drawings of Erzsebet, Akos, Cata, and even Lucifer and Anubis. The spark illuminating them shines through."

Laughing self-deprecatingly, she continued, "But each time I attempt to draw you, what is truly *you* escapes me. Just when I think you are stiff, controlled, self-contained, you surprise me by playing music beautiful enough to make an angel weep, and I want to scream in frustration because I know I wouldn't be able to capture in a drawing the passion you showed me this evening."

"I am not an enigma, Bibi. I am just a man who owes you an apology. I know I upset you this evening by prying into your life, and I sincerely apologize, but at this moment I must apologize for a future transgression."

She drew back, the better to see him. "A future transgression? How does one apologize for a transgression yet to be committed?"

"This way."

Janos cupped his hands around her face and drew her to his lips to bestow a tender kiss. A kiss quickly blossoming into one of passion.

His spicy flavor, indeed, even his tang of fresh-cut pine and leather, made her surrender after a brief resistance. Her conscience surfaced to chide her over her lack of opposition to Janos's seduction, and she made a weak plea for understanding from whichever angel guarded her this evening. She'd kept herself pure before marriage, surely her behavior had garnered some leniency.

Her conscience had its say before any angelic intervention and castigated her. Bibi was surprised when her inner being took umbrage and replied remaining chaste wasn't difficult when temptation came in the form of inexperienced kisses stolen by boys and young men. She further temporized she'd entered into her wedding with every intention of being a dutiful wife, but though she possessed title, property, and status, they meant nothing without a living, breathing husband. She tossed down an imaginary gauntlet to her conscience by thinking, if given the chance, tonight, she would be self-indulgent, and do what young, widowed women of her station had the privilege of doing. She would freely welcome what death denied her.

The overwhelming sensation of her arousal by Janos's talented lips and hands made her wonder if someone in the castle would hear the breaching of the dam of her self-control as it burst with a roar loud enough to shake the gloomy pile of stones the Rackoszis called home. The prince's masterful kiss opened all floodgates, and she met his second kiss with parted lips, and an embrace strong enough to crush his body to hers.

"*Kincsem*, if you continue to return my kisses so passionately, I will not be responsible for what follows. I wanted you from the moment I met you, but I tried to do the honorable thing and keep you at arm's length. However, I will no longer be able to act honorably if you don't tell me to stop."

She cast her propriety to the four winds when he continued to bestow soft, wet kisses on her eyes, her earlobes, and the sweet spot where neck met shoulder. The calloused pads of his fingertips played her body as skillfully as he did the violin, and small, crystal notes of want emerged from her throat to hang in the silvered moonlight of the solar.

She ran her hands through the ebony silk of his hair and held him still long enough to gasp, "I think you need to continue this manner of apology."

A growl rumbled from his throat as he lifted her from the bench and untied her robe. Her thin, cotton nightgown shone transparent in the moonlight, and his fingers trembled as he inched it up her legs and over her head. It was torture to remain still, but if this was moon madness, she did not want to move and startle him back to sanity.

"My God, you are more beautiful than my dreams imagined."

In response, she took his hands and molded them around her breasts. She groaned in unabashed pleasure when he cupped them and rubbed his thumbs over her pebbled nipples. Gazing into his mesmerizing eyes sent a bolt of lust straight to her core, and she began to rain with desire.

"And in *my* dreams, you are clad in nothing but moonlight," she whispered, and unbuttoned his shirt to tug it free of his trousers.

When he stood before her, limned in silver, it took her a moment to find her voice. "My artist's eyes spoke true. Your body is as beautifully sculpted as I pictured it would be. Perhaps my mistake was not sketching you in the nude, first."

Janos spread his shirt over the cold, leather bench before laying her upon it. "I beg your forgiveness, but this apology is going to take hours to deliver."

The prince apologized to her hair, and her nose, and her throat, especially her throat, where he suckled, and laved, and sent shivers down her body. Her breasts were profoundly apologized to by his hands and his warm and talented tongue. Frissons of anxiety made her squirm when he kissed and nipped at the insides of her thighs, and she attempted to deny further access.

"Let me sample you, Bibi. My imagination says your essence will be even sweeter than a rose dipped in honey. I want to give you so much pleasure you will fill my mouth with your nectar."

His reverence eased her fear, and she opened her legs for him, exposing the sweet rosebud of her desire for the first time.

"*Kincsem*, you quicken my hunger with such exquisite flavor. Open your eyes and behold what you do to me."

She obeyed the royal command and wished for pencil and paper to capture a moment worth savoring for the rest of her life. Janos was so aroused, his member wept a perfect tear for her, begging she accept him.

As she sighed her surrender, the prince used his fingers to arouse her, yet again, to ensure his entrance would be welcome. When his warm body covered hers, she squirmed in anticipation.

"Your beauty all but blinds me," he whispered to her as he entered her. The magical mood shattered.

Bereft at the instant withdrawal, she strove for courage to meet his eyes. "Janos, I know I owe you an explanation, but please, dear God, allow me to give it after you finish this apology." She dared to hope when her request sent a shiver of sexual hunger down his body.

"My apology will not come without pain, Bibi, but let us share it. When I enter, bite down on my shoulder. It will be an honor to bear your love bite."

One glance into the prince's beautifully fringed eyes, and she believed the sincerity of his words. She nodded and permitted him to position his body over hers once again.

As he whispered to her in a language she didn't understand, he tantalized her with short strokes. The sensation, while wonderful, made her body yearn for completion all the more, and she grew impatient enough to meet each stroke with a thrust of her own. She wanted the full length of him seated within her, and she voiced the demand. The prince did not disappoint and gave her the command to bite. She eagerly obeyed.

She wanted to upbraid herself for biting too hard but lost the ability to apologize for causing pain when the small, coppery swallow of his blood made her body explode. Each and every stroke of his shaft brought such exquisite sensation, she shattered into wondrous pieces. Immersed for the first time in the experience of a man filling her with his life and joy, she convulsed in wondrous laughter.

When her lover's stillness pierced her self-absorption, she opened her eyes to discover the prince peering down at her, his lips twitching in a lopsided grin.

"Maybe I should be insulted my loving amuses you so, but you have no idea how good your laughing feels while I'm still inside you."

His subsequent demonstration made her laugh harder.

***

He cursed himself as doubly damned by his selfishness and irresponsibility. Although he wanted to give them to Beatrix Baranyi, he kept the bonding words from tumbling out as he took her precious virginity. And because of his silence, rather than being able to look forward to the rest of his life with eagerness, his soul ached with remorse. He took what he had no right to. He was duty-bound to another, and Rackoszis didn't break their promises. Neither did they bed an innocent, knowing they would leave her unprotected the next morning. His punishment? He already knew it. He would be faithful to the honor of his house, and lose the one woman he desired above all others.

The approaching dawn broke his vigil. He held Bibi in his arms as she slept the boneless sleep of the thoroughly sated and spent the time memorizing every feature, every nuance, indeed, every miniscule flaw or natural marking on her body. She managed to imprint herself into his life force in just a few fleeting hours, and the loss of her would be a mortal wound.

With great reluctance to part from her, he dressed and roused her enough to help her into her nightgown to carry her back to her room. It was almost time for the staff to begin rising for the day, and he did not want anyone to discover them wandering the castle's halls *en dishabille.*

***

The prince's violin wasn't in its accustomed spot, and aware of his employer's penchant for playing in the solar long after the staff retired, Akos headed there to retrieve it.

Ah, right where I presumed it would be, he smugly congratulated himself. What he hadn't expected to find was Baroness Baranyi's silk robe lying abandoned underneath the bench.

If I take this back to His Grace, he will be pleased to return it to the baroness. The valet permitted himself a grin of anticipation for the thanks his prince would receive from the artist. Perhaps the prince's bridal dilemma would end happily, after all. Speaking of which, he would be sure to knock and wait for the prince's permission, before daring to enter the royal bedchamber.

Akos's anticipation of a happy ending evaporated when he returned to the prince's suite and found him pacing in agitation.

"Please inform the baroness we will leave later this afternoon for the Szechenyi estate and to pack accordingly. I think it is time I introduced her to Margyth so she can sketch her."

Holding up the baroness's robe, Akos asked, "Wouldn't you care to tell the baroness yourself and return this to her?"

He glared at his valet. "No, I would not. Use your usual discretion and tell Cata to slip it into the baroness's luggage when she packs for her."

Directing his next remark to the prince's rigid back, he made no effort to mask his disgust with the prince's attempt to dodge the woman so soon after their assignation. "Your father would be ashamed to think he raised a coward."

Whirling around, Janos snapped, "You forget your station, Akos."

The valet stiffened and tendered a grudging apology. "Forgive me, Your Grace, but your actions are making it appear as if the baroness did not receive your attentions willingly."

The man halted his pacing so abruptly, Akos could almost visualize the stones in the invisible wall he appeared to hit.

The prince's words were more growled than spoken. "Are you bereft of reason? I would never force my attentions on the baroness, or on any woman."

Not giving himself time to ponder why he continued to poke the prince with his sharp inquiries, Akos persisted. "Then why are you acting so guilty if you did nothing wrong? Does your wish to send Baroness Baranyi away stem from finding her boring in bed?"

"On my honor as a Rackoszi, everything I did was mutually enjoyed, so cease your questioning, Akos. I just think the baroness might find it less awkward if we put some distance between us for a while."

After the prince ceased avowing his innocence of wrong-doing, Akos moved about, tidying the various rooms, until forced to shift his attention to the prince's bed, the disappointingly empty of the baroness's presence bed. The chaotic state of the bed linens made it evident the brief sleep the prince managed, after parting from the baroness, wasn't restful.

While tidying the bed, Akos discovered a shirt entangled with the sheets. Tsking at the mistreatment of such fine apparel, he shook it out, and left the bedroom to inform the prince of his find.

The prince surprised him by whisking it from his hands.

He attempted to retrieve the garment, but Prince Rackoszi wouldn't surrender the wrinkled shirt. "Your Grace, this needs to be laundered. You can't possibly wear it in this condition. Did you cut yourself? Let me send the shirt to the laundress to ply her skills to remove the blood spot."

When the prince still didn't relinquish his tight hold, he conceded the tug-of-war with an, "As you wish, Your Grace."

"No need to trouble yourself, Akos, I'll discard the shirt."

"But this is one of your favorites. Please, Your Grace, give the laundress a chance to get the stain out."

***

"Enough," Janos roared, and stalked back into his bedroom and slammed the door, leaving an astonished valet on the other side.

Gritting his teeth in frustration, he lifted the shirt to his nose and inhaled the scent of virgin blood, Bibi's blood. His frustration turned to pure lust, and he realized he had to put distance between himself and Baroness Baranyi or all his plans would shatter. His resolve to be an honorable man wouldn't last long in the face of such strong sexual yearning.

His stomach tied itself into a painful knot with his resolve to honor his promise to Baron Szechenyi. With clenched jaw, he forced himself to bundle up the shirt to cast it into the fire. He even began the motion but scrabbled to grab an end before it totally left his hand. Furthermore, he refused to consider his motive for ripping the blood spot from the shirt and searching his room for a secure place to cache his memento. He chose his jewelry chest, and pressed the inlaid wood in a certain spot to open a hidden compartment, which held, until this moment, only childhood treasures.

He placed the torn fragment next to a mica-flecked pebble, and the gold baby bracelet he wore until it no longer fit. Snapping the drawer closed, he consigned the rest of the shirt to the flames. Ah, by the ancient gods, he felt the shirt's immolation as if he'd cast his own heart into the fire. Not to worry, he smirked, even if his heart did turn to ash, Margyth would marry him with or without one.

Akos made no comment on the shirt smoldering in the fireplace when he at last gave permission to enter the bedroom. His circumspect valet simply placed the breakfast tray upon the table and held the chair for him. Too late he remembered even discreet valets possessed ways to demonstrate contrary opinions. Akos waited until he filled his mouth with eggs and bacon to confirm it.

"I apprised Baroness Baranyi of your plans, and she requested a brief moment of your time before leaving.

"And if Your Grace thinks I will help alleviate his choking caused, I dare say, by swallowing the wrong way, he is mistaken."

Too busy trying to recover his breath, he didn't comment on his servant's loud bang of the door upon his exit.

May the ancient ones preserve him from annoyed valets, he cursed as he stood over his freshly made bed and studied the ensemble his valet selected for him. Little did Akos realize, his unsubtle choice of garments would suit his present mood. He did feel as if he was about to attend a funeral, and not call on an arranged *fiancée*.

He left Akos's silent censure on the bed and returned to his dressing room to select a bottle-green velvet jacket, fawn trousers, and a whiskey-colored cravat, and dressed without assistance. Being fully dressed, he had no excuse to remain in his rooms, so he steeled himself to confront Bibi as to why she desired to speak with him.

While searching the castle's dim corridors and rooms for the baroness, he vociferously denied his valet's accusation he didn't want to see the woman because he lacked courage. The real reason for his reluctance to confront his artist stemmed from his lack of experience with the social protocols required the morning after deflowering virgins. He couldn't begin to guess what her reaction would be. Would she be happy or distraught over her loss? Would a night of mutual passion lead her to expect more from him than he could give? Gods help him, he sadly lacked experience in both love and dalliance.

His feet, without conscious effort, took him to the castle's main entrance. "Ah, there you are, Baroness, I was told you wanted to ask me a question?"

He looked over her shoulder, where she stood out of the way as her artist's supplies were loaded into his carriage, and poked his head through the doorway to verify his order for a closed carriage had been obeyed. Even though the day was cloudy, he would take no chance of getting caught in an open carriage if the sun made a surprise appearance. Despite the enclosure, he would still need to wear his smoked glasses if the baroness wanted the window curtains to remain open.

Bibi spun around at his question and gifted him with a radiant smile, which all but froze his feet to the stone floor.

"Good afternoon, Your Grace. Yes, I wanted to ask if it would be permissible to bring Shadow along. I'm not sure what Baroness Szechenyi's stable accommodations are, and I wouldn't want to impose."

He noted the formality of the baroness's address, and it made him breathe a little easier. She appeared as eager as he to put some distance between them, so why did such formality send a sudden, painful ping through his chest? Was she signaling an end to their easy friendship?

Unexpectedly hurt at the notion, he deferred to her wish for formality between them and responded in kind. "Not to worry, Baroness, the Szechenyi stables will be able to accommodate Shadow. I will personally make the arrangements when we arrive. If you will permit me to assist you into the carriage, we will leave."

Chapter Nine

Sitting diagonally across from Janos in the enclosed carriage, she had a chance to study him in profile. His dark glasses hid his beautiful eyes, but the clenched jaw told her how uncomfortable he was with being in such close proximity to her.

No doubt he thinks I want to accuse him of taking advantage of me. Well, I intend to banish such nonsense, immediately. What we did together was memorable and liberating. I am free of guilt for the first time in a year, and the prince's frigid reserve cannot and will not ruin it for me.

Leaning forward, Bibi tapped him on the knee and smiled when he jumped at her unexpected action.

"Janos, you needn't be uncomfortable around me, in fact, I want to thank you for last night."

"Thank me? I must apologize for, for..."

She reached out and placed a finger on the prince's wonderfully talented lips before he gave voice to an unnecessary apology.

"Please, no more. I don't think I would survive another one of your apologies for a transgression quite so soon."

At the nonplussed look her remark engendered, she couldn't help herself and laughed until she hiccupped.

"What? Did you expect to be trapped inside this carriage with an outraged, violated virgin? Please give me credit for being a little worldlier."

Regaining a modicum of composure, she continued, "I owe you an explanation, and a sincere apology for putting you into what you must believe to be an awkward position. Truthfully, my particular regret is *you* seem to rue our actions last night, but I assure you, you gave me something my life had been missing, and I truly have no regrets."

Turning to face her at last, Janos removed his dark glasses.

"Bibi, it was more like I *took* something precious from you, and I've been reproaching myself for enjoying what your husband did not live long enough to experience."

She sat back into the leather squabs and tapped her bottom lip with her finger to consider her words carefully before answering. "I am certain, even if my husband had lived, he would never have enjoyed it."

"My dear, you are not making sense. You said Mihaly died in your arms because he tried to shield you from harm with his body. To me, his actions speak of a man in love with his wife."

She turned to look at the passing scenery and seconds elapsed before she responded. "Because you gave me something I will always hold dear to my heart, I will gift you with the truth of what happened on my wedding night."

When the prince shook his head as if to stop her, she protested, "No, let me speak of this, and perhaps I will be able to stop dreaming of it. Everyone in my family avoids asking about it. They think I will become hysterical all over again, but I think it's time to let the horror fade with the light of truth.

"When Baroness Baranyi summoned Mihaly home after

his father's death, I hardly knew him, and both of us were shy in each other's company. It amazed me when he began making a clumsy attempt to court me."

She closed her eyes, and cocked her head to consider her words before continuing. "Did I love him? I'll be honest and say no, but I did hold a certain affection for him. He always managed to raise my spirits when in his company, and, I will admit, his handsomeness attracted me. But the few, chaste kisses he gave me aroused no romantic stirring in me, at all. I did us both a disservice when I agreed to marry him. My family encouraged Mihaly's suit because they believed I would be protected and cherished. As it turned out, they erred in thinking so."

Taking a deep breath, she tried to continue, but her throat had grown tight and dry.

"There is no need to continue this, I don't like upsetting you," Janos offered as he reached across to squeeze her hand.

"You are a very kind man, but believe me when I say recounting it to someone I consider a friend may very well purge it from my memory." She looked away from his concerned gaze and continued, "I assumed Mihaly suffered from nerves as much as I did on our wedding day. He was pale and trembled visibly as we said our vows. However, the look on his face when he entered our bedroom from his dressing room, was more one of a condemned man rather than an eager groom."

She lowered her eyes to study the carriage floor before she continued her recitation of events. "I naively assumed Mihaly was at last eager to do his husbandly duty when he all but jumped into the bed, but when I attempted to kiss him, and embrace him, he stayed my hands and burst into hysterical sobs.

"My husband"—she failed to control her shudder—"kept apologizing, and saying he wasn't brave enough to go through with it. Mihaly babbled apologies for his plan to get me with child, hopefully on our wedding night so he would never need to lie with me again. His aversion was just too strong to let him attempt the act."

She leaned over and patted the prince's knee to calm him when he started to splutter in outrage for her husband's treatment of her.

"His aversion?" Janos snarled. "No man in his right mind would deny himself the pleasure of having such a beautiful and willing wife as you in his bed."

"I thank you for the compliment, but Mihaly was not repelled by me in particular, he had an aversion to all women. Just as the meaning behind his hysteria dawned on me, his valet ran from Mihaly's dressing room and pointed a gun at me. I'll never forget hearing him scream, 'He's mine. I won't share him with you.'

"Mihaly stopped crying long enough to plead with his lover not to do anything foolish, they would work things out. But the valet was beyond reasoning with, especially when Mihaly threw himself in front of me to protect me. Crazy with jealous despair, the valet fired the pistol. The ball caught Mihaly in the throat before lodging in my shoulder."

"Was the valet brought to justice?"

She gazed out the carriage window and cleared her throat

before answering his question. "There was no need. After shooting Mihaly, the valet ran back to the dressing room, and used the other pistol in the matched set to kill himself."

"My God, what a horrible experience," he exclaimed, and crossed swiftly to her side of the carriage to gather her into his embrace.

Putting her hand out to ward him off, she demanded, "Let me finish it. I don't remember the funeral details at all, except I dressed, spoke, and ate when directed to. Shock can be a merciful thing.

"Weeks later, at the reading of the will, the only words I heard were my own as they rolled constantly through my head. I was a fraud, a baroness who inherited considerable property from a man who, according to law, wasn't her husband because the marriage was never consummated. I was a virgin widow, how ironic. I lacked the courage to tell my family such a sordid tale. Nor could I return the title and the estate, because no other living Baranyi relatives were found after both Mihaly and his mother died. I was forever bound by Mihaly's deceit."

She let herself relax into Janos's side for a brief moment. "I want to assure you, by making love to me last night, you gave me a gift beyond price. You replaced a horrible memory with a beautiful one, and you gave me the courage to seek love for my own self."

"*Kincsem*, I am not the one who gave you courage. Your actions after Mihaly's death tell me you possess more courage than most newly widowed wives."

"Janos, what I experienced with you last night was

precious. One night with you opened my eyes to the realization I devalued myself by agreeing to marriage with a man I liked but didn't love. I allowed myself to be cajoled into a marriage based on the fact both Mihaly and I possessed the right bloodstock. It still confounds me I didn't think to point out to my father, or Baroness Baranyi, Mihaly and I were people, not horses. At very least I should have found the courage to insist I wouldn't marry unless I found a man who completed my passions, not make the Horthy and Baranyi stables profitable.

"If I die without ever finding my ideal, I will be thankful I at least experienced such pleasure as you gave me. But I swear to you, I will never give up searching for a man who desires me for just me, and not what property, wealth, or the strength my bloodlines can do for his lineage. I finally understand what passion is, and I want more of it. I want to be ardently in love with my husband, and I will happily spend my life returning his love in full measure.

"You, Prince Rackoszi, have shown me what love between a man and woman can be like, and I thank you for doing so. My goodness, I guess confession is good for the soul, I feel so relieved." Bibi didn't bother repressing her giggle as she relaxed back into the cushioned leather seat.

However, when she cast her eyes toward her traveling companion, she found his eyes closed, and, instead of sitting perfectly straight, he'd withdrawn from her side to slump in the corner of the carriage. "Janos, what is it? Did I upset you with my diatribe?" Taking his hands in her own, she gave them a slight shake until he opened his eyes.

"Oh, Bibi, I think you're about to be very disappointed with me."

She patted the hand she still held and tried to reassure him. "Disappointed? I wouldn't presume to be disappointed with you."

"Not even when it appears as if I am about to marry for all of the considerations you find repugnant?"

The prince reared back when she replied, "I am aware of your need to secure both properties through marriage to Margyth. Akos told me."

Janos grumbled, "Meddling valet."

She hastened to defend Akos. "Don't be angry with him. He was attempting to explain why you sent me such mixed signals. At times it appeared as if you enjoyed my company, and at other times I thought you detested being anywhere close to me."

Tugging on her hands until she drew closer, he held her gaze with a direct stare. "Intense dislike is an emotion I will never ascribe to our relationship, *kincsem*. Please let me explain myself so you don't think I am doing this just for money, or property, or... What was the term you used to describe pedigree? Ah, the right bloodstock."

At her nod, he continued, "The Szechenyi estate lay vacant for years. Baron Szechenyi's father preferred living in Vienna but let the land and the manor house be used occasionally as a hunting lodge. After his death, the son chose to move his wife and daughter here. Baroness Szechenyi, and you will find this quite believable once you meet her, did not fit in well with court society and preferred to live in isolated country splendor.

"Unfortunately, the Baron Szechenyi had a gambling problem, which he kept hidden until last year. I believe he was lucky or skilled enough to win more than he lost, and his estate's farm profits were able to pay for his losses, but he either suffered from a colossal run of bad luck, or he ran into someone very good at cheating and not getting caught.

"When my man of affairs in Budapest alerted me the Szechenyi holdings were in danger from anyone purchasing his markers, I instructed him to buy them back from as many holders as he found.

"The Szechenyis and Rackoszis have a long understanding to keep our noses in our own business. The baron didn't fuss when he spotted Lucifer in his fields, and I made sure Lucifer disturbed nothing on his property. We happily ignored each other until he risked eviction from his home."

At her indrawn hiss, he hurried to explain. "I had no intention of turning the baron and his family out, but I wanted to make sure no one else did so, either. As I said, the baron and I both valued our privacy, a new owner might not be as eager to keep to himself.

"You see, the Szechenyi estate is the cork in the valley bottle leading to the castle, and with the baron in residence, I didn't need to worry about restricting Lucifer's jaunts, or to calm irate villagers demanding he be put down for sheep attacks he wasn't responsible for.

"The baron did not care to keep abreast of what went on in the castle, or even make the occasional neighborly visit, although I always gave him an invitation to any social events.

Invitations he returned with his regrets. Perhaps it was lazy or selfish, but I didn't want to take the time to develop a similar arrangement with a new owner, and so I tried to convince Baron Szechenyi to give up gambling.

"In hindsight, I wish I'd tried harder to convince the baron I wasn't trying to destroy him by buying up his markers, or at least assuring him I had no intention of calling them due. But I did ask for him to stop visiting the gaming hells in Budapest, and work to reestablish the financial footing of his estate.

"I should have recognized him for the inveterate gambler he was, because Baron Szechenyi hedged his bets. He refused to believe my sincerity until I gave my word should he fail to raise enough funds out of his estate to buy back all of his markers, I would marry his daughter to protect his land and his family. I conceded, and gave him my word as a Rackoszi, and less than an hour after I left his residence, he took his own life.

"As you will soon see for yourself, his widow hates me. Indeed, she blames me for being the cause of his death, and I cannot say she's entirely wrong."

Bibi leapt quickly to the prince's defense. "She is wrong. You only tried to help him. The baron's misplaced pride at being found weak is what made him take the easy way out and leave his family to face the consequences of his vices."

"Perhaps, but as you did when you inherited Mihaly's title and property, I must lay claim to a certain amount of guilt. I question whether or not my motives were as altruistic as I've tried to convince myself they were. Especially since I accepted the baron's proposal because I wanted to guard my own privacy. To be honest, if I had even an inkling the baron intended to kill himself after securing my promise, I would never have accepted his terms, for I'm bound by my honor to provide for his widow and daughter through marriage. And I will not go back on my word and turn them out, or let anyone else do so. Indeed, I'm still buying up markers when my man of affairs encounters them.

"The one who truly suffers is Margyth. Her father's self-indulgence assured she would have no dowry, no presentation at court, and no hope to attract a suitor with her family estate so deeply in debt. As her father was clever enough to arrange, marriage to me will give her the status and security he felt his daughter deserved."

He crossed his arms over his chest. "It hasn't escaped the baroness's attention I will inherit the Szechenyi estate through marriage to her daughter and the outstanding markers I hold. As God is my witness, I never expected to secure my privacy and earn hatred in return."

His artist broke the gloomy silence at the end of his confession with her characteristically strange way of looking at things.

"I married for convenience and parental pressure, and you are about to marry for privacy and obligation. Those are not exactly good reasons for entering a life bond. However, unlike me, you can take a bad beginning and make a better end."

"How so?"

"Well, Janos, there are no jealous lovers waiting to shoot

you, and we both know you do not abhor women."

She was encouraged she'd lightened the prince's mood, when he took one look at her twinkling eyes and wry grin, and freed a hoot of laughter he was unable to suppress.

"Beatrix Baranyi, you are incorrigible."

Their mutual confessions came to an end when the carriage entered the circular drive of the Szechenyi estate.

Chapter Ten

"Baroness Szechenyi, may I present Baroness…"

"Szigi!"

Bibi looked on as Prince Rackoszi froze in the middle of his introduction to give his attention to a beautifully coifed and gowned woman who threw her arms around him and kissed him exuberantly on both cheeks.

Stepping away, the prince cleared his throat. "Margyth, let me introduce you and your mother to Baroness Baranyi, the artist I engaged to paint your miniature."

Before she could extend a greeting, Margyth interrupted.

"Pooh, Szigi, why do you need a miniature of me? The real me is a great deal better than a tiny, painted likeness."

Choosing diplomacy, Janos attempted to put the daughter's deliberate rudeness in a better light.

"A portrait is a form of immortality, Margyth, and Baroness Baranyi can make you so by painting your portrait."

At the mention of immortality, Baroness Szechenyi gave an audible hiss. By her pursed lips and flashing black eyes, everyone in the room understood Margyth's mother did not favor the suggestion, or perhaps she disliked the prince himself.

As much to calm troubled waters as to save her commission, she offered, "And what a beautiful daughter for me to paint, Your Grace. Margyth's is the ideal, classical face. I don't doubt I'll paint anything less than a stunning portrait."

The Baroness Szechenyi relaxed her rigid posture a bit at the blatant flattery, but her daughter, while basking in the general agreement of her beauty, turned to focus her feline, green eyes on her.

As Margyth intended, she didn't miss the spoiled chit's unspoken, but crystal-clear message the prince was hers, and she'd brook no interference from an interloper.

Her artist's eyes assessed mother and daughter. Stout, with sallow skin, and dark hair and eyes, and dressed in unrelieved black, as befit her widow's status, the Baroness Szechenyi did not resemble her willowy, golden-haired daughter in the least.

Margyth, however, possessed the much sought-after Hungarian ideal of golden hair and green eyes, and she eschewed mourning dress. Musing there would be a more than a passing resemblance between the deceased Baron and his daughter, she almost missed Margyth's question.

"How long will you require me to pose? I find sitting still boring in the extreme."

Responding before the prince could deliver a sharp retort for the rude remark, she replied, "Oh, all I require is several good sketches of you in different poses. I can be very discreet, and not inconvenience you in the slightest. Once I accumulate enough poses to select from, I'll return to the prince's residence to complete your final portrait."

Not bothering to answer, Margyth grabbed Janos's hand and demanded his attention once again. "Szigi, you didn't compliment me on my new dress, and I made sure to wear it just for you."

She looked to the Baroness Szechenyi to deliver, at least, a mild rebuke for such blatant rudeness, only to find Margyth's mother gazing at her daughter as if she just said something monumentally brilliant.

With the first prick of anger at such terrible social manners, Bibi stopped to analyze her reaction. Did her cold reception by Margyth offend her, or did the deliberate monopolization of Prince Rackoszi's attention by a spoiled debutante offend her more? One, deep look into Margyth's eyes told her the woman did not possess the young, innocent soul she portrayed to this assembly.

Bibi experienced sudden contrition over how she teased Janos about his arrangement with the late Baron Szechenyi, for she excelled at estimating whether or not a horse possessed the qualities worthy to be included in the Horthy-Baranyi stock, and instinct told her Margyth, were she a horse, would not make the cut. She wouldn't offer one forint for such an inferior bloodline, and she didn't think jealousy tainted her assessment.

Even though the prince appeared resigned to give his arranged fiancée what she so clearly wanted, she didn't think Margyth would spare him even a small measure of gratitude for keeping his promise to her father. Furthermore, the spoiled woman erred in thinking she would interfere in any way with the marriage arrangements. Prince Rackoszi hired her to paint betrothal portraits, and she didn't need to be reminded, so blatantly, of his unavailability. However, she didn't bother repressing the unkind thought Margyth's over-the-top fawning on the prince did not impress the man.

She did permit herself a twinge of sympathy for the undesired situation in which the prince found himself when Margyth led him to a love seat, and turned her back on everyone else.

At last recalling enough of her manners to break the embarrassing silence, the baroness bade them all be seated and rang for tea and pastries, just as a tall, very handsome man with dark auburn hair entered the room and drew her interest.

"I say, who owns the marvelous piece of horseflesh tied to the back of the carriage?"

Had her father been present, he would scold her for her lack of charity when she smirked at how fast Janos jumped up from the love seat to greet the stranger, but she did at least keep the unladylike expression from lingering on her face.

"The horse belongs to the Baroness Baranyi. I'm sorry, Baroness Szechenyi did not inform me she had guests." The prince separated his hand from Margyth's to step forward and greet the newcomer.

"Oh, do forgive my rudeness for interrupting." The red-haired man bowed to the group.

The Baroness Szechenyi, with a glare toward her daughter's suitor she didn't bother to conceal from anyone present, made the introductions. "May I present a distant relative of mine, Lieutenant Colonel Eszterhazy."

As Bibi's brow rose at the mention of one of Hungary's most prominent lineages, the colonel hurried to explain. "Come, come, Madame Szechenyi, you must also add I am a fourth son of a fourth son of said illustrious family, and not anywhere in the direct line of inheritance to their immense holdings."

Not to be deterred, the baroness continued, "Pal Anton is a Lieutenant Colonel in the Imperial Hussars."

The baroness but stated the obvious. Bibi took in the plaited braids at each temple, hair swept back into a queue, and a very well-trimmed handlebar mustache, and confirmed the sartorial style *de rigueur* among hussars survived in Pal Anton.

"Yes, and how fortuitous I volunteered to go on a purchasing trip for my regiment, as I was able to combine it with a visit to the Szechenyis." Pal Anton gave Margyth a wink and a grin, and added, "I never knew such beautiful lands housed such a beautiful cousin."

When the conversation lapsed, and the baroness failed to introduce them, she extended her hand. "I am Baroness Baranyi, and this is Prince Janos, er, Szigismond Rackoszi, Viceroy of Transylvania."

Pal Anton's *bonhomie* reasserted itself as he shook the prince's hand and bowed over hers.

"Baranyi, did you say? Your name sounds very familiar. Are you a regular at court?"

She went still, as chills ran over her skin. Janos's smooth response rescued her.

"Perhaps you are thinking of the Horthy-Baranyi horse-breeding concern. The baroness merged her late husband's stables with her father's, and they breed the best cavalry horses for the emperor's use."

Slapping his head in mock consternation, Pal Anton

apologized. "I can be so dense at times. The name is famous in military circles. Is the horse outside one of yours, Baroness?"

She cast Janos a weak smile of thanks before addressing the hussar. "Yes, I bred Shadow myself. He's a marvelous mount."

"Oh, Szigi, did you bring it as a present for me? Come, show me."

The prince halted Margyth's rush from the room by grabbing her hand and drawing her back to the love seat. "Margyth, the horse is not a present from me. Shadow is the baroness's mount. She brought him here for her private use."

Undeterred, Margyth continued, "Well I want to ride her horse so I can determine whether or not it's more suitable than my present mare. The horse you gave me, Szigi, is such a slow poke."

Even though red to the tops of his ears at Margyth's selfishness, the prince still attempted to placate her. "I'm afraid you won't be riding this one. He is a trained cavalry horse, which means he's accustomed to hand and leg signals and can only be ridden astride. Your mother, I am sure, would never permit you to ride astride."

Turning to Pal Anton, Janos continued, "Perhaps, Colonel, you and Margyth can show the baroness the stables so she may get her mount situated. I need to speak in private with Baroness Szechenyi."

Taking the cue, Bibi rose and offered her arm to the colonel, while a sulking Margyth led the way outside.

*****

Janos steeled himself to face the Baroness Szechenyi's palpable hatred of him. Though off-putting, her blatant dislike would not deter him from discussing what needed to be said. He opened with a direct shot across the baroness's corseted bow. "Why do you hate me so? I bought up the majority of your husband's gambling markers so you and Margyth are no longer at the mercy of any creditor who would claim all your remaining possessions and cast you out."

When the baroness responded with the truth, it made him suck in a quick breath.

"From the moment we took possession of this house, I studied you and the people who work for you. I am not ignorant of your true nature, and I hate you, and all such abominations, with my whole being."

Lifting the ornate gold cross from the bosom of her gown, Baroness Szechenyi held the blessed item in front of her face, as she spit her words like an angry cat. "You are very much mistaken if you think I'm one of those people you can enthrall. I'll never give my daughter to you."

He stiffened at the attack but extemporized to cover his anger. "My true nature, as you put it, is nothing more than a man who wants to honor his promise to your husband. I am also your nearest neighbor, the Viceroy of Transylvania, and your daughter, forgive me for stating the obvious, is more than willing to marry me."

His attempt to assuage the Baroness Szechenyi's animosity bore no fruit. The baroness crossed the room and shoved the cross in his face. He stepped back to avoid being cut by the religious symbol.

He made another attempt. "Baroness, I do not understand your animosity. My sole wish is to make things easier for you and your daughter. I replenished the servants you let go to save expense, and I paid off, I am certain, the majority of the markers your husband used to cover his debts, and all without any need for you to request I do so. You no longer have to worry about depending on the largesse of a relative to maintain your lifestyle."

Baroness Szechenyi's eyes shot daggers at him as she exclaimed, "You are *Nesferatu*, the Undead. I will not give my daughter to you so you can drink her blood until she is one of you. You are damned for all eternity, and I won't let Margyth be condemned as well for your perversions."

Though enraged by the baroness's vehement accusation, he kept his temper hidden as he dropped into a chair opposite her. "*Nesferatu*? Me, a vampire? Whatever made you reach such an absurd conclusion?"

"I keep abreast of what goes on in your castle. No one ages as they should, and you do not go abroad in daylight."

At the end of his patience over the baroness's constant waving of her cross in his face, he leaned forward and captured the bit of gold and reverently kissed the religious item, before allowing the representation of the crucified Christ to drop to her sunken bosom.

"You blaspheme!"

"How have I blasphemed? Because I paid reverence to the God of all Gods? Baroness Szechenyi, if I am an undead creature as you claim, would I be able to kiss your cross? And here it is broad daylight and have traveled from my residence to yours for this visit. I have also drunk your tea and eaten your pastries. You've been listening to folktale nonsense, Baroness. Vampires do not exist."

Not to be deterred by logic, the baroness spat, "What about your familiar, the wolf? He roams about my lands as if he owned them. Perhaps the wolf is actually you in animal form."

Taken aback at the baroness's assumption, Janos shook his head. "Did my wolf kill any cattle on your property? Did he attack anyone? Did he ever make a threatening gesture to you, or Margyth, or any of your servants?"

As he assumed she would, the baroness refused to answer his questions rather than lie to his face, and so he continued, "No person or animal on Szechenyi lands will come to any harm from my wolf. First, you call me a vampire and then a shape-shifter. What next, will you accuse me of sleeping in a coffin? You are being ridiculous in the extreme, Madame."

Not permitting logic to alter her beliefs, the baroness drew herself up to her outraged best and snarled, "I've followed your family since we moved here, and I know your household is not normal. Your parents never aged. I don't think they died in an accident, as is the story. I think they ran off before people discovered such abominations lived amongst them. Or perhaps, you drank their blood and killed them."

He stood so fast his chair toppled with a crash. "Baroness Szechenyi, why you choose to believe such outrageous things about me or my family is a mystery, but you are wrong. I'm not a vampire, and neither were my parents.

"If you are finished impugning all things Rackoszi, let me impart some unpleasant information of my own. While paying such close attention to the occurrences at castle Rackoszi, you managed to raise a willful, spoiled daughter. One who is quite vocal in her acceptance of me as her future husband because it ensures she will continue to enjoy an elevated lifestyle.

"And despite your low opinion of me, I will honor the agreement your husband forced on me, and not call due his markers and turn you out. You may continue to live here in comfort after I marry Margyth, but I suggest you refrain from broadcasting such outrageous slander. Remember, I am the Viceroy of Transylvania, with the legal means to silence you. Please excuse me, Madame, I will bid *adieu* to Margyth and Baroness Baranyi."

He worked hard to calm himself as he walked to the stables. What information did Baroness Szechenyi consult to reach such an outrageous conclusion? Undead? He briefly wished the old harridan had witnessed his physical reaction to Baroness Baranyi when she encountered him playing his violin in the solarium, it would disabuse her of the notion he was anything but very much alive. He wrestled with the vexing question of whether or not the mother poisoned her daughter against him by such mad accusations, and his spirits sank at the image of a lifelong marriage tainted by unrelieved acrimony from the both of them.

As he neared the Szechenyi stables, he asked himself what it would take for Baroness Szechenyi to drop her spurious accusations? If he got Margyth pregnant soon after the wedding, her mother would know she erred in calling him

Nesferatu. He curled his lip in disgust, even more annoyed when his salacious musing failed to stir his member into a semblance of interest.

He barely had his temper under control when he encountered Margyth, Bibi, and Pal Anton on their way back from the stables.

"Szigi, Pal Anton suggested we play cards, and you will be my partner."

"Thank you, Margyth, but another time. There is some estate business requiring my immediate attention. Please make my apologies to your mother, and do give the Baroness Baranyi some of your valuable time so she may complete her sketches."

Janos bowed to the trio. "Excuse my hasty visit, but I must go."

***

One look at Prince Rackoszi's white face and clenched hands made Bibi curious over what occurred between the Baroness Baranyi and the prince. By all appearances, Margyth's intended did not find his visit with his future mother-in-law a pleasant one.

She refrained from comment when Margyth's good mood disappeared with her suitor's abrupt departure.

"Drat it, playing with three is boring," Margyth complained.

Pal gave her a wink from behind his cousin's back. "Why don't you ask your mother to join us?"

When Pal Anton's suggestion restored the girl's mood, and she ran ahead to ask her mother to join them, Bibi turned to the Szechenyi houseguest, and with a sardonic lilt in her voice asked, "Are Imperial Hussars always so quick-thinking?"

Pal answered her. "*Mais certainment*, Baroness Baranyi. We are required to be. There isn't much time to dither when your enemy is charging at you with a wickedly sharp saber. May I escort you to the game room?"

At the look she received from Margyth when she entered the game room on Pal's arm, Bibi wondered if the hussar didn't plan the maneuver to tweak Margyth's jealousy, but Margyth being Margyth won the last word.

"Here, Pal, you will be my partner, and the two baronesses will play against us." Margyth's emphasis on the word "baronesses" managed to convey the suggestion of advanced dotage.

After the third hand, she knew the game was rigged as the Baroness Szechenyi and Pal both colluded to feed Margyth winning hands. Losing yet again, and not willing to waste her time catering to Margyth's overinflated opinion of herself, she eased back her chair and suggested, "My luck at cards is abysmal today, so why don't I fetch my sketch pad and do some preliminary drawings while you three are settled at the table?"

Not waiting for Margyth's approval, she hurried from the room and asked a servant to direct her to her assigned room.

She returned, sketch pad and pencil in hand, just as Margyth threw down her cards with a huff.

"This game is beyond boring. The two of you are not

much competition. Why, I won every hand."

The Baroness Szechenyi soothed her daughter. "You deserved to win every hand, *kincsem*, for you are an excellent card player. Since you are tired of this game, why don't you play something for us on the pianoforte?"

At the baroness's suggestion, Pal Anton brightened, visibly.

"You play the pianoforte, Margyth? How wonderful. Yes, let's adjourn to the music room, I am most eager for you to play for us. I grew up with music flowing through our home, and I miss it. My fellow hussars are not appreciative of fine music, so I seldom get the chance to listen to someone who plays well. I shall be delighted to turn the pages for you."

Margyth seated at the pianoforte, and the tall, dashing hussar standing beside her ready to turn the pages, made a perfect tableau to sketch. Bibi surmised she needed to be ready to sketch Margyth wherever and whenever the social butterfly made up her mind to alight for a few moments, so she took up her sketching materials and selected a chair with the best vantage point, while the Baroness Szechenyi seated herself front and center to enjoy her daughter's performance.

Perhaps it was the angle at which she sat or just her artist's keen observation, but she noted the tic in Pal's eye, which began when Margyth struck the first discordant note. Pal's tic increased as Margyth made one mistake after another.

She used her sketch pad to hide her grin when it became evident the hussar had reached the end of his patience and could not bear to hear another discordant note. For herself, she readily seconded his suggestion.

"Margyth, why don't I play and you sing for us?"

"Oh yes, darling, sing for us," the baroness cooed.

"Of course, Momma, I'll sing your favorite song." Margyth surrendered the pianoforte to Pal and gave him the music to accompany her.

Judging from his look of astonishment when Margyth's clear soprano rang out, Pal thought her singing would be equally dismal, but Margyth, her true talent found at last, sang like a nightingale.

Pal played masterfully, and with Margyth totally engaged in singing, she got a very good sketch of the woman. She even did some quick ones of Pal and Baroness Szechenyi, before the baroness reminded her daughter not to strain her voice and the music ended.

Chapter Eleven

Bibi found Pal sitting at the breakfast table with his fork poised over a mound of eggs scrambled with bacon, peppers, and mushrooms.

"Mmmm, your breakfast smells delicious. I was hoping someone, besides myself, was an early riser. I hate eating alone."

Pal rose and held a chair out for her. "Then you are lucky I am visiting, for the ladies of the manor do not arise much before noon. I don't find eating alone pleasant, either, but if I waited until Margyth or the baroness chose to make an appearance, I would waste away to nothing. The kitchen staff is quite unused to having diners this early. If the eggs suit you, I will request they make more."

At her nod, Pal rose and opened the door to the butler's pantry and called to someone answering to "Magda," and ordered more eggs, bread, and coffee.

He then poured coffee from his own pot, and scooped half the eggs onto a clean plate and set it in front of her, despite her protest she could wait until her eggs were ready.

"Please eat, the eggs are warm, and I don't want to be rude and eat in front of you. We can share your eggs and coffee when they arrive."

This was the first time she had been seated so closely to the hussar, and she was delighted to discover Pal had a few endearing freckles sprinkled across his cheeks and nose. His thick, auburn hair had been dressed back into a queue, and he wore civilian riding attire of black breeches, black boots, and not being able to hide the hussar's love for flamboyant color, a sapphire-blue shirt with a black vest alive with vivid floral embroidery.

"So, tell me about yourself, Pal."

"As I mentioned when we first met, I am the fourth son of a fourth son. The family estate is in Pest and will be inherited by my eldest brother. The next oldest is a doctor, and the one a year older than me is a semi-important civil servant at court.

"My father likes to brag I displayed a talent for riding almost as soon as I began to walk, so he bought me a commission in the Imperial Hussars. I do enjoy being a hussar, except having reached the exalted rank of lieutenant colonel, there isn't quite as much fun as commanding a squad and riding to the sound of guns. Lieutenant colonels attack paperwork rather than the emperor's enemies, and I've discovered hussars and prolonged peace are not a good combination. When such men spend too much time in barracks, they go looking for trouble, and I spend my days trying to keep them out of the local jails.

I needed to take a vacation from the usual mayhem, so I volunteered to purchase mounts from a breeder in the area, and I was also curious to meet my distant relatives. I'm glad I came, for this is a beautiful area. Excellent horse country with a lot of open space to ride and relax."

Magda arrived with a huge plate of fresh eggs, and at Pal's nod, served her a too generous helping before dispatching the rest to Pal's empty plate.

"My goodness, I'll never be able to finish all of this."

"Not a problem, Bibi. We hussars don't just ride horses, we eat as much as they do, too."

Looking into Pal's twinkling blue eyes, she conceded and shared the meal with the agreeable man, who was proving to be a formidable trencherman, belying his lithe, long-legged body and trim waist.

Replete at last, Pal sat back and waited for her to finish her breakfast. "I must say, your riding habit is quite daring for a woman. I can't recall ever having met a female *Csiko*. Ah, I've made you blush, forgive me, I am an unrepentant tease, don't be angry with me."

Pal reached across the table and gave her hand a small squeeze while gazing at her with a spurned-puppy look. Forced to swallow her coffee before she spewed it over the linen tablecloth, she half wheezed and hooted at the same time.

"You are impossible. I do possess a beautiful, sartorially correct, riding habit, but I wanted to put Shadow through his paces this morning, and even you must admit *Csiko* attire is made for riding. Shadow is a young horse, and I'm still training him in cavalry drill."

Wiping his lips with his napkin, Pal sprang from his chair. "Well then, let's be away and drill. I would love to be your training partner this morning."

Looking up into Pal's eager face, she asked, "Are you sure your mount is up to carrying the weight of all those eggs this morning?"

It was a good thing the estate walls were thick, as Pal's

whoop was almost loud enough to awaken the sleeping Szechenyi women.

"And you accuse me of being a tease? There is a nice, level meadow not far from here, where we can hack and stab at each other to our hearts' content."

Agreeing to keep their weapons in the scabbards for safety's sake, Pal and Bibi faced each other at opposite ends of the flower-strewn meadow. It was a beautiful day, with bright sun, wildflowers in profusion, and peaceful birdsong. Peaceful until Pal gave a startling war cry, and his huge bay shot across the meadow straight for her.

If Shadow was nervous, he didn't show it but responded to her command with a leap toward the charging horse. When they drew within striking range, Pal leaned forward and stood in his stirrups, and she realized Pal's height put her at a serious disadvantage.

Reacting as she had been taught, she threw herself backward and lay flat in the saddle. She felt the breeze over the length of her body when Pal swung his scabbard and missed her as he thundered past.

She had just enough time to regain her upright position and turn Shadow before Pal reined in and reversed direction. This time, she would not be able to avoid a hit unless she used one of the maneuvers taught to her by the Cossacks.

She held her breath and prayed she wouldn't fall off, as the hussar again descended on her with an eager look on his face. She waited the last second, until Pal was committed to the downward stroke, before she dropped her right stirrup and swung out of the saddle to flatten herself along Shadow's left flank, with all her weight balanced on the left stirrup as Shadow continue to gallop past Pal's bay.

She held in her gaiety for as long as possible when Pal reined in then frantically looked for her in the tall meadow grass. Her peal of laughter drew his eyes to Shadow to find her very much still in the saddle.

"My God, how did you do that? I was certain you'd fallen from the saddle when I swung at you. Where did you learn such a thing, and can you teach me? If I show my regiment how to do this, I'll be the man of the hour."

She nodded her agreement and winked at Pal. "I traveled to Russia to study a painting technique and had the great good fortune to be befriended by some Cossacks. Among other things, they showed me I didn't know all there was to know about riding.

"I'll be happy to teach you, but I warn you, you'll be very sore by this evening. Until you learn to balance on one stirrup, you will fall a number of times."

Pal gave her a devil-may-care grin and responded, "Well then, I'm fortunate this meadow is covered by such thick grass. Is it possible to show me the technique at a slower gait?"

Pal caught the balance and rhythm of the maneuver after several bruising falls. She assuaged his embarrassment over his unseating by admitting it took her far more falls, and on far less forgiving ground than thick meadow grass, before mastering the trick.

"Your horse is very patient with you, Pal. My uncle, an excellent horse breeder, would praise his good lines, spirit, and gait."

"Yes, Ares is a good horse. He makes me look like I learned how to ride, don't you, boy?" Pal praised Ares as he stroked the horse's sweating neck.

"One last ride at full gallop, and we'll pray I can keep from inflicting further pain on my aching body. Come on, Ares, make me look good for Baroness Baranyi and I promise to give you an extra treat."

Ares was more than game, and Pal managed the movement as if he'd been born knowing how to do it.

"Bravo, Pal. I'm amazed at how fast you mastered the trick," she called, as he regained both stirrups and turned to join her for the ride back to the Szechenyi estate.

"All compliments accepted. Thank you for a marvelous workout. Would you believe the eggs are nothing but a memory and I'm famished? I wonder if the sleeping beauties are awake enough to join us for lunch."

She and Pal made short work of cooling down and grooming their horses and left the stable with assurances from the groom their mounts would be fed well after the morning's strenuous exercise.

Relieved to note there was enough time before lunch for her to bathe and dress in a suitable gown, so as not to scandalize Baroness Szechenyi, she hurried to her room.

The hot water and soap, provided by the almost invisible Szechenyi staff, revived her, and with optimistic hope Margyth would agree to some formal posing, she grabbed pad and pencil and descended the stairs.

"And here is my delightfully talented instructress," Pal

proclaimed as he jumped up to kiss her hand. "I confess to regaling the baroness and Margyth with your prodigious equestrian skills, Baroness Baranyi."

She started to demur, but Margyth's acerbic comment made her swallow her words.

"Playing at cavalry, riding astride, swinging swords? I'm sure those are not activities a lady should pursue."

Pal proved he did indeed belong to a diplomatic family by his quick response. "And you, Margyth, are very much a lady and a treasure to behold. I can't imagine you ever doing such a thing. My mind boggles at the picture of you swinging a saber while riding sidesaddle on your sweet mare."

She had to bite the inside of her cheek to keep from laughing. Margyth didn't appear to catch on to the fact Pal's flattery was nothing but a jibe at her own expense.

Accepting what she construed to be a compliment, Margyth smiled at Pal and suggested, "Pal, let's get out of this stuffy house. There is a delightful path running down to a small stream, and we can enjoy the fresh air. I'll tell cook to pack some wine and cheese and those pastries you so adore."

Before her newly discovered fourth cousin responded to her invitation, Margyth turned to Bibi. "I am sure you must be terribly fatigued from this morning's activities. Mother can keep you company after you wake from your nap."

She almost doubled over and howled at the look of astonishment on Pal's face for Margyth ordering a baroness to bed.

If you think I will give you the satisfaction of causing a scene, then you have misjudged the Horthy mettle, she fumed to herself, as she replied with what she hoped was a sincere expression, "Why thank you for your concern, Margyth, I am a bit weary. If you will excuse me, napping is a capital idea."

Turning to the Baroness Szechenyi, she offered, "Perhaps we can share a pot of tea when I awake, if it would suit you?"

Not waiting for a response from the baroness, she left the table but not before seeing Pal raise one finger to his temple to give her a surreptitious salute.

Chapter Twelve

All of the past week's activities caught up with her at last, and Bibi fell into a deep and refreshing sleep after she bid *adieu* to Margyth and her mother.

A soft knocking on her door awakened her, and she rose to admit Margyth's timid maid.

"Here are the fresh towels you requested, Baroness."

"My goodness, I managed to sleep the afternoon away." She glanced out the window to discover the sun in the process of setting.

"Yes, Baroness, I hope your nap refreshed you. What gown is your preference for this evening?"

"You may select one for me. Oh wait, make sure whichever you choose isn't the same color as what Margyth is wearing. I wouldn't want to upset her."

"Mistress Szechenyi chose a sapphire-blue gown for this evening. Would this sage-green gown be acceptable, Baroness?"

She studied the sage-green silk organdy with woven floral pattern. The neckline was quite modest, and the matching velvet belt with amber clasp just below her bosom drew attention to her narrow waist and flat stomach.

"Yes, the gown will suit. I will wear my Russian amber earrings as well."

"Excellent, Baroness. How may I style your hair this evening?"

"Nothing fussy. A simple chignon worn low on my neck will best please me."

Margyth's maid may have been on the timid side, but she was efficient. Dressed and coifed in record time, she picked up her pencil and sketch pad and left her room to descend to the library. She hoped to peruse the shelves for a suitable book to read while she waited on Margyth's pleasure to be able to sketch her.

Pal stood as soon as she entered and complimented her.

"You are a lovely vision this evening, Baroness." Pal took two glasses of wine from the footman's tray and offered her one. "I'm afraid we'll have a bit of a wait before Margyth graces us with her presence."

"You must be much sought out by every woman you meet, Pal. You are extremely adept at flattery, but I would be remiss if I didn't bestow the same compliment on you. You look quite dashing in evening dress." To her utter astonishment, Pal blushed at her compliment.

"Why I can't recall ever receiving a compliment from such a beautiful woman, but while l will admit to being talented with a phrase, in your case, I speak only the truth."

"Oh, you are good, you rascal." She took a sip of her wine before asking, "I hope your picnic *al fresco* was enjoyable?"

Pal had the grace to look a trifle embarrassed at the unexpected inquiry. "Er, quite. Margyth is a very entertaining hostess, and this estate is a marvel to explore. The baron erected follies in interesting nooks and crannies, and we had great fun trying to find them all."

She would've teased Pal just a little further by asking to be shown them at some time, but Margyth's entrance made her grant the hussar a reprieve. She chose to compliment Margyth instead. "What a stunning dress, Margyth. The blue suits your coloring."

Before acknowledging the compliment, Margyth studied Bibi's dress. Apparently mollified the artist's dress in no way eclipsed her own, Margyth performed a small twirl and ended up near enough to Pal Anton to link arms with him. "Yes, most of the jewel tones look well on me. I'm afraid smudgy colors, such as the green you're wearing tonight, would not suit at all."

Pal's deliberate clearing of his throat drew her attention away from the artist.

"May I pour you a glass of wine or sherry, Margyth?"

"A glass of sherry, please." Margyth bestowed a coy smile on her newly discovered relation. "We had such fun exploring the estate, didn't we, Pal Anton? I can't remember when I bothered to spend any time in those rustic follies my father scattered about."

If Margyth hoped to upset her by excluding her, she was going to be disappointed. Bibi turned her back on the company and proceeded to read the titles on the nearest bookshelf. She immediately discovered Baron Szechenyi's taste in books did not extend beyond estate management and animal husbandry.

Speaking of the baron, his portrait, as she discovered, hung between two of the bookshelves. Her assumption Margyth favored her father turned out to be correct. Father and daughter possessed the same blonde hair and green eyes.

Whoever painted the picture chose to represent the man in a larger-than-life pose. Baron Szechenyi wore formal court dress and held, of all things, an ornate, ebony walking stick. As she stood back to study the large painting, she discovered the artist must have held the baron in low regard, for depending on the angle from which one chose to view the portrait, the baron's green eyes were cold, and his lips were drawn up in a smirk rather than a sincere smile. The overall effect was one of venality rather than generosity of spirit. The technique was masterful, and she moved a little closer to try and read the artist's signature.

The Baroness Szechenyi's voice behind her almost made her spill the glass of wine she held.

"My husband was well-favored," the baroness commented, as she stood in front of the portrait of her late husband.

"Oh yes, quite. He's most impressive in his court dress."

"Clothes do not always make the man, Baroness Baranyi."

The Baroness Szechenyi's acerbic comment left her openmouthed in astonishment, and she sipped the rest of her wine to cover her lack of response. Thank heavens the Szechenyi footman rescued her by announcing dinner.

Dinner was, again, a study in dull repetition. If she had to listen to one second more of the baroness fawning over her daughter, or Pal Anton trying to moderate Margyth's not-so-subtle barbs to her wardrobe, looks, or penchant for riding astride, she would leave the estate posthaste and tell Prince Rackoszi just what she thought of his commission. The saints she'd been praying to, to keep a civil leash on her tongue, rewarded her by having Margyth declare the fresh air and long horse ride had tired her, and she would retire for the evening. The baroness gave a barely civil good evening to her and Pal and followed her daughter. Even the hussar declined to remain at the table and bid her good night.

Wide awake after her long afternoon nap, she returned to the library and started a systematic search of the titles for something remotely interesting to pass the evening. Not until she reached the last bookcase, and noticed the books showed frequent use, did she begin to wonder at the interesting, but strange, titles. *Nesferatu, Vampyre, A Compendium of the Undead*, she murmured to herself as she trailed her finger over the leather covers. Someone in the house enjoyed the *macabre* in their reading material. Removing the *Compendium* from the shelf, she returned to her room and hoped the book would be sufficiently boring to lull her to sleep.

Accustomed to undressing herself, she dismissed Margyth's maid after she had unfastened all of the difficult-to-reach hooks and quickly donned her modest nightgown. Carrying her reading choice to bed, she fluffed the pillows and settled in to read until tired enough to blow out the candles and sleep. Despite her plans to read herself to sleep, the book captured her attention from the very first paragraph. The author had a way with words, as if he possessed practical knowledge of which he wrote:

Vampyres often have an animal familiar. It can be a cat or a dog or a bat, and it allows them to roam undetected. Daylight is the enemy of the Undead. He cannot travel by the light of day, and so chooses to sleep the day away. Maidens must be especially careful because their blood; their innocence, is particularly sought by the Undead upon awakening, as their blood is the most fortifying. Once the vampyre has drained the maiden's blood to the point of death, he reveals himself for the hideous revenant he is, but it is too late for his chosen bride, who will appear to die, only to rise from the dead unless staked through the heart with the wood of a holly tree, doused with sanctified water, or burned and her ashes scattered to the four winds. If these steps are not followed, another bride will terrorize the territory the revenant calls his own.

She slammed the book shut. This was not the kind of reading material to inspire sleep. She was about to lean over and extinguish the candle by her bed when a small chiming sound and the light tread of footsteps caught her attention.

Curiosity being a weakness of hers, she extinguished the flame and tiptoed her way to the door. Turning the knob with exquisite slowness, she cracked the door open without a sound and peered out into the dimly lit hallway. Her eyes were drawn to a man standing outside Margyth's suite, four doors down. When Margyth opened her door, the light from inside framed Pal Anton as he bent to kiss Janos's intended and illuminated the wine bottle and two glasses he carried.

Ah, an assignation. She was not at all surprised, since the hussar had made it quite plain he found this area of Transylvania beautiful, and in truth, the prince had not yet placed an engagement ring on Margyth's finger. Well, faithfulness will not be one of the virtues the Baroness

Szechenyi would be extoling for her daughter.

A wave of sadness swept over her for the disservice done to Prince Rackoszi, and she sagged in weariness of this assignment. Give her the straightforward business of training horses, any day. It was more rewarding and less fraught with negative emotion. Closing her bedroom door as softly as she'd opened it, she made her way back to bed and settled in for a sleepless night of trying not to be envious of Margyth, who, undeservedly, was being pursued by two very handsome men.

Chapter Thirteen

"Oh good lord, you startled me!" Akos added additional descriptive adjectives to his exclamation before ending with a remonstrance. "Must you be continually underfoot? Why don't you go outside instead of causing me to trip over you?"

The wolf, Lucifer, drew back his lips in a rumbling snarl.

"Don't take your ill humor out on me. I am very aware the weather is too sunny for the prince to be abroad, but you are not bound by the sun. Why don't you go see what the Baroness Baranyi has accomplished in the week she's spent with Margyth?

"If you will remember, Baroness Baranyi is an early riser and prefers to ride in the mornings. Bestir yourself, and you can accompany her on a morning ride to run off some of your surliness, because I vow, if you snap at one more person, I will banish you to the confines of the deepest room in this castle."

Lucifer cocked his head from side to side, as if he understood the words, and then walked with his tail held high to the door to wait for the valet to open it.

***

Bibi dressed hurriedly. She could not bear to spend a moment more confined to her bedroom after spending the night dreaming of vampires sucking the blood from hysterical virgins, and then moving on to speculating which of the men

Margyth would choose to wed. Her instincts told her Pal Anton did not stand a chance. Margyth would never settle for second best, and Janos was a royal and the powerful Viceroy of Transylvania.

Aware the kitchen would not be prepared to make her breakfast at such an early hour, she chose to forego it. Even the stable staff was not ready for such an early rider, but saddling her own horse was not a chore, especially if she could leave the Szechenyi manse far behind in a morning gallop. What she didn't expect was a wolf waiting for her just outside the stable doors.

"Lucifer, are you waiting to accompany me?" She dismounted long enough to hug the huge wolf. When the wolf deigned to lean into the hug, she gave a final welcoming squeeze and remounted. "Well, let's be away, then," she called as she gave the leg command to Shadow, and the gray leapt forward.

Trusting the wolf to know the terrain, she enjoyed an excellent ride over areas someone unfamiliar with the estate would never think to explore. Janos's wolf forged a challenging course, and both she and Shadow received an excellent workout.

Lucifer seemed to sense when Shadow needed to rest. With a glance up at her, he stopped and dropped down to his stomach beneath a shady tree. The panting of a wolf, and a horse whickering softly before beginning to crop grass were the sole intrusions on the stillness of the morning.

She joined Lucifer under his tree and leaned her back against its rough bark. "How wonderful. I haven't had such a glorious ride since leaving your master's castle. Even riding with Pal didn't pose such a challenge."

At the mention of the hussar's name, the wolf turned his head, and catching her eyes, growled.

She gave Lucifer a quizzical glance. "What are you growling at? The hussar hasn't harmed you in any way, although you might tell the prince he needs to visit more. The Szechenyi's relation is rapidly becoming a competitor for Margyth's affections."

It surprised her when the wolf stalked away on stiff legs and used the back ones to rough up the sod in a fit of pique. Amused by his antics, she praised him. "Defending your owner's claim, are you? You are a most loyal wolf. Well, I must leave you, and please do not accompany me back to the house. The baroness made it very clear at dinner last night she is not enamored of wolves on her land."

She knelt and threw her arms around the wolf to hug him farewell. It pleased her very much when Lucifer leaned into her and licked her hand.

Her self-congratulations for rising early and engaging in morning exercise ceased when she drew near Margyth's room on the way to her own and was assaulted by the sound of raised voices. She froze when she identified the harsh words as belonging to the baroness and her daughter. She hesitated to continue on to her room because Margyth's door was ajar wide enough for mother and daughter to note her presence, her mud-spattered, *Csiko*-attired presence. And she was reluctant to confirm Margyth's belief she was nothing more than an unfeminine hoyden, thus giving her more ammunition for future insults.

Unfortunately, her momentary worry over her state of dress gave way to curiosity when the conversation elevated to a shouting match between the baroness and her daughter, and she risked peeking into the room.

"Margyth, I absolutely forbid you to go forward with this plan. Why don't you concentrate on Pal Anton? I can tell he is greatly taken with you. You would be well received as an officer's wife in Vienna."

"How dare you forbid me, Mother. I want to be a prince's wife, not a lowly hussar's." Margyth shouted back but lowered her voice at her mother's insistence the servants did not need to hear their conversation from below stairs.

The baroness hissed at her daughter's defiance. "Silly, spoiled girl, you are ignorant as to the true nature of the prince. He is a revenant. His soul is damned for eternity, and he will make you the same. You must listen to me for once in your life."

Margyth slammed her hairbrush down on her vanity. "Mother, so help me God, if you spout one word more of vampires and wolf familiars, I will scream this house down. I am going to marry the prince, and you will not interfere. I am tired of being stuck in the country with farmers and peasants. I want to live in a castle, explore Budapest and Vienna from top to bottom, attend balls, and wear nothing but the finest clothes and jewels. Pal Anton cannot give me those things."

The baroness advanced on her daughter, shaking her finger. "Oh, you will live in a castle all right. A castle with no windows. Your tour of Budapest or Vienna will be conducted in the dark, because the prince cannot go abroad in daylight. Who will admire those fine clothes, if you are confined by a husband who never goes out in society and sleeps until the sun goes down?"

"Sometimes, Mother, I think your grief over father unsettled your mind. The prince does, too, visit us in the daylight, and you can't say he refused to eat or drink in your presence." Margyth, carried away in her anger, spat out, "If my blood is so attractive to this revenant of yours, why hasn't he even kissed me yet?

"And as to my social life, I will convince Szigi to model our marriage in the same manner as yours. It will be the price he must pay for my giving him an heir and a spare. It won't take much effort to convince Pal Anton to be my most special friend, as father did of numerous women. And if Szigi turns out to prefer sleeping until sunset, Pal will give me the daylight outings my husband shuns. I will demand a town house in Budapest, and one in Vienna, and there I will hold a salon for artists and interesting people. And if my husband objects to being surrounded by such people, he can rusticate here in his dark castle.

"Help me select a dress, Mother. I intend to sit for Szigi's artist this morning because the sooner she finishes her drawing, the sooner she is out of this house. I do not need her spying on me and reporting back to him. It will be a relief to show her the door. She constantly smells of horses. Has no one in her family ever given her a bottle of perfume?"

Bibi thought she'd missed her opportunity to pass by Margyth's door when the argument slowed, but the baroness refused to give in to her daughter's wishes so easily and resumed the topic of the prince's unsuitableness.

Her curiosity inflamed, she dispensed with her wish to make a clean escape and vowed, if discovered, she'd let her temper have free rein and enter Margyth's bedroom to defend Janos. Curiosity overriding the wisdom of returning to her room, she remained frozen against the wall. However, she did cross her fingers to ward off having her eavesdropping discovered by a servant venturing down the hallway.

Baroness Szechenyi clasped her hands and bowed her head. "I regret my parents did not choose my husband with more attention to his bloodline than his title."

With a whine of exasperation, Margyth asked, "And just what are you trying to say, Mother?"

"Only this. If I had married a man with sense and self-discipline, you might not have inherited such wildness and self-indulgence."

Margyth screeched. "For God's sake, Mother, I've shown admirable discipline for twenty-one years, thanks to my father's profligate spending. I've missed my coming out and being courted by young, handsome men with impeccable social standing. Being confined to this estate with peasants and farm animals for company is the only inheritance father left me, and I swear to you, I don't intend to be labeled as being on the shelf, so to hell with your cautions, Mother.

"After we wed, the prince can remain here, if he desires, and watch his prized bulls mount cows, or he can listen to the grapes grow in his vineyards, but I intend to be in Budapest or Vienna, listening to music and drinking champagne. If Szigi, as you claim, wants my blood, he can put his name on my dance card for an opportunity to drink it."

"Margyth, you are being indelicate. A lady does not refer to the mating of bulls and cows."

"I doubt it has escaped your notice we live on a farm, Mother. Roosters mount chickens, stallions mount mares, and men mount women. Even as prudish as you are, I doubt I was born by any other means. Thanks to your reticence on the subject, I was forced to do my own experimentation. Peasants are quite willing to engage in the sexual act, especially if a few coins are tossed their way."

Bibi, outraged on Janos's behalf, had enough presence of mind to stop herself from kicking the door wide and announcing herself. How could Prince Rackoszi even consider marrying such a wanton? She would get her drawing finished today and be gone. The sooner she completed the commission, the sooner she could return to the Baranyi estates. Her heart ached for the prince, but it was not her place to interfere.

And so what if she smelled of horse? At least she did not reek of venality, and she was not delusional enough to believe the prince a vampire. The sound of the baroness's wordless sputtering covered her return to her room. Letting some of her temper free at last, she almost tore the tapestry bell cord from the wall as she called for more water. She would not be offending Margyth's olfactory sense when she sketched her this morning.

By the time the spoiled, self-indulgent woman deigned to seek her out, she had regained her composure. The sight of Margyth, dressed in the ice-blue gown she intended to wear at her betrothal party, gave her the exact image she would paint on the miniature. The folktale sprang into her artist's mind, and all she needed to do was sketch the design of the gown. For all Margyth Szechenyi was a despicable human being, her portrait would be magnificent. And though she kept telling herself she shouldn't interfere, her heart was urging her to do so. The chit's lack of anything close to gratitude for the prince's sincere attempt to protect her and ensure she would want for nothing made her Horthy temper rise at such an injustice.

She experienced a second of dizzy astonishment as a revelation rushed through her mind. Had she fallen under the prince's spell after just one night of lovemaking? Damn, maybe he really was a vampire and she was in his thrall. Spell, thrall, love, lust, she didn't care for those particular labels, but from this moment on, Szigismond Emre Janos Rackoszi had someone who would fight to protect him from the worst of Margyth Szechenyi's machinations.

***

Janos tapped his valet on the shoulder, and the room erupted in linen shirts. Once again, he inadvertently surprised the man, this time while in the act of putting his shirts into the armoire.

"By all the gods, great and small, first it is the wolf who startles me, must you do so as well?"

He held his silence and waited until his valet regained his composure.

"And how may I assist you, Your Grace?" Akos gritted through a clenched jaw.

"Please draw my bath as soon as possible. Today is going to be cloudy enough for a drive in an open carriage, and I intend to show Margyth around the estate. Oh, tell Cook to prepare a picnic basket. The little trout stream should serve to chill a bottle of wine quite well, and it is a very picturesque place to do some courting."

He should've known, if it involved Margyth, his valet would obey him to the letter and not a scintilla farther. When he climbed over the tub's rim to sit in the bath water, he heaved himself out again as quickly as a cat falling into a pond and glared his disapproval at Akos, who turned a blind eye on his obvious displeasure.

"You did say as soon as possible, Your Grace. It takes time to heat water. I was under the impression you were in a hurry to keep your appointment with Margyth."

Akos bit his lip to keep the smirk off his face but failed miserably, when he replied, "The ardor to do so has cooled considerably. You may leave and tell the coachman to ready the phaeton."

Thank heavens he chose the two-seater carriage, elsewise, his coachman would think it extremely odd the Viceroy of Transylvania carried on such a vigorous dialog with himself. The central topic was just why was he so reluctant to court Baron Szechenyi's daughter? She possessed beauty in abundance, youth enough to bear his children, and marriage to her would secure the safety of the valley for his subjects. On the other hand, she was spoiled, she was vain, and she was, she was, ah, he didn't exactly know what she was, but he couldn't picture Margyth as the princess to his prince.

You're a damned liar, Rackoszi, you know exactly what you want your wife to be. Bibi's statuesque, Valkyrie form appeared like a mirage in the road, and he jerked involuntarily on the reins. Apologizing to the carriage horse for his erratic driving, he next found himself listing the attributes he particularly desired in a wife and quailed inwardly when none of them were to be found in Margyth's possession. But her lack thereof didn't matter. Duty was duty. He understood and accepted the obligation, although he didn't need to be happy about it.

As he steered the carriage under the Szechenyi portico, he counseled himself to oust all doubts from his mind. He was here to court a woman, and court her he would. He managed to stifle a gasp when the baroness answered her own door.

"If you are here to visit Margyth, this is an inconvenient time. She is sitting for the painter you hired. As it is by your direction my daughter pose for her, you must choose another day compatible with her schedule."

In his best Viceroy of Transylvania voice, he informed the baroness, "Your daughter can sit another time. I wish to show her my estate. My cook prepared a picnic luncheon so we will be gone several hours. Do you intend to keep me standing on the doorstep, Madame?"

He had to hand it to the dragon, his rebuke didn't embarrass her in the slightest. Well, two could play ill-mannered games. He brushed past the woman and called out, "Margyth, it's Jan, er, Szigi. I'm here to take you for a drive and a picnic." His eardrums vibrated painfully at the high-pitched squeal of delight issuing from above stairs.

"Szigi, what an unexpected pleasure. Yes, just let me fetch my parasol and I'll be with you in a trice," Margyth called over the balcony as she passed by with a swirl of skirts.

Baroness Szechenyi was not to be deterred in disappointing his plans and her daughter's enjoyment of them. "I am sorry, Your Grace, but this is quite unacceptable. I feel the beginnings of one of my headaches, and I will not permit Margyth to accompany you unchaperoned."

"Surely, you can permit me to drive Margyth in an open coach on my land? How else will we get to know each other?"

He wanted to kick himself for giving the old trout such an opening.

"It is my fervent hope you will remain strangers, and I for one do not intend to ride anywhere with you, and neither will I let you drive about with my daughter unchaperoned."

The Baroness Szechenyi didn't get a chance to continue voicing her displeasure, for Margyth stormed down the stairs and rudely silenced her mother.

"Pooh, Momma, there's a simple solution to the chaperone problem. Pal Anton can accompany us and serve as the chaperone."

"But Pal Anton is an unmarried man, Margyth."

Indeed he is, but as you so often point out, he is our relation, and thus quite suitable as a chaperone. He's resting in his room. I'll just pop upstairs to ask him. Besides, I am bored, and an outing is just the thing to put me in a better mood, especially if Szigi and I get better acquainted."

Returning so quickly neither the baroness nor he had had a chance to trade more barbed comments, Margyth grabbed him by the hand, and tugged him through the door as she called over her shoulder, "Pal Anton is quite happy to serve as my chaperone. Rest well, Momma."

He had to rush to assist Margyth into the coach. The hussar's arrival did not surprise him, as he was to be the chaperone, but his accompaniment by Baroness Baranyi did give him pause. By the frown gracing his intended's face, Bibi's presence was also a surprise to Margyth.

Pal grinned and apologized. "I hope you don't mind, but I invited the baroness along as well. If I'm to chaperone you two, it would be nice if I also had someone to converse with. It will ensure you some privacy if I'm engaged in conversation with my riding companion."

Janos did appreciate the gesture, but he suddenly felt angry at himself for dreaming up this outing with Margyth. He wanted to be riding over his lands with Bibi. A cold bottle of wine, her head in his lap... Pah, this was getting him nowhere. But it would be nice to speak to Margyth without having her mother listening to every word he spoke while trying to find nefarious intent in each syllable.

He thus offered the hussar more freedom from his chaperone responsibilities. "I know the coach will go too slowly for you, but I intend to picnic at the trout stream I showed the baroness when last we rode. You can range ahead, and when you tire of riding, you can meet us there and share our picnic. I'm sure my cook packed enough for the four of us."

As the carriage pulled away, he deliberately refrained from hunching his shoulders at the imaginary daggers the Baroness Szechenyi was hurling at his back from her position in the library window. He waved to the dragon out of politeness, but she didn't return the gesture.

Damn, he was as uncomfortable in Margyth's solitary presence as if he were a callow youth on his first outing with a girl. If his posture was any more erect, his spine would snap. Mercifully, his intended's brazenness saved the awkward situation. She put her hand over his and gave it a squeeze. He tried but failed to disguise his small jump of surprise.

"Be at ease, Szigi, my mother isn't about to pop up from those bushes ahead and scream about impropriety. I'm so glad you had this idea because we do need to get to know each other better. The brief moments my mother permits me to be in your presence are not enough for us to become comfortable in each other's company."

He turned to face Margyth because he almost didn't recognize the mature voice she was using to address him, and he had to admit, this version of her was far better than the simpering girl he endured on previous visits. Maybe this union would work after all.

He relaxed in slow degrees. And relaxed even more when he pointed out the beautiful attractions to be found on his lands. Disappointingly, when he stole a glance at his silent companion, he found her lack of comment wasn't due to rapt interest in the scenery. He caught Margyth stifling a yawn behind her gloved hand, and her inability to care about something important to him rankled to the core. He stopped the carriage and turned it around as he mentally compared Margyth's response to Bibi's. The artist had shown nothing but enthusiasm as he had pointed out the beauty of his lands to her.

"Why are we reversing direction, Szigi?"

"I mentioned the trout stream running through my property to Pal Anton as a nice picnic spot. I did point it out to you when we passed by. Perhaps Pal and Baroness Baranyi are there already. Are you hungry?"

"Not so much hungry as thirsty. I look forward to sharing a glass of wine with you. I hear nothing but praise for the wines from your vineyards."

Not for life or limb would he play the prude and demand Margyth remove the hand she so boldly placed on his thigh, but he did wish she would recall a smidgen of propriety. His wish was not granted. His second wish failed as well. He hoped to find Bibi and Pal Anton at the designated spot, but it was deserted enough to satisfy any courting couple. He assisted Margyth from the carriage, all the while wishing she were not the one he was courting.

As he led his intended into the shade of a large oak, he wanted to vent his temper and kick the innocent tree, knowing full well he needed to stop wishing for what he couldn't have. It was a moot point anyway. Honor demanded he court Margyth, not Beatrix Baranyi.

***

Margyth noted the cloth Janos spread upon the grass was

quite small. Just enough for the two of them. The image of the Baroness Baranyi having to seat herself on the grass pleased her. It also pleased her to note Szigi would not be able to put much distance between them. She intended to break through the prince's reserve, and seated closely together would be a good start.

She managed to check her mother's obvious attempt to keep Szigi away this day, but she didn't think such freedom to have the prince all to herself would continue. The old tartar was very good at stifling her wishes. It was one of the reasons she wanted to leave her childhood home, and so she would by giving Szigi a small taste of what he could expect as her husband. She wouldn't grant him such exclusive freedom with her person in the future, but he didn't need to be aware of her plans until after a priest baptized the prince's heir.

She refused the prince's offer of a glass of wine and waited until he swallowed his first sip. She took the glass from his hand and winked at him as she took a small taste.

"I did offer to pour a glass for you, Margyth."

"No need, Szigi. Don't you think it more romantic to share a glass?" She offered the glass back, but as the prince leaned forward to accept it, she deftly held it from his reach and kissed him directly on the lips. She was pleased when he returned her kiss. She expected the withdrawn man to retreat from her advance, and his positive response encouraged her. Szigi was surprisingly good at kissing, and his tongue was doing marvelous things to her mouth while sending very interesting sensations much lower. So much so, she tossed the wine glass to the four winds and ran her hands up his firm chest to relieve him of his coat. She suddenly wanted to explore what was under all of those formal clothes the prince wore.

The sound of pounding hooves made her swear every lurid curse to herself she learned from the stable hands and scullery maids when they didn't know she was near. By the time Pal Anton and the artist joined them by the stream, both she and Szigi had regained their proper composure and state of dress.

Well Szigi's loss was Pal's gain. Having whetted her appetite, Margyth intended to slake her arousal with the hussar after Szigi's stodgy artist retired this evening.

***

Knowing Pal Anton was a mischievous imp was not a new discovery to Bibi as they turned their horses to head to the trout stream. She laughed when he teased it might behoove him to fulfill his chaperone duties, and save the prince from the necessity of a hasty wedding if they were to discover the couple *au naturel*.

By the extremely displeased look on Margyth's face, and Prince Rackoszi's guilty one, she could well believe the hussar had been quite prescient to return so soon.

"You are a devil, Pal," she whispered when he winked at her as he helped her dismount, and gave her an exuberant hug in the process.

"Well, if I am, I'm an extremely hungry one. Let's see what the Rackoszi cook packed for us, shall we?" Without so much as a by-your-leave, Pal threw himself down on the grass then unloaded the wicker hamper.

She chuckled at his audacity and followed his lead, passing out plates and silverware. "My, I'm positively famished. Pal and I had an excellent ride." She smiled as she uncovered a dish of cold chicken and offered it to Margyth, who surprised everyone by the way she viciously stabbed a piece and placed it on her plate.

When it was evident the chit did not intend to play hostess to anyone other than the prince, she fixed a plate for herself and Pal Anton and then passed their wineglasses to Janos to fill. It earned her another malignant glare from the prince's fiancée.

Perhaps to make up for her small temper tantrum, or maybe it was the piercing look she received from the prince, but Margyth sweetened her attitude, and the conversation was light and teasing as they dined. It was a short respite, as the spoiled woman grew tired of not being the center of everyone's attention and broke into the conversation to demand, "Szigi, why don't you offer a toast to our coming union?"

Bibi cast Pal a grateful look when he rescued the flummoxed prince. "My dear, how can Janos offer a toast when he is intimately involved as a recipient of the good wishes? Do allow me. Here's to a happy union, beautiful children, and all the joys life can hold."

Pal's toast was sincere, and the timing of it even more perfect. The day had been growing steadily darker, and with a clap of thunder, the *al fresco* luncheon was all but washed into the trout stream by a torrent of rain. It galvanized everyone into packing up and running to their various mounts, everyone but the spoiled woman, who stunned her intended into white-lipped disapproval with a string of vulgar curses on the stupidity of dining in the open air with dirt, insects, and boring people, as she stood under a tree and used a napkin in a futile attempt to dry her hair. Bibi castigated herself for her secret enjoyment of Margyth's obvious discomfort and became more contrite when a loud crack of thunder called attention to her uncharitable thoughts.

***

Baroness Szechenyi waited until the carriage disappeared from sight to begin pacing the carpet in the library. Stupid, selfish, self-indulgent girl. Her daughter acquired more of her father's distasteful characteristics as she grew. Yes, she and the baron had had an arrangement. He was free to indulge in his vices, as long as he kept them out of their house and did not besmirch her reputation as a good wife. She, blind to her husband's faults, foolishly believed the man possessed a modicum of restraint, or at least sense enough not to endanger his estate. And for her misguided trust of the man, she and her daughter were practically penniless and had an ax, in the form of Prince Rackoszi, hanging over their heads. Only the fact her husband had had the grace to kill himself first kept her from doing the deed herself.

The silly chit had yet to learn the lesson every wife was forced to—it was the man who held all of the power. If Margyth married the prince, she would soon find herself confined to his castle with no way to achieve her freedom. Prince Rackoszi controlled the money, the land, and who she could associate with. Men had the freedom to go where they would and do what they wanted. The naïve woman, for all she professed herself to be worldly, was wrong to think she could enthrall a man with just her body. Only if she possessed monies of her own could she possibly achieve some independence, but her father squandering his fortune destroyed any chance of independence.

While it would be the path of least resistance to submit to the vampire's wishes and give him her daughter in exchange for financial security, it was not her way. The prince was about to discover she had a steel spine when protecting what was hers. Margyth was her child, and despite her spoiled daughter's wishes to the contrary, she would never permit Prince Rackoszi to marry her.

***

The picnic did not begin or end well. In spite of Pal and Bibi's excellent conversation, and the beautiful setting, the old gods combined their powers to show their displeasure with his plan to go forward with the betrothal. The cloudy day suddenly turned from misty gray to solid black, right before the skies opened up.

While everyone but Margyth accepted the impromptu bath with good grace, the Szechenyi brat did nothing but complain about the ruination of her new dress, the abysmal state of her hair, and the folly of anyone using an open carriage in such uncertain weather. She never stopped her tirade long enough to let him apologize for the unfortunate ending to the day. When he at last reached the Szechenyi portico, the enraged woman hopped, unassisted, from the carriage and slammed the door behind herself. He didn't bother looking into any of the windows he passed on the way out. He didn't want to see the baroness's gloating face at such a dismal ending to the day. Perhaps the woman was indeed the witch she appeared to be and could summon storms when she wanted them.

At least Erzsebet had sense enough to hold her tongue when he encountered her in the kitchen. He used the rear entrance due to the state of his clothes and the fact he left small puddles wherever he trod.

"There is a freshly brewed a pot of tea, Your Grace. Would you care for a cup or would wine suit better?"

"Thank you, a glass of my special wine would be most appreciated."

"I'll send it directly, Your Grace. Akos has a warm bath ready for you. You may relax and sip your wine while the warm water takes the chill away."

"Just the ticket, Erzsebet," he replied as he headed upstairs, his boots squelching with every step. Perhaps his housekeeper had a bit of witch in her as well. How else would she know he would be home in time for the water to still be hot in the bath? He opened the door to his suite and discovered his valet adding bath salts to a steaming tub of water.

As Akos helped him undress, not a comment was made

about his drenched state. Janos didn't think his valet possessed any warlock powers, but he did possess a healthy instinct for self-preservation, and so there were no questions on the success of his outing, just a silent offering of the bath sponge and the glass of wine. He accepted both and sank into the soothing water. He needed to do some serious thinking and what better place than a soothing bath.

He stretched out in the tub and poked at the sponge with a fingertip as it floated by. Sip of wine, poke at sponge, sip of wine. This activity soothed him until he could order a mind as muddied as his boots.

He finally grasped what was troubling him. It was Margyth's boldness. It was she who initiated the kiss, indeed, it spoke of experience. He was far from a prude, but he assumed she'd led a sheltered life with her sharp-eyed mother overseeing her exposure to the opposite sex. The heated kiss they exchanged made it evident the daughter managed to elude her mother's over watch, but with whom? Pal Anton? Yes, most definitely with Pal Anton, if Bibi's remark to Lucifer concerning the hussar's attentions to his promised fiancée was correct. But the colonel's visit to the Szechenyi estate was too recent to make Margyth so practiced in her seduction. Indeed, she boldly stroked his leg to just within touch of his manhood and had even begun undressing him after a kiss which involved stroking his tongue with hers. While he could credit Pal's experience in wooing the opposite sex, he didn't believe the hussar was Margyth's instructor.

He took another sip of the dark wine and grimaced. Not at the wine's flavor, but at the sour knowledge the woman he would marry must be practicing her technique with male servants.

So, was this to be the mother of his sons? He groaned and slid under the water to wet his hair. His body was washed clean, but he couldn't wash away the distaste he was developing for the bleak future he imagined for himself.

He surfaced with soap-free hair and a dark stab of jealousy. Perhaps his intended's foul mood could not be solely blamed on the weather. Maybe it was due to his imitation of a clam as far as supporting his end of conversation, and he put the onus for his boorish behavior on Pal Anton. No one could miss the way the hussar's hands eagerly sought Bibi's waist to help her dismount, and he grumpily thought the hussar made the courteous gesture when there was no need for him to do so, the baroness was practically a *Csiko*, for God's sake. She could dismount and remount in the time it took anyone else to just throw a leg over the saddle.

And he also noted his artist lingered longer than was proper in Pal's arms. Her lips were suspiciously close to kissing the man's ear as she spoke to him before joining them for the picnic.

He was surprised to find the sponge back in his hands and once again full of soap. What was he doing? He'd already washed his entire body. Janos launched himself up and out of the tub when his ablutions were interrupted by the distinct voice of his good angel.

Why don't you use the sponge to wash those nasty thoughts out of your mind?

Chapter Fourteen

The squeak of leather and jingle of harness made Lucifer stretch himself low to the ground. He would ascertain who belonged to the noise before he exposed himself to the Szechenyi stable hands. Lifting his nose to scent the wind, the wolf bared his teeth in lupine displeasure.

"Ah, the slug-a-bed has finally risen," Pal called to Bibi as his horse, Ares, touched noses with Shadow. "I didn't wait for you to accompany me this morning. I assumed you would be sleeping in after consuming such a heavy meal last night."

"You assumed correctly, Pal, but I don't think this early hour constitutes playing lazy. Did you enjoy your ride?"

"Very much, but I'm glad I found you. Baroness Szechenyi warned me last night a huge wolf has been spotted on her property, so I wanted to tell you to be careful when riding through the woods. The baroness said this beast has been known to hunt indiscriminately on her estate, and she's afraid he might get brazen enough to attack unwary riders."

She scoffed at the warning. "No need to worry, Pal. The wolf belongs to the prince. Lucifer, as he is named, is quite domesticated and won't hurt you. In fact, he's accompanied me on my morning ride on more than one occasion, and I've never known him to attack so much as a squirrel."

"Well then, I'm glad I didn't encounter him. I might have killed the prince's pet and earned royal displeasure. I'm ready for breakfast. If you ride fast, there may still be some eggs left for your own breakfast."

Lucifer waited until Pal Anton was away before showing himself and was pleased when Bibi reined in Shadow as soon as she spotted him.

"Good morning, Lucifer. I take it someone has told you of the Baroness Szechenyi's dislike of you on her property, but I'm glad it hasn't dissuaded you from our morning exercise."

As the baroness used a slight leg pressure to urge Shadow into a ground-eating canter, he loped after her, eager for the morning's run.

They'd reached the very edge of the Szechenyi estate, where it bordered the castle's grounds, when he smelled it, the distinctive metal tang of a large trap, and horse and rider were heading right for it in blissful ignorance.

Gathering his haunches, Lucifer launched himself and hit Shadow squarely on his left foreleg. When the horse reared in fright, his ears rang from Bibi's outraged exclamation.

"Lucifer, what the hell has gotten into you?"

But it was too late for making amends. The trap snapped shut and his body was caught in its wicked teeth. He'd ricocheted off Shadow and fallen right into the maw of the deadly trap. And even though it was making things worse, he couldn't stop his violent back and forth twists to free his badly wounded body.

***

Kicking her feet free of the stirrups, Bibi jumped from Shadow's back and ran to the wolf's aid. "Lucifer, stay still. I know how to free you. I just need to find a large stick to pry the trap open. Please, please, be still. I'll have you out in a second, I promise."

When she spotted a branch of sufficient strength, she blessed her uncle Andris for showing her how to set and release large traps. Andris took no chances with newborn foals if there was even a hint of marauding predators in the Horthy fields.

Using the tree branch, and considerable strength, she worked the stick into the trap and jabbed the central release until the jagged steel teeth parted. Even though she feared Lucifer's injury would make him bite her for having to cause him more pain, she persisted in extricating the wolf and dragging him to safety.

"Lie still, your struggling is making your wound worse. I'll be right back after I spring the second trap. My uncle always set two traps, and I'll bet the baroness's gamekeeper has done the same."

Muttering to herself, she swept the ground with the sturdy tree limb and was gratified, and not a little startled, to have it captured in the second trap's evil mouth. The silence behind her frightened her. Where the wolf had been growling and thrashing in pain, the absence of sound was ominous. She was afraid Lucifer had expired from such a fearsome wound, and cursing the Baroness Szechenyi for such a vile act, she reluctantly turned to go back to the body.

"Wha...holy hell...Janos? Where did...?" Her eyes refused to make any sense of what she saw. Instead of the broken body of a wolf, there was a very naked and bloody prince lying on the ground, and in full sunlight.

She didn't hesitate to drag the moaning prince into the nearest thicket. Having at least saved the prince from terminal sunburn, she cast about for something to bind his wounds, but the only thing she had with her was a rain cape rolled tightly on the back of Shadow's saddle. Judging by the gaps in the bushes, it would be more useful as a temporary sun shade than a wound dressing.

She was gratified when the shade deepened after she tossed the cape over the bushes. When she stooped to enter the makeshift tent, the prince's command halted her.

"Please, Bibi, proceed no farther."

"Don't be ridiculous, I need to attend to your injuries."

"Just ride to the castle and send Akos back to me. He'll know what I need. I'll be fine until then."

She might have believed the prince, if his words weren't panted as if he was in great pain and having trouble breathing.

"I'll do no such thing, your injuries are severe, and it will take too long to fetch Akos. You must let me help you." She knelt and wedged her head and shoulders into the impromptu cave.

"You must listen to me," he ordered. "I'm not safe to be around at the moment. Leave me and fetch Akos to..."

She might have listened to the prince if he hadn't been writhing in agony from the pain of his wound, and so she held her ground at the entrance to the makeshift shelter, and thus witnessed his mouth draw back in a grimace of pain, exposing fangs, and everything suddenly clicked. All of the tales the baroness had been filling Margyth's head with were true.

Nesferatu, the Undead. The need to drink blood to survive. The animal familiar. The aversion to sunlight. She sat back on her heels as her mind swam with the outrageous comparisons.

Despite what her eyes were telling her, her mind refused to believe it. Janos was not undead. She had felt his heart beat when he held her close. He'd made love to her and never taken her blood. There had to be another explanation. Ignoring the prince's repeated requests to leave, she proceeded into the shelter to examine him.

Moving very gently, she supported his head in her lap. "I know what you need, and I am willing to give it. You may have my blood freely for saving Shadow."

A close inspection of the wound told her it was worse than she'd imagined. The writhing he'd done while trapped had left great tears in his abdomen, and blood flowed freely. "Please, Janos, take my blood. I don't think you can wait for me to return with Akos."

"No, I'll wait. I don't want to hurt you. I am in too much pain to be able to ease the pain of my bite."

God save me from chivalrous and stubborn vampires, she swore to herself. Removing the small knife she always carried in her boot, she took matters into her own hands and sliced her wrist quickly before she let fear change her mind. But the prince refused to drink until she actually dipped her finger into her blood and rubbed a few drops on his lips. The strike was so fast she almost missed it, but he hadn't lied, it hurt. Afraid he would stop drinking if she made a sound, she sat patiently while he fed.

It was obvious, from looking down the length of his body,

taking her blood had a most arousing effect on Janos. His shaft was fully engorged when he licked the wound closed and settled back into her lap. Whether it was her blood or embarrassment, he had a faint blush on his face, but she felt her own arousal when he kissed her wound closed and looked directly into her eyes.

"I thank you for your gift, Bibi. Taking blood is a very sensual experience for my kind, as you can no doubt observe. Unfortunately, at the moment, I am without sufficient clothes to hide the reaction and without sufficient strength to repay your kindness with pleasure."

"Your kind?" As soon as she'd asked the question, she flashed back to her uncle Andris's supposition the prince would eat, sleep, and make love like any other man. He'd been very wrong about Prince Rackoszi, and she hoped she'd live to tell him so. Hoping her curiosity would not be a contributing factor in her death, she chose to ignore the prince's repeated requests she leave him. She really wanted to hear his answer before she did her best to save him.

He answered her question with one of his own. "What do you know about the lost city of Atlantis?"

"Do you mean the mythical city the archaeologists are hunting?"

Speaking through a spasm of pain, Janos continued, "As a direct descendent of the Atlantean ruling family, I can assure you it isn't mythical."

"Okay, not mythical, but supposedly destroyed by an earthquake with total loss of life."

The prince attempted a laugh but it came out a wheeze.

"This isn't an ideal time to deliver a lecture, but if you know a little of Atlantean history, it will help you understand me. Atlantis was definitely destroyed. Some say it was destroyed by an earthquake and it sank beneath the waves, while others say the ancient gods did the deed because the Atlanteans were too powerful with their use of magical, energy-producing crystals. If I had to hazard a guess, I say the gods chose to raze it because we had somehow discovered the secret to prolong life."

At the mention of powerful, she looked down the length of him, and his well-defined chest, powerful thighs, and long legs had her picturing him as an Atlantean noble. The prince's physique was one of a warrior, and she re-dressed him as such in her mind's eye. Short, white chiton with a purple edging befitting his noble status. Perhaps a gilded belt to emphasize his broad shoulders, narrow waist, and flat stomach. Sturdy, well-made sandals fit for marching, and a *chlamys* or cloak pinned with a jewel-encrusted pin on his right shoulder to keep him warm.

Continuing her mental sketch, she asked herself whether or not Janos, the Atlantean, would he have a beard? Yes, he would. A well-trimmed one, making his face look dark and dangerous. The prince would have been a power to be respected in his ancient homeland.

"Do I have blood on my face?"

She snapped back to attention at the unusual question. "Blood? No, why do you ask?"

"Because you are looking at my face so intently."

Not willing to tell him of her fantasy of him as an

Atlantean warrior, she extemporized. "Ah, I am fascinated by your tale of Atlantean society. Tell me more."

"Atlantis," Janos continued, "was originally a scientifically advanced warrior state. In fact, the Atlantean mages were the ones who discovered a microscopic organism they called nanos. Injected into the bloodstream, the nanos were able to correct any illness or injury. The major defect, if you can call it a defect, was the nanos lived on a person's blood supply. It soon became obvious the nanos needed more than its host could naturally manufacture, especially when repairing injuries or sun damage. Hence the need for an outside blood source.

"While Atlantis was at its greatest glory, finding willing donors was easy. There were plenty of slaves captured in battle, and they were well rewarded when they opened a vein and gathered their precious blood into a cup for their masters to drink.

"When the earthquake hit, there were some who managed to escape to the mainland. They soon found, without willing donors, they had to adapt or die. The canines, designed to descend and pierce a vein to take what is needed, are one of the adaptations. Unfortunately, it took a certain amount of trial and error to perfect the new feeding method and not kill the donor, thus the tales of vampires were born."

Prince Rackoszi would have made a good university lecturer. His history lesson was abating her panic over his condition, and it was keeping his attention away from his wound. Encouraging him to continue, she asked another question. "Aside from growing fangs, what other adaptations have your kind made?"

Janos actually grinned up at her before continuing her edification. "The power to cloud minds and implant a pleasant memory or forgetfulness is not an adaptation but one of the talents we inherited from our Atlantean roots. However, lest you think we are amazingly powerful, I must tell you we are not truly immortal. We can be killed by fire, decapitation, prolonged exposure to sunlight, a stake or bullet through our hearts, or in the present situation, exsanguination. Our numbers are small. There are pockets of Atlanteans all over Europe, but my family was among those who eventually found a place in the Carpathian Mountains where we've chosen to live isolated enough to not draw attention to our existence."

"Aside from the blood drinking, you make Atlanteans out to be upright citizens. Why then are books written about you being revenants and soulless? Baroness Szechenyi has several books on the subject, and they are not at all flattering to your kind, Janos."

The prince grimaced at the mention of the baroness's reading choices. "Bibi, I think you've known me long enough to know I bear no resemblance to any of those descriptions. Once in a great while, one of us does go mad with blood lust, but those we hunt down and destroy before they make themselves widely known to humans. None of my kind want to be hunted down in the same manner as feral animals, so we put a swift end to their madness. We aren't soulless or damned. We do age, but very, very slowly. As you can attest, we can eat and drink regular food, but after a century or two it loses its appeal.

"Here's a fact I'll wager isn't in the baroness's books. We do drink blood, but it doesn't have to be human, although human blood is more fortifying. In fact, the drink you've seen Akos hand me each morning is wine mixed with bull's blood from the herd grazing in the castle's fields.

"We avoid spending too much time in the sun because it makes the nanos work harder to repair our bodies. And so, we prefer, but aren't actually required, to sleep during the day so our bodies can heal from the previous day's exertions."

The prince, who'd lain quietly in her lap, stiffened suddenly, and his feet dug into the ground as a loud groan was torn from his throat. "It begins," he panted.

"W-what begins?" she stammered, suddenly afraid she was losing him.

Blood-red tears escaped from Janos's eyes as he squeezed them shut against the pain. "The healing begins."

She had no idea how to help the Atlantean, except to let him hold onto her arms when the spasms overtook him and talk soothing nonsense as he did so. In between bouts of agonized healing, she found he relaxed if she ran her fingers through his hair and massaged his temples with slow, circular strokes. To distract him from a particularly long spasm, she braided the hair over his temples and was gratified to discover he'd fallen into a shallow sleep.

Now you resemble a proper hussar. No self-respecting hussar would be caught in public without braids. But what are we going to do about a moustache? Hopefully, the merciful God will not prolong this healing until you've grown one.

Her nonstop prayers for the prince's survival were

interrupted by Janos's husky voice.

"You must leave me and go to the castle and inform Akos I need the carriage. It's imperative, Bibi. I need more blood to heal than you can afford to donate."

Her fingertips eased the frown from his face before she replied, "I've been thinking of a plan while you slept. I *could* go and return with Akos, but he'd never get the carriage anywhere near this thicket. The woods are too deep, and he would have to carry you through the sunlight. In less than an hour, the sun will begin its decline, and these woods are thick enough so I can mount you on Shadow and keep him in the shade. You can wear my rain cape with the hood up, and I'm positive we can make it back to the castle."

"I'm surprised Shadow is still here. I would've thought he'd bolt after the scare I gave him."

"Shadow is well trained. I left his reins trailing so he won't go far."

"There is a small fault in your plan, my dear. I don't have the strength to mount a horse, and I doubt you have the strength to boost me into the saddle by yourself."

At her giggle, the prince leaned far enough back to look into her face. "What amuses you so? This is hardly a laughing matter."

"Forgive me, Your Grace. I was just picturing where I would have to place my hands on your, um, bare derriere, to get you into the saddle. Not to worry though. I've trained Shadow to kneel, so you will be able to mount him quite easily. I'll ride behind to hold you in the saddle so I can catch you if you faint. If we take it slowly, I'm confident I can get you to the castle sooner than my leaving you here and coming back with Akos."

"May the ancient ones help me," Janos intoned, "But I'm too weak to argue with you. If we're going to do this, it were better done immediately. And if I don't survive the journey, know you have my heartfelt thanks for all you've done for me. Call Shadow, and let's see how willing he is to accommodate two riders."

Maneuvering the Viceroy of Transylvania into the saddle was not as easy as she'd imagined, but the mounting was eventually accomplished, and she winced when he hissed in pain as Shadow lurched upward to stand again on all four hooves.

As promised, she kept to the shadows, and they'd been making steady progress when the prince stiffened in her arms and panted for air.

"Hold up. I need a minute."

Bibi felt him shudder as another bout of healing threatened to overwhelm him.

"As much as I hate to ask this, could we go a little faster? I need more blood, and I need it soon."

"But won't the jarring cause you more pain?" she asked in concern.

"Yes, but I'll risk it. I don't want to expose you to the nastier side of an Atlantean whose blood loss makes him willing to hurt the friend who rescued him. You need to get me to the castle and Akos as expeditiously as possible, Bibi."

She touched her heels to Shadow's flanks and picked up the pace. "Okay, but it will be a fast walk, not a trot. I won't risk opening your wounds again.'"

Janos grunted his assent and changed the subject. "I'm truly amazed the old dragon had the temerity to strike a blow if she truly believed I was a vampire. Whatever her source of information, however, she had the right of it. Killing the wolf would've killed me."

"Are you going to retaliate?"

"Not the way you think. I would never hurt Margyth's mother. What I will do is advance the date for our engagement ball. Do you have enough sketches of Margyth to begin the miniatures?"

"Yes, I do. I can begin them tomorrow, if you wish."

"Perfect. After you leave me in Akos's tender care, return to the Szechenyi estate and inform the baroness you've completed your sketches of Margyth, and I offered to send my coach for you early tomorrow morning. And if by chance the baroness should inquire as to my health, tell her you found me quite hail and hardy."

Janos's loss of blood must be affecting his reasoning ability, but she refrained from saying so. What Margyth's mother had just done to the prince was beyond her capacity to forgive. Rather than give voice to her disapproval, she merely clucked to Shadow and urged him forward. It wasn't until they had the castle in sight, he called another halt.

"Let us rest here a moment. I need to gather my strength to dismount. Take the path circling to the rear of the castle and I'll guide you into a secret entrance. I don't need the entire staff to witness my predicament. But before we move, I confess to being curious. After everything you've witnessed today, you haven't tried to convince me not to wed Margyth. Why not?"

Here was her chance to sway Prince Rackoszi from his path, but at the last moment her courage failed her. "While I think you and she are not well suited, I would never presume to try and change your mind. I do understand what duty is. You aren't marrying for love but duty, and I think you are well aware of your fiancée's shortcomings. As your friend, it saddens me to think you probably won't find love in this marriage, but I understand your reasons for carrying through with it."

What unmitigated twaddle you spout. You don't understand it at all. If Margyth were out of the picture, you and Janos could be happy together. Maybe you should enumerate the long list of her sins. The prince couldn't possibly want to marry her after he hears them.

And maybe you should enumerate your own as well. Start with coveting another woman's intended.

Janos interrupted her mental castigation, and she was more than relieved to let it go.

"Well, you are the only one who does. Give Shadow a nudge and let's get this over with before I fall out of the saddle and embarrass myself."

Chapter Fifteen

Bibi hid her look of relief when the carriage stopped under the portico. She'd spent the last ten minutes making desultory conversation with the baroness while waiting for her means of escape to arrive. She'd wanted to leave the Szechenyi manse without notice at this early hour but, alas, the baroness uncharacteristically remembered her duties as a hostess and rose early to bid her goodbye.

As she walked through the door without a backward glance, she was surprised to find Shadow already hitched to the prince's carriage. However, the hand opening the carriage door from the inside made her jump back in shock.

"Why, Prince Rackoszi, I'd no idea you'd come in person to convey me to your castle."

She would've said more but was rudely elbowed aside by the baroness who thrust her head into the carriage, making Janos move back with alacrity.

"Good day to you, Baroness Szechenyi. I hope you slept well."

"I slept as I always sleep, Prince Rackoszi. I sleep with a clear conscience and a righteous purpose."

"Indeed, Madame, I, too, am a sound sleeper. How is your list of invitees coming? I am advancing the date of the betrothal dance. Baroness Baranyi assured me she can have the miniatures finished by month's end."

Bibi was gratified on Janos's behalf to note Baroness

Szechenyi's reaction. Upon hearing the news of the changed date, the woman grabbed the large, gold cross she wore around her neck and held it in a white-knuckled clench.

"It is finished. There is just one person I care to invite. Pal Anton will serve as our chaperone for the ball."

"As you wish. I'll be sure to tell my housekeeper to place him near the rooms I've reserved for you and Margyth. And before you refuse to stay the night, let me add the festivities are sure to continue into the wee hours, and I wouldn't want you and Margyth on the road at such a time. I do care about your safety, despite what you may believe of me."

It would appear the prince had won this round with the Baroness Szechenyi, for the old besom backed away as if she'd been smacked, and Bibi furtively pinched herself for the uncharitable wish the viceroy had actually done so.

Bibi turned to make her farewells and was amazed to find only the retreating back of the baroness. The firm thud of the front door closing put paid to her attempt at courtesy, and she climbed into the carriage with a wry grin on her face.

Her comments as to the baroness's execrable manners were stilled by the groan the prince gave as the carriage jerked into motion.

"Janos, are you mad? You aren't well enough to be traveling this morning."

"Perhaps, but it was necessary as a show of strength. The baroness needed proof her plan to kill me hasn't worked."

"She only has proof her plan hasn't killed you *yet*," she shot back in a reproving tone. "If you continue to neglect your health this way, the baroness may still win."

Further remonstrance was cut off when the prince sought her hand and gripped it hard as another surge of pain took him, and she jumped to his side of the carriage to support him as another bout of what she hoped was healing overtook him.

"Oh, do forgive me. I will refrain from chiding you. What can I do to help?"

"Nothing you aren't already doing, Bibi. Just keep me upright until Akos can get me out of this damned bouncing box. I just need another day or two of healing and I'll be right as rain."

Despite her worry for the prince, the farther the carriage drew away from the Szechenyi estate, the lighter she felt. The baroness's sourness and Margyth's selfishness had cast a pall over her usually cheerful demeanor. It was ironic, where once she'd dreaded entering the prince's castle, she now looked forward to being inside its strong walls.

Akos was the first to reach the carriage and threw open the door. "Let me assist you, Your Grace. I've turned down your bed. You are to rest for the remainder of the week. Here, drink this straight down, and I'll help you inside."

Bibi nodded approval as Janos tilted the goblet and drank the dark wine because she knew what it contained and was relieved to see a flush of color bloom in his cheeks. She waited while the prince gathered his strength and exited the carriage unassisted.

She gasped in consternation when the stubborn prince stopped and extended a hand to help her from the carriage. She didn't waste the prince's small cache of strength by arguing but flung herself from the conveyance after taking his hand.

"Thank you, Janos. I'll visit you after you've recovered sufficient strength." And she marched into the house and never looked back. She couldn't bear to witness the pain on his face the small courtesy had cost him.

Even though she didn't expect the prince to be up and about the morning after her return to Castle Rackoszi, she was still disappointed to find herself the sole occupant of the solar. Erzsebet, ever the efficient chatelaine, had already carried all of her art supplies to the room and had included a large, cloth-covered table to serve as her work surface. Since the miniatures wouldn't be worn, she had settled on a larger, saucer size. She'd prepared them with the multiple coatings of black lacquer before leaving for the Szechenyi estate, so with the light at its brightest, she painted the first, delicate stroke.

Bibi hadn't been aware Erzsebet had entered the solar until she sensed her presence. Just how long the woman had been standing there, she'd no idea, but it wasn't until she straightened with an audible crack of her spine, and a small groan of relief, the housekeeper spoke up.

"Your lunch, Baroness. Please take a moment to eat, you'll need your strength to continue painting."

She was nonplussed. Kindness from the taciturn woman? "I, er, thank you. Yes, I find I am quite famished. Your kindness is..."

"Unexpected? I know we got off on the wrong foot, and I apologize. I can be overprotective of the prince. I was, and still am, against his course of action, but I also wanted an opportunity to thank you for saving his life. Prince Rackoszi told me what you did for him and I wanted to thank you for saving us."

"I'm not sure what you mean by 'us'? My only action was to give him a small amount of my blood. It was the least I could do for his gallantry in saving my life as well as my horse's."

"Ah, the stubborn man may have explained what he is, but he hasn't told you what he does for the rest of us. By saving the prince, you saved everyone in this castle. Every year, on our birthdays, we drink a celebratory glass of wine with the prince, and in our glasses is our present, a few drops of his blood. It is a gift he, and the Rackoszis before him, gives to each of us. It keeps us healthy and able to live longer lives in service to the Rackoszis. Since they cannot function in bright sun, they need a staff who can."

Bibi stared at her in amazement. "Everyone? You, Akos, Cata?"

Erzsebet gave a rusty cackle. "Right down to the scullery maids and the stable boys. By saving Janos, you've saved all of us."

Bibi groped for and found the chair then sat herself down with an ungraceful plop. Before she could formulate a reply to such an amazing announcement, Erzsebet placed the tray in front of her.

"Please eat and rest for a few moments before resuming your work. I'll collect the tray after the light has faded. I've already instructed the staff not to disturb you, and the prince has promised not to enter the solar even during the evening hours. He wants to be surprised by the finished portraits, so he won't peek until they are on display for the engagement party."

"How is the prince?"

"He's recovering. It will take a few days for his system to restore his energy after such a blood loss, but Akos is guarding him like a mother hen. The prince will not be permitted to overextend himself with Akos on duty."

Erzebet turned to go but swung back around. "The Baron Szechenyi and his wife and daughter may have been made noble by royal decree, but they never had or will have what the prince has in abundance, and I'm not referring to the nanos in his blood."

"And what does Prince Rackoszi have in such abundance?" she asked.

"They will never have nobleness of spirit. Janos and his father, and his father's father, have all had it. And it is the very reason I am so vehement in my objection to him marrying Margyth. That spoiled, self-centered woman will drain every drop of his spirit in his attempt to find the tiniest spark of goodness within her. You may soon be dancing at his engagement party, but the rest of us in this castle will be mourning the loss of a very fine man who gave up his happiness to protect us."

Bibi sat in stunned silence for several moments after Erzsebet's departure. When she did take a sip of the soup, she discovered it had grown cold while she'd pondered the housekeeper's gloomy prediction.

Always the optimist, Bibi formulated and cast aside several ways she could help to avert the doomed marriage. She could tell the prince what she'd gleaned from the argument between Margyth and her mother but quickly rejected the plan. Telling him would expose her as a sneak and an eavesdropper, and having Janos think less of her character was repugnant. Nor would she tell him of the tryst between Margyth and Pal. She didn't think the prince would much care to leave Margyth for a tattletale. The sauce on her fish congealed, and the roll grew stale, and still no solution. She had to admit she was a terrible tactician. Even as hard as she was presently thinking, she hadn't invented a decent strategy to save Janos from his noble course. And so, she returned her concentration to the miniature. It was the only thing she could think to do. Like the prince, if she accepted an obligation, she fulfilled it.

Chapter Sixteen

Disgusted with lying in bed and having the reoccurring dream of Bibi as his bride and the mother of his sons torment him, Janos eased the curtains back and swore when he discovered his room, even at this early hour, bathed in the pale light of a rising sun. It would be another gloriously sunny day. Two weeks and there hadn't been a cloud in sight.

Casting off the covers, the Viceroy of Transylvania padded nude to the window and defied the gods to finish raising the sun and fry him on the spot. It would be merciful, and quick, and not the constant pining he'd endured since he'd healed enough to get out of bed. Despite being housed in another wing of the castle, he felt her. Her blood was calling to him, and it had taken more strength to resist answering it than it had cost him in closing the wounds from the wolf trap.

He needed to get out of this stone prison before his self-control broke and he took what his heart was demanding. He knew when she opened her eyes for the day. He felt her concentration when she painted. He followed her scent when she strode to the stables, and his heart throbbed in pain when she galloped out of sight and the wind dispelled the bouquet of tuber rose, musk, and horse.

Any more of this madness and the king would be sending hunters after him. Looking upward at the *trompe l'oiel* cherubs on the ceiling, he addressed the ancient gods with far less deference than usual.

"Well, ancient ones, why are you keeping these cupids affixed to the ceiling and not freeing them to pierce my heart with arrows of love for Margyth? Why are you so hellbent on tempting me to ignore my duty? It wouldn't kill you to send a few cloudy days my way and permit me to visit my intended. The very least you could do is give me one, miserable, cold, and rainy day to slake some of this bloodlust with a punishing ride on Anubis."

Hearing Akos enter the suite with his morning beverage, Janos fell silent. His valet already considered him to be daft for honoring his word when being wed to Margyth would be the result, he didn't need to be found communing with plaster angels to compound it.

***

Akos wasn't surprised to find the prince awake. Ever since he'd been wounded, the prince hadn't slept but a few hours. His body was mended, but his spirit was still bleeding. Well, he'd had enough of this. He was not afraid to run straight toward danger. Indeed, he'd followed the prince into actual battle as his orderly when the emperor had needed their local militia to keep the Italians from grabbing any more territory.

Akos opened with a volley of big guns. "This has got to stop, Your Grace. Your actions will have dire consequences."

"My actions? What actions are you referring to, Akos?"

"Perhaps I should have said your non-actions. You haven't left your suite or this castle in two weeks. You haven't eaten anything at all. The solitary action you've taken is to play your violin, and doing so, has also had negative consequences."

"And just what consequences have my nonactions had? Pray enlighten me."

The prince's silky tone of voice didn't fool him. Akos recognized it was but a cover for building rage, but he was no coward and stood his ground.

"You've snapped at everyone who has had the misfortune to enter this room. The poor between-stairs maids, who replenish the coals for your fireplace, are afraid to enter even after knocking. The chambermaid has had an inch of skin flayed from her body by your abrasive tongue. And the cook is threatening to quit because she thinks you no longer care for her cooking since you've sent every meal back without sampling anything. And for the gods' sake, didn't your gypsy instructor teach you how to play anything except funeral music? The parlor maids are weeping at the sound of it and leaving tear stains as they polish the furniture...and...and worst of all, you've annoyed Erzsebet."

"And just why is annoying Erzsebet such a dire consequence?"

"Because, Your Grace, annoying her makes everyone in this castle afraid to breathe. Your family may have built this castle, but it is Erzsebet who makes it work."

"And what of you, my stalwart valet? What dire consequences have befallen you as a result of my abominable behavior?"

After handing the wine goblet to the prince, Akos turned his back and straightened the bed linens. "Those consequences have yet to come to fruition, Your Grace. But if you don't eat something soon, my valet services will be called into question when you appear at your own wedding with a withered body, and too-large trousers sagging from your shrunken waist as you lead your new bride to the bridal reception."

Ignoring the outraged sputtering behind him, Akos delivered the *coup de grace*. "No one is confining you to this room. Find the misplaced balls you were born with and go out. You are healed. Change to wolf and go outside and do what you need to do. Chase butterflies, mark your territory by pissing on every bush and blade of grass, or hunt something down and kill it to relieve your anger, but for the sake of everyone who loves you, regain your balance."

Akos didn't draw breath again until he plucked the cover from the breakfast tray and the prince lifted a loaded fork to his mouth. Apparently, his employer would permit him to live despite his impertinence. Not wanting to interrupt the first meal the prince had consumed in two weeks, the valet waited until the prince wiped his mouth and shoved back from his chair to inform him, "The baroness left for her morning ride not ten minutes ago. If you hurry, you can catch her up."

"It's doubtful, I don't know which direction she's chosen to ride this morning."

"While *your* nose may be lacking, Your Grace, I know Lucifer's is not. A wolf's sense of smell will tell him the path she's chosen this day."

It wasn't until he opened the door for the silver wolf and closed it behind him, did Akos relax his rigid posture and let the shakes overtake him. Unwittingly mimicking the prince's earlier action, he shook his fist at the plaster ceiling and urged the gods to give the prince a small measure of relief for this one morning.

***

Janos found her at the trout stream and loped to a nearby bush to study her unusual antics. Bibi had taken off her boots and rolled the legs of her trousers above her knees. She was bent over in midstream with her hands cupped beneath the water. He was about to make his presence known, but she gave a great whoop and thoroughly drenched herself when she scooped her hands quickly from the water. His artist-in-residence was attempting to fish without a pole.

While wolves couldn't laugh, per se, they could draw back their lips in a fierce simulation of mirth. His sneeze of derision alerted Bibi to his presence, and she spun around in surprise and fell into the stream. With any other woman, he would have had to close his ears against shrill shrieks and vituperation, but Baroness Baranyi hooted and splashed water in raucous delight.

"Lucifer, how good to see you. I was wondering when you would leave the castle. What's the matter, are wolves afraid of water?" Bibi punctuated her question with great gouts of water thrown in his direction. "Oh, do join me, the water is quite refreshing."

It was downright miraculous. As each wave of water hit him, he felt his black mood drain away and his natural playfulness take over. With a great leap, he left the bank and did the wolf version of a cannonball hitting water. If his artist hadn't been already drenched, it would have drowned her.

They splashed and played tag until they were both beyond wet and out of breath. He was pleased Bibi had to grab his ruff to wade from the water. Her riding clothes were so heavy, she had a difficult time climbing the small bank.

"Oh my, Lucifer, I think you will need to show me your secret entrance again. I don't think Erzsebet will approve of my present disheveled state." She took off her vest and wrung it out.

The sun was beginning to dry his fur, and he sought the shade under the tree where he'd hosted the picnic for Margyth. No, he was not going to recall the dismal scene. Today was for sunshine and the company of a good friend, and he intended to make the most of it.

As if sensing his silent resolve, Bibi rubbed his ears in absentminded affection. At first, he found it soothing, but soon he found it to be less soothing and more arousing. But he wasn't so focused on her touch he could block out his evil angel's suggestion.

Go ahead, turn over and let her rub your belly. You know you want to. When you are sufficiently aroused, you can change forms and strip her naked and do what you've spent nights thinking of, you can drink her sweet nectar and take what is yours.

Shut the lascivious hole you call a mouth, you evil spawn. Szigismond Emre Janos Rackoszi, unless you want to experience Hell with a fallen angel as your guide, heed my advice. Run!

Despite the strong urge to cast himself forthwith into the path of temptation, Janos ran.

Chapter Seventeen

Bibi sat in miserable silence and propelled the strips of bacon she'd been served around on her plate in random patterns. What on earth had she been thinking? She'd embarrassed herself, and the sting of embarrassment warmed her cheeks when she recalled how she'd cavorted in the stream with a prince of Transylvania. And her blush deepened when she also remembered how she'd rubbed his ears, and his face, and his chest as anyone would a common house pet. Oh, *please, God, let mortification kill me so I won't have to apologize for such asinine behavior. And here I've been casting aspersions on Margyth's acting the simpering schoolgirl. Petting Janos as if he was a lapdog had to have been just as off-putting to the prince.* Thank God the prince had had enough self-control to run away before he bit her in outrage for such an insult to his person.

She muttered her resolve under her breath. Beatrix Celine Baranyi, this is going to be painful, but Horthys don't breed cowards. *You will find the prince and apologize.* She started to leave the table to find the prince and make her apology when a footman entered the dining room.

"Baroness, you have a visitor, Lieutenant Colonel Esterhazy. Shall I show him in?"

Wincing at her instant delight for the momentary reprieve, she gave her assent and resumed her seat.

Bloodstock

"Good morning, Pal, are you here to ride with me this morning?"

"A delightful suggestion, Bibi, but I've come to bid you *adieu*. My leave is up and I have to report back to my regiment. Ah, your crestfallen look tells me at least one person in this region will miss me. I dare say the Szechenyis were relieved by my departure. They didn't even bother rising to give their farewell."

She and Pal stiffened in surprise at the unexpected sound of Janos's voice from behind them.

"There is another person who will note your absence, Pal. I will miss your presence as well. Please, have a seat and join Bibi and me for breakfast. I would count myself a terrible host if I sent a hussar home without a decent breakfast."

She was too shocked by the prince's early rising, and his actual appearance at breakfast, to comment as the two men helped themselves to the selections at the sideboard. In all her time at Castle Rackoszi, she had never seen the prince eat breakfast. Perhaps he'd risen early to chastise her for her lapse of manners. She hoped he'd wait until Pal left before doing so.

Bibi noted Janos's plate almost matched Pal's in quantity of food, but before her tongue could form a tease, the prince opened the conversation.

"I overheard you telling the baroness your leave is up. Has Baroness Szechenyi informed you of your invitation to the engagement dance?"

Pal cocked his head at his host's question. "Not exactly. She mentioned something about accompanying them as their chaperone should I care to return by month's end."

"Well let me make it a formal request, then. You are invited by the Viceroy of Transylvania to attend his engagement dance at the end of this month. If you need an official request sent to the commander of your regiment, I will be happy to do so."

"You are very kind to invite me, Your Grace. My commander will be quite amazed by the company I've been keeping. I'm sure he'll grant me leave. I accept with delight."

Janos nodded as he shook out his napkin and placed it in his lap. "It's settled, then. Come join me in showing my cook how much her culinary skills are appreciated. You've a long ride ahead of you, and I wouldn't want you to expire of hunger."

Bibi held her silence as the two men emptied their plates. But when Pal put his fork down and wiped his mouth, she gave Pal Anton a parting tease. "Poor Ares, he must bear the weight of well-packed saddle bags and a well-stuffed hussar. I do hope he isn't sway-backed by the time he reaches Vienna."

Both Pal and Prince Rackoszi roared with laughter at her sally.

"Ah, Bibi, I will miss your wit, but I look forward to returning to bear the brunt of it. Thank you for the excellent breakfast, Your Grace, but I must be on my way."

"Please, Pal Anton, call me Janos. I've enjoyed knowing you and hope you can return often. Although I can't ride on sunny days, I would be happy of your company on the cloudy ones."

"Bibi has told me of your riding skill and the remarkable Arabian you ride. I will look forward to riding with you when I return. *Adieu.*"

"I'll walk you to the door, Pal," she offered. She'd be lying to herself if she said she hadn't done so more to delay her face-to-face with the prince than out of courtesy.

But it wasn't much of a delay. Pal played the gallant and kissed her knuckles before vaulting into the saddle. He was gone before she could even raise her hand in farewell.

It was no surprise to find Prince Rackoszi waiting for her in the shadows of the main entrance. If she hadn't been so nervous, she might've noticed the prince squaring his shoulders at the same time she did.

"Janos, I—"

"Please, Bibi, let me apologize for my rude behavior yesterday."

She was confounded. "Your behavior? I think it is I who owe you an apology for my appalling lapse of good manners. I can't imagine why I let the notion of wading into a trout stream and cavorting about like a madwoman overcome my good sense. I'm sorry for my lack of decorum. I forgot Lucifer is, um, a royal wolf. I acted inappropriately, and I'm sorry."

"Don't be, *kinczem*. I refuse your apology because you've done nothing wrong. Let's just agree yesterday was fun and be done with it. Come, I'm all ears to hear how your work is progressing."

***

Bibi relaxed her rigid posture, and her face lit up in her eagerness to tell him of her painting. Janos listened as she explained the Russian use of lacquer and gold leaf paint and vibrant colors. He chuckled along with her as she coyly refused to tell him what the actual pose of the painting would be. Indeed, he hung on her every word, every slight change of her face, and the graceful gestures her hands made as they demonstrated painting techniques. His concentration was so keen, he almost missed her question.

"I hate to ask this, but could I do one more sketch of you? Although I have several, I'm still not satisfied with your face."

Janos brayed in self-derision. "You and Akos. My valet has grown tired of looking at my face. He so informed me just yesterday and again this morning."

"Oh, my Lord, Your Grace, I've done it again, haven't I? I've insulted you by my awkward phrasing."

"Ah, Bibi, you could never insult me. You don't have a mean enough spirit. Stop sputtering, I know what you meant by the remark. If you need me to sit for you, I'd be happy to do so.

He allowed her to steer him into, of all places, the kitchen. His quirked eyebrow forced an explanation from her.

"Yes, odd, I know. But I've tried sketching you in formal poses and it just hasn't worked. I'd hoped, maybe, if I could pose you in a more, um, normal setting, you would relax enough to let me discover the inner you. The kitchen is the one place I could think of with strong but indirect light."

He pretended not to see the look of amazement and then consternation passing over his cook's face. He hoped his dinner wouldn't be burned as a result of having had her domain breached by his august person.

The normal kitchen routine resumed when Bibi drew a chair over to the bank of windows. Since the kitchen was shaded by a massive oak tree, the windows cast a dappled light. He found it not at all discomforting to sit there.

"Please turn the chair around and straddle it. Yes, exactly. I want you to look past me, say, to the rack of pans hanging from the ceiling. Okay, keep looking there, and no more thinking of estate business. I don't want to have to paint you with a scowl."

How about a leer? Think of her luscious body spread beneath you as you thrust into her and make her yours.

He felt his face go rigid with displeasure at the persistence of his evil angel.

"You're doing it again, Janos. Remember, happy thoughts, cheerful thoughts. Think of riding Anubis, if you must," Bibi cautioned.

It's not a horse you want to ride, is it?

The damned imp just refused to give up. He swore there'd been a gargling sound before the interruption of his good angel.

I did warn him what would happen if he didn't shut up. Calm yourself, you won't be hearing from Satan's garrulous spawn anymore today. Despite what you may think, you haven't angered my master. Your sense of honor is pleasing to him.

Janos sat up straighter in the chair and pretended he was playing cards for money to keep his facial expression neutral, but the good angel's advice to run from Bibi was not sitting well with him in retrospect, and if the celestial messenger

188

hadn't picked up on the anger in his mind, he was about to.

Well, if you have the power of intercession with the God of all gods, perhaps you can induce him to send some cloudy weather my way. I need to put distance between my desire and my duty, or your mission to keep me honorable will fail. And I don't mean to be impertinent, but tell him to make it soon because I don't give a tinker's damn about being dutiful anymore.

"My goodness, Janos, I don't know what you were just thinking of, but I swear I saw fire shooting from your eyes."

He groaned and rested his head, facedown, atop his arms. "Sorry, Bibi. I guess I'm just not patient enough to hold a pose. Please tell me you've got what you wanted because I don't think I can sit still a moment longer."

"Yes, of course. I should be able to paint a good representation of you from what I have. If you'll excuse me, I need to get back to Margyth's painting. I have some finishing touches to add, and there's enough light left to complete it today. Thank you for posing this morning."

Janos stood and gave a slight bow as she passed him to leave the kitchen. He wasn't at all curious to see the result of her sketching. He was well aware she was trying to be diplomatic about it having been a successful sitting.

Janos groaned at the screech the curtain rings made as

Akos opened the bed drapes. He must make a note to have the damned things oiled. Another day spent wanting the woman he couldn't have did not appeal to him, at all.

"You are in luck, Your Grace. It's a misty, cold, cloudy day. Unusual for this early in the summer. Shall I ask Baroness Baranyi if she'd care to accompany you for a ride this morning?"

A vigorous ride is just the thing you do want this morning. Go ahead, let your servant bring your heart's desire to your bedroom, and you can gallop beneath the sheets for the entire day.

Don't listen to him. A morning run with your horse is just the ticket. It will get you away from temptation. And you, you uncouth imp, are damned for your persistence. You don't have sense enough to back off unless...

Unless what? You try cramming your halo down my throat again to muzzle me, and I'll show you how painful the sharp end of a pitchfork can be when it's embedded in your ass. Satan save me from do-gooders. Run? Is that the best advice you can give the man?

Ah, wait a moment, I begin to discern your strategy. You had him running from the artist, and you presently have him running with a horse. What's next, will he run all the way to the woman his duty says to wed? Not a bad plan at all. Keep him running, and he'll be too exhausted to do anything with a woman except collapse and gurgle like a plague victim. I must salute you, no woman would find such behavior attractive.

Menj az anyad, *and I'm including both of you in the curse,* Janos roared at the two mental pests. He'd had his fill of being driven crazy. The extremely vulgar imprecation worked, for his head was blessedly empty of competing suggestions.

"Your Grace, did you hear me? I said it was cloudy out."

"Yes, yes, I heard you the first time, Akos. I just had to order my, er, my schedule for the day," he replied, testily. "There is a note on my dresser. I want it delivered to Baroness Szechenyi immediately. And tell the messenger he is to wait for an answer."

"But what about Baroness Baranyi? Will you ride with her this morning?"

Akos, who comprehended a promise of mayhem when he heard it, dropped the subject and handed over the goblet of wine as soon as he stopped his deep growling.

"I want you to choose suitable clothes for an outing. I intend to take Margyth and her mother to the coffeehouse in the next village. It's time we discussed wedding arrangements."

He wished he'd used the words "wedding arrangements" sooner, for they did the trick in locking his valet's lips. Not another word was uttered by the man as he selected his clothing for the day, seated him, uncovered his breakfast, and handed him his hat and gloves when the messenger returned to say the Szechenyi women would be waiting for him at his convenience. It was unfortunate he couldn't keep himself from cringing every time he said the word *wedding*. Realizing he was dawdling in the hallway, he squared his shoulders and descended the stairs.

***

"Szigi, you've rescued me. I swear I was about to expire of boredom. Since Pal Anton returned to Vienna, I've had no one but mother for company, and though I love you, Momma, you aren't a very good conversationalist. Hurry up, Mother, so we can be away. I'm tired of the inside of this house."

She ignored the dagger glare her mother sent her way when she chose to sit next to the prince after the coach started to roll. Turning to her intended, she began her quest to learn the answers to questions the prince had, so far, avoided answering. An enclosed carriage traveling at a good clip was the perfect place to interrogate the prince. The man would have to throw himself from the carriage if he wanted to escape answering her questions.

"Szigi, where are we going? Your message was quite cryptic."

"It is my pleasure to treat you and your mother to some coffee and pastry this misty morning. There is a coffeehouse in the next village, and the owner's wife makes excellent pastry to accompany the freshly brewed coffee. It's not as grand as those coffeehouses you would find in Budapest or Vienna, but it makes up for it in the quality of its baked goods."

"Oh, how delightful. I swear, Momma and I haven't been out exploring in ages. It will give me something to compare to the ones in Vienna. You will take me to Vienna when we're married, won't you?"

She quirked an eyebrow as color rose in the prince's cheeks and he fussed with his cravat.

"I suppose we can visit Vienna, Margyth. I dislike traveling because of my sun allergy, but if we travel by night, it might be accomplished with minimal discomfort."

It sounded to her like the prince was consigning her wishes to the maybe category, and this she just would not tolerate. She ignored her mother's small tsk of disapproval when she put her hand over the prince's, which was resting on his thigh, and gave it a small squeeze.

"But what of our honeymoon? You don't expect me to leave Momma's house for your gloomy castle without at least a honeymoon? I want to go to Vienna, and Paris, and Rome, and—"

"Oh look, we've arrived," Janos called out.

Her recitation of the world's capitals was halted in mid-word as the prince flung open the door and dove from the conveyance. She fumed as she waited for her mother to alight, but before she could hold Szigi's feet to the fire, she was forestalled yet again.

"Margyth, permit me to introduce you to the proprietor. You will have a hard time making a selection, for everything on the menu is a treat for a sweet tooth."

The prince opened the shop door and all but shoved her mother and herself inside. Well, if he believed she could be put off for long, he was mistaken.

Her second attempt to get her intended to agree to a world tour was thwarted by the proprietor of the pastry shop. She didn't appreciate being ignored as the prince and the proprietor exchanged pleasantries.

"Szigi, I've asked you a question and I want it answered.

Send this man about his business."

"Margyth, I was but listening to the menu selection. What would you care to sample? My personal favorite is the plum and apricot preserves lattice cake. It will melt in your mouth."

She shuddered at the combination. Plum preserves did not appeal to her with their black color. "What a dreadful combination. I'd prefer something a bit more sophisticated. Is there anything resembling cream cake or custard tarts?"

***

Janos hadn't missed the proprietor's crestfallen look at Margyth's insult. He knew better than to look to Baroness Szechenyi to smooth over her daughter's appalling lack of good manners, so he offered the man an excuse in her stead.

"My apologies. Mademoiselle Szechenyi has a penchant for cream. Why don't you serve your wife's cream cake? I think four layers of cake with cream filling in between should assuage her craving. As for me, I'll have the lattice cake. As a matter of fact, please box up four more pieces for me to take home. I know my house guest would love to try it. Turning to Margyth's mother, he asked, "And what would you care for, Baroness Szechenyi?"

"I care for nothing."

He had to steel his face into one of calmness rather than rage. The old dragon was doing her best to make this an unpleasant outing. Turning once again to the pastry shop owner, he ordered, "Let us have three cups of your special blend of coffee and chocolate with fresh-whipped cream on the side to go with our pastry selections."

Once the proprietor sped away from the table, he was left with nothing to say. It was a pity his intended wasn't lacking words as well.

"Szigi, you haven't answered my question. Are we or are we not going to have a honeymoon? I want to visit the world capitals. I want the entire month to be spent traveling from one exciting place to another, and I don't want to just do it at night."

Perhaps some of his anger at her blatant selfishness appeared on his face, for she stopped demanding and pretended to play coy maiden again.

"Prince Rackoszi, I'm beginning to think you are ashamed of me. Aren't I attractive enough to appear in public with you?"

"I don't have to tell you how pretty you are, my dear. I'm sure your mirror does so every day. It isn't I don't want to escort you; it's just I can't do it in bright sunlight. I have town homes in Budapest and Vienna, and I will be happy to escort you anywhere you care to visit after sunset."

"Oh, Szigi, after sunset I should think the only place you'd want to escort me is to the bedroom."

"Margyth, you are being indelicate." The baroness reprimanded her daughter.

"At last, the mother remembers her duties," he whispered to himself.

Ignoring her mother's glare of disapproval, Margyth placed her hand atop the prince's and asked, "Szigi, just how soon after the engagement party do you intend to announce the bans? I think it nonsense to wait for an entire month while they are called. After all, we've known each other forever, so why wait?"

Before he could even answer one question, the overindulged girl forged ahead with another, and he refrained from twitching as nervous perspiration made his shirt stick to his back.

"When can my mother and I inspect the Mistress Suite? I'm quite sure I'll want to redecorate it to suit my tastes. Even if you insist on calling the bans rather than a special license, I'll need time to redecorate it to suit myself."

Janos forced himself to keep his displeasure from showing. The Mistress Suite? His soon-to-be wife was implying he would occupy his father's rooms. He'd never even considered moving from the rooms he presently occupied to the master suite in the west wing. Damn it, he was comfortable in his present rooms and hadn't even given a moment's reflection on what changes marriage would have on his day-to-day routine. He quailed at the knowledge the woman would have free access to him via the master suite's connecting door. Well, if there wasn't a lock on the door, there would be soon. It was ironic to be saved from having to answer her persistent questions by the baroness herself.

"Margyth, I'll have no talk of a special license. It implies the need for haste. I'll not stand for the Szechenyi name to be subject to gossip and speculation as to the reason for such unusual haste."

Ah, thank the ancient gods, the desserts arrived and he could stuff cake in his mouth rather than answer any more questions. But the baroness quashed even this small enjoyment.

"Daughter, do remember how well the gown you intend to wear to your betrothal dance fits you? If you finish all of your cream cake, I doubt the gown will be quite so flattering if we have to let out the seams."

Janos held his silence as venom spilled from the girl's eyes, but she did put her fork down. Giving her mother a cold shoulder, Margyth turned to him once again.

"Will there be any other royals invited to our wedding?"

He must have appeared confused for she enlightened him.

"What I mean to say, Szigi, is you are a prince. Can I expect other royals at our wedding? I want to make sure my gown is on a par with the status of the people attending, after all."

Akos must've tied his cravat too tight this morning, he complained to himself as he inserted a finger to give himself breathing room. "I dare say my godfather will attend. He's our, um...he's the ruler of Wallachia."

"A ruler? Do you mean a king?"

He didn't have the energy to go into details and so just nodded. He was relieved when she didn't press for further elucidation.

"Mother, a king, a real king will attend my wedding. You'll have to invite your second cousin the Marchioness, and isn't there a Viscount or two on the Szechenyi side? We can't be seen as peasants in comparison."

His intended's gushing snobbery had the Baroness

Szechenyi's face frozen with disapproval. But when the woman returned her cup to its saucer with a loud clack and turned to face him, he was astonished to find her disapproval wasn't directed at her daughter but himself. What little hope he'd had for a pleasant morning gave its death rattle as it died from a thousand bloody cuts. Admitting defeat, he called for the bill and settled it quickly. He added a generous gratuity to cover the Szechenyis's boorish behavior.

The one bright moment to the whole outing was the baroness's request they be driven straight home. He didn't linger over his farewells.

***

What a disagreeable day this was turning out to be. Bibi had arrived at Janos's suite to suggest a ride, since it was far from sunny, but was told the prince had taken the carriage to visit Margyth.

Without a riding partner, she opted to exercise Anubis, which ended on an irritating note. Spooked by a hare shooting from under a bush, the Arabian hopped sideways, pinned her leg against the rough bark of an oak tree, and ripped the skirt of her best riding habit.

She stood gazing down at all the sketches she'd made of the prince, and despite the weak light coming through the solar windows, she could tell none of them would suit, and forced herself to walk away from the displeasing efforts before she consigned them all to the nearest flame. She was thoroughly frustrated by her inability to capture him in anything but the stiffest of poses. As she stared pensively at the castle's courtyard, Janos's carriage returned. She started to wave at the prince when he stepped from the closed carriage and glanced up at the watery sun.

Bibi arrested her greeting because the prince's unguarded pose was perfect. She believed it to be a glimpse of the man few people had ever had the privilege to observe. She almost tripped over the hem of her dress as she ran full out to the work table to snatch up her sketch pad and pencil. *Please, please hold that position just a moment longer. Yes, perfect, it's perfect.* She sent a silent thank you winging to heaven when the prince, miraculously, obeyed her.

When she studied what she'd drawn with such haste and fiendish concentration, she wanted to both whoop with delight and weep. She'd captured the essence of him at last. The portrait would be a masterpiece, and if she couldn't think of a way to change the prince's stubborn sense of honor, it would break her heart. She almost wavered in the promise she'd made to herself to always paint what she saw because, if she held firm to her convictions, the prince's miniature would reveal her own feelings as well.

***

His first inkling the prince had returned from his outing with Margyth was a shouted command.

"Akos, where the devil are you hiding? Attend me."

"Yes, Your Grace. I was in your dressing room polishing your riding boots and brushing your jacket. There is still time to go riding with the Baroness Baranyi, if it pleases you."

"No, it does not please me. What I want you to do is follow me to the Master Suite. It's time I changed rooms as befits my status of ruler in this castle. I want to see what will have to be cleaned or changed or discarded to accommodate some of the furniture I favor.

"Also, I want to have a look at the Mistress Suite. Margyth will be visiting tomorrow to see if it suits her taste. She will want to do some redecorating before she occupies it. At the very least, it should be thoroughly aired and dusted before her visit."

Akos could do nothing but follow the prince's rigid back down one hallway and through another until they reached the rooms his parents occupied when they were in residence. Not knowing if he should remain in the hallway or follow the prince inside, he found himself dithering just outside the door. It was an unusual sensation. Good valets, and he prided himself of being one, didn't dither. His employer solved the dilemma for him.

"Why are you standing out there? Make a note of the furniture I want taken away. You can also have all of my father's personal effects packed and taken to the attics. I don't even know why they are still here."

"I believe it is because you ordered it to be left so, Your Grace."

The prince cocked his head then glared at him, but he stood his ground. "I assume you will want your mother's things packed as well."

"Yes. I want everything personal to her gone from the suite. The family portrait is to be removed as well."

"Your Grace, you can't mean to consign it to the attics? It is the only portrait you have of your parents."

Akos was immediately sorry he'd spoken before thinking when Janos stifled a curse and threw himself down on the massive, four-poster bed with the dark-blue canopy dripping with silver fringe.

"No, of course not. Tell Erzsebet to find a place for it somewhere else in the castle. You may leave me and arrange for the servants to begin making the furniture transfer."

"As you wish, Your Grace. Can I be of any further assistance?"

"No, no thank you. I just want to spend a few moments alone. Oh, there *is* one more thing. Do you know where the key is for the door connecting my suite with...with Margyth's? It isn't in the lock."

"I do not, Your Grace, but I'm sure Erzsebet does. She is the one who supervises the cleaning of these rooms. I will go and ask her immediately."

The moment the prince flapped his hand at him in dismissal, Akos absented himself. He needed to find Erzsebet, and he needed to do so forthwith. Their plan to derail the wedding needed to be advanced immediately. He almost tripped over his own feet in his haste to descend the servants' stairs in search of the castle's housekeeper. Especially when he recalled he and Erzsebet hadn't really formulated a plan which would work on such short notice. He was out of breath by the time he found the woman in the family breakfast room, laying out a formal place setting.

"Erzsebet, the prince has..."

"Yes, I know. He wants to have the Mistress Suite tidied up. As if it needs tidying. I've kept the room spotless, and the Master Suite as well. Aside from the dungeons, which haven't been used in this century, there isn't a speck of dust in this castle. Oh, don't look at me like I'm some sort of witch. What I am is a good listener. The coachman overheard Margyth confirm her desire to inspect the Mistress Suite on the morrow, and the coachman told the stable master, who told the cook, who told me. If the Szechenyi woman intends to occupy the Mistress Suite, then it follows the prince will occupy the other. I've already told the stable master to send some of his hands up to begin transferring furniture, and Cata is overseeing the packing and storing of the clothing and personal mementos. It's about time those things were packed up and the wing occupied."

"You can't mean you want Margyth to occupy the Mistress Suite? Her very presence would sully the memory of Janos's sweet mother. The tales I've heard from the Szechenyi servants would blister your ears. We must think of a way to prevent this marriage from ever happening."

"Calm yourself. I'm aware of the tales as well. I don't want such a spoiled woman to occupy any part of this castle, either, except perhaps the dungeon. What I meant is, it's about time the Viceroy of Transylvania accepted the perquisites of his rank. He's always accepted the duty, but he's far too modest. He needs to rule and be seen to rule, and being in the Master Suite will announce he has taken over from his father and isn't just a placeholder."

When the housekeeper set a second formal place at the

breakfast room table, Akos's curiosity overwhelmed him. "What are you about? Aren't those place settings a little formal for tomorrow's breakfast?"

"Yes, they are, but they're not for breakfast but the formal dinner the prince and Baroness Baranyi will have this evening."

What dinner? I wasn't informed of any dinner plans."

"You are so informed. You will march back to the Master Suite and inform the prince he is hosting dinner in the breakfast room. Since everything is at sixes and sevens in his old suite, and the Master Suite equally chaotic, the breakfast room will have to do. The formal dining room is just too large to carry on a quiet conversation, unless he enjoys the sound of his own voice echoing off the walls."

"But what if the prince doesn't want to dine with the baroness?"

"Must I think of everything? You will suggest to him the baroness is feeling a trifle neglected. Since we've had so many days of unrelenting sunshine, she was able to finish the miniature of Margyth.

"This was the first day the light was not too strong for the prince to be abroad, and did she not visit his rooms to request his company for a ride this morning? Yes? Well then, find a way to suggest she misses his company. The way his eyes follow her when she is in the same room, I doubt you'll have to work very hard to convince him to dress for dinner."

"Dress for dinner? Do you mean evening dress?"

"You're the prince's valet. Far be it for me to tell you what the appropriate clothing selection should be. I've already told

Cata to choose the gown she thinks is most, shall we say, subtlety seductive when she dresses the baroness this evening. It just wouldn't do if the prince showed up in informal attire. While the Baroness Baranyi is quite attractive when wearing the proper attire, our prince, with his father's dark good looks, can match her. It is beyond time he used his handsomeness to his advantage. He just needs a little nudge from his valet.

"Be off with you. I've got to go tell Cata how to convince the baroness the prince is anxious to spend an evening over dinner with her."

The valet turned to go but remembered to ask about the key to the connecting door. "Ah, do you know where the key to the adjourning door between the suites is? His Grace requested it."

"Of course I know, and I don't blame him for wanting to lock it." The housekeeper jangled her key ring and, without hesitation, selected the correct key from the dozen or so on the metal ring.

Akos returned to the Master Suite to find his employer sitting cross-legged on the bed. The prince's mood hadn't improved a whit, and he was issuing terse commands to the stable hands, who groaned and sweated as they carried the heavy furniture about.

The valet quailed at the evidence of temper. *This is not going to be easy. When His Grace is in a bad mood, he tends to wallow in it unless distracted.* Hoping what he carried in his hand would do the trick, he spoke up. "The key you requested, Your Grace." He tossed the key on the bed, and the prince snatched it up and marched to the door to insert it.

"Ah, it works. Bless Erzsebet for keeping the locking mechanism oiled," the prince praised with notable relief in his voice.

Saying a silent prayer he'd live to reach his own bed at the end of this day, Akos commenced his plan to get Janos and the baroness together. "I'm sorry, Your Grace, but it is almost time for your bath. You don't want to keep the baroness waiting for dinner."

"Keep Bibi waiting? I know of no dinner plans. With everything so disarranged, I don't think it appropriate to use my old suite. I plan on having a tray sent to this room. Give my apologies to the baroness and tell her we'll dine another night."

"I am terribly sorry, Your Grace, I don't know where my mind has been. It's unusual for me to forget a message. The baroness sought you out this morning. She was feeling somewhat neglected. She's been working for a week straight and hadn't seen hide nor hair of you.

"When she requested your company for a ride this morning, I had to tell her you'd already left. She was most disappointed to have missed you. She asked if she might have the pleasure of your company for dinner this evening, and I assumed you would agree to dine with her. Of course, I didn't know of your plans to change suites. I'll go to her immediately and make your apologies."

When the prince's face softened from its harsh lines into one of eagerness, the valet breathed a little easier.

"Baroness Baranyi was asking for me? No, wait, don't cancel the dinner. I guess she won't be too upset to dine in less than pristine surroundings just this once."

"As usual, Your Grace, Erzsebet has saved the day. Dinner will be served in the breakfast room. Oh, and I have it on good authority the baroness will dress for the evening. Shall I lay out your evening attire as well?"

"Yes, you may. I'll join you in my old rooms, shortly. The men are almost finished carrying in the pieces I've selected."

Akos quit the room. He didn't want to have to answer a closer questioning. It was success enough the prince was muttering his pleasure over the baroness missing him. He was relieved His Grace could see nothing more than his back. He'd have a hard time explaining the reason for the huge grin wreathing his face.

***

Janos accepted a goblet of his special wine from a footman and stood staring at the beautifully arranged table. Erzsebet had worked a small miracle. The flowers, delicate white roses, were arranged in a bowl of water low enough to permit conversation between Bibi and himself. The sterling silver with the Rackoszi crest shone so brightly, it sparkled in the candlelight.

Just as he was beginning to think everything was just a little too formal, she entered the room and all such musings left him. It was unfortunate sensation hadn't accompanied them, for his member stood at attention as the sole survivor, and he had an imbecilic moment when he found himself comparing his cock to a hunting dog on point. It made him want to smack some sense back into himself. He wrestled the ridiculous image into a strong box and turned the key with a vicious twist. He wanted no visitation from the pestiferous imps to harangue him for his prurient thoughts.

"My goodness, Your Grace, is something the matter with my gown?"

"My dear, words fail me. I've never seen such a stunning gown. The color suits you." And indeed, it did. The apricot satin overlaid with creamy chiffon accentuating her full breasts made his heart increase its palpitations. Bibi looked as succulent as the ripest of peaches with her rosy, flawless skin, and his mouth watered with a need to bite into this peach and suck the juice from it until it ran down his face. *Aaargh, get a hold of yourself, man.*

Some deity from somewhere must've taken pity on him, for he found his voice, and his missing sanity. "Would you care for an aperitif?"

His fingers touched hers as he handed her the small glass, and he had to fight off the dizziness caused by the speed of his renewed arousal. Silently cursing his deplorable lack of self-control where his artist was concerned, he put distance between them.

No more touching her, he admonished himself, or the table would be used for a most unusual first course, and he wasn't thinking of food. Gods, but this was going to be an excruciating dinner if he wasn't successful in clamping down on the signals his body and his soul were sending him.

The baroness, heaven bless her, helped him divert his singularly focused brain.

"Janos, when did you hang this picture in here? I don't recall ever seeing it."

He spun around to follow her gaze and gave a fine imitation of a simpleton, when he gaped in openmouthed astonishment. "Oh, Erzsebet must've hung it this afternoon."

It's quite beautiful. This artist had much better success than I in capturing you in a natural pose."

He studied the portrait of himself and his parents. It featured his mother seated in one of the castle's gilded chairs, with his father behind her. She was looking up in amusement at something his father had said. His father was portrayed with a devilish grin on his face, and he was seated on a footstool at his mother's feet. There was no mistaking the grin he wore as coming from anyone but his father.

He allowed it to appear on his face again to assuage Bibi's disappointment in his less than stellar attempts at posing for her. "He was probably more successful because I was a mere boy when this was commissioned and hadn't my present responsibilities."

"It's a fantastic portrait. Where was it hanging before moving it here? I know it wasn't in your suite because I would have noticed it."

He wanted to throttle Erzsebet. His taciturn chatelaine did nothing without purpose. He just wished he'd be lucky enough to dodge any other surprises she might spring on him in the coming days. Realizing he hadn't answered her question, he rushed his response. "Ah, it hung in the Mistress Suite. My mother loved the painting. I requested it be hung elsewhere because, while it is an excellent representation of my parents, I don't think my wife will enjoy waking up each morning under the eyes of her departed in-laws."

He cursed himself as seven kinds of fool when Bibi lowered her eyes to look everywhere but at him. What could he say to cover his gaffe? He'd just managed to freeze all communication with the mere mention of Margyth's future occupation of the Mistress Suite, and, by inference, her rights to the Master's. This was not the direction he'd wanted the evening to take.

"May I serve, Your Grace?"

He wanted to kiss the footman for the rescue but restrained himself. "Yes, you may." He waved the servant away and seated his dinner companion himself.

***

Bibi masked her desire by studying the prince from beneath lowered lashes. Seeing him for the first time in evening attire had stunned her. It put her previous imagination of him in a short, Atlantean chiton to shame. At their first dinner together, he'd worn a well-tailored jacket and trousers, and an elaborately tied cravat, but this evening's black-on-black with dazzling white shirt and onyx studs took her breath away. She was very glad she'd lost the argument with Cata about what to wear this evening.

Maybe it was watching the man eat oysters with such relish for the first course, but when Janos picked up a spoon to begin the soup course, her eyes were drawn from admiration of his impeccable table manners to an intense concentration on his lips as he puckered them and blew gently on the hot soup. She had to swallow past a dry throat as she shivered with desire to have him use those very same lips to drink her down spoonful by spoonful.

Wanting to stand in for a bowl of chicken soup had to be the height of insanity, and she rolled her head from side to side as unobtrusively as possible to prod her absent brain into choosing a safe topic of conversation. As a businesswoman, she prided herself on her ability to talk to anyone, but at the moment her skill was somewhere below the trout on her plate where it stared up at her from its bed of rice. Alas, the fish was as stymied for a topic as she, and she gave a small sigh as she selected her fish knife and beheaded the fish to vent her frustration.

A moment later, she almost embarrassed herself by projecting masticated fish on the tablecloth as Janos ended the silence.

"I missed riding with you this morning."

Swallowing, she responded in kind. "As did Anubis and I. He gave such a silly, sideways hop after a rabbit startled him. As a matter of fact, I think he put the rabbit to shame. Anubis's hops were much higher."

And giving thanks to whichever Christian saint was responsible for inane conversation, the dinner proceeded without another hitch, until the footman returned with a maroon-and-white striped box tied with a green velvet bow and set it before her.

"What a beautiful box. What's inside, if I may ask?"

"A small gift I purchased this morning."

"A present for me? How kind."

"I visited the coffeehouse in the next village, and the owner's wife makes one of my favorite desserts. I purchased some for you to sample."

Touching the soft, velvet bow, Bibi grinned. "Is it another piece of *dobos torte*? You said it was your favorite, as I recall."

Janos, in an uncharacteristic gesture, used a finger to stroke the back of her hand and sent a small shiver up her arm.

"I said it was *one* of my favorite desserts. This is the other. Open the box and you'll discover what's inside."

She tugged on the ribbon until it slipped the knot and fell from the box. She didn't lift the lid but pretended to guess. "Could it be a cherry tart? No? Well then, it must be a sinfully rich chocolate and hazelnut cake."

She attempted to play keep away with the prince so he couldn't take the box from her hands but gave in with good grace when he captured it.

"You could go on guessing, Bibi, but I'm anxious to have another piece of my favorite dessert." And he handed the box to the footman to serve the pastry.

She raised her eyebrows at the rather plebian slice of lattice cake the footman placed before her, and the prince defended his choice of pastry.

"Perhaps it lacks culinary panache, but plum butter is a favorite of mine. I'll have the footman serve something else if it doesn't appeal to you."

"You will not. My aunt Margareta makes this cake as well, and it has always been a Horthy favorite. Prince Rackoszi, you are not playing fair by eating so fast," she complained. "In case you are planning on eating the rest, I will stake my claim to one of the remaining slices, even if I have to let out the seams of my *Csiko* trousers tomorrow."

***

And there it was, the chance reference to letting out seams returned him full circle to the Baroness Szechenyi's comment to her daughter. What in the hell was the matter with him? He was involved in a promised marriage to one woman during the day and flirting with another one by night.

Damn Erzsebet's interference. He'd forgotten about the pastry and left it in his carriage upon his return. The coachman must've found it and given it to the housekeeper, who was needling him, first with the family portrait and again with the pastry. Recalling Akos's last admonition concerning his recent temper tantrum, he ruefully equated the present situation as a consequence of annoying Erzsebet.

He worried he'd been silent too long while contemplating his housekeeper's inventive revenge after Bibi put down her fork and dabbed her mouth with her napkin.

"Let me guess, estate business again, Janos?"

"Estate business? What connection does that have to dinner?"

"It has nothing to do with this excellent meal, but you are frowning, just as you do when I try to get you to pose, and you always use estate business as the reason for ending the session. Have I said anything to anger you?"

"No, don't be silly. I, er, just a spot of indigestion from gobbling the cake. Perhaps some of my special pear brandy will cure it. Will you join me? It really is very good brandy."

He wanted to kick himself. Must he give up card playing as well as the sun? Allowing his emotions to be writ large on his face during a card game would quickly bankrupt him. Perhaps Baron Szechenyi had lost his estate that way.

"Another stomach spasm, Janos? The pained look is back. Are you sure you're quite well? It's late and you might feel better if you retired," Bibi said with concern.

"Sorry, this time it was estate business, *just not my estate*. I promise to think of nothing but your delightful company henceforth." Janos felt the heat of mortification warm the back of his neck. Could he just stop with the cursed Szechenyi flashbacks? He was single-handedly ruining what had been a wonderful dinner.

As the footman placed a small glass of the crystal-clear brandy before the baroness, he picked up his own and offered a toast. "To your friendship, Bibi, it means a lot to me."

"And yours to me, as well, Janos. Oh my, this is excellent brandy. Might I take a bottle with me when I return home? My father and uncle would love it."

He wanted to say, absolutely not. You may not take it home because you aren't leaving, ever, but the politeness his ancestors bred into him made him say, "Of course. You must take two, one for each of them."

As if he'd given her a prompt, his dinner companion stood and thanked him for the evening. No, he didn't want it to end, but what excuse could he invent to make her stay with him a little longer? Whichever part of the brain responsible for conversation failed him again, and he stood to move to her side.

In a last-ditch effort, he found himself offering, "Let me escort you to your room. I've changed suites, and your room is on the way to mine."

Oh, what a scintillating conversationalist he'd become. Perhaps he should carry the decanter of brandy along with him so he could blot out this evening's loutish behavior in the privacy of his new bedroom. Yes, capital idea, and he caught the footman's eye and pointed to the brandy bottle and then at the ceiling after she turned her back on him to lead the way out of the makeshift dining room.

His inattention made him step on the back of her gown when she stopped in front of her bedroom door. He'd been berating himself for the many tense pauses he'd engendered during what should have been a meal filled with witty *repartee*. "Oh, I beg your pardon."

He was immensely relieved when Bibi smiled and cupped his cheek with her hand.

"Let me guess, your brown study was caused by more urgent estate business."

Janos put his hand over Bibi's and grinned. "You know, my mother, had she been present at the dinner we just shared, would be waiting for me in my room to box my ears for such deplorable treatment of such a beautiful woman. She really did teach me better manners."

"She'd be absolutely correct to do so. I believe you owe me an apology, Your Grace."

His artist surprised the hell out of him by stepping into his arms and offering her lips for a kiss. It was an offer he would never decline, and he covered those sweet lips with his own, and swept her into his arms. He maneuvered their bodies so he could reach the doorknob to enter her room, when the voice in his ear froze him.

Mmmm, she tastes of your favorite brandy. Bite into her and drink her dry. The spoiled Szechenyi girl doesn't give a damn who you take for a lover, as long as you ignore her visits to the stable lads, and other men who want to tup not wed. Hell, you could set your artist up as your paramour in one of the castle's many rooms, and your wife would never find her. You could have Bibi by day, and do your duty to Margyth by night. It's a wonderful arrangement. Like the dessert you shared at dinner, you could have your cake and eat it, too.

Baron Szechenyi got you to promise to marry his daughter, but he didn't make you promise to be faithful to her.

He snapped back to awareness when the object of his desire went rigid in his arms. Just what the hell was he doing? Even thinking she would agree to be his mistress dishonored her. She was a good woman, not a hardened one. Her first experience with a man had left her wounded. Was he so selfish he could deliver another such emotional injury?

He broke the embrace at Bibi's request and stepped back. He tried to form an apology but found himself bereft of words.

***

Bibi fought with herself the whole time she and the prince

walked back to her room. Dinner had been fun and, at times, painful. She wanted this man as she'd never wanted anyone before. Mihaly was but a dim memory, while Janos was the living embodiment of everything she needed to be happy for as long as she drew breath. Perhaps it was time to stop mouthing platitudes about understanding his promise to Margyth. The woman deserved to lose him.

She almost swooned when he looked down at her and grinned during his apology for his inattention at dinner. It made her want to kiss his entire body, starting with his adorable dimple, and she could see no reason not to do so. If he gave her the slightest indication he felt the same, she would open her door and lead him straight to bed, and she wouldn't give a damn who found them in it the following morning. She stopped thinking and just reacted when Janos picked her up and searched for the doorknob, only to freeze when a very small voice spoke clearly in her head.

Is coveting another woman's intended the kind of person you are? Make him break his word and what will people think of you, of him? Oh, you think you'll settle for an affair. Hah! Could you give him up in a month, a year, a lifetime? If you can, you don't deserve him.

You were hired to do a job, so do it and get the hell away from Prince Rackoszi, Margyth, and this castle. Go back to doing what you do best. Horses are easier to understand than humans. They simply need to be ridden, groomed, fed, and stabled. But the prince is not a horse and so much more than human. Do you think you could keep him interested as you grow old and withered while he remains young and virile?

This is a lesson you should allow the Szechenyi woman to learn. Use the common sense bred into you and stop before you turn a budding love into enduring hatred.

She backed away from the prince. "Janos, I'm sorry, but as much as I want to go where this evening is headed, I won't. I've forgotten my position here. You hired me to paint two portraits, and so I shall. I think it would be better for the both of us if I finish them and return home. I've made a muddle of things and overstepped my license, but I'm going to be honest with you, and I hope you won't think less of me for doing so. If I had had the good fortune to have met you before Baron Szechenyi extracted such a vile promise from you, we'd both be making mad love in my room, but I didn't, and so we won't.

"I don't want you to ask me to accompany you on rides or to dine *en suite* with you. I think doing so would be too painful for both of us. I'll confine myself to the solar on sunny days and ride alone on cloudy ones, and just as soon as I finish the paintings I'll leave."

The stunned look on the prince's face had her reaching up to smooth the hurt away. "Please, Janos, I am not trying to hurt you. I just don't want to tempt you into doing something both of us will regret later on."

She bit her knuckle to keep the sob inside when he put space between them.

"I'll respect your wishes, *kinczem*, but tell me, do you love me, even a little?"

In a voice gone husky with unshed tears, she gave him the truth. "I love you more than I can bear. I may leave this castle, but my heart will remain."

She reached blindly for the doorknob and was inside with the door closed behind her before the prince could utter a word. Unmindful of her beautiful gown, she sank to the carpet with the bitter knowledge she was a coward. She'd put a solid oak door between herself and Janos without waiting for his response to her declaration. Because, had he even hinted he'd wanted her to stay, she would have agreed to any arrangement allowing her to remain, but if he didn't give her the words, she'd be completely and utterly crushed.

A running nose got her up and moving to her bedside in search of a handkerchief and the bell to call Cata to help her undress. Her last exhausted reflection before sleep claimed her was horses really were so much easier to understand than men.

***

Janos curtly ordered Akos to bed before his valet could render assistance in undressing him, and his valet's face mimicking an abused puppy's, only added to his disenchantment with the way the evening had turned out. And he was enough of a lout to think if he was going to be unhappy for what remained of this evening, and more than likely his life, then having company in his misery was welcome.

Ah, gods bless the perspicacious footman, the pear brandy decanter was on his nightstand. Yes, it was rightly *his* nightstand and no longer his father's. He was the lord and master of this castle, and if he wanted to drink himself into a stupor in the master's bedroom, no one could stop him.

Bibi had declared her love at the same time she'd given him her farewell. How the hell was he supposed to behave with such mixed signals? He didn't know, and he never got a chance to figure it out because she hadn't waited for him to tell her of his own love but shut the door in his face.

Loathe to continue poking that sharp stick into his sensitive ego, he concentrated on removing the studs from his shirt and flicking them carelessly onto the tall dresser. Akos would have to count them in the morning to tell if all were present, but he didn't give a fuck whether they were or not. He called the nearest chair into service as a closet substitute, and his trousers soon joined the shirt he draped there. Shoes? A quick toe to the heel and then a vicious kick sent them winging to the farthest edge of the room. He chortled at the thought his valet would have to go on a treasure hunt in the morning to find this evening's ensemble. He poured himself a generous measure of brandy and dropped his small clothes by the bedside.

Propped up in bed, Janos had a clear view of his nude body and toasted his rampant cock. "Here's to us. Too bad neither one of us will get what we want this evening, or any other evening until my wedding night."

His dark humor might've made his conscience shrivel but not so his member. Pouring another glass of the pear liquor, he drank it down in one gulp and waited until the fire in his belly extinguished itself.

Looking down, he discovered his stomach was no longer generating heat, but his cock was. *Are you trying to tell me something? Could it be you won't let me sleep until I put you to bed?* "Angels preserve me, I'm talking to my prick," he muttered. But once the idea entered his mind, he considered it.

"Okay then, let's give you what you want. No, I know it's not what you or I *really* want, but Baroness Baranyi has just made it abundantly clear you and I will have to settle for a poor imitation of satisfaction."

After gulping a third brandy, he drew the first long, soft stroke, and the twitch his prick made felt quite good. Snuggling down into the pillows, he continued the stroking, increasing the pressure just a bit. As for second choices, this wasn't half bad he mused, and ratcheted up the pressure and speed as he rubbed the head of his cock with his thumb. Its velvet softness made him think of Bibi's lush breast and her signature scent of tuber rose, musk, and the undernote of horse.

Ahhh, so good, he could feel his sac draw up in preparation for his release, but he was rudely jerked back from the brink of pleasure. The damned demon was back in his head.

Demon? Excuse me, you have me confused with the fallen angel. I'm the one who's been given the onerous duty of saving your sorry ass. Is this how you intend to treat the bed you were conceived in? If so, go right ahead. Sully the sheets and your royal bed with your lascivious desires and reprehensible actions, but any satisfaction you manage to achieve will be temporary.

He was not in the mood to listen to angelic counsel and said so. Well, temporary is better than not at all. I'm good with temporary, but you are ruining the mood. Unless you want to remain in this room and play voyeur, return tomorrow morning and remind me why I need to keep my word and marry a woman I detest instead of the one I most desire. But I warn you, if you even so much as use the word duty I'm going to...I'm going to... What? Maybe the brandy was acting as a barrier to sentence composition, but he couldn't even formulate a decent threat.

When his head no longer rang with the sound of angelic displeasure, he looked down at his deflated cock and swore. Hell, he wasn't even allowed the pleasure of himself this evening. The way the entire evening had gone, he was not at all surprised. Maybe it was through the intercession of the god Morpheus, but he fell sound asleep shortly after blowing out the candle on the nightstand. His nightstand, his canopy, his, damn-the-angel's-interference, unsullied bed.

Chapter Eighteen

Janos woke refreshed but unhappy. His excellent hearing allowed him to catch Akos's mutterings about the wrinkled condition of his evening dress, but he wasn't going to inform his valet he was awake. He was too busy plotting. While he'd mutely nodded his agreement to Bibi's terms last night, this morning was another matter. He couldn't bear to part with his friend, and even though it was but the one time, Janos considered her his lover. He just would not, could not accept not ever holding her in his arms again. He would grudgingly accept platonic, if it was really her wish, but he would never accept absent.

An idea tickled the back of his mind, and he almost had it, when Akos shoved the bed curtains aside and offered his morning libation.

"Good morning, Your Grace. May I inquire as to your plans this morning? At the moment, it is sunny, but I believe there is a chance of rain in the afternoon. Shall I inform the baroness you desire to ride today?"

"No, the baroness is concentrating on my miniature, so I won't disturb her. Oh, and I'll be taking my dinners on a tray in my suite. The baroness has voiced her intention to work nonstop until she completes the painting."

He was not surprised when a look of frustrated disappointment washed across his valet's face. Indeed, it mirrored his own. Not waiting until Akos could interrogate him for more information as to why Bibi was hastening her efforts, he spoke up. "You may choose suitable attire for a visit from Margyth. She wants to view the Mistress Suite in the early afternoon. I'm assuming her mother will accompany her. Tell Cook I'd like tea served in the formal parlor. And sometime before they arrive, refresh my memory as to the parlor's location. It's been quite some time since I've had occasion to use it."

Janos was amazed at how fast the castle's information system worked. By the time he'd dressed, eaten breakfast, and followed Akos's directions to the formal parlor, a general pall had fallen inside the castle. Evidently, a visit from Margyth and her mother was not a cause for celebration.

It was with great relief he nodded his head at Erzsebet's terse announcement the Szechenyi carriage had arrived. Margyth's possession of the ebullience of a magpie saved him from having to make more than a brief welcome.

"Szigi dear, did you miss me?"

Before he could respond, Margyth turned to Erzsebet and fixed her with a haughty glare.

"You may leave us. If Szigi hasn't already ordered it, you may return with tea."

His anger at such high-handedness froze him in place. He had never been in attendance when anyone had nerve enough to address his housekeeper in such a way. Certainly, his parents hadn't wanted to destroy the efficient running of their domain by giving her unnecessary and demeaning orders. He would've tried to smooth over the incident, but Erzsebet had already left the room. Damn, how long would it take to unruffle those feathers? Margyth's next question snapped him back to attention.

"It's so dim in here. Are you trying to save candles, Szigi, or have your servants become lax in their duties? I've never been in a room so lacking in windows. I'm sure we can fix the light problem after we're married. A competent stonemason can knock out a few of these stones to construct more windows. Sunshine is better than gloom to maintain my cheerful humor. This castle is much too gloomy, no wonder you have a melancholy air about you."

"I wasn't aware you considered me to be melancholy, Margyth. Must I remind you yet again I suffer severe burns in direct light? Your wish to let more light into my residence will not come to fruition."

Margyth was about to respond to his rejection of her suggestion, but Cata's entrance with the tea tray forestalled her.

"Oh good, I'll play mother, shall I?" And without waiting for anyone's permission, Margyth poured the tea. "I know just how to fix yours, Szigi. Two lumps and a touch of cream. Here, just the way you like it."

Although he accepted the cup, he wouldn't drink it. If Margyth had paid the slightest attention on his previous visits, she would know he hated cream in his tea and took one lump. And if she stopped chattering long enough to look into his eyes, she'd see his annoyance at her writ large.

"Szigi, we must talk staff. I'm afraid the surly housekeeper you employ just won't do. Also, I will need a real lady's maid. I want one who's been trained in Vienna or Budapest. I'm weary of having peasants attempt to dress me. They have no sense of style."

In an attempt to defend Cata, Janos praised her. "Cata, who delivered the tea tray, is also an excellent lady's maid. She dresses Baroness Baranyi, and the baroness has had no complaints."

"Well she wouldn't, would she?" Margyth said in a sugary sweet voice. "The Baroness Baranyi knows horses, not style. For God's sake, the woman smells of horse for most of the time and has been seen wearing men's riding apparel. I wouldn't want my maid's inexperience to mark me as a country bumpkin when we go to Vienna or Rome."

Noticing the Baroness Szechenyi, who'd yet to utter a single syllable, had finished her tea, he stood. "Permit me to lead the way, to the Mistress Suite, ladies." He hadn't missed the baroness swiping a finger over the polished occasional table as she passed him. If she was looking for dust, she wouldn't find any. His servants were well trained in their duties and their places. He wished his intended had been as well instructed.

He also didn't miss the avid look in Margyth's eyes when she entered the suite. It really was a beautiful room with its rose damask window hangings and matching bed canopy. Margyth headed directly to the one piece of furniture he'd always admired, a delicate, inlaid rosewood writing desk. It wasn't hard to recall his mother seated there making out invitations or writing a letter to their far-flung relatives. But the memory was sent packing as efficiently as the family portrait had been.

"My, what a useless piece of furniture. It's far too impractical for a writing desk. I want something larger. Something I can keep my correspondence in. I am a terrific letter writer, and I'm sure we'll make many friends over the course of our honeymoon.

"Oh, and these draperies will have to go. I detest dull colors. I want crisp, bright ones. God knows this room is as dark as all the rest. Perhaps bright-yellow curtains will help, or maybe we can forego curtains altogether and purchase some Flemish tapestries while we're traveling."

Janos counted to ten in an attempt to keep his anger behind his teeth. He'd gotten to five when Margyth astonished him by clapping her hands and crossing the room to bounce on the bed.

"Szigi, I've just had the most amazing idea. I've been reading a book about King Louis the XVI's wife, Marie Antoinette. She had the king build her a folly. It was a complete house in miniature, and she could go there whenever she wanted, and she decorated it to suit herself. She pretended to be a shepherdess and had sheep roaming the palace grounds. She dressed up in pretty gowns, and carried a shepherd's crook, and made the courtiers dress up as well. Wouldn't it be wonderful if you built a folly for me? The castle's lawns would more than accommodate one, and my folly would have large windows and all the sunlight I wanted. You could pretend to be my peasant lover."

"Margyth!"

Either there was an echo in the room, or the Baroness Szechenyi had been shocked enough to silence her daughter's drivel at the same time as his own temper burst forth. "You will have to make do with just the castle, Margyth. Concerning the sheep, my pet wolf would make short work of them, I assure you."

He received no reply because his bride-to-be had left the room. He found her in the Master Suite.

"Szigi, my you do love your gloom. Perhaps a nice cherry red for curtains would liven this room up. Also, gold tasseling to replace the silver. Silver is dull. Gilt has an uplifting effect, don't you think?"

"What I think is, this is my room and my domain. I want nothing changed in here. You are free to decorate to your heart's content in the Mistress Suite, but all changes stop at the connecting door."

In a desperate attempt to get her out of his room, he suggested, "Shall we continue the tour? I know you don't want to climb all the way to the servant's quarters, how about the nursery?"

Oh, gods strike him dead. Had he really suggested visiting his old nursery? His sole excuse for blurting out the fact the castle even had one was the woman's insane prattling had raised his blood pressure high enough to liquefy his brain.

"Nursery? No, I most definitely don't want to visit the nursery. There will be time enough to see it when we've been married for a while. Perhaps we can take in another wing."

Baroness Szechenyi stopped her daughter's headlong rush to the door. "I don't think we have time to explore all the wings today, Margyth."

Would the baroness die of apoplexy if he kissed her for

ending this torturous visit? It was very tempting to try it to observe the result, but he merely offered, "Well then, let me lead the way out. The castle's passages can be quite confusing until you get to know them."

He tried to hurry Margyth past the solar, but the strong sunlight attracted her as forcefully as a lemming to a cliff. He had to hurry to catch her elbow and stop her from entering.

"I'm sorry, Margyth. The solar is off-limits. The Baroness Baranyi has commandeered it for her studio. She is working diligently to complete my portrait in time for the engagement ball."

"Oh, pooh, Szigi. This is your castle, not hers. If she's working on your portrait, it means she's completed mine. I want to see it." Margyth shook off his hand and entered the solar.

Embarrassed by the necessity, he groped for his mother's parasol before he entered. His mother always kept one at the entrance for when she wanted to know who was approaching the castle. The solar offered an ideal view of the courtyard and the avenue leading to it.

After donning smoked glasses, he opened the parasol and followed his visitors into the, for him, blindingly bright room. The three of them didn't get very far. Bibi was standing in front of her makeshift easel and preventing Margyth and her mother from moving any deeper into the room.

"I'm sorry, Margyth, I cannot show you your miniature. It is meant to be viewed in conjunction with the prince's, and I'm still working on his."

"I don't know why it should matter. It's my portrait, after

all." Margyth swung around to face him. "Szigi, tell your hired artist she's to show me my portrait. If she won't show it, I'd suspect she is pulling the wool over your eyes. After all, you are paying her to paint them, and you should be able to tell if they are worth the money before you send her on her way. I wouldn't want to show an inferior painting to our invited guests."

The shocked sound Bibi made at such an affront to her worth and honesty aroused his temper yet again, and this time, he spoke without a brake on his tongue to soften his words.

Turning to the Baroness Szechenyi, he addressed her. "Madame, since you've abdicated your duty in instructing your daughter in the social graces, it falls to me.

"Margyth, you've insulted a guest in my house. Baroness Baranyi is not hired help. She is a member of the peerage, a talented artist, and the owner of an esteemed horse-breeding enterprise. You've inferred she is inferior to you, but the reality is, it is you who are the inferior. I have invited Baroness Baranyi to our engagement ball."

He didn't look at Bibi for confirmation because he didn't want to find refusal in her eyes. "It was always my intention she attend. I want my guests to enjoy her work and have the opportunity to engage her services should they so desire. It is the least I can do for her willingness to travel quite a distance to paint our likenesses. Furthermore, any changes you care to make in any of the rooms will have to wait until after the wedding and only with prior approval from me."

"If you find my daughter so lacking in manners, Your

Grace, perhaps this marriage is a mistake. If we cancel the ball immediately, your guests will receive notification in time to change their travel plans."

At last, the ghastly apparition speaks. But before he could put voice to his sarcasm, Margyth all but elbowed her mother aside and turned to Bibi to offer an apology.

"I'm truly sorry, Prince Rackoszi and Baroness Baranyi. Do forgive me. My exuberance to be the lady of this castle has overwhelmed my common sense. I didn't mean to offend anyone. Please, please stay for our engagement dance, Baroness Baranyi. It will be nice to have someone I know there."

At Bibi's slow nod, he hurried the Szechenyis from the room. "I think we've explored the castle enough for one day. I'll assist you to your carriage, Margyth."

***

Bibi almost believed Margyth's apology until the chit tossed a poisonous look over her shoulder as she left the room. Not surprisingly, it was mirrored by her mother. Well, if glaring at her was the best they could do as a warning to make herself scarce, they'd never tried to intimidate a Horthy.

As her uncle Andris often said when he was teaching her how to deal with potential buyers for their horses, "interfering in a fight between two stallions can hurt you. Standing your ground in the face of a marauding wolf or bear can hurt you. But receiving a mean look from someone who doesn't know you, won't hurt you in the slightest."

She'd be at the engagement dance with bells on. It would give her great pleasure to upstage the spoiled girl on the evening she expected to outshine everyone. She chided herself for her meanness but quickly reasoned Margyth needed to be on the receiving end of retribution just once in her life, and so she would be made to pay for the myriad slights and insults she'd distributed so lavishly to Baroness Beatrix Celine Horthy-Baranyi.

She set about cleaning her brushes and made sure to protect her work in progress before she returned to her room. Giving Margyth a lesson in being careful how you treated people because they might return the favor would require some careful planning, starting with a stunning dress.

She needed to inventory her wardrobe. She hoped her aunt Margareta had included the dress she had in mind when she'd packed for her. She'd purchased it in Paris. It was a conversation stopper, and it would outshine anything Margyth had in her own wardrobe, and maybe, just maybe, it would make the prince reconsider his plans.

She jumped in surprise when she turned away from her work table to find Janos standing, once again, under the parasol at the entrance to the solar.

"I didn't mean to startle you, Bibi, but I wanted to offer my own apology. I know I agreed to let you return to your home upon completion of the portraits, but hear me out. You shut the door so quickly, I wasn't able to say it would be a fair trade."

"Fair trade? I don't understand."

"You said, when you left you would be leaving your heart

behind. It would be a fair trade because you'd be carrying my heart with you."

"Janos, I don't think..."

"No, let me get all of this out. I agree we can't continue to torture one another by pretending we don't want each other, and I'm certain we would make love in every room of this castle, if we were free to do so. I'll be honest and say I want to cast duty and honor and fidelity to the winds when I am around you, but such behavior would do you a great disservice when the engagement is announced. And it *will* be announced at the damned engagement ball.

"You probably think I am a weakling who can't make up his mind. One minute I'm courting Margyth, and the next I am holding you in my arms. I detest myself for such behavior because I know I've wounded you, but if I could make you understand, just a little, how great my dilemma is, it would be enough.

"I've given my word, Bibi. If Baron Szechenyi were still alive, I would be in his study refusing to leave it until we found another way of supporting his family without marriage. But I gave my promise to marry his daughter and I must keep it. A man is only as good as his word, and the Rackoszi word has been as good a currency as gold for centuries. I wouldn't be able to live with myself if I tarnished the family name because of personal preference.

"However"—he reached a hand out to her—"please, please, I beg of you, don't deny me your friendship, your affection, while you are still here. Since your arrival, I've realized how lonely I am. You've shown me how to have fun and how to put aside my responsibilities for an hour or two to just enjoy doing simple things. Please, Bibi, stay and help me make memories that will warm and encourage me when I most need them. All I'm asking is you ride with me on cloudy days and dine with me, and do silly things such as fishing in a trout stream with a wolf."

What could she say to such a request? She could tell him she had no talent for keeping her own feelings from showing whenever she was around him, and she might lose her mind if she had to keep her hands off his body for the remainder of her time here, or she could do what a Horthy would do when their heart was certain of the path it wanted to take, despite any pain to follow.

She ran into the prince's arms and hugged him. "It would be my greatest pleasure to do those things with you." As a cloud dimmed the solar, she forced a giggle. "Oh look, I think someone has been listening in on your request. The day has turned quite gloomy. Why don't we take Anubis and Shadow out for some exercise?"

***

His artist spun out of the room with her usual rush. Good, she wouldn't be witness to his reaction. His entire body shook with the emotion his request had wrung from him. He'd lied, to her and himself. He wasn't at all content to settle for half of Bibi. He wanted all of her, but if half was all he could have, then he'd make the best of it. Having her prolong her stay was better than her immediate departure. Having her at his engagement would be a taste of hell, but not having her there would be insupportable.

Janos closed the emasculating parasol, returned it to its accustomed holder, and walked back to his suite with all of the agility of man recuperating from the ague. He'd been successful in his mission to keep her here, but at what cost to himself? The longer she stayed, the crueler their parting would be.

Well, at least I've managed to make someone happy this day, but he refrained from patting himself on the back after informing Akos he was to ride with Baroness Baranyi this afternoon. The beaming smile his valet presently wore almost made him reach again for his smoked glasses.

As much as he tried to slow time down and savor every minute he spent in her company, the sands in the hourglass wouldn't be stopped. Nor would his increasing need to have her in his arms and in his bed, but he'd learned to find excuses to put distance between them and so hadn't been plagued by his guilty conscience in over a week. But here he was, sitting under an apple tree with Bibi, and irony of ironies, a damned apple broke his resolve as completely as Adam's in the Garden of Eden.

Janos lost his reason as Bibi took a healthy bite from the crisp apple and juice ran down her chin. Before he even had a chance to search for his lost wits, or seek the counsel of his good angel, or even the damned fallen one, he grabbed the apple and tossed it away, and took her in his arms to lap the juice from her mouth and whisper all of the words of love he'd kept to himself these last two weeks. It surprised him to hear her return them word-for-word. They were both as naked as Adam and Eve in seconds, and the lost paradise was rediscovered a heartbeat later.

In consideration of her beautiful body and the rough ground, he used his own body as her barrier against discomfort. Looking up from his perusal of her rose-tipped breasts, he groaned with lust. "I want you to ride me, Bibi. I want your thighs to squeeze my body as you canter, and then I want you to lean into the gallop. I want to experience what it feels like to be made love to by such an accomplished rider as you, my darling *Csiko*."

At his command, she started into a slow, rocking canter, and he felt her muscles squeeze his shaft with every forward pelvic tilt, and the slap of her flesh on his as she sat firmly in the saddle of his lap made him work hard on his control. It was exquisite torture, but he wanted more, and by the gods he'd get it.

He sat up and positioned her body chest-to-chest with his, and used his hands to guide her into a fast gallop that drove him to the peak of his endurance. "Bibi, oh gods great and small, Bibi, I'm not going to last much longer with such a talented rider. Let me drink from you and give you an equal amount of pleasure."

With the last syllable of her hissed yesss, he gifted her with a sensual memory before his fangs struck and their apple-strewn paradise exploded.

He regained his senses with her luscious body melded to his and her soft breath ruffling the hair at his temple, and the Viceroy of Transylvania had to open his eyes to let the tears escape so he could bring into focus the woman he would miss for centuries.

"Janos, I…"

"No, don't say it, *kincsem*. I won't apologize and neither should you. We both wanted this. I even think it was inevitable."

She rose and wiped her own tears from her eyes. "Yes, perhaps it was. I wondered how we would say our goodbyes and this was perfect. I think our time of making memories is finished. Your portraits are completed, and the memories we've made together are beautiful, so we must end this before we do something monumentally disastrous."

He would've tried to cajole her, but he admired her will and so desisted. But when she'd dressed and vaulted into Shadow's saddle to ride away without looking back, he dressed slowly and returned to the castle with despair as his companion.

He should've known he'd be held accountable for his lapse of self-control. After an evening spent in his room, dining upon a tray and not even tasting what the cook had prepared, he couldn't sit still, and he wasn't sleepy enough to go to bed.

He rose and paced barefoot in front of the fireplace until he stepped on something sharp. He hopped on one foot and swore creatively until he reached a footstool and sat to see what caused the injury. It was one of the onyx shirt studs he'd unfastened so carelessly the night he and she dined in the breakfast room. Here was evidence Akos hadn't been successful in finding all of them.

Janos withdrew the small stone from his foot and opened the wooden chest on his dresser to add it to the rest when the vision of her in the peach confection of a dress she'd worn sprang into his mind's eye. A peach, an apple...gods save him from ever eating another piece of fruit. In a spurt of temper, he slammed the lid closed so hard the secret compartment popped open, and in an instant, he doubled over in lust.

He wouldn't have credited it as possible, but he'd forgotten all about the small square of linen stained with her virgin blood. Forgotten until this moment, until the scent sent him straight to his knees, and with head back and fangs exposed, he howled his excruciating need. He wanted, no he needed her. Just her. No one else. Never anyone else.

Grabbing the remnant from its hiding place, he staggered to the bed and fell upon it, curled in pain. Thank the gods, the room's thick draperies would keep the sounds of his grief from attracting the unwanted attention of his valet.

Her scent was driving him mad. The bed offered no solace, and so he resumed pacing. Soon even his large suite couldn't contain his grief, and in blind frustration, he picked up a small table and smashed it to pieces against the thick stone. Better, much better. Even better was the decanter of pear brandy sitting by his bed. Picking up one of the small cordial glasses, he considered it before he sent it winging into the fireplace. For this he needed no glass, just the decanter itself, and upended the bottle.

Remembering one of the last kisses he'd had from Bibi had tasted of this very same fruit, Janos tossed the empty bottle to the floor, and spying a long, jagged piece of wood from the ruined table, picked it up and had its point centered on his chest before reason returned in the company of his nagging demons. Here at last was a worthy target for his anger, and he hurled his hurt at the unfairness of having to do what was right into their faces.

"You say you are angels and have been sent here to help me. Well, help me, I beg of you. There must be a way I can have what I want and not dishonor my word. You say you are the messengers of great masters, well prove it. Make it so. Stop this pain."

Oh, there are several ways of stopping the pain. You can use the pointy end of the stick you're holding and avoid getting married altogether, or you can have your cake with a cherry on top. No one but you gives a fuck about your precious word. Your staff doesn't, they hate the Szechenyi brat. Bibi wouldn't give a damn about lofty words after you'd pleasured her to within an inch of her life and planted a child in her womb. And Baroness Szechenyi would be ecstatic to have her daughter untouched by your fanged self. Margyth is a clever minx. My master believes she shows great promise. She won't even miss you once she lands another rich man to warm her bed. Just give me your permission and you'll have Bibi in your bed from tonight until you are called to meet my master.

Put the stake down. Don't be stupid by listening to the false promises of the imp. There is only room in hell for one Lucifer, and it isn't you in your wolf form. And that is exactly where you will end up if you let this fallen rogue take control.

I am here to help you, but you must have patience. Your situation is a difficult one, but with a little faith, you will be granted what you desire. And it won't have eternal damnation attached. Go to bed and say your prayers. You are forgiven for this one temper tantrum, but you will still have to suffer the embarrassment tomorrow morning when your valet discovers what you've done to this room.

Oh, and, um, either burn the scented memento or return it to its hiding place. You've had all of the temptation you can handle for one night.

Drained dry, Janos did as he was bade and returned the spotted linen to its secret drawer. What he did consign to the fire was the remnants of the table, starting with the jagged stake, and he stared into the flames until it was consumed. He wondered, inanely, how long it would take Akos to work up the courage to ask him the table's whereabouts.

Janos experienced a small measure of God's mercy by falling into a deep, dreamless sleep when he closed his eyes after apologizing for his behavior.

Chapter Nineteen

Akos's announcement King Draculesti's carriage, with entourage in tow, had just turned into the long approach to the castle, made his gut clench in dread. The last grain of sand in the waiting game had fallen. The festivities leading to the engagement ball were about to commence. Festivities? His stomach was making unhappy churning motions more in keeping with incipient illness than in anticipation of what should be a happy event in his life.

"Akos just told me King Draculesti of Wallachia and his wife have arrived. Are they related to you?" Bibi asked, as he passed her in the hall on his way to greet his guests.

"Yes, His Majesty Alexandru Draculesti is my godfather. I'm sure he is accompanied not only by his wife, Queen Lucretia but also by my cousin, Countess Krisztina, and assorted other distant family members. Although my immediate family isn't large, we are rich in interconnected marriages. Quite honestly, I have a hard time figuring out who is related to whom on the best of days. They do me great honor by traveling during daylight hours to attend my engagement."

She hooted, "Now I know how you heard of my work. I wasn't aware you and Countess Krisztina were related."

When she turned to leave, Janos rushed to her side and stayed her with a light touch on her arm. "Please, Bibi, there is a favor I need to ask of you."

"Of course. How may I help?"

"First, you can accept my apology for asking it so late. I guess I hoped I would find a way to end my engagement without breaking my promise to Margyth's father.

"Ah well, since I haven't found a reprieve, let me ask for your assistance in entertaining my guests. Not all of my godfather's retainers have the sun affliction. I humbly ask for your help in leading the events scheduled for those days when the sun is shining. I've planned for several riding and hunting events, but what I can't plan for is always having cloudy weather so I can be there."

"But shouldn't Margyth or her mother be in charge at those times?" Bibi asked.

"I don't think Margyth is mature enough or generous enough to lead without trying to monopolize the event, and heaven help me, the Baroness Szechenyi would scare them more than entertain them."

"I begin to perceive your dilemma, Janos. Of course, I'd be happy to stand in for you on the sunny days, but I want you to tell Margyth I will be doing so. I don't want her to think I'm usurping her right to act as your hostess."

"Of course, Bibi. I will make it very clear she will be needed by my side for those activities I've planned for those who need to avoid the sun. Margyth will readily accept when she learns the king and queen will be among them."

His relief at her consent faded somewhat when she murmured perhaps Pal Anton might assist her. He was very sure the hussar would jump at the chance to have Bibi in his company without Margyth's or his own interference. Disliking his jealousy, but unable to voice approval of the suggestion, he changed the subject.

"When will I be able to view the miniatures?"

She grinned cheekily at him. "Why? Are you worried I won't show them to you before anyone else? Of course, you'll be able to view them in private. I've already promised to have them to you the night before the ball. I will even include a brief description of the Russian folk tale inspiring each portrait. I assure you, there will be plenty of time to have Margyth study them before the dance. Even if I do say so myself, Margyth will have no reason to find fault with her portrait. She is a very attractive woman and I've captured her beauty quite well."

"And what of me, Bibi? Have you captured me? I know I was not a very cooperative subject." He was sorry he asked when her smile dimmed.

"Yes, Janos. I've captured you. Are you fishing for a compliment? Do I think you as handsome as Margyth is beautiful? You know I do. Your guests will not be disappointed on your behalf.

"Please excuse me, I have to get my ball gown ready, and you must see to the comfort of your guests."

***

From his position in the place of honor at the head of the dining room table, King Draculesti noted a variety of emotions race across his godson's face. Something was eating at the man and it had to do with his artist. Whenever Janos looked in Baroness Baranyi's direction, his eyes softened for a moment, and then he used a monumental amount of will to keep from displaying anything but polite interest.

His concentration on his godson's quixotic emotions was broken when the women excused themselves and left the men to enjoy their after-dinner port. Finally alone with Janos, he prepared to deliver the dressing down he composed while suffering the bumpy carriage ride to be by his godson's castle for his official engagement.

Just what in the hell was his godson playing at? He hadn't been notified of his godson's engagement until the last possible moment. Unless he was losing his ability to read tells, his godson was in love with his artist.

King Alexandru could be intimidating when he set his mind to it, for he wasn't just the ruler of Wallachia, he was king of the Atlantean descendants. His word was law in their circles and his godson was definitely part of the circle. Alexandru held his temper in abeyance until the servant handed him a glass of wine and closed the door behind himself. If his godson needed him to smack some sense into him, he wouldn't shirk his duty. As a godfather, it was his responsibility to do so in the absence of Janos's father.

"Janos, first of all, let me offer my apologies for keeping your parents away from this happy event. As you know, I called them back to my service to serve as hunters, and they are doing an admirable job. It is most irritating our kind don't go mad until after they've lived long enough to become truly clever and inventive in escaping capture. Count Armand Lefebre is leading your parents a merry dance in France, and so far, he's managed to remain free. At least your parents prevented him from killing another human. I know they'll get him, eventually, but I'm afraid it won't be in time to attend your engagement festivities."

"Apology accepted, Your Majesty," Janos replied.

"I think it's time you told me why you've chosen to wed a stranger and not one of our kind, and without my prior approval."

Janos took a gulp of wine and blurted out, "It is a matter of honor, Your Majesty."

"Honor you say? Have you gotten the woman with child?"

"No, no, nothing so dishonorable," Janos spoke hastily. "I gave her father my word I would protect his daughter by marrying her."

"Well then, go back to him and work out another arrangement. I am not pleased you have chosen a local woman. I had hopes to align your family with the Braganza line. Their bloodline is becoming a trifle weak, and an alliance with a Rackoszi would infuse new life into it. We are not so large we can squander our Atlantean blood on a person who will give us pleasure for but a fleeting moment. Remember, you can only change one human in your lifetime. Is your fiancée the one you've chosen?"

He was surprised when his godson shuddered at his question.

"No, Your Majesty, she is not. I have no intention of making Margyth one of us."

"Then why in the hell are you marrying her, Jancsi? Is she wealthy or in possession of something you need?"

245

His calculation of using Janos's childhood name to ease some of the tension his godson was carrying, failed. If anything, it made him even more disinclined to open up, based on the frozen expression on his face. He got the ball rolling by delivering a withering, "Explain to me exactly how you come to be in this predicament, Jancsi."

"Margyth Szechenyi has no wealth, Your Majesty. It is the reason why I gave my word to protect her."

"Well, find another way to appease her father," he commanded before draining his port.

"By all the ancient gods, I wish I could, Your Majesty. Her father committed suicide right after he secured my word. Truth be told, I do not even love his daughter, but I've given my word."

The king curled his lip and put his empty glass down with a solid thump. "Well, we are getting to the root of the problem at last."

"I don't understand, Your Majesty."

"Enough, Janos. If you call me 'Your Majesty' one more time, I won't be responsible for my temper. What happened to Uncle Alex? Are we no longer to enjoy our special relationship just because you take a wife?" He held his place until Janos sighed and walked into his open arms for a long-delayed hug.

"I don't understand what you mean by 'getting to the heart of the matter,' Uncle Alex."

Patting his godson's back, the king said, "Better, much better." The ruler of Wallachia lifted his empty glass and handed it to his godson for refilling. "You had me confused by the heated glances passing between you and Baroness

Baranyi. They were hot enough to toast bread. I thought you might leap across the table and take her right then and there. You must've had to work to chew your dinner without having your fangs punching holes in your lips, and this was not the reaction of a man in love with his fiancée.

"You and Baroness Baranyi are lovers, aren't you? Do you intend to make her your mistress after doing your duty to this other woman's father?" Alexandru was surprised when his godson put his glass down with a snap and forgot all of his protocol lessons by turning his back on a king.

His godson walked to the fireplace and stared into the flames. "Yes, Bibi and I have made love, but it was always with the understanding she would leave after the engagement ball. If I had been free to do so, I would've already proposed to her. She understands my obligation, and she has made me understand she is not the type of woman to accept being a mistress. Had she agreed to it, I would not be so desperately unhappy at the thought of never being with her again. And before you ask, yes, I would gladly make her one of us if she'd consent to it."

Alexandru didn't miss the painful swallow Janos made, and so he held his temper until his godson got whatever troubled him off his chest.

"Um, Uncle Alex, there is another problem with my engagement besides not being in love with my intended."

He tried softening his voice to encourage the prince to continue. "Do I need to be sitting down to hear this?"

He had to hand it to his godson, the man didn't shy away but stood his ground.

"Sit or stand at your preference, Uncle Alex. The Baroness Szechenyi, the ancient gods themselves only know why, has concluded I'm a vampire, and is thusly opposed to this engagement. So much so, she's tried to kill me."

"She what?" He forgot his vow to remain calm and headed for the door.

His godson took his life in his hands by putting himself between him and the door in an attempt to keep him from confronting Baroness Szechenyi. The only reason he didn't bodily remove Janos from his path was his godson's plea for him to hear the complete tale before he did anything rash.

"Whatever the source of her information, Baroness Szechenyi learned she would end my life if she killed me when I was in wolf form. She set two large traps and I was caught in one. If it hadn't been for Bibi, I would have died of my wounds.

"She gave me her blood, voluntarily, to save me. She knows what I am, Uncle. I could hardly have hidden it when I changed back to human form the moment she freed me from the trap."

He used the old language to swear violently, and none of his curses were to wish the Baroness Szechenyi a long or pain-free life. When he had the breath to do so, he asked his godson, "Then why are you even thinking of wedding Baroness Szechenyi's daughter?"

"Because the Szechenyi estate is the bottleneck to my valley. If I don't marry Margyth, and allow someone holding the baron's outstanding notes to oust her and her mother from their lands, the baroness will search the world to marry her daughter off to someone who will listen to her outrageous beliefs.

"And, if Margyth's husband is at all susceptible to persuasion, the baroness will make it her mission in life to convince him to burn me out of this castle. I'm not afraid of going up against torch-waving mortals, but even you will have to admit it's far easier to marry her daughter and secure the estate and have the women under my control. I am not without the political power to keep the old witch silent after the marriage. And, thanks to our longevity, I will outlive them."

King Alexandru studied the ceiling a moment before he approached his godson's side and lifted Janos's face with one finger under his chin. "You'll outlive them if you learn to sleep with one eye open. However, I can make your obligation go away and you'd be free to marry Baroness Baranyi. Picture yourself dressed in deep mourning and walking behind two horse-drawn coffins."

"No, Uncle. I can't... I won't visit such grief on Baroness Baranyi. How would it look, if Margyth and her mother were to die of mysterious circumstances, and I proposed to her before the Szechenyis' bodies were even cold? Bibi knows what we are, and she is intelligent enough to put two and two together. Having blood on my hands is not the way I want to start a marriage."

Frustrated, Alexandru threw his hands up and exclaimed, "Damnation, Janos, your parents did too good a job of instilling honor and duty in you. It saddens me to know you will not have the joy of a love match. Your parents have it, and even though mine was an arranged, political marriage, Lucretia and I were blessed to grow into love."

Another thought struck him. "Are you certain the Baroness Baranyi can be trusted with the fact of our existence?"

"Absolutely, Uncle. She's had plenty of time to run screaming from here and she hasn't done so. She appears to have taken it in stride. After all, she told me she'd chalked up Baroness Szechenyi as mad when she started raving about vampires, so I doubt she'd attempt telling anyone about Atlanteans to avoid having people think the same of her."

"And what of you? Have you shown her all of the differences between our kind and hers?" King Draculesti could tell by the shocked look on his godson's face, he hadn't but stubbornly waited for the denial. He was perturbed enough at his godson to punish him just a little.

Janos spoke past a clenched jaw. "No, Godfather, I haven't. I may be in love with the woman, but I still retain a measure of common sense."

Alexandru cocked his head and held up his hand. "Ah, speaking of love and women, the queen is about to join us. I'll support you in doing your duty, but I can't promise to be pleasant around Margyth's mother for her attempt on your life. I'll be sure to warn everyone in my retinue to be extra careful when in her presence. We don't want to give her the knowledge she needs to be successful in a second attempt. However, should you change your mind..."

His godson cut him off before he could put words to the offer.

"No, Uncle Alex, thank you, but no. It's just one week to the engagement ball. I think I can keep Baroness Szechenyi's attention focused on the activities I've planned. She will be too busy dancing attendance on her daughter to have time to wonder whether any of my guests are vampires."

Alexandru lifted an eyebrow at Janos's snicker. "What's so amusing?"

"I was just wondering what the baroness would do or say if she ever discovered the Emperor of Austria and his son, the Grand Duke, share our bloodline. I was half tempted to tell her when Margyth started insisting on going to Vienna to be introduced at Court on our honeymoon."

Queen Lucretia broke up the uncomfortable *tete-a-tete*. "Just what have you two been discussing? Have you been telling ribald jokes? You are both wearing smirks on your faces. Attend me, Husband. It's quite late and I'm weary. After such a long carriage ride, I am desirous of a soft bed."

"Is a soft mattress all my queen desires?" The King of Wallachia waggled his eyebrows and made the queen sputter, but he willingly retired with his bride after one last couched offer of assistance. He was disappointed yet again by having the offer refused by his stubborn godson.

***

Queen Lucretia was well aware her husband's feathers had been ruffled over the last-minute summons to his godson's engagement party, but she didn't think the dressing down Alexandru gave his godson was the reason for Janos's nervousness. Like all Atlanteans, she could spot unease a mile away, and their godson was broadcasting it as strongly as a lighthouse beacon. And so, she made excuses to retire early to hear if her husband had been successful in learning the cause of her godson's discomfort.

Nestled in bed with her royal husband, Lucretia commanded, "Tell me. Is it as bad as we speculated? I was very glad to reach the end of our journey today because each mile had us creating new reasons why our godson delayed so long in inviting us."

Alexandru sighed and scrubbed his face in irritation. "In a million years, love, we would never have guessed the reason for it. Our godson is deeply in love but not with his fiancée. He loves the Baroness Baranyi, and if I haven't gone blind in my old age, she loves him as well, but it is a doomed affair. Janos has pledged his word to provide for the Szechenyi women by marrying into the family.

"Can't you offer your assistance in settling the matter short of marriage?"

"Ah, beloved, I have already done so, but our godson is a stubborn man who insists on settling his own problems. I need to caution you concerning Baroness Szechenyi. She thinks Janos is a vampire. The silly woman has no idea vampires or revenants, as she thinks he is, are quite rare. She doesn't know about Atlanteans, and she never will if Janos has any say in the matter. He has no intention of making his bride one of us. As he said, he'll eventually outlive her."

"How awful for him." Queen Lucretia commiserated with her husband. "His parents will be most unhappy to learn of this. I just wish they were here to offer him their advice. Maybe something can be done to prevent such a disaster."

"Short of draining those Szechenyi women completely dry, I'm at a loss to assist my godson. He has refused any help along those lines. At least, compared to us, humans live but a moment. Damn it, Lucretia, even though I've been engaged in important matters, I should've made time to visit more often or chosen someone other than his parents to be hunters. Maybe then he wouldn't have such a bitter pill to swallow."

"Well, husband mine, we have many powers, but fore-knowledge isn't one of them. Our godson is a strong man and he'll get through this. It's a shame he'll lose Beatrix Baranyi. I quite like the woman. Krisztina speaks very highly of her. Maybe I'll invite her to paint our portrait. The last artist we hired made you look cruel."

King Draculesti kissed his wife soundly, and surprisingly agreed with the artist's interpretation of his character as he settled Lucretia under his chin. "But I am a cruel man. Just ask anyone who's had the misfortune to make my fangs show."

"Oh, I don't know, Xandru, I don't think you look a bit cruel when you display your fangs. In fact, it makes me want to do wild and wicked things to you when you show me them."

Queen Lucretia Draculesti matched her husband's fanged smile and sighed as he bent to her neck. "Yes, Husband, I very much love it when you show me your fangs."

***

Janos lay in bed and pondered how a man could be

relieved and embarrassed at the same time. He was relieved his godfather hadn't delivered the dressing down he deserved. It was true, he'd waited until both of his feet left the cliff's edge, and the ground was rushing up to meet him, before he invited any of his relations to his engagement party. He should have known he'd get no reprieve from his hasty promise to Baron Szechenyi, and likewise, in lieu of his parents' attendance, his godfather would move heaven and hell to represent the family.

He was also embarrassed to admit telling his godfather he'd never have occasion to be with Bibi after the announcement of his engagement had sent a shriek of denial through his soul. He wanted the comfort of his parents. Hell, here he was a powerful ruler, a viceroy for the gods' sake, and he wanted his mommy.

His face flamed at the admission, and he rolled over and punched his pillow and clutched its mate to his chest. He drifted to sleep thinking it too bad it wasn't his artist he held in his arms. Her very scent of tuber rose and horse would calm him.

Her scent made his fangs punch out, and his prick quivered with impatience to enter her again, and again, and again, until, satiated at last, they both collapsed with satisfaction. He focused on the delicate coral flower of her sex dripping with honey when she opened for him, and he drank his fill and gave her the bonding words. He scored his chest and cradled her head to let Bibi drink from him. He'd planted his heir in her body and—

The abrupt intrusion of light into the curtains

surrounding his bed made him roar in outrage, and he grabbed the culprit by his neck and threw him to the bed.

"Your Grace, Your Grace, oh, do wake up. I'm sorry if I've startled you, but this is the hour you requested I wake you."

The prince blinked back the red haze and jumped back from his valet's prone body when he realized he'd been choking the man. "It's morning? How is this possible? I don't even remember going to sleep."

Akos edged his way across the room after he'd extracted himself from the twisted sheets, and Janos was immediately ashamed of himself for attacking the man. He felt even worse when he was handed his morning drink, and he noted his valet's shaking hands as he offered the goblet.

"Do forgive me, Akos. I was in the throes of a dream. Which in no way excuses my behavior, but you startled me from a deep sleep. You may leave me. I'll dress myself this morning. Tell the king and queen I'll join them for breakfast."

While he struggled to tie a decent knot in his cravat, Janos vowed he would avoid Bibi's company unless it was absolutely necessary to be in her presence, and only then when there was someone else present. He had to stop this yearning for her. It served no purpose to want something he couldn't have. Part of being a responsible adult was avoiding what was bad for you. If he had to make a vow, this was an excellent one. One he'd continue to remind himself of until he believed it or made himself crazy. He was good with whichever came first. After his behavior this morning, he was probably more than halfway to crazy. Akos, he was sure, would agree with him.

Chapter Twenty

Bibi delayed entering the breakfast room until well past the usual hour. She hoped to avoid a repeat of last night's uncomfortable dinner. Witnessing the prince with his family about him had sent surges of pain through her heart. Henceforth, Margyth would be the one dining each night with him, not her. She needed to tell Cata to have her traveling trunk sent up to her room this morning. The sooner she packed her belongings, the sooner she could depart Castle Rackoszi after the engagement ball. She should never have agreed to remain for the event. The miniatures were finished. They were damned good, and not even the Szechenyi's would be able to find fault with them. Upon further reflection, she admitted to herself Margyth could and would disparage them just to be contrary, but Janos would never let her get away with not paying her artist's commission.

If she'd remembered, as her father frequently chastised her, to raise her head in the correct posture for a baroness, Bibi would've had enough time to note the presence of the same diners from last evening's meal, with the added fillip of the Szechenyi women, the sight of whom had her calling up her *Csiko* vocabulary. *Ah, damnation. I must've been horrible in a former life to merit such punishment this morning.* She came to a hesitant stop at the room's entrance, but Countess Krisztina's exuberant greeting kept her from executing an immediate about-face.

"Bibi, I assumed you'd breakfasted much earlier. I

remember what an early riser you are. Please join us."

Wanting to decline breakfast, as much as one of the ancient Greeks would've declined the offer of a drop of hemlock being added to their morning beverage, she reluctantly chose the remaining chair and seated herself. Well to be more accurate, the King of Wallachia seated her. Unused to having such an exalted person do the honors, she blushed and sputtered through a thank you. Strangely, it was Margyth who rescued her. Strange because it was more of an insult, but it got her away from present company for the rest of the day.

Margyth waited until she'd taken a healthy bite of the paprika-cured bacon before firing the first shot across her bow with the accuracy of a seasoned naval gunner.

"Baroness Baranyi, Szigi just informed me you will be assisting us on the sunny days. Since today is not at all sunny, your assistance will not be needed. My darling prince is naming a beautiful rose in my honor, and the ceremony is to take place this afternoon in the formal gardens. The entire family will be present, so you are free to do whatever it is you do for the rest of the day."

Although it took two tries to swallow the bacon, Bibi managed it on sheer anger. She had to hand it to the chit. Margyth succeeded in thanking her and belittling her in one fell swoop, but she gathered a modicum of courage from Countess Krisztina's outraged glare at Margyth. Wiping her mouth with her napkin, Bibi placed an insipid smile on her face and a lie on her lips. "Why I do thank you, Margyth. I did want to exercise Shadow today. I always enjoy a good gallop, don't you?" *Hah, the spoiled twit wouldn't know a gallop from a trot because the gentle mare the prince gave Margyth would never think of unseating her mistress. And no, she would absolutely not cast her eyes in his direction after mentioning the word gallop.*

Janos surprised her by remaining unaffected by the unsubtle jab. He didn't correct Margyth's high-handed dismissal or her blatant inference she wasn't family. She was well aware she wasn't, but having someone point it out so publicly was, in her opinion, *déclassé.*

"Well, Margyth, I'm sure you will enjoy the afternoon. Such an honor. Do keep a lookout for bees. I'd hate for your face to be swollen at your engagement ball. Your Majesties, it has been a pleasure sharing breakfast with you. With your permission, I must attend to my horse. I'm training him to be a cavalry mount. If your godson hasn't already mentioned it, the Horthy-Baranyi stables provide the best."

And she was gone and marching to the stables before anyone could discern the hurt on her face from the prince's failure to defend her. It had been humiliating to have Queen Lucretia cover the awkward moment by changing the subject. Janos hadn't even spared her a glance but just sat there with his head bowed over his plate.

Bibi left the stables in full retreat. Shadow, bless his stalwart heart, was delighted to put the stables behind them. After several minutes of full-out galloping, her love for her horse overtook her outrage, and she reined Shadow in to a walk before he got overheated. Perfect, just perfect, she castigated herself as she took in her surroundings. Without conscious volition, she had returned to the trout stream. She led Shadow to the bank and let him drink after she slipped from the saddle.

When Shadow had quenched his thirst, she let the reins trail so he could crop grass. She needed to get a handle on her temper before returning to the castle. Too restless to sit, she found herself walking round and round the tree where they had picnicked, and hoped it didn't take another dowsing in the stream before her temper cooled enough to return to the castle.

If she hadn't been wearing spurs, she might've tried to kick herself in the ass. It was more than obvious she'd overstayed her welcome. Janos's failure to chastise Margyth this morning was proof positive. If she hadn't given her promise to stay, she could make an early morning getaway and he could put her bloody payment in the post. Bibi snorted at the ludicrous plan. She was howling angry, not howling crazy. A woman traveling alone was the height of idiocy. Her death at the hands of bandits or rapists would kill her father, and she couldn't be responsible for visiting such sorrow on him.

Noticing a well-trodden ring in the grass around the tree, she shook her head at the obvious sign she'd paid more attention to trying to divine an enlightened solution to her problem than in placing her feet. Her anger had kept her from reaching the simple solution before walking herself dizzy. It was indeed simple, she'd just avoid Margyth and Janos. After all, she wouldn't have to be with either one of them on sunny days. Knowing she was being more hypocritical than devout, Bibi fell to her knees and prayed for nothing but sunny days until the day of the ball.

She let Shadow have his head on the way back to the Rackoszi stables. Her self-absorption was broken by the sound of heavy hooves thundering toward them. She had just enough time to flatten herself over the back of her saddle as a sheathed cavalry sword passed within inches of her body. Her brain caught up to her right before she drew her own weapon.

"Pal Anton, you are deranged," Bibi called, after she turned Shadow to face her attacker. But she was so glad to be in the cheerful hussar's company, she couldn't stay angry.

"Bibi, you know I missed on purpose. I would never hurt you." Pal Anton guided Ares alongside Shadow and leaned from the saddle to give her a smacking kiss on the cheek. "I just couldn't help it. You were so unaware of your surroundings I had the advantage of surprise."

"Yes, I was, and so you did, and I'm very glad you've joined us. Have you eaten? The family has already had their noon meal, but maybe we can persuade the cook to give up some leftovers."

"No, I haven't eaten. I pushed on from the miserable little inn I stayed in last night to make it here before dark. I'm starved."

"Why does the fact you are hungry not surprise me?" She snickered.

"Be nice to me, or when I cajole more than just cold leftovers from the cook, I won't share with you."

Looking into Pal's cheerful face, the realization dawned on her that, with Pal's help, she could get through this week, Margyth and Janos be damned. She had a friend she could rely on. She would keep her promise to stay for the ball, and Pal Anton would be at her side. Although she wasn't a hussar, she understood cavalry, and thus she and Pal had a bond of friendship and easy camaraderie.

She hung back while Pal worked his magic on Castle Rackoszi's cook. The woman was so flattered by his attention, she tittered in eagerness to feed the handsome hussar. Bibi just shook her head in amazement when they were directed to a private alcove off the kitchen to await whatever culinary offering the cook cared to deliver.

The excellent luncheon lost its flavor for her when Erzsebet appeared in the kitchen to inform the cook there would be two more people for the evening meal. The Baroness Szechenyi had relented about staying in the castle for the week prior to the engagement ball when she learned how early she'd have to arise to allow Margyth to supervise the next day's activities with the prince.

"Why are you smiling, Bibi? I shouldn't think you were looking forward to spending time with Margyth."

"No, I am not enraptured over sharing space with your spoiled fourth cousin or her grim mama. I'm smiling because Erzsebet is giving her the green room in the south wing. I know from recent experience the bed is supremely uncomfortable. I suppose gloating at Margyth's discomfort makes me a bad person."

"No, not bad." Pal grinned. "Just human. Margyth gathers enemies as adroitly as bees gather pollen. I just wish I could warn the prince, but it's not my place."

She matched the hussar's frown. "Yes, I know. It isn't my

place, either. I wish I hadn't agreed to stay for the engagement ball, but I do enjoy Countess Krisztina's company. Since you've finished gobbling your luncheon, why don't we go find her? I'll make the introductions."

"Is this Countess friend of yours married, by any chance?"

"Oooh, you devil, you. No, she is unattached, and she's an excellent rider. Perhaps the three of us can go riding tomorrow."

"Well, then, lead the way. I am most anxious to meet your friend, Baroness Baranyi."

The next morning Bibi had to turn away to keep her wry expression to herself. Pal Anton was delighted to have Countess Krisztina join them for a ride until the queen and six other women asked to be part of their party. She'd wager good money the hussar was beginning to regret not joining the prince and King Alexandru to shoot pheasant on this cloudy day. It had surprised everyone when Margyth proclaimed herself an excellent shot and took up her hostess duties for the hunt with enthusiasm.

Bibi organized the riding party as Queen Lucretia mounted her horse. "Good morning, Your Majesty. Might I suggest we follow the prince's bridle paths for a relaxing ride this morning?" She stopped when Queen Lucretia, after an obvious nudge from Krisztina, held up her hand.

"My dear, Krisztina has regaled us with your skill as a rider, and I for one would like a demonstration. Can't we do something more strenuous than trot down flat paths this morning?"

With one glance at Pal Anton's quirked eyebrow and

wicked grin, Bibi vaulted into the saddle and set Shadow to a gallop. And they were off for a reprise of the steeplechase she'd enjoyed with Janos. By the time they reached a willow-fringed pond, the horses were lathered and blowing hard. It was an excellent spot to cool them down and have the picnic the castle's cook had labored hard to provide.

Bibi couldn't help but compare the impromptu picnic she'd enjoyed with the prince and this one being provided for a queen. There were white, cloth-covered tables with chairs, wine cooling in silver urns, and silver trays heaped high with chicken, and bowls of vegetables. Unlike her previous steeplechase, there were warm, damp cloths to clean the mud from everyone's face and hands, while a trio of stable hands saw to the horses.

She had no idea how Erzsebet had coordinated this in such a short time, but she took her seat when Pal Anton held it out for her. She was famished from the ride, and judging by the oohs and ahs of appreciation, so was everyone else.

"Such a wonderful ride, Bibi. May I call you Bibi?" Queen Lucretia leaned in to thank her, startling her from her bemusement.

"Yes, Your Majesty. I prefer it. I married into my title and was widowed very soon after, so I'm still not comfortable being addressed as Baroness Beatrix."

"I'm very sorry for your loss, but I'm not sorry to have you here today. You gave us a magnificent ride. I haven't had such fun in eons." Poking fun at herself, Queen Lucretia gestured to her empty plate. "My goodness, I've eaten everything and I'm still ravenous."

No sooner had the queen uttered the words than a fresh plate, with a sampling of everything, was placed before her. Bibi smiled as the queen's wineglass was filled with Janos's special blend. Paying closer attention, she noted, along with hers and Pal Anton's, there were two others drinking wine of a lighter hue.

Queen Lucretia was in no hurry to end the picnic, and so they dawdled until the afternoon waned. At the queen's nod, the horses were mounted and the party returned to the castle in a much more sedate fashion than they'd left.

Bibi wished she was disingenuous enough to fabricate a worthy excuse to absent herself from dinner this evening. Dining with Margyth and the Baroness Szechenyi always upset her digestion.

**

Margyth turned her head to see what had stopped Szigi's effusive compliment of her shooting skills, and her lips pulled back in a snarl. She caught herself before she did something unforgiveable like slapping the prince back to attention. The damned artist had made her appearance, and the ruby velvet gown she wore had Szigi all but drooling into his wineglass. As the Baranyi woman was the last to be seated, she surmised the artist had delayed her entrance to garner every man's attention. The fact the ploy was successful left her wanting to rake her nails down the baroness's cheeks. This was her week to shine and no one, certainly not a woman who rode about in male attire, was going to upstage her. Even Pal Anton earned a share of her ire when he jumped up, like a marionette whose strings had been jerked, to seat the tart.

She took a sip of wine to cool her temper and to study the cut of the gown. It was magnificent, even if it was draping the artist's body. The gown had *haute couture* stamped all over it, and she made up her mind in a snap. She was going to wheedle a trousseau buying trip to France from Szigi, whether he accompanied her or not, and then she planned to burn every last country bumpkin gown in her wardrobe.

At least, at her insistence, Erzsebet seated the woman far below the salt so she had the royals all to herself. Turning her back on the artist's half of the table, Margyth smiled at King Draculesti and complimented him on his prowess in shooting flying game.

"I should be the one complimenting you, my dear. I don't believe I've ever been in the presence of a woman who could shoot so well."

"My father taught me. He enjoyed hunting and so do I, but I haven't had a chance to enjoy it lately," she simpered.

As the footmen entered with the first course, King Alexandru earned another smile from her by tapping his wineglass with his fork and telling the diners they were enjoying this evening's pheasant dinner, thanks to her shooting skills. And everyone tittered when he cautioned Szigi not to make her angry if there were firearms present, as she was an excellent shot.

***

As much as Margyth tried to monopolize his attention, she wasn't successful. He was playing the cad by turning his attention to what was happening at the far end of the table and not paying sufficient attention to the Szechenyi women, but he didn't have the volition to stop. He wouldn't be at all surprised if his intended lost patience with him entirely, and poured a glass of wine over his head as a reminder of which woman he was about to marry. He was so absent from his present surroundings, his godmother had to step on his foot under the table to remind him to answer the question Margyth had just asked him.

This dinner was interminable. The royal half of the table had fallen into almost total silence, while the lower half was quite loud with conversation. It was a relief when the footman entered with the port. Janos cast his eyes skyward in a brief thank you when the queen herded the women into the formal parlor and Margyth begged off.

"I'm sorry, Your Majesty, but the day's shooting has made me very tired. With your permission, I'll retire for the evening. I'll join you for breakfast. Szigi has a day of cards planned for tomorrow, and I'm so looking forward to it." At the queen's nod, Margyth, accompanied by her mother, made her curtsy and left before anyone could delay her.

The flinty look his intended cast his way as she turned to leave brought him a smidgen of guilt. But he knew Margyth hoped to make a favorable impression on his godparents, so she would wait until she was behind closed doors before she loosed a string of curses at his head for his inattention.

The longer this hellish week lasted, the more his manners

deteriorated. Janos was not ignorant of the fact he behaved quite boorishly at dinner, but he'd been physically unable to keep his eyes away from Bibi. Her red gown was the one she'd worn the first time they'd dined together, and it had made one hell of a permanent impression. He was also very cognizant of the fact he'd made one hell of an unfavorable impression on his godparents. Indeed, the sharp reminder Queen Lucretia gave him to pay closer attention to Margyth's conversation still smarted.

He'd been trying to catch Bibi's eye, but, alas, his efforts were unsuccessful. She steadfastly refused to return his attention during the dinner, and he knew why. His plan to keep his distance from the artist was succeeding better than he'd planned, and he was reaping his just desserts for not putting Margyth in her place when she insulted his artist by pointing out she, Margyth Szechenyi, was soon to be family and Bibi was not.

Without the women present, he was able to tear his mind away from things he was helpless to resolve and remember his manners. "King Alexandru, may I present Lieutenant Colonel Pal Anton Esterhazy. Pal Anton is one of Emperor Franz Josef's hussars and a distant cousin of the Szechenyis. Pal Anton, may I present King Alexandru Draculesti, Ruler of Wallachia, and my godfather."

Pal saved him from having to carry the burden of polite conversation by launching into a play-by-play of the last fracas with the Italians when the king mentioned it. His godfather loved discussing military tactics, and doing so with an Imperial Hussar pleased him. Janos shamelessly kept the conversation and the port flowing until it was time to rejoin the women.

His attempt to seize an opportunity to approach Bibi and tender an apology failed. She saw him coming and quickly made her apologies to the queen and received permission to retire. It was as blatant a snub as one of the many ones Margyth had delivered her, and the burning ache between his ribs made him aware of how much they must've hurt.

Maybe the ancient gods were not as upset with him as Baroness Baranyi, Margyth, and his godparents were, for the gods took pity on him and made the evening end when his godfather stifled a yawn behind his hand, and the queen caught him at it. Between walking the fields in search of game, and the queen's vigorous ride with Bibi, there was a general consensus to call it an early evening.

Needing to be alone with his own thoughts, he dismissed Akos for the evening and settled into a wing chair by the fire. However, it was soon evident he wasn't to be left alone, and whatever thoughts came wouldn't be his. The damned demons had found him again.

Demons? How many times must I remind you, there is one demon and one angel in this room? I am not the one who has fallen.

I can arrange your fall, Mister Holier than Thou. You might earn a permanent place in my neighborhood if you displease your master when you fail to find a solution to the prince's little problem. Especially since you naively think he can keep his honor, and do his duty, and have the woman he really wants. Not even Lord Lucifer himself would bet on those odds.

Janos felt his dinner and his temper rise, but, hell, he had nothing better to do for the remainder of the evening. He might as well sit back and let the imps insult each other. It would serve as entertainment.

He'd planned to remain just a bystander to their bickering, but a question presented itself. If maintaining his patience didn't result in a solution to his predicament, what would? And no, he would *not* ask his godfather to turn the Szechenyi women into dry husks of their former selves. For once, the demon had the better suggestion.

Patience is for weaklings. You haven't asked Margyth for her hand yet. Tonight is the last night you will be free to do what you want to do, and you know exactly what it is you want to do. Stop hiding in your room and change forms. None of your servants will think anything amiss for a wolf to be prowling the castle's corridors this late at night. Follow the maddening scent of tuber rose and horse to Bibi's door and scratch at it until she lets you in, and then you can change back to your human form, a very nude human form she appears to have a weakness resisting. You can spend the rest of this night making love rather than let her continue the packing she is presently engaged in. Go to her. Show her she is mistaken in her belief you no longer care for her, it's just you've temporarily misplaced your Atlantean balls!

He changed forms before the good imp could even stop calling down outraged imprecations on the demon. With practiced ease, he had the door to his room open and loped down the hall to put distance between the quarreling sides of the conscience he left behind in the Master Suite.

The wolf caught the clink of glass on glass as he passed the south wing's corridor and turned back to investigate the noise. He found Margyth walking the hall attired in a flimsy night robe and carrying two glasses and a bottle of wine.

Lucifer folded himself into the deep shadows between the few candles still alight in the passage and followed the woman. He flattened himself to the stone floor when she stopped to knock on one of the bedroom doors, a door not hers or her mother's. He was not surprised when Pal Anton answered the summons. Rather than leap snarling from his concealment, the wolf crept closer, the better to hear her explanation for visiting a man's room so late at night and in such a state of undress.

***

Margyth stood in the dark hallway dressed in her night robe, and with her golden hair undone and streaming in waves down her back. She held the wine bottle and two glasses at the ready as she waited for Pal Anton to come to the door.

"Well, are you going to invite me in, Pal?" She was very aware of Pal's similar state of *dishabille*. It was more than obvious the hussar had begun his preparations for bed. She was titillated by the sight of his bare, muscular chest and narrow waist.

"Margyth, it's very late and you shouldn't be here. I'm sure your fiancé would not approve."

Pal did not budge from his blockade of the doorway when

she attempted to edge around him, and she was forced to continue the conversation in the hallway. "Szigi? What he doesn't know won't hurt him. I'm sure that stick-in-the-mud is sound asleep by now."

She held up the bottle and glasses. "We can enjoy this bottle of wine, and then we can enjoy each other, if you are open to suggestions on how to pass the night." When she tried again to pass into his room, Pal stopped her.

"Margyth, whether the prince is awake or asleep, he's still your fiancé, and your being here is extremely improper. Return to your room before you are discovered."

"Pooh, when did you become such a proper hussar? You had no objections to our late-night games when you were staying in my house, Pal Anton."

"Yes, I did enjoy them, but the prince had yet to make it evident he was courting you, and you hadn't made it clear you would accept his suit. Since we are both enjoying the prince's hospitality before your engagement announcement, it's crystal clear you've accepted his suit. I have this rule, cousin. I never cuckold a friend in his own home."

Margyth rolled her eyes at the hussar's sudden recovery of his morals. "Well then, you can be my special friend when I open my salon in Vienna. I doubt Szigi will care what I do once I give him his heir. He is disinclined to travel, and I am even more disinclined to remain in this drafty, dank pile of stones. I want bright city lights and interesting people around me. People who don't wear perpetual frowns on their faces like his dwarf of a housekeeper. We will make quite a splash in Vienna, Pal, with my beauty and your elan."

Pal left her openmouthed in surprise when he didn't agree with her, and she found it offensive when he made shooing motions at her.

"I'm sorry, Margyth, but becoming your special friend would violate another personal rule of mine."

"God in heaven, Pal, how many of these idiotic rules do you have?" She was becoming bored with the conversation and chilled by the cold air in the dark corridor.

"I only have two rules. The second of which is never, ever, become involved with a married woman. I've worked too hard for the rank I have to become romantically linked to a noble's wife. Janos outranks me and could destroy my career with a mere crook of his finger. Besides, I like the prince, and I'd never betray his friendship in such a manner. Return to your room, and we'll both forget this conversation ever took place. We've been lucky no servant has wandered down this corridor on some errand or other."

Enraged, she stamped her foot. "I don't give a fig about servants. Let them discover us, it won't make a difference. They'll keep their mouths shut or I'll have them dismissed without reference."

Pal shook his head at her display of temper. "Margyth, if you would stop equating servants with insignificant objects, you'd know they notice and hear everything, and loyal servants such as the prince employs, report it. I bid you good night. Sleep well."

She was incredulous Pal had the effrontery to close the door in her face, and anger at being denied made her consider kicking the door, but she desisted and spun on her heel to return to her room. She squeaked in fright when she encountered a snarling wolf blocking her way.

Slipping into her natural haughtiness, she snapped at Szigi's pet. "Get out of my way, you mangy dog. I hope you are enjoying your last days of freedom because when I'm the mistress of this castle, I'll insist Szigi keep you chained outside."

Her temper, already at the boiling point, spilled over when the animal snorted and brushed against her, almost knocking her over as it passed by. The wine bottle she threw after it made a satisfying sound as it shattered on the stone floor. *Let the damned servants report that*, she fumed as she marched back to her room.

***

Janos became cognizant of his low growling and stopped dead in his tracks after rounding the corner. It had taken all of his strength to restrain his wolf from ripping Margyth's throat out when she'd rounded on him. He'd suspected she wasn't chaste or pure or faithful, but until he'd borne witness her blatant disregard for conventional morals, and been made aware of her low opinion of himself and his staff, he'd fooled himself into believing it didn't matter. Well, the blindfold was off. He became nauseated at the thought his children would have such a mother and had to stretch full out on the cold stone floor to break the paralysis in his chest so he could breathe. Was the damned Rackoszi honor more important than the welfare of his heirs? There had to be a way of solving this conundrum, there just had to be.

The wolf shook its fur to rid itself of the crawling disgust then ran full out to the north tower and Bibi's room, until a small voice in its head stopped him with the same force as the Szechenyi wolf trap had done.

Why are you so angry with Margyth when you are about to do the same thing? You are headed to a woman's bedroom who isn't your intended. Coupling with her will be just as wrong as Margyth would have been if Pal Anton had been agreeable. In fact, doing so brands you the rake to Margyth's whore. It gives you and Margyth something in common. Perhaps Baroness Baranyi will have the strength of will Pal Anton had and turn you away, but do you want to put it to the test?

With dragging steps, the wolf returned to the Master Suite.

Chapter Twenty-One

Bibi played a card and winced when it was snatched up by Countess Krisztina, who gave a whoop and, with a broad smile on her face, displayed the winning hand.

"I'm perturbed we aren't playing for money," Krisztina teased. "I believe I'd own the Baranyi stables if we totaled points."

She grinned at the countess as she refuted the boast. "If we were playing for money, I would pay closer attention to my cards. Aren't you bored with playing card games? It has been raining all afternoon and you, Pal Anton, and I have been relegated to the farthest table to keep us out of Margyth's circle of power. But I'm not complaining."

The conversation ended when Pal Anton returned carrying three punch cups.

"Ladies, unless my eyes deceive me, the Countess has won all of my tokens, and all of yours as well, Baroness. Why don't we suggest another activity? I think some music might liven things up. Too bad the rain shows no sign of stopping or I'd suggest a brisk walk."

Turning to Countess Krisztina, Pal asked, "Do you play an instrument or sing, Countess?"

Krisztina displayed her pretty dimples for the handsome hussar as she answered his question. "I play the harp quite well, but I sing horribly. I can't even hum on key."

Bibi just couldn't stifle the nasty comparison that popped

into her mind. Krisztina was the exact opposite of Margyth, who sang beautifully, but played the pianoforte horribly.

Pal warned them of Margyth's approach with a tilt of his head, and called out, "Cousin, have you won everyone's tokens at your table?"

"No, I have not. I was winning until Szigi made us play a game I'm not familiar with and I lost all of mine. I'm bored, Pal. Why don't we go and do something fun?"

Krisztina smiled sardonically at Margyth's suggestion, and it didn't take Bibi but three seconds to understand Margyth's plans had not included the countess or herself. Pal, displaying his diplomatic skills yet again, suggested, "Capital idea. Why don't we adjourn to the prince's music room and liven the day up with music? You can sing for us. Has the prince heard you sing yet? No? Well then, come along. He's in for a rare treat. I'll play for you, and perhaps Countess Krisztina can accompany us on the harp. Why don't you ask King Draculesti if he'd consent to attend our impromptu entertainment?"

As Margyth brightened and sped off to inform the king of their proposed musical performance, Bibi clapped one hand gently with the other. "Bravo, Pal Anton. You've saved the day."

As she neither sang nor played an instrument, she seated herself at a chair where she could observe the performers but not be in the front ranks. Tired, she wanted to close her eyes and let the music release some of the tension she'd experienced during this never-ending week. With the first fluid notes of the harp, she felt herself relax. Margyth held her audience in thrall with her beautiful voice, and Bibi wasn't mean enough to find fault with perfection. However, on the first shivery note of a violin, her eyes flew open and she listened as Janos, with his eyes shut, plucked a hauntingly romantic tune. It had to be one of his own construction because she didn't recognize the magnificent piece, and he was playing without music.

Bibi panicked. The room closed in on her, and she fled as quietly as she could. And once out of sight, and with no decorum whatsoever, she picked up her skirts and ran back to her room to lock herself in.

Flinging herself facedown on the bed, she tried but failed to erase from her mind the bittersweet expression on the prince's face as he played the violin. It was yearning, and she recognized it because she was trying to wash the same one off her face with copious tears. Wanting Janos was etched into her soul. It was irremovable. Not even a lifetime apart would fade the mark.

Typical of her odd reaction to startling or unhappy events, she got mad rather than wallow in misery. She jumped up and vented her anger on her helpless travel trunk. She circled the inanimate object and kicked it until the pain in her foot registered, and she ceased as rapidly as she'd begun.

Regarding the myriad scuff marks she'd placed on the good leather, she covered her face with her hands. Out of breath and embarrassed, she apologized to the insensate trunk for her tantrum.

She considered undressing and crawling into bed, but she was too energized by her recent physical activity. Energized and perspiring. The realization sent her to the washbasin to eradicate such unpleasant evidence of temper. However, while scrutinizing her appearance in the mirror over the washstand, she spotted the two miniatures resting on the gilt easels she'd had one of the Baranyi carpenters make to display the finished paintings.

Bibi washed her face and put her hair to rights before running to the door and unlocking it. With everyone in the music room, it would be the perfect time to place the paintings in the Master Suite for Janos's private viewing. She wanted him to have privacy to study her work. She wanted him to absorb the message she'd painted into them, even though he'd never change the course he'd set for himself. For herself, she didn't want to be present for the refusal in his eyes or cause him more pain when he saw the sorrow in hers.

Carrying the miniatures so they wouldn't touch each other, she walked as fast as she could down the corridors until she reached the prince's suite of rooms. Hoping Akos was inside, she knocked and held her breath until the doorknob turned, and she saw Akos's surprised face as he stood aside to let her enter. She rushed to explain her purpose. "I've the miniatures for the prince's viewing, Akos. If you think it acceptable, I'll place them on the mantel so His Grace can study them from afar or close up as he desires."

"Oh please, Baroness, display them to their best advantage. If you need me to rearrange anything, I'd be happy to do so."

"Yes, please. Would you put those candlesticks on another table, and slide the clock to the far end?"

"As you wish, Baroness."

She set each miniature into its easel, and placed the small cards she'd copied from her book of Russian folktales each miniature was patterned after in front, but as she began to cover them with a linen cloth, she was halted by Akos's question.

"May I, Baroness? I'll completely understand, if you'd prefer the prince to be the first one to view them."

"Of course, you may." She hesitated as the prince's valet approached the mantel. She wanted to flee, but the artist in her wanted to know how her work affected the man. If she lived to be an old crone, she still wouldn't have guessed his reaction.

The valet stared at each miniature for a good five minutes and then covered his face with his hands and burst into tears. Before she could offer any words of concern, Akos flung himself into her arms and sobbed as if he'd just been told Janos had expired.

"Oh, Baroness, you've done it. You haven't just painted their faces, you've painted their souls. His grace couldn't possibly...couldn't possibly. Oh, do forgive me. The miniatures are so hauntingly beautiful, I can't find words enough to describe them."

Bibi was weak-kneed with relief when the man caught hold of his emotions and dried his tears with his spotless handkerchief before placing a clean cloth over the miniatures. She made her escape when he had his back to her. She didn't think the valet was even aware he was once again alone in the prince's rooms.

Shaken by the valet's reaction, she wondered if she could avoid Janos for the rest of the day. What excuse could she invent for not dining with everyone this evening? The answer was none. She was an artist, and as such, she painted what she felt about what she observed, and therefore, she'd be damned if she'd hide in her room. She'd done nothing wrong. She'd created two masterpieces, and so would show Janos, and everyone who viewed them, she was proud of her talent.

But it wouldn't hurt to go to dinner wearing a stunning gown to help bolster her resolve. Bibi picked up her pace and headed back to her room to make her dress and jewelry selection. It wouldn't be long before the women retired to their rooms to dress for dinner, and she wanted to be well rested when Cata arrived to help her dress.

***

Oh, what to do, what to do? Akos wandered aimlessly about the Master Suite trying to come up with a solution to his dilemma. Should he hide the portraits until after the prince left for the evening meal? Could he get away with such license? The baroness would expect the prince to comment on her work at dinner. But having seen them, he would never forgive himself if he let the prince appear at dinner before he had time to recover his emotions.

Glancing once again at the shrouded miniatures, he made up his mind. Gods help him, the prince was more than just his employer, he was his friend, and he just could not allow his friend to appear in public with his heart painted on his face for everyone to comment.

The valet picked the paintings up and gently carried them to the prince's dressing room, where he secreted them on a top shelf behind the box containing a top hat Janos used on the rare occasions his employer attended the Viennese opera. They would remain there until the prince left for dinner, and then he'd restore them to the mantel.

He reminded himself to send a note confessing his perfidy to the baroness. He was more than sure she'd understand why he felt the need to delay the viewing.

Akos almost fainted when the prince entered the suite with a thundercloud painted on his face. *His Grace has come to view the paintings* was his first panic point. His second was, *he's going to dismiss me without references for attempting to hide them.* He stood rooted to the carpet as the prince walked to the fireplace and banged his head on the wooden mantel, the mantel absent of Bibi's art. Only when the prince barked out Margyth was the cause of his anger, could he walk without his knees knocking together.

"I swear to all the gods, Margyth has a real knack for putting everyone in a foul mood. Her few redeeming features are singing and a fair face. The woman cheats, Akos, she cheats at cards, she has been cheating on me, and she doesn't care who knows it. She took all of the king's tokens at cards by cheating, and he and I both were aware she was doing so. Honest to God, I..."

Akos shifted his eyes away from pouring bath salts into the water for the prince's bath when the sound of growling filled the room. He was afraid a wolf would be climbing into the warm bath water. He huffed his relief to find the prince still in human form.

"Why don't you let me undress you and you can climb into your bath. The water should relax you, Your Grace."

"Capital idea, Akos."

The prince unwound his cravat and stood still long enough to be divested of coat, shirt, trousers, and boots, before he dropped his small clothes and walked to the bathtub.

"Akos, before you select my clothes for this evening, pour me a generous amount of whisky. Perhaps the fine Scots distillation will take the edge off my temper."

He complied with alacrity but had to pick up the prince's hand to fit the glass into it, for Janos was stretched out in the tub with a damp washcloth over his face.

Saying a fervent *Te Deum* to the gods for the prince remaining ignorant of the location of the miniatures, he all but ran back to the dressing room and selected the appropriate clothes. He just couldn't help one, last, upward glance to reassure himself the cause of his fear remained securely hidden.

As it was, he paced between the bedroom, dressing room, and sitting room in perpetual motion for one hour after the prince departed, dressed elegantly for dinner. Certain the dinner had commenced, and the prince wouldn't be popping back in unexpectedly to demand to know why the miniatures had been hidden from him, the valet retrieved them from behind the hat box and placed them back on the mantel, and once again leaking tears of sympathy for His Grace, covered them.

It was with a heavy heart he closed the door of the Master Suite and returned to his own room. He doubted, once the prince discovered what had been left for him, he'd be summoned for the rest of the evening.

***

Receiving the valet's note untied the giant knot in Bibi's stomach. She at least would be able to eat dinner without fearing she'd embarrass herself by losing the contents of her stomach in public. If her luck held, tomorrow morning would dawn sunny, and she could escape for a long ride before having to face the prince's reaction to the miniatures. She'd stay away from the castle until it was time to rest in her room for the evening's dance.

Cata's knock on her door ended her dithering. "Come in, Cata."

"Oh, Baroness, I was hoping you'd choose this gown. I've wanted you to wear it from the moment I saw it."

The gown Cata was referring to was one which, at its worst description, could be described as a dead leaf color. It was saved from further unfavorable comments by the gold thread running through it, and the daringly scooped neckline. Bibi would never have worn it if she hadn't had a magnificent, four-strand choker of amber beads to cover some of her exposed flesh.

"Oh, please, Baroness, I know you don't enjoy having your hair fussed with, but please let me try something different this evening. It will be your last evening dining with the family before the engagement ball, and I know it's prideful of me, but I want you to outshine the rest of the women this evening."

At the mention of the word "last," a wave of sadness crashed over her, and Bibi, not trusting her legs to hold her, seated herself at the dressing table. "As you wish, Cata."

Despite her dejection, she sat still in fascination as Cata wound her hair into a figure eight pattern, and secured it high on the crown of her head. It was severe but it suited her. When the maid added the matching amber earrings and bracelet to the choker, her ensemble was complete.

She watched in the mirror as Cata stood back and surveyed her work with a critical eye before crossing the room to hold open the door to the bedroom.

"Since I've already helped Margyth with her gown this evening, I know she won't be able to come close to topping yours. And you can scold me, Baroness, but I don't care. I hope she gets instant dyspepsia when you walk in and stun everyone with your beauty."

Not being able to scold her maid for wanting to deliver a set down to the spoiled Szechenyi brat, Bibi winked at her and left to join Janos for his last dinner as an unengaged man.

Chapter Twenty-Two

The first hint he had of Bibi's arrival in the library for a pre-dinner aperitif was his godfather's exclamation of, "The Baroness Baranyi is one attractive woman," and Pal Anton's low whistle of agreement. At least their comments allowed him to school his face into one of polite agreement with his godfather's judgement. Janos had to put his whisky glass down on the table after one glance at Bibi. He didn't want Margyth to notice how much his hand was shaking with the effort it took to remain at her side.

He took a slow, deep breath as his godfather left his side to go to his artist and wrap her arm around his own to lead her to where he stood with Pal Anton and Margyth.

"Isn't the baroness looking especially fine this evening, Janos?"

He nodded mutely. His tongue was stuck behind his teeth and just wouldn't obey his command to form words. Gods bless his godfather for the skilled conversationalist he was, for he leapt into the breach.

"I swear, Baroness, your ensemble calls to mind the time I visited the Tsar in St. Petersburg, and he and the Tsarina were gracious enough to show me the amber room. It was quite something to experience, and you would have added to its beauty had you been there as well."

"Thank you for the compliment, Your Majesty. Indeed, the amber I am wearing tonight is from Russia. I purchased it while I was there to take art classes."

"Oh, I'm so glad you mentioned art, Baroness." Margyth smiled innocently to excuse the interruption. "As I recall, you said you would have our miniatures ready for viewing the night before the engagement ball."

Janos's intended threaded her arm through his and gave his bicep a small squeeze. "Has your artist shown you the miniatures yet, Szigi? No? Perhaps we should have the baroness fetch them so we can all give testimony to her talent. I'd hate for her to leave without anyone being able to give their comments on her efforts."

He cleared his throat to come to Bibi's rescue but once again found himself without words to respond to Margyth's obvious attempt to denigrate his artist's efforts.

Bibi responded to Margyth's challenge. "The miniatures are in the prince's suite, Margyth. I had his valet place them on his mantel. The prince will be able to view them at his leisure after dinner. I'm sure he'll permit you to glimpse them when you rise for the day tomorrow, and everyone else will have access to them during your engagement ball."

The awkward silence following her announcement was broken when the footman threw open the doors to the dining room, and Janos cast a grateful glance to Pal Anton when the hussar offered Bibi his arm, and drew everyone's attention when he avowed with great conviction, "Thank God, I was about to expire from hunger."

All he wanted was to sit back and feast his eyes on Bibi, but it just wasn't possible. Margyth was bent on capturing his sole attention, and even though she deserved to be cut to the quick, he couldn't find it in him to be so cruel. Neither was he strong enough to be able to swallow past the lump in his throat. Janos was well aware this was his last dinner as a free man. Ha! He wasn't free at all, and the sooner he admitted this to himself, the sooner he could erase it from his mind. Maybe he couldn't eat solid food, but the wine flowed down his throat quite easily.

King Draculesti waited until his queen engaged Margyth in conversation before he leaned in his direction and whispered exclusively for his ears, "Slow down, Janczi, do you want to stagger away from the table? If you aren't going to eat anything, then you should refrain from having anymore wine. Honestly, I've offered my assistance, you but need to ask."

Perhaps it was the wine, but he did give a fleeting thought to changing his mind before he rushed to apologize to the good angel for the wicked yearning. He wanted no other buzz in his head but the one already caused by the wine he'd consumed.

Responding to his godfather's *sotto voce* reprimand, he whispered, "If you want to be of help, make sure this evening ends early. I think I've exhausted my ability to engage in polite conversation for the evening."

He was not at all surprised, therefore, when his godfather, just as soon as the women rejoined them after the port had been served and consumed, stood and announced he and the queen were for bed. The king even managed to include Margyth in the royal announcement.

"Margyth, tomorrow is your big day and it will be quite a late one. Why don't you let my godson escort you and your mother to your rooms so you can get a good night's sleep? He tells me tomorrow is free of activities. Everyone can sleep as late as they want, and there will be no fixed times for breakfast or lunch. He has arranged for everyone to serve themselves at whatever hour they find convenient. As you know, dinner will be served as part of the engagement ball."

Janos grinned wryly at his godfather over the top of Margyth's head. Leave it to a Draculesti to take a suggestion and make it a royal command. He bowed to Baroness Szechenyi and took Margyth's arm as he asked, "May I escort you back to your rooms?"

He could sense the waves of anger radiating from Margyth, but he would go to his grave before asking her what had sparked her temper. As it turned out, he had barely closed the bedroom door behind the Baroness Szechenyi when Margyth rounded on him as he escorted her to her room.

"I will not have your whore live in this castle. If you must continue the affair with your trumped-up artist, you will do so far enough away from here to keep up appearances."

Janos was taken aback at such a blatant attack. "Baroness Baranyi is not going to be my mistress, Margyth, she—"

"Oh, don't lie to me, Szigi. The lust in your eyes each time you look at her is embarrassing, and she all but undresses you every time she casts her eyes in your direction. You can't think I'm so naïve I'd believe you two haven't had each other in every room of this cold pile of stones, but she is not the one marrying you, is she? I demand you respect me by being discreet."

Margyth's harsh words set his heart aflame, and it

warmed his frozen heart at last. Her direct attack required a response, and, by the gods, he was happy to deliver it.

"Respect is earned, not demanded, and you have not earned it. You want the truth? The truth is I despise you, but I gave my word to your father to marry you, and a Rackoszi keeps his word, even though he might find it personally repugnant.

"Have Baroness Baranyi and I made love? Yes, we have, although not in every room of this castle, but I wish we had. She has refused to be my mistress, and after she leaves, it would have compensated for the few times I intend to take you to my bed. You will stay in this, as you've called it, cold pile of stones, until you give me an heir, and once you have, you may do whatever you damned well please in Vienna. Oh yes, I know quite a bit about you, Margyth Szechenyi. I know you are a wanton, a greedy, grasping woman, and one who has a very poor opinion of the man she is to marry. The wine bottle you threw after my pet the other night was observed by one who saw you walk back from Pal Anton's room. Even stone walls have eyes, my dear.

"As long as we are being honest with each other let me say, I don't care for you enough to place a lot of restrictions on you, save one. I will not countenance you foisting another man's bastard on me. I don't intend to live with you in Vienna, so you will have to practice a modicum of discretion with any lover you take. A word of warning, should you find yourself pregnant by any of them, I will cut you off without a forint, and you and your mother can walk the streets to keep body and soul together."

At the mention of Vienna, Janos noted guilt flit briefly over Margyth's face. "You are not as discreet as you think you are, my dear. I know of your plans to live the high life in Vienna. I also know you are many times past being a virgin, so there will be no need to use a vial of blood, which I am sure you have brought with you to dupe me into believing you come to my bed unsullied.

"Let me give you a further lesson in the differences between us. Once we announce our engagement, I can continue to have congress with other women, should I so choose, but you cannot. Why? Because if you deliver a child before nine months after our official wedding, I will declare it a bastard and you an adulteress. I will dissolve the wedding and your income with all the speed a Viceroy of Transylvania has at his disposal."

Janos had to close his eyes from the zing of pain sent right between his eyes when a solution to this whole entanglement came to him. "There is a way to enjoy the life you want, Margyth, and I don't know why I didn't think of this sooner, except to say I couldn't get past the fact I'd given my word to your father. While you might have to walk down the aisle, you don't have to say yes at the end of it. Be truthful for once, Margyth. You don't like me, much less love me. You don't want to live in my ancestral home or even in this part of Hungary, or with a man who will hold you in contempt for as long as we both draw breath. Say the word, and I will craft a story to take all the blame for a broken engagement."

Conflicting emotions raced across Margyth's face, and he dared to hope she'd, for once in her life, think of someone other than herself. Hope fled when she used her index finger to prod him in the chest.

"I know exactly why you want me to call our marriage off. You want to keep your damned honor intact and have the Baranyi bitch with a guilt-free conscience. Well, I'm not in a mood to be generous, especially after the things you've just said to me. You, Szigi darling, are my passage out of this boring backwater. If I don't marry you, I'll be stuck marrying some country bumpkin and raising his lumpish heirs. I'm serving notice, if you attempt to break your word, I will see to it a very large, very black blot stains the Rackoszi escutcheon, my oh-so-honorable prince."

Janos squared his shoulders and reached around Margyth and opened the door. "I bid you good night, then. Sleep well. Tomorrow will be a very, very long day." He didn't bother waiting for her to enter her room as was polite. He just didn't care anymore.

His satisfaction with having delivered Margyth's much-deserved set down evaporated as he undressed for the evening. The truth was, making her aware of his contempt for her had changed nothing. It wouldn't make her change her ways, it wouldn't prevent his engagement or marriage, and it wouldn't keep Bibi in his arms.

Tired of introspection, Janos crossed the room and poured himself a healthy glass of whisky to cajole his brain into giving him some relief from his painful catalog of injustices. But just as he seated himself in front of the fire, he spotted the covered miniatures on the mantel and his one-sided dialog continued. Uncover them or wait until the whisky gave him some liquid courage? He remained seated and sipped the whisky until he emptied the glass. Sufficiently numb around the edges, he stood and uncovered the first of the tiny paintings.

It was Margyth's painting, and he picked up the printed translation of the traditional Russian folk tale to read: Long years ago, Faerie Spring and Mighty Winter were lovers. Although their love faded and died, they were bound together by the child born to them, the lovely Snegurochka, The Snow Maiden. She was safe from death by the sun's rays only so long as love for a man did not enter her heart.

Janos backed away from the painting, the better to study it. And here was Margyth in all her splendor. Bibi painted her in an ice-blue, fitted-waist coat, trimmed at collar, cuffs, and hem with ermine. The Snow Maiden was walking in a forest whose fir trees were heavy with snow, and the sun shining down was so bright it made him want to squint. The sole dab of warm color in the entire portrait was a grinning red fox impudently peeking from around the hem of Margyth's coat. He had to shake his head at the artist's cleverness. She'd given the fox Pal Anton's grin, and the same shade of red as the hussar's own hair.

Even though there was little love between Margyth and Bibi, the artist had not stinted on reproducing her natural beauty. The Snow Maiden had the long golden locks Margyth took such pride in, and adorned them with a diadem of diamond snowflakes. The effect was a cold, ethereal beauty which captured her perfectly. She was breath-catchingly beautiful, and bone-chillingly cold. No man would ever capture this Snow Maiden's heart.

He was about to uncover the remaining painting, but his eyes detected another small spot of color. Drawing closer, he discovered it was centered in a gray shadow under the low boughs of a snow-laden fir tree. As he concentrated on it, he discerned a wolf, one with yellow eyes and fangs exposed in a snarl. A wolf who would forever be consigned to the shadows of Margyth's overexposed life. His realization forced him away from the miniature and back to the whisky decanter.

He didn't know how long he sat there just sipping the smoky liquid and staring at Margyth's portrait. One hour? Two? He almost wanted to check himself for a mortal wound because it felt as if his life-blood was draining from his body. "Damn you, Bibi, you see too much." After uttering the oath, he surged from the chair and uncovered his portrait. He returned to his seat after snatching the printed explanation from beneath the painting.

She had chosen to paint him in military attire, complete with half cape and saber, but the light illuminating his portrait was the opalescence of the moon. He was astride Anubis, whose haunches showed the strain of maintaining the difficult angle of a perfect levade. From this position, the rider would be able to survey the terrain before him.

Janos whistled in admiration of Bibi's skill. His portrait was designed to be viewed as if the moon was shining down on him. Remembering the printed explanation, he began to read.

Prince Elisey had traveled to the far corners of the kingdom in his search for his beloved. Long did he grieve, and everywhere he visited he asked if anyone had seen his princess. But alas, no one had. In desperation, he waited for nightfall, and when the moon rose, he asked, "Moon, dear Moon, have you seen any trace of my beloved?"

As the gods were his witness, he did not want to look at the face Bibi had painted for him, but he was helpless to keep himself from doing so. The empty glass fell from his nerveless fingers, and he slid from the chair to kneel in front of the fire with his hands covering his face. He'd seen what he'd expected to see. Frustration, yearning, love, but most of all, a deep sorrow for what would never be. This Prince Elisey was not destined to find his beloved. To anyone else who viewed the miniature, he would appear handsome, rather stern-visaged, but altogether a heroic figure. Janos closed his eyes in shame at the self-realization he was far from being a hero and closer to being a coward.

The large amount of alcohol he'd consumed this evening must be the reason for his inability to stop the tears pouring from his eyes as he regained his seat and stared at the light and dark paintings revealing the unfortunate truth of his life.

Chapter Twenty-Three

Akos replaced the delicate teacup into its matching saucer with an audible click and earned a silent rebuke from Erzsebet. "Sorry, I'm worried about the prince. It's time to wake him, but I don't know what emotional state he'll be in after he's seen Baroness Baranyi's paintings. They are exquisite in detail and color, and she's painted the prince quite handsomely, but there is something in his visage which suggests sadness. I tell you, Erzsebet, she is an extremely talented artist for she captured Margyth's soullessness perfectly. How the prince will be able to marry her after seeing the miniature is beyond me. I wonder if he even got any sleep. Today will be a very long one if he isn't rested. It would be bad form to appear at his own engagement with a pale and drawn face."

Erzsebet interrupted his fretting. "Here, if you discover the prince has had a bad evening, put this in his wine before you hand it to him."

He hesitated before taking the twist of paper from the housekeeper.

"Stop looking at me as if I'm giving you poison. It is a sleeping potion. A very weak one. The prince should sleep for a few hours and then he'll be refreshed enough to play gracious host to the invited locals and his godparents. I'm sure Margyth will be too busy basking in everyone's attention to notice whether or not the prince is at the top of his form."

Akos hesitated in the hallway outside the prince's door and checked the pocket of his waistcoat for the draught Erzsebet had given him. Yes, still there. After taking a deep breath, he opened the door and gave a small gasp of fright when he discovered the prince seated before the ashes of the previous evening's fire. The miniatures were uncovered and still on the mantel.

"Come and have a look, Akos. Baroness Baranyi paints beautifully, doesn't she?"

His voice quavered as he responded to the prince's command and drew near the mantel. "Yes, yes she does. Here, Your Grace, I've your morning drink. Please drink all of it. It will give you the strength you need to face the day."

He'd emptied the sleeping potion into the special wine when he heard the deadness in the prince's voice and seen the prince's eyes devoid of their usual spark. The distraught man had not been to bed at all. Well, between himself and Erzsebet, His Grace would at least have several hours of rest before the sun retired on this day.

***

What the hell? He was still abed, and, judging by the darkness in his bedroom, the sun had set. The last thing he remembered was Akos placing a warm, damp cloth over his face in preparation for his morning shave.

"Oh excellent, Your Grace. I was coming to wake you. It's time for your bath and then I'll dress you for the evening."

Janos threw the covers off and peered up at his valet in

consternation. "How is it, Akos, I'm still wearing my clothes but I'm in bed?"

Akos had a guilty look as he replied, "I was preparing to shave you, Your Grace, but when I unwrapped the towel from your face you were sound asleep. So sound asleep, you didn't even wake when I had a footman help carry you to bed. I assumed you hadn't rested well and needed more sleep. This evening will be a busy one for you.

"Here, your bath is ready. Why don't you enjoy a nice soak while I retrieve your decorations?"

"Decorations? Why, for God's sake, are you trotting those out?"

"It is your godfather's request. He sent a note around while you were asleep to remind you he intends to wear his and wants you to do the same. I'm assuming he wants you to shine as much as Margyth will this evening, Your Grace."

He gifted his valet with a grimace. So, this evening was going to be interminable and a parade of peacocks. Could his life descend to even lower depths of absurdity? Noooo, he wouldn't think such thoughts. He pointed his mind in another direction before his mental imps could chime in with an answer.

Janos held still while his valet fussed with the crimson silk sash edged in green, where it bisected his body from right shoulder to left hip. After satisfying himself it hung correctly, Akos affixed the Order of Saint Stephen to it at the hip and the eight-pointed star on his left breast. Even his muttered, "Damned heavy baubles," wouldn't deter his servant from adding the decoration of a red dragon ouroboros underneath the collar points of his stiff white dress shirt.

He suffered in silence because his godfather would be disappointed if he didn't wear the Order of Saint Stephen of Hungary. He was a Grand Cross Knight, and as such, the Austrian Emperor had to address him as *Cousin*. He'd been told many times by his godfather how proud it made him to have Janos, and his father before him, be recipients of Hungary's highest decoration.

As to the Order of the Dragon, King Draculesti wore his award proudly, as it seemed aptly named for himself. Draculesti meant dragon in Rumanian. He'd received his award for his continued alliance with the Austrian Emperor. Janos suspected he himself was a recipient because of his service to the emperor and some backstairs campaigning by his godfather.

"Well, am I dazzling enough?" He held his hands away from his body and did a slow turn for his valet's inspection.

"Yes indeed, Your Grace. Margyth will have to share your guests' admiration with you."

A knock on the door cut off further conversation, and Akos withdrew as he waved him away, before he bade whoever it was to enter. He was surprised when Erzsebet, followed meekly by Cata rather than Margyth and her mother, entered his sitting room. He'd sent word earlier to the Szechenyi women they could view the miniatures when they were finished dressing.

"Good evening, Erzsebet, Cata. Is there something you need?"

"Yes, Your Grace, I need to tender my resignation."

The prince stared quizzically at his housekeeper when Erzsebet placed the keys of her duty as housekeeper on his desk. "Erzsebet, whatever are you about? Have I done something to offend you?"

"No, Your Grace, *you* haven't, but your intended has." Erzsebet turned and called Cata out from where she'd been hiding behind her skirts. "Show him, Cata. The prince needs to see this for himself."

Janos caught his breath in dismay at the sight of the ugly burn on the girl's arm. "How did you burn yourself, Cata?"

But before the maid could respond, Erzsebet answered his question.

"Cata didn't burn herself, Margyth burned her. She was angry because Cata accidentally pulled her hair when she was dressing it for the evening and used the hot curling iron to punish her.

"I've held my tongue concerning your intention to marry Margyth, Your Grace, but I'll do so no longer. I am giving notice. It's time I retired. I prefer to be the one giving notice rather than have Margyth tell me my service is no longer needed when she becomes the lady of this castle."

When he opened his mouth to protest, Erzsebet held up her hand. "No, Your Grace, I'll not stay to witness your intended practice her cruelty on anyone else. I, at least, have a small cottage to retire to, but the rest of the people who serve you may not. They will be forced to stay and suffer.

"It is time to ask yourself, Prince Rackoszi, whether keeping your word to Baron Szechenyi, a man who took his own life because he'd irretrievably shamed himself, is more important than ensuring the people who depend on you for their livelihoods are treated with respect and kindness."

The forceful tone of voice used by his mental prod made him pay closer attention as he seated himself ungracefully at his desk.

Your housekeeper has just pointed out what you should have been considering all along. You wanted a way out of this intolerable dilemma, and she has just given you a greater justification than Margyth being a bad influence on your children. Is the desire of one, dissolute man, who failed in his duty as husband and father, more important than the needs of the many people who are loyal to you and depend on you? What good is it to keep your word if it harms many and benefits only the one who doesn't deserve to profit from it?

From long experience, Janos waited for the fallen imp's input, and he wasn't disappointed.

Damn, I was hoping you never had such a question put to you, but I never foresaw Margyth herself would be the one to precipitate it. Oh well, I may be fallen, but I'm not a sore loser. Besides, the abnegation of your promise will make Margyth and her mother easier to win over to my master's side. I doubt I'll be punished for this loss when I return with two souls.

As suddenly as the voices started, they stopped, and he felt clearheaded for the first time since Bibi entered his domain. Clearheaded and lethally resolved. Glancing at the miniatures on his mantel, molten steel flowed through his veins as he picked up the dagger he used as a letter opener and nicked the end of his finger.

"Come here, Cata. I will take the pain away." When the

timid maid held out her arm, he rubbed it with the blood welling from his finger and smiled at her obvious relief when the nanos in his blood repaired the burn. "There, all better."

After licking his small wound closed, Janos picked up Erzsebet's keys and handed them back to her. "Your resignation is not accepted. You will go to the Szechenyi rooms and inform mother and daughter I have requested their presence in my suite.

"Once they leave their rooms, I want you to inform the stable master to have the Szechenyi carriage ready for immediate departure, and then I want you to pack up all of their possessions and have them transferred to the carriage. You will return here and inform me when all is completed. I don't think I need to tell either of you this is not a subject for dissemination. When the time is right to give an explanation for the Szechenyis' sudden departure, I will be the one to do so."

The prince had to admire Erzsebet, she didn't comment or gloat at her victory but picked up her keys and shepherded Cata from the room.

"Shall I leave before Margyth and her mother get here, Your Grace?"

Janos spun around at the question. He'd forgotten his valet had been in his dressing room and had heard the conversation between Erzsebet and himself. Smiling ruefully, he shook his head. "No, Akos. I want you to stay but remain hidden in the dressing room. I might need your immediate assistance to repair my clothing after Margyth and her mother hear what needs to be said.

"After they leave, please have a footman carry the miniatures to the small room off the ballroom. I'm sure my guests will enjoy them."

When the knock sounded, he waited until Akos withdrew to call, "Enter."

Margyth swept into his rooms as if she was already in residence in the Mistress Suite. Before she could rush to his side, Janos diverted her attention. "Margyth, the miniature Baroness Baranyi painted of you is above the fireplace." He pointed to the mantel, and she and her mother swept past him as if he weren't in the room.

"Oh, come and look, Mama, aren't I beautiful? The baroness has more talent than I'd credited her with."

He noted Margyth did not bother reading the printed explanation of the folk tales. It was just as well. He doubted she'd get the symbolism. Margyth gave voice to displeasure when she inspected his portrait. "Szigi, I take back my praise of your artist. She did not do you justice. Your painting is dull compared to mine."

Having given Bibi's miniatures all the attention she felt they deserved, Margyth crossed the room to stand before him after completing a twirl. "Well, what do you think? Am I not a sight to do you proud as your fiancée?"

Margyth was choosing to believe she'd won last night's argument, but he would set her straight. "Sorry to disappoint you, Margyth, but you are not." As he'd expected, his comment earned him the instant wrath of both women.

Baroness Szechenyi stepped forward, and with a red, mottled face demanded, "Explain yourself, Your Grace. What do you mean by this insult to my daughter?"

With a coldly indifferent stare, he noted the baroness had eschewed deep mourning for a dress of dove gray. He almost laughed in her face when the aberrant comparison popped into his mind the Baroness Szechenyi was, in dress as well as fact, a true eminence grise. And since she was, he needed to confront her, not her self-indulgent daughter.

"I mean exactly what I say, Baroness. Your daughter is not worthy to be my wife. Her mistreatment of one of my staff this evening has unmasked her cruelty, and I won't condone having such a viper in my house, even if it means going back on my word as a Rackoszi."

Margyth interrupted in a shrill voice. "But she tugged my hair. She probably did it deliberately, the stupid cow."

"And for such a piffling injury she deserved to be severely burned rather than given a reprimand?" Not letting Margyth respond, he once again turned his attention to Baroness Szechenyi. "I've already pointed this out to your daughter last evening, but you, Madame, have raised a selfish, spoiled, cruel, wanton child. Your daughter believes the world revolves around her and demands it continue to do so. I'm sorry, but I find such behavior quite objectionable.

"I gave my word to your husband I would marry his daughter, but her continued despicable actions outweigh a promise made out of sympathy for a ruined man. It wouldn't surprise me at all to discover your husband killed himself so I couldn't change my mind once I got to know her character. Although the both of you deserve to spend the rest of your lives in poverty, the generosity my parents instilled in me requires I do not cast you penniless from this room."

Janos held up his hand to stop the baroness's remonstration. "Pay attention, Madame, for your future well-being depends on it. I am calling in the baron's markers. Your husband legally gave up his ownership of his property when he signed those gambling chits, and I became the legal owner when I bought them. I intended to give them back to you as a wedding present, but due to your appalling behavior, I will retain possession of them. Though you are unworthy of any good will on my part, I will still provide you a decent income."

"If you are trying to insult me by offering charity, Prince Rackoszi, you'd best beware. I am not one to take an insult lightly."

"You think I'm insulting you? If I am, I am taking a page from your own book, Baroness. You have done nothing but insult me by calling me a revenant, trying to kill my wolf, speaking disparagingly of me to your daughter, and being rude to my staff and guests. You have no right to be insulted. Do not let your misplaced pride speak for you before you consider the repercussions, Madame, or I will happily show you how a Rackoszi repays such attempts at intimidation."

Margyth all but pushed her mother aside. "Szigi, darling, I know we had words last night, but it was just pre-wedding nerves. If you don't care for my mother, you needn't worry. After we are wed, Momma can go live with one of her relatives and she won't bother you at all."

Prince Rackoszi turned a sardonic eye on the red-faced baroness. "Such a loving daughter you've nurtured at your breast, Baroness. Margyth, perhaps you were so busy twirling around in all of your finery, you failed to take the meaning of my words. I am not marrying you. I am evicting you from your home."

Seeing his words had at last made an impression on the self-centered woman, he continued, "Since you voiced a desire to live in Vienna, I will grant you your wish. I will instruct my man of affairs to purchase a town house in a good section of Vienna, and you and your mother will live there. You may inform anyone who cares to ask that you are my ward. I will provide a dowry of sufficient size to attract suitors."

Janos held up his hand to silence the lie before Margyth could give it to excuse her behavior. "I suggest you find an older man to wed who has sufficient wealth to afford you, and one who will sacrifice having a faithful wife for the pleasure of being seen in public with you on his arm. Oh, and I would do so quickly because my offer of a dowry has a two-year limit. I want you and your mother gone from here within the month, and, Baroness, once your daughter is wed, you will not return. You'd best hope Margyth manages to find a small reservoir of filial kindness to provide for your welfare after she secures a husband."

He had to admire Margyth's sense of self-preservation, for the woman wrung her hands and pleaded quite prettily with her eyes as she addressed him in a forlorn voice. "Szigi, how can you embarrass me so in front of all our guests? What will they think when I don't appear by your side in the ballroom?"

"They will think you have begged off the engagement. I will take the blame for this, Margyth. I will tell anyone who cares to listen you wish to experience more of the world before settling down to married life. You are young and attractive, so I doubt people will find fault with my explanation."

Janos was relieved when, with one knock, Erzsebet entered his suite to announce the Szechenyi carriage was ready.

Bowing to the silent women, he swept his hand to the door. "Your carriage will take you home. Erzsebet will lead you down the servants' stairs and out through the kitchen. The guests are starting to arrive and I would spare you the embarrassment of having to explain your departure. You will also find all of your possessions have been packed for you and are on the carriage as well."

Finished with the mother and daughter, the prince turned his back on them and did not turn around until the door to his suite slammed closed. "You may show yourself, Akos."

For an instant, he almost lost his composure at the sincere appearance of concern on his valet's face. "Don't fret, Akos. I'm quite all right. In fact, I think this calls for a celebratory drink, and pour one for yourself as well. It isn't often one can start a day off badly and have it end so happily.

"What should we toast to? Any suggestions, Akos?"

"I think, Your Grace, we should toast to a woman, a very beautiful and talented one. To the Baroness Baranyi."

"Here, here. I couldn't have come up with a better toast." Janos clinked glasses with his valet and drained his glass. "Wish me luck, I go to play the dejected, spurned man."

"I doubt you will have to play the part long, Your Grace. Every unmarried woman at the ball will do her utmost to brighten your spirits."

***

At any other time, Bibi would have been fretting at Cata's late appearance to help her dress but not this evening. She had no wish to attend the engagement ball. If her dresser didn't arrive until midnight, it still would have been too soon to suit her.

The maid's flustered arrival, and voluble apologies for her lateness, soon had her more intent on soothing the maid than dwelling on her own problems.

With all of the preparations her special dress needed, there was no time to worry about what the evening would hold in store for her or Janos. At least she would have friends there, Pal Anton and Countess Krisztina would quash any blue mood she had. Besides, she adored dancing, and Pal Anton would partner her for one waltz at least.

"Upon my honor, Baroness, every woman at the ball will be green with envy. I've never handled such a beautiful gown. You will have every woman, even the royals, marching to Paris to find your *modiste*. But even if they found her, they still wouldn't be as lovely as you. Your beauty comes from within, not through fabric and jewelry."

"I know you don't wear curls, but you should. You are over-the-moon beautiful with your hair styled this way."

At such effusive praise, Bibi was almost afraid to approach the full-length cheval glass to discover what miracle Cata had wrought this evening. She couldn't believe it was her own image staring back at her.

The gown had a pointed waist done in dark-rose silk brocade with a wide open *décolleté* and short sleeves with a lighter shade of pink silk rose affixed to each shoulder. The widely belled silk brocade skirt, courtesy of several petticoats, was the same shade of deep rose, but it was layered with three colors of pink silk organza in shades of bright to palest pink, with the outermost being the very faintest blush.

She turned her head slightly, and the ringlets Cata fashioned swayed with the movement. Cata had fashioned long ringlets with the curling iron, and they were held away from her face by a deep-rose, velvet ribbon with another lighter silk rose sewn to the band at her temple.

Not wanting to lessen the effect of the dress, Bibi had chosen a single strand of pigeon-blood rubies at her throat, and matching teardrop earrings. Her dancing slippers were also silk and a coordinating shade of pink with roses gracing the tops. Opera-length gloves of pale-pink kidskin completed her ensemble.

It had been her intention to upstage Margyth this evening, but one sight of the magnificent stranger staring back at her from the mirror, and she was certain she'd upstaged herself. The total package was over-the-top, and she didn't think she had the sophistication to carry it off.

As if sensing her self-doubt, Cata placed a leaf-green lacquered fan in her hand and turned her toward the door.

"Go join the other guests, Baroness. It would be a sin to waste this gown on the inside of this room. This may be an engagement ball, but it is also to showcase your work as a talented artist. I haven't seen your paintings yet, but Akos hasn't stopped singing your praise."

Before Bibi had a chance to protest, she found herself in the hall with her bedroom door closed behind her. Ah well, who was she to disappoint her maid?

Her nervousness left her at the first sight of Pal Anton in his dress uniform. The hussar was, simply stated, magnificent. The white of his uniform was brilliant enough, but the amount of gold trim on the dolman he wore blinded the eye. A leopard-skin half cape, tied diagonally across his chest, was sure to make even married women forget themselves and flirt outrageously.

She almost dissolved in giggles when she caught sight of the bevy of young ladies the hussar had already attracted to his side, but Pal was at her side and swinging her onto the dance floor before she could even form a compliment.

"What on earth are you doing, Pal? The musicians haven't started playing yet."

"What I am doing is giving everyone here the chance to admire a beautiful woman. You take my breath away, Baroness Baranyi. My cousin will scream in rage when she spies you."

"Well, my attractiveness has good company, Pal." Bibi pointed to one of the floor-to-ceiling, gilt-edged mirrors lining the ballroom. If I am beautiful, then you are handsome. Your dress uniform does you justice, Pal Anton. No woman will turn you away when you request a dance."

Pal favored her with a wide grin and backed away just enough to bow and twirl to show the half cape he wore over one shoulder to good effect. "Do you really think so?"

"You scamp, you don't need my opinion, you already know so." Bibi offered the small dance card she'd hung from her wrist. "Here, my friendly peacock. You can be the first one to sign my dance card."

"Would it be uncouth of me to fill in all of the slots?" Pal winked.

"Yes it would, and you well know it. Oh, the prince has entered with his godfather, King Alexandru."

"Well the sooner they open this dance, the sooner I can claim you as my partner," Pal teased but fell silent as Prince Rackoszi held up his hands to quiet the general murmur of conversation.

"Friends and honored relatives, a moment of your attention, please. You've come here tonight to honor me by celebrating my engagement. Unfortunately, I must apologize. There will not be an engagement. My intended has had a change of heart. She wishes to travel before settling down to be a wife and mother."

As the assembly voiced their shock, the prince again pleaded for quiet. "Please, do not be concerned for either of us. Margyth will, I am sure, eventually find someone who will complete her, and I intend to just spend this evening enjoying the company of good friends and close relatives. I also want to give you the opportunity of viewing the miniatures painted by a very talented artist who's become a dear friend, Baroness Beatrix Celine Baranyi."

Bibi blushed when the prince pointed her out to the assembly before continuing.

"Baroness Baranyi's miniatures are on display in the room immediately to the left of the dining room, and you can view them at your leisure before the midnight meal is served. I'm sure the baroness would be happy to entertain requests for painting your own portraits, should you desire to do so.

"Come friends, let me open this dance on the arm of my godmother, Queen Lucretia." The prince swung his petite godmother onto the floor and the dance was officially opened. Not to be out shown, Pal waited the correct amount of time before leading Bibi onto the floor, and it was the signal for everyone to do likewise.

As she expected, he asked her if she had any idea what had happened to occasion the unexpected announcement. She shook her head to say she hadn't, but she was surprised, and not a little shocked, when he whispered an unusual sentiment in her ear.

"Well, I for one am relieved on the prince's behalf. He is too good a man to deserve spending a life of misery with Margyth."

***

Janos stopped dead the moment he entered the ballroom and spotted Bibi. He was unable to resume motion until King Alexandru's hand clamped down on his shoulder and propelled him forward with a whispered admonition.

"Think, Jancsi. You're about to announce being rejected as a suitor. You will send the wrong message if you immediately fly to Baroness Baranyi's side, and then everyone will think they know the reason for Margyth's rejection."

Although annoyed to be reined in, his godfather had the right of it, and so he vowed to behave with decorum this evening as he continued to the middle of the dance floor to make his announcement.

As it was, he had to apologize to his godmother, Queen Lucretia, for stepping on her toes when Pal Anton whirled by with Bibi on his arm. Her dress was as much a masterpiece as her paintings, but what had his fangs punching out and nicking the inside of his mouth was the sight of the single strand of blood-red rubies she wore. They resembled drops of blood on the whiteness of her neck, and he remembered all too well the sweetness of the essence of Bibi.

He closed his eyes against the distraction, the better to keep the tempo and his feet from hurting his godmother yet again. But it was a futile attempt to keep the sight of Baroness Baranyi from his mind. It was as if his gardener waved an enchanted wand over one of his prized roses, and the rose became a most beautiful woman. Even her scent lingered in his nostrils. Tuber rose and musk. No faint horse aroma this evening, although, truth to tell, he wouldn't have found it off-putting. The dance ended, and Janos looked down at his godmother's unsmiling, serious face.

"Alexandru was right to caution you, Janos. There will be time enough tomorrow when all of your guests are gone to pay your suit to the baroness." When her godson's eyes searched the ballroom for Bibi, she tugged at his sleeve to center his attention once more. "But you are free to dance with her this evening, just not every dance."

His godmother needn't have worried. Baroness Baranyi was much sought after as a dance partner. It wasn't until just before the midnight dinner he had the opportunity of asking for a dance. Janos handed her punch cup to Pal Anton and bowed to Bibi. Her blush was adorable, and he instantly wanted to be alone with her to watch as it suffused her entire body, but he restrained himself and offered his arm to escort her onto the dance floor. At his signal, the musicians played the waltz he'd requested.

Janos leaned closer and whispered into her ear. "You are the most beautiful woman here this evening. Indeed, you are the most beautiful woman I've ever had the privilege of holding in my arms, Bibi. I'll admit to being jealous of every man who's danced with you this evening."

Bibi smiled up at him and teased, "Even the portly mayor of the village with the frizzled mutton-chop side whiskers?"

"Especially him. He doesn't deserve to hold such an exquisite jewel so close to his belly."

"Prince Rackoszi, you are being most indelicate."

Janos was relieved to discover Bibi was teasing rather than reprimanding him. "I will forgive him because having you in his arms was probably the high-water mark of his life."

"How outrageous to think so," Bibi tried to state with a straight face.

"Outrageous? Definitely not. Have you not met the mayor's wife?"

"Yes, I have. She was the one you charmed with little effort as you danced the *czardas* with her. Your decorations were making stars in her eyes as you spun her around the floor."

He snorted at the sally and changed the subject. "My dear, I've wanted nothing more than to shock everyone by dancing every dance with you this evening, but I didn't want to embarrass you."

"For my part, I am sorry about your broken engagement, Janos. I know you didn't want to marry Margyth, but I'm sorry you had to suffer the embarrassment of announcing it."

"Thank you. Bibi, the dance is about to end, so let me say this quickly. I will explain everything if you will come to my room after everyone departs. I know it will be quite late, but there are things we need to discuss. Please say you'll come?"

"As you wish, Prince Rackoszi."

He would keep his distance from Baroness Baranyi for the remainder of the ball, but not for life or limb would he keep himself from kissing the back of her hand as the dance ended and he escorted her back to his Cousin Krisztina's side. Knowing he'd have her all to himself at the end of this day energized him enough to enjoy the formal dinner. He was even able to restrain his growl of jealousy when he noted Pal Anton making his artist blush with his teasing and singular attention from his place at her side.

Chapter Twenty-Four

Bibi was grateful for the late hour and Cata's tiredness. It meant she didn't have to explain why she was dismissing her as soon as her dress was unbuttoned. "Thank you, Cata, you may retire. I think I'm quite capable of getting myself into my nightgown."

"But, Baroness, what of your hair? I will brush it out for you."

"Not necessary, Cata. If I can brush out the tangled manes of horses, I believe I can do the same for my own locks. Goodnight, and thank you again for being such a wonderful lady's maid."

Ah, thank God, the tired woman did not need to be cajoled but withdrew without further protest and closed the door behind herself.

Reminiscent of her late-night raids to the Horthy kitchen in search of a sweet treat, she ducked down the servants' stairs and cut a generous slice of the first cake she'd happened across. Her hand shook, and the fork rattled against the delicate porcelain plate, as she carried it to her rendezvous with the prince.

Grasping the dessert plate more firmly, she wondered if her hand trembled because she was nervous about visiting Janos's suite so late at night with the offer of a shared sweet, or perhaps it was anticipation of making love with him one last time. Yes, it would be the last time, considering what she'd overheard when she sought out King Draculesti to bid him goodbye after he'd announced to all at the table he and his queen would be leaving as soon as the ball ended to get an early start on their journey back to Wallachia.

She hadn't meant to eavesdrop, but she arrived on the terrace just off the ballroom in time to hear him tell his godson, he would insist the newly free prince find a wife from among their kind. She withdrew before Janos could respond. She didn't want to be discovered, and if the prince acceded to his godfather's wish, she didn't want to hear it.

As Janos opened his door to her soft knock, she noted the prince had thrown his silk dressing gown over his trousers. Proffering the plate, she asked, "May I come in?"

Swinging the door wide, Prince Rackoszi replied, "Of course, please come in."

Such formality between them gave her pause. Was Janos rethinking his earlier request she visit him in his rooms? Was he in agreement with his godfather's earlier dictum?

"I'm sorry, Your Highness, if you've changed your mind and want me to go...."

"Gods no, of all things I want, your absence is not one of them." Janos stared pointedly at the *dobos torte*. "You've come bearing dessert, may I ask why?"

Cutting a small bite, Bibi lifted it and stopped just short of his lips. "The first night we dined together you gave me a taste of bliss, so I'm returning the favor."

"Oh yes, please." And he wrapped his arms around her waist as he closed his eyes and opened his mouth.

The tug of his lips on the fork did wonderful things to the

very center of her as she waited for the prince to open his eyes. She was startled when Janos began shaking like a leaf and hurriedly placed the plate on the nearby fireplace mantel.

"Your Grace, you're trembling, are you unwell?"

Moving again into her embrace, he nestled closer. "Truthfully, I have never felt so lost. Even after making love to you, I believed I could still marry Margyth. I'd given my word, after all. I thought it would be the best course after you discovered what I really am. Even though we've made love several times, I didn't believe you would accept a husband who was not exactly human, especially since I haven't shown you all an Atlantean can be.

"Margyth, on the other hand, was more than agreeable to marriage, despite her mother labeling me a revenant. I have little doubt she'd care if I was an immortal or a two-headed circus freak, as long as she had a title, generous funds, and lovers on the side. It was poor Cata who showed me how wrong I was to continue to cling to my word."

The prince continued his explanation when Bibi made a quizzical sound. "Margyth used a hot curling iron to burn Cata's arm as punishment for causing her a small discomfort. You know Cata would never have done so deliberately, but Margyth enjoys being cruel. I couldn't honor such a woman with the Rackoszi name."

"But here you stand offering to feed me with your own hand, and I, a being of immense power, am left shaking with regret for even thinking of giving you up. I want to devour your body until you will cleave only to me, Bibi. I want to give you so much pleasure you will wake the castle with your screams. Will you let me make love to you in the manner of my people? I would show you ecstasy as you have shown me love."

Bibi disengaged and stepped back. She was dismayed when a cold mask descended to hide the prince's emotions. It dismayed her to think he had interpreted her small retreat as a rejection, and before he could speak, she untied the sash of her robe and shrugged it off her shoulders.

"I know taking blood is very sensual for you. I also know, having experienced your lovemaking, you can be very gentle and giving, so your offer does not frighten me. Make love to me, my prince. Show me how a descendent of Atlantis makes love."

As the prince's hands started to loosen the belt of his robe, she stilled them and untied the robe and opened the buttons of his trousers for him. When he stepped out of his clothes, she knelt and ran her hands up his legs and around his waist to cup his ass. She took her time to survey him with a saucy grin and a tease. "Of course, if you'd rather finish your cake first..."

***

The physical pain of his erection blossoming so quickly made Janos hiss. Bibi stood before him completely nude and waiting for him. She was waiting for whatever he had to show her with an assurance he would have been hard-pressed to duplicate.

He felt his fangs descend, and he called upon all of his

self-discipline to go slowly enough not to scare her with the transformation about to overtake him. But show her he would. Honesty was suddenly immensely important to him.

"Bibi, look at me."

He expected her to shrink away from him in fright, but once again his artist surprised him as he showed her a face sculpted into something so unique, she would have had a hard time duplicating it on paper. Her husky voice startled a shiver from him, as did the sensual touch of her fingertips as she sketched him with the only implement she had.

"Janos, words fail me. Your cheekbones are razor sharp, and my image in your eyes is surrounded by tongues of fire."

When she lifted his chin and touched the tip of one finger to a fang, a scarlet drop welled up.

As the rich, distinctive scent of her blood hit him, he groaned. "Bibi, you are destroying me. I want this to be a memorable evening for you, but I don't think my sanity will be safe if I can't have you right this very minute."

"Are all Atlantean males similar to stallions, then? Do they rush to cover the mare just once, and then have to be helped, staggering and weak-legged, back to their stall?"

Licking the blood from her finger, he responded, "Perhaps you can compare us to stallions in our virility, and the length of our organs, but we have much longer staying power. But why speculate when a third and fourth demonstration would be better proof?"

Giving him back his earlier words, she lifted her arms and embraced him. "Oh yes, please."

He had her in his arms and in his bed before she could

change her mind. A small nip at her earlobe, a sip at her breast, a taste of her navel, and one on the inside of her thigh set her squirming, but when he dipped his head to suck the nectar from the very core of her being, she began to plead. It pleased him, but he wanted more.

Although her signature scent of tuber rose and musk was driving him steadily mad, the memory of the sweet, coppery taste of her blood made him feral. In a last-ditch effort to slow things down, Janos captured her head between his hands and demanded she focus her attention on him.

"Do you truly want me?" He bared his fangs for her decision.

Thrusting her hips forward, she impaled herself and looked into his eyes. "How could you doubt it?"

He had no idea what happened after he bit her and took the first full, sinfully rich sip of her blood. They'd both climaxed, but whether she came first or he did was a moot point. If his hoarse shout or her scream woke anyone in the castle, he hoped they would be well trained enough to resist the temptation to investigate the noise.

He reluctantly loosened his arms when she turned to face him.

"Can you fly?"

With a startled exclamation, he asked, "Fly? No, I can't fly. Why? Do you think I turn into a bat and fly about the castle at night?"

"No, I don't think you turn into a bat, silly man. Although the image of you hanging upside down from the bed canopy as you slept paints an intriguing mental picture. I was just wondering how we got into this bed. I don't recall moving after you kissed my finger."

"Ah, let's just say I can change locations incredibly fast if the incentive is there." And he demonstrated by fetching the plate of cake from the mantel and returning to her side before she even felt his absence. He grinned at her huge, rounded eyes, and placed a small piece of the torte into her open mouth, and waited for her next question as she chewed and swallowed the cake.

"What other talents do you have? If I may be so bold as to inquire."

He smiled widely enough to display his full complement of fangs and waved the fork in a small arc. Immediately, the fire rose higher in the fireplace, and all of the candles in the room were suddenly lit.

"Impressive, very impressive."

"Child's play." Placing the empty plate on a side table, he rolled her over onto her stomach. If you want to be dazzled, I will show you how an Atlantean male covers his woman."

He lifted her hips from the mattress. "Hold on to the headboard and do not let go. I promised you ecstasy this evening and you shall have it."

Parting her legs with his knee, Janos entered Bibi's core with one finger and then two, assuring himself she was again ready to accept the full length of his cock. As he pinched her nipples into hard pebbles, he slammed the length of himself into her until he felt her honeyed nectar on his balls.

Amazing him yet again with her responsiveness, she groaned as she ground her hips into him again and again in counterpoint to his thrusts. He could tell by the trembling of her sheath she was very close to shattering, and leaned forward to cup her full breasts as he whispered into her ear. "You will feel what I feel while I am inside you. You will experience every sensation I feel as we make love. This is the real talent of Atlanteans, *kincsem*, and it's got nothing to do with nanos." He bit his wrist and made a small wound with his fangs. Offering his wrist, he commanded, "Drink, Beatrix Baranyi, and know me."

***

Bibi sipped and felt it all, and it was...she had no words. How do you describe the indescribable? With a keening wail she shattered, and everything exploded into white light. She felt him in her mind, as he felt her body making love to his. She felt his taut chest at her back, and even the sweet tension in his balls the moment before his hot sperm geysered into her, and then she felt nothing at all.

She awoke to the feel of Janos's arms around her, and his lips trailing featherlight kisses at her temple. "Did I faint?"

"I believe so, my love."

Snuggling farther into the prince's embrace, she asked, "Is it so overwhelmingly wonderful every time a male and female of your species make love?"

"Yes, it is, and until we become accustomed to each other, we usually both faint. The bonding is very intense for a while."

"Oh, Janos, I hope you find your bond mate. I would not wish you to be deprived of such an experience."

***

Bibi's sincere wish all but overwhelmed him. He wanted to tell her he had almost given the words to the bonding while he was deep inside her. Truly, with the very first taste of her blood, his mind had screamed *Mine!*

He tried to tell her he desired no other, needed no other, but he was unsure, and so the words remained unspoken. Would she mate with him and willingly tie herself to the limitations of his life? He hadn't told her any of the intricacies of what being bonded meant. Would she run from him if he told her bonded mates died if they lost their mate? Would she willingly submit to the arrogance and jealousy and protectiveness of an Atlantean male?

Realizing she had fallen asleep while he dithered, he gathered her into his arms and joined her in worshiping Nyx. Tomorrow morning would be soon enough to discuss things.

***

Bibi woke in the short time between the end of the night and the beginning of the day. Shifting away from the prince's embrace, she left the secure warmth of his arms and stood at the edge of the bed, and not being able to help herself, gazed down at her own, personal fallen angel. Janos lay with his chest and arms above the covers, and with those extravagantly long eyelashes gracing his closed eyes.

Smoothing a lock of ebony hair from his brow, she whispered, "You will remain in my heart always, Janos Rackoszi."

With a sweet uplift of his kissable lips, the prince responded, "As you will be safe in mine, *kincsem*. But why do you leave me?"

"It is almost dawn, and I don't think it would be quite the thing for anyone to discover we had spent the night together after your announcement yesterday. I would spare both of us the embarrassment."

"Sleep is soon upon me, Bibi. After such a glorious night, the nanos will have to work extra hard this day. I am eager to hold you again when I wake, but at least let me bid you sweet dreams, *kincsem*."

And with a smile he was gone, and she was free to gaze her fill and draw a memory to last a lifetime. This was one picture she would paint just for herself.

He lay on his side with one hand tucked under his cheek. His ebony hair was spread upon the white linen, and the dark stubble of a morning beard accented his high cheekbones. The faintest hint of the dimple, evident when he smiled, graced his cheek as if he were having the most pleasant dream. The portrait would serve to remind her of Atlanteans, and ecstasy, and a noble and loving man when the nights grew long and she wondered if he'd ever found his bond mate. She loved him enough to sincerely hope he did.

Unable to deny herself one last kiss, she took her time and kissed the prince's forehead, cheek, and, finally, his sweet lips. Her last memory of Prince Szigismond, Emre Janos Rackoszi would be the fresh-cut fir and leather smell of his cologne. It was a scent she had only smelled on him once before, but she'd recognize it instantly, if she were ever fortunate enough to encounter it again.

Bathing hurriedly and changing into her *Csikos* attire, she arrived in the breakfast room, relieved to find Pal just finishing his meal. "If it wouldn't be too much trouble, can I accompany you as far as Budapest?"

"Your company will be most appreciated, but I want to go on record as having said the Viceroy of Transylvania is an ass. Why isn't he here to stop you? I'd have to be blind to miss the way he devours you with his eyes or the way you return his regard. The two of you are made to be together. Why is he letting you go without a protest?"

She couldn't meet Pal's direct gaze, and so stared at the toes of her riding boots as she answered him. "Let's just say the prince needs and deserves a mate who will complete him, and I do not fulfill his requirements. If you are finished your breakfast, let's be away. I've made arrangements for the coach to follow us with my trunk. We can ride in it part of the way to save our mounts."

He stood and took her hand in his and placed a brief kiss on her knuckles. "You would have made a good hussar, Bibi, for you always consider the welfare of your horse. Since the prince does not appear to value you, I want you to know I am very interested in continuing our friendship. Perhaps you will allow me to visit your family when time permits?"

She favored him with a brief smile and a considering tilt of her head. "You would be welcomed, Pal Anton. Shall we broaden our friendship on the long road back to Budapest?"

***

Upon learning of Baroness Baranyi's departure, Akos carried the prince's morning drink to his suite with a trembling hand. It was not fear but anger making the dark blood shiver in the crystal goblet. How could he let her go? The baroness completed him as no other could, and he just slept on while another man accompanied her on a lengthy journey. A man who would be sleeping in the same inns, sharing meals, and perhaps more with her. And why shouldn't the hussar wheedle his way into Bibi's affections when it was obvious the prince had cast her aside? No, he would not let this happen. If it took putting his hands on the prince's body and shaking him out of his morning lethargy, then by all of the ancient gods he would do so.

Opening the door to the bedroom, Akos's senses were assaulted by the redolence of the prince's bonding scent, and it infuriated him his master had not completed the ritual. If he had, the baroness would still be in the prince's bed, and he would have been overjoyed to back silently from the room.

After placing the goblet down with enough force to endanger its fragile stem, Akos threw the covers off Janos and shook him until the prince's eyelids fluttered with the beginning of awareness. Not satisfied to wait for a leisurely awakening, the valet threw restraint to the four winds and pinched the prince's bare buttock. It had the desired effect. The assaulted man leapt from the bed and turned in a fighting stance to ascertain who had dared interrupt his sleep in such a rude fashion.

"Akos, have you gone completely around the bend? What

is the meaning of this insult?"

"You ask if *I* have gone mad? You must be howling mad to stand there reeking of bonding scent while the woman you should be bound to is, this very moment, riding to Budapest with another man, a very dashing, handsome man, and unaware you even care for her."

At the mention of Bibi with another man, a savage growl escaped his prince, and his fangs descended as he bared his lips in a snarl.

This was the reaction the valet had hoped for. A bonded Atlantean was an extremely jealous and possessive creature. Perhaps the prince would be given another chance to recite the bonding words, if they could catch the baroness before she reached Budapest and back into the arms of her family or, worse yet, those of the hussar.

Chapter Twenty-Five

The sudden appearance of bright sunlight made Margyth sit up with a start, and the book in her lap fell to the ground with a loud thump.

"Oh, forgive me, Mistress. I never imagined you would be in the library. I've just come to open the drapes for the day."

Sleeping in a chair had not put her in a good mood, and the maid was a convenient receptacle for her anger. "Why can you not imagine I would be in the library? Do you think I cannot read?"

"Oh no, Mistress, I never meant to suggest..."

She found the maid's voice even more irritating than the fact her robe and nightgown were wound around her body in uncomfortable constriction. "Stop your bleating this instant and leave the room."

Good, the Szechenyi help always responded quickly to her orders, and this maid was no exception. She almost stubbed her toe on the damn heavy tome when she made to stand, and the previous evening's events rushed back.

She remembered tossing and turning until the idea of verifying some fact in the library made her leave her bed. But what she'd been searching for remained just out of recall this morning.

Shaking herself fully awake, she recalled with absolute clarity the scene in Prince Rackoszi's rooms, and the ignominy of being cast out of the castle. The fact she and her mother were sent down the back stairs, and out through the kitchen like servants, stung, but not as much as the slap her mother delivered to her in the carriage on the way home.

Even though the red mark had long faded, she rubbed her cheek in remembrance of the unexpected assault. Her mother had never laid a hand in anger on her before last night.

Margyth picked up the book and sat down. It was suddenly important to recall every word she and her mother exchanged on the ride back to their residence. Her mother had said something significant, but what was it? Rubbing her face with her hands to chase the cobwebs from her brain, she put her head back and closed her eyes in concentration.

Her mother had opened the conversation with, "How dare an undead, soulless, revenant treat us with such disrespect. He will rue the day he insulted us, Margyth."

Her response to her mother's complaint had earned her the unexpected slap. "Us? He hasn't insulted you. I'm the one who is embarrassed. He has broken the engagement. I will be a local laughingstock until I find someone else."

Thank God the carriage had been a closed one. She wouldn't have wanted the coachman to witness her mother slap her or hear the dressing down her mother launched into.

"You have embarrassed yourself, you silly girl. The prince was correct in his assessment of you. You *are* a spoiled, wanton, selfish, cruel woman, Margyth Szechenyi, and it was you, who broke the engagement. If you hadn't let your temper run free, you would have refrained from punishing the maid, and you would still be dancing at your engagement ball. However, I think Prince Rackoszi was wrong to hold me responsible for your deplorable behavior."

She recollected quite well her shock over such a pronouncement. "If not you, then who, Mother dear?"

"If you don't want me to mark your other cheek, you will cease the back talk and listen to me. Your father is responsible. He believed his handsomeness gave him license to indulge himself in any profligate activity he happened upon, and you, Daughter, are exactly like him. You were too blinded by his larger-than-life presence to realize he had feet of clay. Your father was spoiled, wanton, selfish, and cruel, as are you, Margyth. He whored and drank and gambled all of our lives away, and the man you so admire didn't give a damn he ruined our lives.

"Oh, yes, I am very aware he consorted with prostitutes, and had massive gambling debts, and I also knew of the prince's offer to not call them due if he would stop going to gaming hells. And do you know what your father's response was? No? Well, he bragged about laughing in the prince's face. You might be interested to know your father made a counter offer. He offered your body for his gambling debts. He told the prince he would keep to the straight and narrow if the prince would take you as his wife. The disgusting man didn't deserve your adoration."

"Well Papa must have felt some remorse after the prince accepted, he killed himself, after all." It was the sole rejoinder she could think to make to put her father in a better light.

"So he did, but I doubt it was remorse over using his daughter as a gambling token. Here is the truth I've kept hidden from you, and lest you heed me, you will earn the same awful fate as your father, if you continue to spread your legs for any man who takes your fancy. Your father was driven to suicide, not because he felt guilty for having bartered you away, he shot himself because he had the French disease, the French pox, and didn't have the courage to spend the rest of his life watching his handsome face rot by slow degrees.

"Although I became quite good at playing the grieving wife, I actually rejoiced the day he shot himself. You and I were free of his gambling. If we lived frugally and sold our valuables to cover his debts, I was positive we'd eventually recover, and then we'd leave this place and start a new life in whichever city or town your father hadn't soiled the name of Szechenyi. What I didn't take into consideration was the word of a Rackoszi. The prince had given his vow and he wouldn't break it."

"Then all of your nonsense about him being the undead is a lie? How could you ruin my chance at happiness? Do you think I want to be stuck with you and grow into a withered spinster? I want to travel the world, and I want to do it on the arm of a young, wealthy, handsome man, not my bitter, sour-faced mother."

Margyth recalled the shock writ large on her mother's face right after she'd delivered her set down. Her mother had drawn her head back into the carriage squabs as if she'd just been the one slapped.

"You, Daughter, are singularly remarkable in your selfishness. I've just told you your father committed suicide because he had contracted a disgusting disease due to his profligate lifestyle, and all you can think about is your personal comfort. I don't think you are capable of hearing the truth unless it happens to coincide with your own goals. But no, I did not lie. I am convinced Prince Rackoszi is a revenant. There are too many telltale signs for him not to be so, I set a trap for his alternate form. The abomination you want to marry takes the shape of a wolf so he can move about in daylight. Although the trap failed to kill him, I believed I'd scared him off for good. I gave him incontrovertible proof, if he continued to insist on marrying you, I wouldn't rest until I saw him back in his grave where he could never rise again. But I was wrong, it was his valet I should have gone after."

Margyth stopped listening to her mother's angry ravings. But the baroness's last words had struck a chord in her mind and swept her to the library at an ungodly early hour to search the book entitled *Nesferatu*. Why the valet and not the wolf?

She studied the book on the floor and smiled. She'd found the answer. Leaving the book where it lay, she hurried from the library and started up the stairs to her rooms to dress but stopped on the third step and changed directions. She needed to visit her father's study first to retrieve his pistols. She considered it more than fitting to use the same weapon her father had used to end his life on the man who'd rejected her.

The stable lad gawked when she handed him the pistol in its leather carrier and ordered him to secure it to her saddle. "Well, you do know how to attach it, don't you? And be quick about it, I want to be gone before my mother awakens."

She didn't bother thanking the servant for the hand up into the saddle he gave her before she sawed the reins on her mare and kicked her in the ribs to set her galloping to the

Bloodstock

Rackoszi castle.

As a rapid means of transportation, the mare was a disappointment. No matter how many times she kicked the dumb beast, it just would not maintain a steady gallop, and using her quirt repeatedly about the creature's neck made it shy sideways rather than go forward at a faster gait.

She wanted to reach the castle during early morning while the valet was in the prince's rooms dressing him. But thanks to Szigi's miserable choice of a mount for her, she'd be lucky to reach the Rackoszi dwelling before nightfall. She tried throwing curses at the poor mare to encourage more speed, for she really didn't want to confront the prince after sundown if what she'd just read about revenants was true.

Chapter Twenty-Six

Bibi didn't draw a full breath until she and Pal Anton turned away from the long drive leading to Castle Rackoszi. To distract herself from descending into a moody travel companion, she centered her attention on the hussar and offered, "I should paint you, Pal. You'd make an excellent miniature."

"I would, wouldn't I?" He pretended to preen for her, and then slyly added, "But you've already painted me."

At the quizzical look she gave him, he enlightened her.

"Aren't I the red fox in Margyth's painting? Very clever of you, my dear artist, to show the fox in the henhouse, so to speak."

Bibi doubled over in laughter so hard she lost one of her stirrups. "You are very perceptive for a mere hussar, Pal. Yes, the fox is you. And I'm sure you noticed the fox was enjoying himself."

"Oh, my dear I am not a *mere* hussar. I am an extraordinarily magnificent hussar. I think you should paint a full-length portrait of me. It isn't possible to show all of my manly beauty in miniature.

"And hussars have to be perceptive, don't you know? A hussar lacking in perception would soon find his head estranged from his body."

The scream of a horse in pain extinguished conversation, as hussar and artist attempted to find the source of the sound.

Pal Anton put Ares into a levade, the better to see farther down the road, and pointed. "There, off to the right."

Bibi followed Pal's arm and squinted in the direction he pointed. "It's Margyth. I've a mind to throw her from the saddle. She's abusing the animal." She spurred Shadow forward, but soon drew him in when she lost sight of the woman, who'd veered down a shortcut to the Rackoszi property. Pal broke her concentration when he reined in beside her.

"Judging from the hurry she is in, she has a thing or two she wants to get off her chest. I don't know how she and the prince parted last night, but I can't think it was particularly cordial. Ah well, I'm sure the prince is more than capable of dealing with her. Come away, Bibi, neither of us has the right to interfere."

The hussar spoke the truth, and so she gave Shadow the signal to advance. But there was something bothering her about Margyth, and she closed her eyes, the better to suss it out. Perhaps her perceptive companion had caught it as well.

"Pal, did you notice anything strange about Margyth or her mount? My brain is buzzing over an oddity, but I can't quite make it out."

"Oh, a guessing game. What fun. Let's see, my distant cousin was wearing a riding habit she's worn before, so I can't say there was anything different there. I can also say I've seen her bad riding form before as well. She did appear to be abusing her sweet, gentle mare more than usual. The chit blames the poor horse for her execrable riding, but she will never be a good enough rider to handle anything but a gentle horse."

Bibi asked, "Was she riding side-saddle or astride? She was bouncing around so much I couldn't tell."

"Hmm, let me think a moment. She was riding side-saddle, but her leg kept catching on the pistol case and throwing her off-balance."

Pal Anton echoed her exclamation of "pistol case?" Turning Shadow around, she shouted to him to stop the coach following them and have it turn back before following her back to Castle Rackoszi. She didn't know what Margyth was up to, but a rejected woman carrying a pistol didn't point to a friendly visit.

It didn't take Pal long to catch her up, and they leaned low over their horses' necks and rode like the entire Turkish cavalry wanted their heads. Neither one of them bothered to use the hitching posts in the castle's stable yard but slid from their horses and let the reins trail as they dashed through the kitchen and up the back stairs.

***

Margyth slipped into the kitchen and entered the servants' stairway without discovery. The castle's servants were so busy putting to rights the disorder caused by many guests and a late formal dinner and dance, no one paid her the slightest attention.

The castle's many corridors confused her, but following the rigid back of Szigi's unnatural freak of a housekeeper as she'd led them from the Master Suite, had allowed her sufficient time to etch in her memory every twist and turn she needed to take this morning. A Szechenyi did not forgive an insult, they paid it back twofold. And she would repay Prince Rackoszi for his rejection of her this very morning.

She soon found herself outside the prince's closed door. Should she knock? No, she would savor the surprise on Szigi's face. She opened the unlocked door and stepped inside to discover none other than the prince himself. He was sitting in a chair with lather on his face, and the valet, with straight razor in hand, was about to shave him.

"Margyth, what are you doing here? I thought I made it crystal clear you were not to darken my home again."

"Yes you did, Szigi, but even princes don't always get what they want." She removed her father's ornate dueling pistol from where she'd hidden it in the folds of her riding habit and pointed it at the valet.

Janos wiped the shaving soap from his face with the towel Akos had dropped into his lap in shocked surprise. "Margyth Szechenyi, what mean you by this? Put the pistol down before you hurt someone."

"I know you don't think highly of me, Szigi, but I am more intelligent than you give me credit for. Since you shamed me in front of everyone by discarding me as you would a piece of tattered clothing, I've, for once in my life, taken my mother's counsel to heart. I've been reading her books on *Nesferatu*, and they are most informative on how to rid oneself of an abomination before God. I learned I don't actually have to shoot *you*, I merely have to shoot your valet. Oh, don't bother lying, I know you must have a human blood source, and there is no one more convenient than your valet. He is the one member of your staff closest to you. He wakes you each morning and undresses you for bed at night. If you kill the blood source, *voila*, you kill the vampire."

She turned the dueling pistol in Akos's direction and centered it over his heart.

"Margyth," Janos protested, "this is madness. I am not a vampire or the undead or whatever name your mother's execrable reading material has for such mythical creatures. If you shoot my valet, you will be committing murder, and I will have you punished to the extent of the law. You will not escape punishment because I will still be alive to administer it."

When the prince stepped toward her, Margyth pointed her pistol at him and stood her ground as he spread his hands wide to shield his valet. "Punish me? Oh, I think not. I merely have to run into the bright sun after I shoot your servant, and you will be unable to follow. Your aversion to sunlight is how I know you really are a vampire. The books all say prolonged exposure to sunlight will kill a vampire, so I know you won't follow me outside. I just need keep away from you until you shrivel up and die of starvation after the death of your blood source.

"If you will recall your godfather's praise, I am a most excellent shot. I won't miss from this distance." She stepped to the side and once again pointed the pistol at Akos but was distracted when the door flew open with a loud crash, as Baroness Baranyi and Pal Anton rushed in.

"Margyth Szechenyi, have you lost your reason? If you are upset with the prince, just tell him so and leave. You needn't do anything as drastic as this. With your beauty, you are sure to find another suitor very soon," Bibi pleaded from the doorway.

"You stupid bitch, I don't want another suitor. I want the prince dead. I stayed up the entire night reading about vampires, and the books told me just how to kill this one." At the baroness and Pal's incredulous protestations, Margyth cast an evil glare their way and used her pistol to direct the interlopers to stand with the prince and his valet.

Pal Anton drew Margyth's attention to himself. "Margyth, put the pistol down and I'll take you back to your house. I'm sure the prince understands why you might've imbibed more wine than you can handle."

She refused to let the hussar distract her from her purpose. "Since you and the baroness weren't present to hear the full explanation for my presence here this morning, I'll say it but one more time. I didn't come here to kill the prince, I came to kill his blood apple, his valet, the one person he drinks from to be able to function among us. When Akos dies, the prince will die."

Janos edged forward but stopped when she again leveled the pistol at him.

"Stop, Szigi, not another step. You know I don't miss what I shoot at."

"Well then, go ahead and shoot me and be done with it, Margyth. If I am indeed a revenant, kill me and let my innocent valet go. This nonsense about me using him as some sort of walking meal is ridiculous. I daresay the poor man would be quite anemic if I did."

"Even though you want me to shoot you, Szigi, I won't. I want your death to be a slow, agonizing one as you waste away from hunger."

"Margyth, you must be drunk. Your reasoning is as sound as a rum pot's."

"You dare insult me again, Szigi? Well, after I send you to hell, you will have ample time to rue having done so." Her hand didn't waver in the slightest as she pointed the pistol at the hapless valet and fired.

"Noooo!" Bibi screamed and threw herself in front of Akos. The infinitesimal delay after the striker hit the flint and caused the spark to ignite the gunpowder was enough to save the valet's life.

***

The room erupted in chaos, and Janos couldn't reach Akos before he collapsed under Bibi's weight then struggled to disengage himself from the baroness. It took longer than he wanted for him to leap to untangle his valet. He cradled Bibi in his arms and discovered the spreading stain on the front of her shirt.

In a voice constricted by fear, he touched her cheek with trembling fingers. "Bibi, why? Why did you put yourself in such danger?"

She gave him her characteristic response to an unusual occurrence and laughed weakly as she replied, "I have the most dreadful luck around valets."

He had served in battle and could identify a mortal

wound when he saw one. Margyth had shot true. Akos would have been killed if Bibi hadn't thrown herself in front of him, and for her selfless act, she was the one dying. Margyth would be brought to justice for this, and he would volunteer to serve as her executioner, but first they had to apprehend her. She'd escaped in all of the confusion.

Janos placed a kiss on Bibi's forehead as a coldness settled in his heart. He ordered the hussar, "Go after Margyth, and when you find her, use whatever means necessary to confine her to her room. If the Baroness Szechenyi gives you any trouble, tell her to desist or stand trial as an accomplice. I will deal with the Szechenyi women after I've done what I can for the baroness."

Akos, who'd been kneeling by Bibi's side wringing his hands in silent distress, spoke up. "You have to save her, Your Grace. I couldn't live with myself if she dies because she tried to protect me, a man she barely knows. Why did she do something so...so...?"

"So dangerous? So foolish? So brave? I believe she did so because she has a generous heart. And you aren't the only one who won't be able to live with himself if she dies. Fetch me the letter opener on my desk and be quick about it. I don't think we have much time if we're going to save her."

Janos's attention was drawn back to the woman he loved when she started struggling to breathe. "Listen to me, my darling. I can save you by giving you my blood. If you accept you will live, but you will be like me. Please, please, darling, say yes. I love you with my whole heart and soul, and I want no other woman in my life. Please, for me, Bibi, say you'll accept my help."

When Bibi gave a small nod and weak squeeze on his hand, he breathed easy. He tore off his shirt when the valet handed him the sharp weapon and made a deep gash over his left pectoral. Gently lifting her, he placed her lips over the wound and commanded, "Drink, *kincsem*, let my blood be the agent to heal you."

As soon as she took the first swallow, he said the words he should have given Bibi the night before. "I claim you, Beatrix Celine, as my bond mate..."

He bared his fangs when Akos interrupted with an anguished cry.

"My Prince, no, not the bonding words. If the baroness dies, you will follow her."

He rebuked his valet with a deep, snarling growl. "If she dies, I will willingly follow her. Bibi is my heart, how can I live without one?"

It was fortunate Akos had sense enough to cease his protestation. It would have been a shame to kill the valet for interfering between him and his bond mate, after she had given her life to save him.

Janos resumed the bonding oath. "You are my life mate, as I am yours. We belong to each other. I freely offer my life to you. I give you my protection, my allegiance, my heart, and my soul. I give you, and only you, my body. I will protect what is yours as I know you will protect what is mine. We will always be in each other's care until we follow each other into the afterlife. As your blood sustains me, mine will be the rock of your well-being. Drink from me and be one with me."

It was mere moments, it was an eon, but he sat there with Bibi cradled in his arms until Akos crouched down and whispered, "The baroness has stopped drinking, but she still breathes. She's merely unconscious, Your Grace. It is in the gods' hands now."

Janos again focused on his valet when Akos touched him gently on his arm.

"Your Grace, you need to close your wound."

It took him a few seconds to understand what his valet was referring to, and looked down at the blood continuing to pour from the gash in his chest. He spit in his hand and wiped it over the wound and then gathered Bibi in his arms to carry her to bed. He did not refuse his valet's support when he wobbled from blood loss as he stood.

"Akos, ask Erzsebet and Cata to come to the Mistress Suite. I need them to undress Bibi and remove the pistol ball from the wound. It must come out if she's to heal properly."

Gods bless his valet, although white-faced and shaking, the man had the presence of mind to pour him a glass of the fortified wine before he ran from the room in search of the housekeeper.

He had done everything he physically could for his bond mate. The one thing left was to pray to the entire pantheon of gods for her safe recovery, or if she was not fated to survive, he be permitted to follow her into the afterlife as soon as possible.

***

Pal Anton didn't need to guess if Margyth had gone through the kitchen to make her escape. There was a scullery maid down on her knees picking up broken bits of crockery and muttering about ladies running without paying attention to where they were going.

Dodging around the mess, the hussar gained the courtyard and halted abruptly so his eyes could make sense of what they saw. The stable master, eyewitness to the accident, ran up to him to explain.

"Oh, sir, it was horrible. Mistress Szechenyi ran out of the kitchen as if she was being pursued by all of hell's devils. I don't even know why she was here, the prince told us she'd begged off the engagement, after all."

Pal waved his hand in a circular motion to get the stable master back on track.

"Well, she flew from the kitchen door and tried to mount her horse, but she couldn't do it. The poor beast was very frightened of her. It wouldn't stand still long enough for Margyth to mount. It just kept shying away and whinnying.

"I tried to stop her, I really did, but she said...she said..."

Pal forced himself to cajole the man into continuing rather than bark an order as he would to one of his hussars. "Go ahead, you may repeat whatever she said. I'm sure it has some bearing on this."

Red-faced and unable to meet Pal's eye, the stable master repeated Margyth's words. "She said, 'It was fitting she take the bitch Baranyi's horse, since she'll no longer be needing it.' I don't know why she was so upset, but she wouldn't listen to me at all when I told her she shouldn't mount Shadow because she didn't know how to ride astride a cavalry horse and it would be dangerous for her to do so. Sir, I don't think she was quite right in the head when she said some nonsense about finally having a horse that didn't emulate a snail.

"Since Shadow is a tall horse and Mistress Szechenyi is very, um, short, she led him over to the stone water trough and used it as a mounting block. I foresaw this happening, sir. Mistress Szechenyi didn't even let me shorten the stirrups before she kicked Shadow and he reared into a courbette.

"Mistress Szechenyi, as you probably know, was not a very good rider, and so wasn't able to stay in the saddle. She fell backwards and broke her neck when she hit the water trough. You can't blame the horse, sir, he executed the order he was given."

Pal followed the stable master to the group of stable hands ringing Margyth's body and gabbling in shock. Butting past them, Pal was surprised to find she appeared to be sleeping, and not the victim of a violent death. There was no blood, no real disarray of her clothing, no rictus of horror on her face, save the unnatural angle of her neck. Shaking his own head at the crazy path this day had taken, Pal spotted Bibi's horse, Shadow, where he stood with reins trailing and ears straight back in reaction to the excited voices in the courtyard, and spoke soothingly to the gray as he led it back to the stable master. "Well, Shadow old man, you have avenged your mistress."

Pal Anton used his command voice to get everyone moving in the right direction again. He ordered the stable master to have one of his lads secure blankets from the castle to wrap Margyth's body, find a flat-bed wagon and driver to carry her back to her home, and, finally, another stable lad to feed and water Shadow and treat any injuries Margyth may have inflicted on her mare.

Having returned the prince's stable to its normal routine, Pal mounted Ares, and when the wagon carrying Margyth's broken body began its journey to the Szechenyi estate, he followed it. The wagon's slow pace would allow him time to create a means of telling Baroness Szechenyi her daughter had died without being overly cruel. It was Prince Rackoszi's right to punish the woman for the evil she had caused, not his.

As the Szechenyi butler showed him into the breakfast room, Pal Anton cleared his throat and steeled himself to begin his rehearsed offer of condolences to the baroness. He'd expected instant tears, perhaps a denial of the event, but not the keening wail which set the hairs at the back of his neck standing at attention. Never did he expect the baroness to jump up from her seat at the table and stare at him in mad horror as she used her nails to gouge bloody trails in her cheeks.

"Baroness, cease hurting yourself this instant. It won't bring your daughter back to life." Pal Anton used his long legs to advantage to cross the room and forcibly hold the Baroness Szechenyi's hands away from her face. Twisting around, he spotted a footman rooted to the wall in shock. "Find the baroness's maid and tell her to prepare a sleeping draught for the baroness, and be quick about it."

Thank God the baroness ceased struggling and allowed him to return her to her seat at the table, where she did nothing but stare, unseeing, at the opposite wall. Suddenly aware the butler was in the room, Pal addressed him. "You there, I'm sorry, your name escapes me at the moment."

"It's Lazlo, sir."

"Very good. Lazlo, please arrange for the bod...um...Mistress Szechenyi..." He'd started to say body, but he didn't want a repeat of the baroness's extreme reaction upon hearing again her daughter was dead.

Pal continued his instructions in a much lower tone of voice. "Have her maid prepare Margyth for viewing and send someone to the village to notify the priest, and then you may inform the staff the house is in mourning, and to act accordingly."

"Immediately, sir. I will have the formal parlor arranged for the viewing. It's where the baron was laid out, but of course it was a closed casket due to the baron having shot himself." The butler, casting sympathetic eyes toward the distraught baroness, whispered the last for Pal's ears only.

"Yes, yes, get on with it." Pal gave a sigh of relief when he spotted the maid, carrying a goblet of wine, enter the room as Lazlo left. He didn't know what type of drug the maid used, but it was very effective. It was an even greater relief to relinquish his attendance on the baroness to two footmen, who held her upright as they led her back to her bedroom, trailed by her maid. As for himself, he headed for the baron's study and his own glass of spirits. It was going to be a very, very long day, but first he needed to ensure there were no other weapons not under lock and key. He didn't know if the baroness was as good a marksman as her daughter, but he wouldn't give her the chance to demonstrate the talent.

Pal was impressed by the efficiency of the Szechenyi staff. He'd been interrupted once in his temporary headquarters in the study by a maid drawing all the drapes and putting veiling over the one mirror in the room. He'd even been served a light meal around noon, and a footman replenished the whisky in the baron's decanter for his convenience. When he was summoned to the baroness's side, he was therefore not surprised to find the entire house bedecked in funeral gloom. What he was surprised to find was the baroness herself sitting vigil at her daughter's temporary catafalque atop the dining room table servants had carried into the formal parlor.

Either the baroness or a maid had washed and dressed Margyth in a high-necked dress of white with sprigs of palest pink. Her long, golden hair was brushed and arranged to spill over her shoulders. It was ironic Margyth appeared more virginal in death than she ever had in life. Pal pinched the bridge of his nose hard as punishment for his irreverence. The poor woman died a nasty death, and having been one of the ones who'd sampled what she'd offered, he had no right to cast stones at her character. Pal's guilt was interrupted by Baroness Szechenyi's harsh command.

"You will tell me how my daughter died. My butler tells me you were present when it happened."

"Your servant misspoke, Baroness. I arrived mere moments after the event, and the Rackoszi stable master, who'd witnessed the accident, told me how it occurred."

Baroness Szechenyi left her chair to shake her fist under the hussar's nose. "Accident? Pah, whatever the means, it is the prince who is responsible for the death of my daughter. Well, he will..."

"Stop, madame. If anyone is to blame for her death, it is yourself. It was you who filled her head with the utter nonsense about vampires. She forced her way into the prince's private suite this morning and held him and his valet hostage with the threat of killing them both. Baroness Baranyi and I were on the road back to Budapest when we happened to spot her riding to the castle. I fervently believe noticing the pistol case strapped to her saddle was a fortuitous act of God. We turned our horses around and followed her to the prince's rooms. As it was, we were unable to deter Margyth from firing her pistol."

"Then the prince is dead? Good, at least I will have something to relish for the rest of my life. A life without my daughter."

He shook his head in disgust at the overwhelming hatred the baroness was displaying. "You are to be denied your unholy pleasure, madame. Baroness Baranyi threw herself in front of the valet and took the bullet Margyth meant for him. Before she fired her weapon, she had been babbling some nonsense about, if she killed the vampire's *pomme de sang*, the vampire would die an agonizing death.

"In the ensuing confusion after she shot the baroness, Margyth ran back to her horse to make her escape. She'd abused the poor creature in her haste to reach Castle Rackoszi, and the horse wouldn't let her mount, so your daughter added horse thievery to her list of sins for the morning. She mounted Baroness Baranyi's horse, and not knowing the importance of where one puts their feet when riding a cavalry horse, she gave it an incorrect command, and the horse reared and she fell off and broke her neck on a stone watering trough."

He gave up the effort to put the blame for the tragedy on Margyth's shoulders when the baroness turned her gaze away and began rocking in her chair as she vowed, "The Rackoszi abomination will pay for this. People have a need to know what he is."

The need for fresh air and sanity made Pal leave the house in search of the Szechenyi staff member responsible for constructing Margyth's coffin. Having assured himself it was coming along as fast as possible, Pal retired once again to the study and requested a dinner tray be delivered to him there. He wanted no part of dining with the mad baroness this evening.

It felt like he'd just gone to bed when Pal was roused from his weary attempt at sleep by the frantic pounding on the bedroom door. "This had better be good," he muttered to himself as he threw his robe on and flung the door open.

The footman he'd ordered to fetch the baroness's maid stood in the hallway wringing his hands in extreme agitation. "Oh, sir, please come, it's the baroness!"

"What about the baroness? Has she fallen ill?"

"No, sir, she is not ill, she is dead. It was my turn to sit vigil over Mistress Margyth, but when I entered the parlor, I found the baroness lying on the floor, and she had this clutched in her hand."

Pal took the letter from the servant's trembling hand.

"What does it say?"

"I do not know, sir, I cannot read. What should I do with the baroness? It isn't right to leave her on the floor next to her daughter's body."

Briefly noting the letter was addressed to him, Pal stuffed the letter into the pocket of his robe and followed the servant into the parlor where the baroness had kept vigil. The servant had not exaggerated, the baroness was well and truly dead, and lying on the floor next to the table holding Margyth's body.

"Here, take the baroness's feet, and I'll take her shoulders, and we'll carry her to her room. Let's do this quickly, I don't want to encounter anyone on the stairs. We'll place her on her bed, as if she was napping and died before she could summon help. I know this will be unfortunate for her poor maid, but it would be better for the baroness's dignity if she were discovered tomorrow morning lying abed rather than dead on the floor of the parlor."

"Yes, sir, you are correct, sir, the baroness was indeed one to observe the proprieties. Thank you for respecting her."

Fortunately, the baroness had not become so stiff in death they were unable to arrange her limbs into a dignified pose. When the servant withdrew to take his place at Margyth's vigil, Pal took the letter out of his pocket and read it.

The vituperation, the blame, the wild accusations leveled at Prince Rackoszi almost leapt from the scrawled pages. The final paragraph confirmed the baroness's death as a suicide via opium overdose rather than a naturally occurring heart attack, and the added injunction to rid the world of the vampire calling himself Prince Rackoszi.

Pal's shoulders sagged in weariness. What a fucked-up mess. What was he going to tell the prince when he next saw him? He hadn't for a moment believed Margyth's absurd accusation the Viceroy of Transylvania was a vampire, and having her mother attempt the same hadn't changed his mind.

Pal relaxed again in preparation for falling asleep when another knock had him crossing the room, yet again, to discover who'd dared disturb him at this ungodly hour at the risk of their life. It was the butler, Lazlo.

"What else could have happened for you to roust me again from sleep?" Pal reined in his temper when the man took a step back at his harsh tone.

"The viceroy is downstairs and asking for the baroness, but she isn't answering my knock on her bedroom door. I hate to wake her; the poor woman is exhausted. What would you have me to do, sir?"

"I will speak with the viceroy." Pal hurried downstairs and found Janos standing in the formal parlor, gazing at Margyth's body. He turned when Pal joined him.

"I will tell you truthfully, Pal Anton, viewing Margyth's body has engendered but one emotion in me, and it isn't regret but anger. I am angry I won't be the one to take her life for what she did to Bibi."

By the thundercloud expression on his face, Pal feared the worst had occurred. "Is Beatrix...?"

Janos whirled to face him. "She is still breathing, but only time will tell if she will recover. Where is the baroness? I want to tell her just what her evil accusations have wrought. She and she alone is culpable for her daughter's death."

"Impossible, I'm afraid. The baroness is dead by her own hand." Pal reached into his robe's pocket and proffered the letter the footman had given him earlier. "The baroness left this letter for me, and it concerns you. Come along to the baron's study. You will need privacy to read it."

Pal closed the study door and sat at the baron's desk while the prince strode to the fireplace to read the letter. Judging by the way the viceroy crumpled the paper in his hands, he was not at all pleased with what the baroness had had to say.

"Would you care for a brandy?" At the prince's nod, Pal poured for them both. Crossing the room, he handed Janos a snifter then resumed his seat behind the desk and waited for the viceroy to speak. He was prepared to tell the prince how mad the baroness must have been to make such accusations.

"What have you to say about the baroness's accusations, Pal?"

"I had no idea she was so steadfast in her conviction you are a vampire, of all things. I never took her seriously. It was obvious to me her ravings were just the hysterical scheme of a deranged woman to keep you from taking her daughter away. What shall we do about her suicide? If it becomes known she took her own life, she will not be buried next to her daughter, and the scandal will be enormous. Perhaps we can say she died of grief?"

Janos sat down to face Pal across the desk. "Has anyone else read this letter?"

"No, the servant who found it on her body cannot read."

"A small blessing at last on this horrible day." The prince

sighed. "The baroness was not mad; she was correct to a certain degree. I am too weary to explain the difference between Atlanteans and vampires, but let me assure you, I am not a soulless, undead creature who kills without reason or mercy. You are a warrior and have been witness to many frightening things in battle, so I think you will be able to handle the truth." Janos let his fangs descend and displayed them for Pal's enlightenment.

"I don't mean to offend you, Your Grace, but I'm going to need more of an explanation than a show of long teeth," Pal demanded with the bravado he'd developed to not display his fear to the men he led into battle. As he hoped he would, the prince relaxed and grinned at his sally.

"Atlanteans have become a breed apart from humans. We are descendants of the original people of Atlantis, and we do have some of the characteristics of vampires, as we drink blood and cannot tolerate bright sunlight. But we don't kill people when we drink from them, and it doesn't have to be human blood, although human blood is more nourishing. Our bodies can heal most injuries, but it takes more blood to do so. If we drink from a human, we cloud their mind and leave them with a pleasant memory and no remembrance of their donation. And, before you ask, I have never taken your blood."

"Have you taken Bibi's?"

"Yes, but it was willingly given. The baroness, may the devil take her, set a trap for my wolf, which is the form I assume when I want to be abroad in bright sunlight, and I was grievously injured. Baroness Baranyi saw me change back to my man form, and rather than leaving me alone in the sunlight to die from exposure and blood loss, she donated her blood and kept me out of the sun until I was well enough to get back to the castle. She is a very courageous woman."

Pal was convinced Janos was telling the truth. He had not hesitated with any of his answers, and the tone of his voice wasn't glib but sincere. "Did you give your blood to the baroness after she was shot by Margyth?"

Janos hung his head, and Pal had to lean forward to hear his response.

"Yes, I did. I could not bear to lose her. I love her. I did offer her the choice, though, and I would have respected her wishes if she had chosen to die rather than become like me. But I'll not lie to you and say my heart could continue beating if she had refused. It will take several days before I know if she'll survive the transition. I'm counting on her strong will and excellent health to pull her through."

Pal eased back in his chair. "Good, I would not care to lose Bibi, either. I know you will take good care of her. She does love you, you know. Even if she had given me a chance to know her better, I'm certain I would've been a pale second choice for her. What shall we do about the baroness and her letter?"

Janos rose and tossed the letter into the fire then faced Pal. "If anyone asks about the letter, tell them it was merely a list of things the baroness wanted to accomplish for her daughter's funeral, and you've taken the list to ensure her wishes are carried out. I wouldn't correct anyone who surmises the baroness died of a heart attack due to overwhelming grief at the accidental death of her daughter."

He gazed into the hearth. "I have a business proposition for you, Pal Anton Esterhazy. For your silence concerning these bizarre events, I will give you the Szechenyi estate."

"Give *me* the estate?" Pal blustered. "The baroness is sure to have a relative closer than a fourth cousin who is more entitled to it. And you insult me if you think you need bribe me to keep silent. I consider you my friend."

Janos continued to stare into the fire, and his voice was raspy as he responded, "Your sincere support and friendship is almost too much to bear on this horrible day. I thank you for it. Forgive me, I meant no insult, but I am so weary, my wording was tactless. The baroness may have a closer relative in line for the inheritance, but the truth is, she no longer owned the estate. Her husband gambled it away and I bought up his markers. Among my parting words to Margyth and her mother when I broke the engagement was the admonishment they were to leave this house and never come back."

The prince held up his hand to forestall a protest from the hussar. "You've no need to chastise my actions, Pal Anton. Even though I detested them, I wouldn't have cast them out without a forint. I planned to establish mother and daughter in a town house in Vienna and provide a suitable dowry for Margyth. My sole restriction was neither one would return to this part of Hungary.

"Apart from the fact Baron Szechenyi tricked me into giving him my word to secure his daughter's protection through marriage, my ultimate consideration for giving my word was to protect my land and my people. This estate is the entrance to my domain and acts as a barrier to the outside world. I do not want anyone living here who might pay too close attention to the fact I, and the people who work for me, appear to live very long lives. I would have been able to control Margyth and her mother via marriage. However, you, and I hope you will not be offended, you, I will need to be sure of before allowing you to take over the estate."

Pal sat up straighter in his chair. "It sounds as if you want to put me through some sort of test. What would it take to convince you I would be your ally?"

"It would entail a show of faith, a contract sealed with blood to be exact."

Pal did not immediately accept or reject the proposal but kept the prince waiting as he considered the terms.

"I don't think I'm a greedy person, but I have come to love this estate, and I know I will never be able to purchase anything of this magnitude on what I earn as a hussar, and as the youngest of several siblings. If taking my blood will convince you of my loyalty, then take it."

He cautioned the hussar. "Be aware, Pal Anton, once I have taken your blood, I won't control you or hold you in thrall per se, but I will be able to locate you wherever you go. If you betray anyone I hold dear, I will find wherever you hide, and I will kill you. Make no mistake, I will pursue you to the ends of the earth if you break your oath to me."

Pal stood and wrapped his robe more securely about his body. When he extended his hand, Janos took it in a strong, forearm grip. "As an Eszterhazy, and as an officer in His Imperial Majesty's Hussars, I, Pal Anton Eszterhazy, swear to forever hold secret the knowledge of Prince Rackoszi's origins and to protect this valley from intrusion by anyone who would seek to do him harm. So help me God."

He accepted the oath with a firm squeeze to Pal's forearm. "We need to seal the agreement. Would you prefer pleasure or do you want the pain?"

"I've experienced enough pain as a hussar, thank you very much. Pleasure would be welcome, but I will admit to being ignorant of the process. How will you take my blood so I experience pleasure rather than the pain of being bitten, and forgive me for the impertinence, but where do you intend to bite me?"

His sardonic tone had the prince chortling, but he listened closely as Janos explained.

"I will take a small sip of blood from the large vein in your neck, and I will give you the sensation of pleasure when I do so. But first, I will lick your neck. My saliva both softens the skin so my fangs slip in with little resistance, and it then heals the wound so you will not see any blood afterward, and the wound will be gone in a few hours.

"Turn around, please. I am going to come up behind you and put my arm around you to grip you tightly, so if you jump or try to jerk away in fear, my fangs won't tear your skin. Relax, I am very good at this. I've had a great deal of practice, after all."

Pal regained his senses with a total body shudder, intense satisfaction, and the embarrassing sight of his shaft tenting the front of his robe. Totally flustered, he babbled an apology. "I'm sorry, um, I don't... I'm not attracted to...I'm not a..." Rather than offend the prince, his red-faced blathering amused him.

"Be at ease, Pal. I promised you pleasure and I gave it to you, and, no, I'm not attracted to you, either. As you can see, I experienced the same pleasure by taking your blood." The prince adjusted himself to ease the fit of his riding breeches. "It is a side effect to the pleasure, and not an indication of your sexual preference."

Stepping back, Janos tilted his head and closed his eyes. "The dawn fast approaches. I must leave and trust Anubis to get me home before full daylight. Let me know this evening if you need help with any of the burial details, and I will keep you posted on Bibi's condition as soon as I know the outcome."

It took several moments after the prince's departure for the reality of the last few hours to settle in. Pal reached the desk chair just as his legs gave way at the realization he'd been made a landowner with a beautiful house and tilled fields and orchards. Spotting the ink well, he then searched the desk drawers for paper. He needed to inform his superiors, effective immediately, he would resign his commission to manage his unexpected windfall. Thank God he had gotten a few hours' sleep, for today would be a busy one.

Chapter Twenty-Seven

His late-night visit to the Szechenyi estate left him weary to the bone, but Janos still found the strength to run up steps and through corridors until he reached the Mistress Suite. He hadn't wanted to leave Bibi to ascertain how Pal fared with Baroness Szechenyi. Indeed, he'd wanted, just once, to tell duty to go to hell and ignore everything and everyone except for the sleeping woman who held both their futures in abeyance, but his rank and position couldn't be ignored. He wasn't surprised to find Erzsebet seated by Bibi's bedside, but the presence of Akos did give him pause. His valet spoke in a whisper before he was fully in the room.

"The baroness is resting well, Your Grace. Her breathing is even, and she doesn't appear to be in pain."

Incapable of speech, he just nodded. The sight of Bibi dressed in a snowy-white nightgown, with her long, blonde hair brushed and arranged over her shoulders, and her form so very, very still, was too close to his last sight of Margyth. His stomach clenched, and he fell to his knees beside the bed and reached for her hand. "Leave us." When he tore his eyes away from his bond mate to reinforce his command, the room was empty.

His prayers, like his emotions, were all over the place. He prayed for her recovery. He prayed he'd given her enough of his blood to affect the change. He prayed he wouldn't have to write her father to tell him he'd gotten his daughter killed before he died. He prayed Margyth and her mother suffered terribly in hell, and then he prayed he wouldn't join them there for petitioning the gods with such a horrible wish.

Janos was shaken awake and caught his shout of outrage just in time to keep it from leaving his throat. He'd fallen asleep with his head on Bibi's bed, and when he jumped up to face whoever dared disturb him, he was surprised to find no one to upbraid. It hadn't been Akos who'd dared disturb his vigil, he discovered when he had to bend down to identify the culprit who was offering him a drink and a reprimand.

"Mind your temper and drink this. Do not turn away from me, Your Grace. You need the sustenance and you need a bath. I will not have the baroness's first scent of you to be off-putting. You smell of horse. I know you don't want to tear yourself away from her side, but you are not helping her. You need to bathe, eat, and rest so you can be strong when she wakes."

"Will she wake up, Erzsebet?"

"She will, if the gods listen to all of the prayers they are receiving from the entire Rackoszi estate. Honestly, Your Grace, I am encouraged. Her breathing is not labored, and this morning, there is a very faint amount of color in her cheeks."

He spun around to check for himself if his housekeeper spoke the truth. Was there a bit of color to her soft, soft cheek? Or was it incipient fever from her wound? He kissed Bibi's forehead and drew breath easily again when her skin was cool to his lips. No fever, then. Perhaps the gods wouldn't take her from him...this day at least.

Janos was surprised to find he'd been led back to the

Master Suite. He made up his mind then and there he would not sink the castle into the gloom one encountered when mourning a loved one. Everything would remain normal.

However, on one matter, he would not budge. There wasn't anyone in the castle strong enough to make him return to his bed to sleep each evening. He could not be apart from his bond mate, for it was her wordless lullaby of inhale, exhale that would give him any hope of sleeping. His valet didn't offer the least resistance to his demand for a mattress to be placed next to her bed but walked from the room in search of brawny hands to carry it.

The day of the Szechenyi double funeral dawned sunny, and he was forced to wear his smoked glasses and carry an umbrella like most of the women in the funeral cortege. Sometimes, his sun allergy could be damned emasculating, but not to attend the funeral would have given rise to too much gossip.

Janos caught the eye of his stable master, who'd asked permission to attend to pay his respects since he witnessed the accident. He drew an easier breath when the man nodded his silent confirmation none of the Rackoszi hands would speak a word of why Margyth had visited him on the day of her accident.

Pal Anton, as a Szechenyi relation, joined him at the head of the procession when the priest gave a nod and the line of mourners formed up. Pal would walk with him behind the wagon drawing the caskets to the Szechenyi family plot. At least the route would take them through a cherry orchard. It would offer welcome relief from the sun.

"Whew, damned hot day already. At least it is a bright one. I don't think Margyth would appreciate getting rained on." Pal used his hat to fan himself.

"Perhaps it's hot to give Margyth and her mother a foretaste of the heat they can expect in hell." He was instantly sorry. "Forgive me, I shouldn't have put my thoughts into words, but I couldn't help noting the Szechenyi plot will presently contain two suicides and a would-be murderess. Not exactly hallowed ground, is it? I should have kept my tongue behind my teeth, but my nerves are wound a little too tightly. Bibi hasn't awakened, and no matter how many people tell me she doesn't appear to be failing, I can't help worrying."

"Apology accepted. I think you've done an admirable job of keeping a stiff upper lip. I'll treat you to a double whisky after the funeral. God knows we'll both need one by then. Come, Your Grace, let's put paid to this sad affair and attend the good father as he performs the graveside ceremony."

Pal was spot-on in his calculation of the need for a drink, a very generous double whisky. If he had to listen to one more sincere offer of sympathy over Margyth's death, he'd show everyone how an Atlantean dealt with grief. Everyone who'd heard of the broken engagement offered their condolences and tried to cheer him up. They were under the misapprehension he was doubly grief-stricken to have Margyth break his heart and then die suddenly. If they knew the sense of relief he'd felt after both occurrences, they'd be looking at him with horror rather than sympathy.

He was about to ask Pal for another drink when he felt it. He felt Bibi open her eyes, and he dropped the glass from nerveless fingers.

"What is it, Your Grace? Are you unwell?" Pal rushed to the prince's side to catch him should he faint. He'd been close enough to the prince to notice him lose color and sway where he stood.

"You must excuse me, Pal. I have to return to the castle. I'm not ill, I am, in fact, most extraordinarily well. I'll explain later."

Pal shrugged his shoulders at the inquisitive looks the mourners gave him as Janos threaded through them with such a show of speed, it left them openmouthed and whispering about the viceroy's hasty exit. Pal didn't bother correcting the woman standing next to him when she opined the prince was too overcome by grief to stay another moment.

***

Bibi, thinking herself alone in the room, stopped her silent admiration at the loveliness of the Mistress Suite when she was surprised by Erzsebet's exclamation.

"Oh, bless all gods, you are awake. Are you experiencing any pain?"

Bibi took a moment before responding to the question to assess her health. There was no pain at all, just a fizzy sensation like she had enough energy to climb a mountain. She was also curious to know why her nose could smell the flower arrangement on the far side of the room or the acrid residue of ashes in the hearth. It was as if she'd been reborn with all new internal organs.

When she made to sit up, Erzsebet moved to her side and gently propped her up. "I'm fine, Erzsebet. Have I been unconscious so long my wound no longer pains me?"

Her unthinking mention of being wounded made her brain catch up to the present, and she frantically batted the covers away to discover nothing more than a beautifully embroidered nightgown. Patting her chest, she felt no thick bandages or even any tenderness.

"Please, Princess, calm yourself. Your wound has healed. The prince was able to give you sufficient blood to stop the bleeding and heal your wound."

She noted the prince's absence from the room for the first time. "Where is Janos? Is he...?" And with the question, she became frightened. She had no idea what had occurred after she'd been shot.

"Be at ease, Princess. His grace is well, but he had an engagement he couldn't avoid this morning. I'm sure he'll be along very soon, very, very soon. Once he senses you are awake, nothing will keep him from your side. Would it be impertinent if I asked why you put yourself in harm's way for Akos?"

Bibi was taken aback by the question. The truth was, she hadn't stopped to consider the result of her actions, but even with the advantage of hindsight, her reaction would've been the same. "Janos told me if the baroness had been successful in killing his wolf familiar, it would have ended his life. When Margyth boasted she'd learned from her mother's books, killing his valet, or his *pomme de sang,* would kill him, I had to act. Even though I know the prince does not use Akos in

368

such a way, I just couldn't take the chance there might be a kernel of truth in her wild conjecture. And I just couldn't let her hurt Akos. I know Janos values him as a friend.

"And I have a question for you. Why do you keep addressing me as princess?" She was treated to a rare smile from Erzsebet.

"Ah, thank you for explaining your actions. As to your title, you are the prince's bond mate. It is the same as marriage in its permanency. Here, drink this, Princess, you will need the strength to greet your bond mate for the first time."

She was reluctant to take the glass of Janos's special wine the housekeeper was offering her. Cognizant the wine's added fortification was bull's blood, she hesitated to take a sip until her nose caught the bouquet, and her instantaneous hunger made her newly acquired fangs descend. The wine was the best thing she could ever recall drinking. It was exotically spiced, and she caught top notes of cherry, and...and lavender, of all things.

She would've returned the empty goblet to Erzsebet but found herself quite alone until Janos burst through the door and ran to her bedside to wrap her in his arms and kiss her thoroughly. She had to grab his face in her hands to stop the exuberant greeting. "Janos, stop for a moment and let me breathe. I want you to tell me what I've missed since I've been asleep."

"What do you remember, *kincsem*?"

She felt a trifle guilty for having her question wipe the joyous smile from Janos's face, but she wanted to understand why she felt so...so damned good, given the circumstances sending her to bed in the first place.

"Before I lost consciousness, Akos warned you not to say the bonding words. What is bonding, and why was your valet so insistent you not give them?" She wanted to withdraw the question when the prince's face, previously wreathed in smiles, reversed itself into a frown.

"For my kind, when two people love each other, they bond. The man gives the bonding words, and the woman accepts by taking his blood. Once she has drunk from him, they are joined eternally. If one dies, the other will follow shortly."

Bibi inhaled in dismay. While the words were hazy, she definitely recalled putting her mouth to the prince's bleeding chest. "Oh, Janos, why would you do such a thing? You had to be aware I was dying from Margyth's bullet."

"Because, my beloved, you once told me you would only accept a man who would give everything for you. What greater gift is there to give than a life? If you had died, I would have followed, and we would be together in eternity. After dispensing with my vow to Baron Szechenyi, to have you snatched away at the hands of his daughter would've killed me as efficiently as another of Margyth's bullets. Quite simply, we both live or we both die. I want it no other way and I'm hoping you feel the same because I can't undo what's been done. The quantity of nanos in your blood makes you as much an Atlantean as myself, Bibi."

She stared in wide-eyed awe of the prince. He'd actually given his life into her safekeeping. How did one respond to something so gallant? Misunderstanding her silence for disapproval, he started to apologize.

"I'm sorry, Bibi. I did ask your permission to save you. There wasn't time to explain about the transfer of nanos and becoming an Atlantean. Margyth, damn her evil soul, really was an excellent shot. You were dying, so I acted quickly. Giving you the bonding was selfish of me, but there was a better than average chance you wouldn't survive, and I couldn't bear living without you."

She held her arms open, and he filled them immediately. "You silly, silly man. I am not upset about being saved, and I'm not upset about the bonding except to say I wouldn't have wished for your death."

She debated asking the next question, but her innate curiosity wanted to know. "What is to become of Margyth and her mother? Will they be punished for the suffering they've caused?"

"They have already been punished. I buried both of them today." At his bond mate's distressed hiss, he rushed to explain. "No, I didn't kill them. When Margyth ran from my bedroom, she tried to remount her horse but she'd abused it too heavily on her ride here, and it wouldn't let her mount. She grabbed Shadow and tried to make her escape using your horse. As you can imagine, she was unable to stay in the saddle and was thrown and broke her neck. I assure you, I felt it was quite a fitting punishment for her crime."

"And Baroness Szechenyi? How did she die?"

"Some would believe she was unhinged when she took her life because she couldn't bear such another loss so soon after her husband's. For myself, I think she did so to stir up more trouble. She drank poison and left a suicide note condemning me as a vampire and responsible for her and her daughter's deaths. Pal and I agreed, however, to tell people she had suffered a heart attack."

She was instantly outraged on her bond mate's behalf. "I'm glad the harridan drank poison. She saved me from having to kill her if she'd been successful in harming you."

"I have a question of my own, my ferocious protector. Why did you leave me? I was awakened by Akos to be told the woman I loved was riding away with Pal Anton. Were you unaware of how much I loved you? Did I do such a terrible job of conveying my feelings the night before?"

Bibi blushed in remembrance of the night of passion. "No, Janos, you didn't. I left because I loved you so much I wanted you to find the woman who would complete you." At his protest, she held up her hand to silence him. "I'd followed you and your godfather out to the terrace after the dance. I wanted to bid him goodbye and thank him for the commission to paint his and Queen Lucretia's portrait. I'd just stepped outside when your godfather told you, as your engagement to Margyth had been broken, he would find you a woman of your own kind. I lost my nerve and withdrew before I was noticed."

"Ah, what a comedy of errors. Had you stayed but a moment longer, you would have heard me tell my godfather I was finished with letting other men choose a bride for me. I told him I was going to marry you and no one else, and there wasn't a damn thing he could do or say to make me change my mind. My mistake was in not giving you the bonding words that evening. Not being able to see the future, I believed we would have time to get to know one another, and I could explain what it meant to be bonded so as not to frighten you. Knowing you will die if your bond mate dies is not something to just spring on someone."

She laughed, and Janos's face relaxed. "No, I don't suppose it is. Are there any other aspects of being a bond mate I should know?" She sharpened her focus on the prince's face when he started to look sheepish. "Out with it," she demanded.

"Bonded males are jealous creatures. If you want your friend Pal Anton to continue to draw breath, never ever try to tease me by trying to make me jealous. He'd be dead before he ever returned your affection. I'm sorry, but it's the God's honest truth. It is one reaction I would not have time to reconsider. And I am telling you this because Pal Anton will be our new neighbor. I've signed over the Szechenyi estate to your hussar friend."

"So glad to know. I'll be sure to just shake hands with the man when next we meet. Pal will be so disappointed." She guffawed at the rumbling growl Janos gave and punched his arm. "I will behave myself. You have no reason to worry, you are the only man I'll ever want to flirt with.

"My next question is, are we really married? I know we are bonded because I can feel the connection in here." She rubbed her chest. "Although I wouldn't have wanted them to witness the circumstances of our particular bonding, is it silly of me to want a special dress, and my family present as you said the bonding words, or have a following ceremony in a church?"

"My darling, Bibi, if you want to be married in Notre Dame Cathedral and invite all of Paris, I will arrange it. Yes, Princess Beatrix Celine Rackoszi *nee* Horthy, we are married according to my kind, but we can have a ceremony more in keeping with your beliefs."

She pretended to consider the outrageous offer. "I don't think Notre Dame is for me, unless they let me ride Shadow down its long central aisle. No, just a small ceremony in the castle with my father and aunt and uncle in attendance will suit me fine."

"And I will invite my parents, Viktor and Irenka. I think they will be relieved to know I have finally found the love of my life."

"Your parents? I thought they were...?"

The prince chuckled at Bibi's consternation. "Dead? No, my parents aren't dead. They serve King Alexandru as hunters."

"Hunters? What do they hunt?" Her question had the prince so overtaken by mirth she had to wait for him to compose himself.

"Oh, my dear, they hunt vampires. No, don't blink at me as if I've finally lost my mind. It's true. You must've forgotten me mentioning this, but sometimes one of our kind does go mad and kills a human by taking too much of their blood. The mad creature must be hunted down and killed before it can find another victim. As you can imagine, the rare occurrence of vampires among us is dealt with silently and swiftly, despite what Baroness Szechenyi's books would have you believe."

At the mention of blood, she experienced a moment of disquiet, and Janos hadn't missed it.

"You have a question concerning feeding, don't you? Ask away, my darling, there will be no secrets between us."

"Will I have to drink from humans? I know you've done so, but didn't you tell me our kind can fare just as well with animal blood?"

"I will teach you how to drink from a human in case you find yourself in extremis and without access to any other source. But one of the advantages of being bonded is you will always be able to drink from me. Part of the bonding words are, 'As your blood sustains me, mine will be the rock of your well-being.' You will take my blood and I yours when we make love, and there is always the fortified wine. Are you hungry, Bibi?"

She felt the blush rush up from her toes. "No, not hungry at the moment. Erzsebet gave me a glass of wine right before you burst into the room. Oh, stop giving me such a disappointed frown, you rascal. I have another question."

She gave him a toothy grin when he groaned in mock weariness. "Since Atlantean blood runs in my veins, I won't be able to ride on sunny days, will I?" She sighed. "I'm going to miss being able to ride whenever I want."

Janos placed a smacking kiss to her forehead. "How is it a woman who breeds horses for a living doesn't know how good their night vision is? Soon you will see just as well as they do at night, and we'll ride wherever you care to after sunset.

"*Kinscem*, I've had some time, in between moments of abject fear you would not recover, to consider what our life would be like if you did. I'm going to build you the largest indoor ring ever constructed. It will surpass even the one at the Spanish Riding School. You will be able to train horses on any day, and you won't have to worry about bright sun. Also, you mentioned putting Anubis to stud, and I've been talking to the stable master about it. He suggested raising a breed called Shagya for either cavalry or carriage use. What do you think?"

"Shagyas? The very same breed the emperor and his imperial guards ride? They're beautiful and elegant and quite brave."

"They are indeed, and with my cousin being the Emperor of Austria-Hungary, I'm sure I can borrow one of his Lipizzaner mares to entice Anubis to do his duty. With such a line, I'll bet we can surpass the Horthy-Baranyi farms in a few years."

Bibi frowned. "Yes, we could, but as a Horthy, I am reluctant to compete with my family."

Janos groaned. "I'm sorry, my dear. I'm an idiot. We don't have to raise horses at all. It was just a suggestion."

"And a very good one," Bibi countered. "You said the Shagyas can be trained as carriage horses, so why don't we concentrate on the carriage trade and leave the cavalry business to the Horthys? The Rackoszi stables can concentrate on breeding Shagya carriage horses, my darling husband."

He placed delicate kisses on each of her cheeks. "You don't know how many nights I've gone to bed pining to hear the word husband fall from your lips. But you haven't told me where you want to go on our honeymoon. Since you are uninterested in Paris, what about Greece or Italy?"

Bibi snuggled down into the bed sheets and grinned up at Janos. "Hmm, Greece and Italy are much too sunny. I'm thinking we should honeymoon in the Misty Isles. I've always wanted to visit rainy, foggy London. But I think we should not stay very long. I don't think we can afford to neglect the other breeding program I have in mind for too long."

"Other program? Weren't we going to breed Shagya carriage horses?"

"We *are* going to breed Shagyas, beloved, but I want to begin breeding the Rackoszi line first. I know the Rackoszi stallion comes from nonpareil Atlantean bloodstock, and the Horthy mare has similar credentials."

Janos's nostrils flared the moment he picked up her bonding scent, and she was amazed to find herself equally affected, and wet with arousal, when his signature scent of fresh-cut pine and leather wafted to her.

She had mere seconds to squeal in unabashed glee as the Rackoszi stallion ripped every single piece of clothing from his body in his haste to mount her. But when he sank his fangs into her neck and drove his seed far into her womb, Bibi exulted in the certainty this bloodline would be the best the Rackoszis would ever produce.

An Excerpt from Basket Case by C.L. Hadyn

Chapter One

A rivulet of sweat escaped from the small reservoir in the hollow of his throat, ran down the valley between his pecs to follow the narrow channel between his abs, and joined the moisture already pooled in his navel. The array of lights for the photo shoot fried his skin as he held the pose. When another small stream of perspiration ran down his spine and made its way between the cheeks of his ass, Gunner North broke the pose and allowed his discomfort to show on his face.

His friend and fellow model, Fletcher Wright, had warned him this photographer was an unholy blend of sadist and genius, but, after seeing samples of the man's work, he realized his cachet would skyrocket if one of the full-page ads, featuring his own face or body, hit the cover of *GQ* or *Esquire*, or one of the big women's magazines.

"Shiiiit! What kind of expression is that?" The photographer's howl of outrage seemed to increase the heat in the room. "Your grimace ruined my shot. Lose the ugly expression, and, this time, I want to see sexy bedroom eyes and a pouting mouth. Not an 'I stepped on a dog-turd' one.

"Makeup," the photographer bellowed. "Blot him down. He looks like he came in last in the Rio Marathon. His sweat is screwing up my lighting."

He gave the man, who reminded him of a weasel-faced elf, a placating smile, and when the photographer returned his attention to his camera, rolled his eyes at Fletcher, who shook his head and gave him an *I told you so* grin. Their silent communication went unnoticed by the elf, who fiddled with the placement of the lights.

He understood the source of the elf's Rio dig. While he got his Arctic-blue eyes and platinum-blond hair from his Norwegian father, his mother, a full-blooded Spanish Basque, was responsible for his Latin swarthiness. No need for tanning beds. An hour or two in the sun and he tanned a deep, rich, mahogany. He credited his naturally tan skin for making him much sought after for winter shoots. His 6'3" frame and six-pack abs were added career assets.

Although his modeling agency was based in New York City, he was here in Miami for an ad premiering a new line of designer underwear. Yesterday's beach volleyball scenario, featuring himself, Fletch, and the next superstar female model named Jamyson, gave him the idea he'd have some fun in the sun—until the photographer moved everything indoors when the wind kicked up. He cared more for his precious camera lenses than the comfort of his models. So now the three of them, despite being clad in various styles of underwear, were being sweated to dehydration by the artificial lights. The photo-shopped backdrop of a Florida beach added insult to injury.

Yeah, this is so much more fun than being in fresh sea air. He bit the inside of his cheek to keep another grimace from giving the photographer apoplexy.

He suffered through the blot down. Sometimes, he had to disassociate himself from being touched so familiarly by strangers, both men and women. The woman presently dabbing a towel between his legs had her face level with his dick, and when she raised only her eyes and bit her lip in blatant lust, he blushed, adding to his natural coloring.

Sorry, sweetie, I'm taken. He moved into place and resumed the pose.

"No, extend your front leg another inch, and turn your right shoulder toward me." Two more rapid-fire clicks of the camera and the photographer yelled, "Let's take a break. I want to look at those last shots."

Gunner straightened and stretched to relieve his total body kink. He had the fleeting hope the Marquis de Sade was finished for the day, but hope died a fiery death when the evil elf disappeared behind the camera again and sent his minions scurrying by calling for the other models.

"Get Jamyson on the set. I want to do a shot with her and Gunner and Fletcher, and damn it, dry North off again while I reset the cameras."

While he'd worked with Fletcher Wright several times, this was his first time with Jamyson, a model who only used one name, and she, like himself, was closing in fast to catch up with Fletcher as one of the top paid models in the fashion world. The next shot called for her to model a sports bra and a boy-leg matching panty with the designer's name quite visible at the waistband. The same logo was equally visible on his and Fletcher's single item of clothing.

The photographer wanted Jamyson to drape her hands over his shoulder and give the camera a smoldering look, while he assumed an aloof, *I have beautiful women clinging to me all the time* expression. The elf positioned Fletcher on the ground at their feet, a volleyball placed in a strategic spot, with the designer's logo visible should anyone care to lift their eyes above the prop. His trademark sardonic grin would make the shot.

They held their poses until...right before the photographer clicked the shutter, Jamyson threw herself in front of him, and he caught her in his arms with a surprised laugh.

Looking down at her, he spoke softly, not even trying to keep the laughter out of his voice. "Oh, you're in for it. Our sadistic master is going to have a cow for you ruining his shot."

Jamyson stood and kept herself between him and the photographer, who ceased spluttering to examine the unchoreographed shot. "You owe me. I actually like you, as opposed to most of the male twits I usually work with."

Fletcher cut in to ask, "Surely, I'm not included on your twit list, love?"

She smiled and blew him a kiss. "Never, Fletch. You never hog the camera when shooting with others."

"I hate to break up this love fest, but why do you think I owe you for messing up the shot?" He tried to move away from Jamyson but stopped when both she and Fletch moved with him.

"You owe me for deigning to serve as your modesty shield, and you owe Fletch for coming up with the way to do it."

He quirked his eyebrows to signal he still didn't get her meaning.

Jamyson leaned in and spoke for his ears only. "Your briefs are soaked enough to be transparent, and your, um, smaller head is stealing the shot. Mind you, I in no way find the display offensive, as it is quite lovely to behold. However, if I can see it so clearly, the camera will bring it into maximum focus. Too bad you aren't modeling black briefs. I think you need to call for a fresh pair."

This time, she let him move away from her to call for a wardrobe change. But he never got the chance to make the request because the photographer clapped his hands and danced toward them in short, bouncy steps.

"Unbelievable, I got the perfect shot! This is going to be a full-page ad for sure. Jamyson, what a brilliant move. You even kept the logos visible.

"It's a wrap for the day. North, I have all the shots I need from you. I'll work with Jamyson and Wright tomorrow and you again at the end of the week. Great shoot, Gunner. The designer is going to really like these shots."

Gunner swept the female model into his arms and gave her a kiss on her lips, eyes, and both cheeks. "My fair damsel, I do indeed owe you one. How can I ever repay you?"

"You can agree to another photo shoot with me. As I said, I like working with you because you let *me* be the prima donna."

"Done. I'll tell my agent to expect the request."

As she moved away, Fletch approached. "So, are you going to spend your days off wooing the fiery redhead you showed up with?"

He grabbed Fletch around the neck and deliberately messed up his perfect hair. "That's the majority of my plan. The rest is to try out for a professional jai alai team."

Fletch broke the hold and gave him a *you fried your brain under the hot lights* look. "Have you told Stephanie of your plans?"

"Nope, and I'm not going to until I find out whether or not I make the team." He stopped speaking when Fletch started to shake his head. "What?"

"I might be wrong, given I have no experience with dating the opposite sex, but Stephanie doesn't strike me as a sports fan. She's too high-maintenance to be found sitting in the bleachers, cheering for her man, especially if it means giving up her corporate law position in New York City."

"All valid points, Fletch, but the men of my family can be

very persuasive." Gunner patted the small, ring box bulge in his pants pocket then hugged his friend goodbye. "Don't let the Marquis de Sade fry you beyond redemption tomorrow, and good luck on the *GQ* shoot you have coming up," Gunner called to his fellow models and left the studio.

As he inserted the key into the ignition of his rental car, he glanced at the thin Omega watch on his wrist and grinned when he discovered his early release put him two hours ahead of schedule. He and Steph could take a dip in the pool of the five-star Miami hotel, courtesy of the designer who'd contracted for this shoot, or catch the sunset on the beach, and then go to dinner at one of Calle Ocho's edgier restaurants. They'd end the night with a few hours of dancing. One of the reasons Stephanie agreed to meet him in Miami was for the salsa dancing. They were both extremely good at it.

Stephanie, a striking redhead, was the flame to his candle. She set his life on fire when they managed to balance their schedules. They were as compatible in bed as they were on the dance floor, plus Steph knew a lot of movers and shakers in the Big Apple. And when she let her luxuriant mane of hair free of its corporate French twist, she stunned any man who got close enough to notice her unusual chocolate eyes. Though he was the professional model, the camera loved Stephanie equally well. They made a head-turning pair whenever they walked into a restaurant or club, and his ego swelled whenever he caught envious looks from men as they strolled along New York City streets.

This evening he planned to ease into telling Stephanie of his accomplishment, and it had nothing to do with modeling.

He'd been chosen for a tryout to play professional jai alai in Miami. He grew up with the popular Basque sport and played on an amateur team during college in Bridgeport, Connecticut, close to his alma mater, Yale University. He surmised a scout for one of the professional teams from Miami caught one of his games and kept him in mind, for he recently made an offer for a tryout.

While he loved the camera, jai alai offered more of a personal physical challenge with the added bonus of warm weather, tropical breezes, and sandy beaches. And while jai alai fans were conspicuous by their small numbers—as compared to the faceless millions who saw his face or body in a magazine—the rabidity of their devotion to the sport's top scorers appealed to the ego he usually kept buried. His agent scoring this photo shoot put him in the right place at the right time, and he would definitely show up for the tryout. After all, no model stayed youthful-looking forever.

His stomach grumbled, reminding him it contained nothing more substantial than whatever remnants remained of the soy latte he drank on his way to the shoot location. He grinned at the thought, if he actually made it on a professional team, playing jai alai would likely keep him in physical shape without having to follow a model's calorie-free diet. Not needing to diet placed one more check in the plus column for his decision to leave modeling.

So far, the only bump in the road to his new career was getting Stephanie, a high-powered corporate tax attorney, to move from NYC to Miami. The purchase of a glittering three-carat diamond ring should be more than enough to override any objection she might have. As he rode the elevator up to their suite, he anticipated her show of love and support for his career change, especially after he slipped the designer ring on her finger. He also intended to use this free week to show her the best of what Miami had to offer.

Stephanie blew his happy thoughts and amorous plans for the week sky high as soon as he opened the door to their luxurious suite.

"Ah, damn, I wanted to be gone before you returned from your shoot today."

He studied the suitcase by Stephanie's feet. "Gone? Where are you going, Steph? Has your office requested you return to work?"

"No, I'm not going back to work, at least not right away. I'm taking a cruise."

"A cruise?" He couldn't get his head around the fact his girlfriend booked a cruise, and he wasn't invited.

"Another reason why you and I won't work, Gunner, is you never check your email or texts. I texted you this morning and told you exactly why I'm breaking it off between us."

"Texted me?" He sounded like a learning-challenged parrot because his brain wasn't moving as fast as Stephanie's mouth. He needed more clarification if he had any hope of understanding why he seemed to be the villain here.

"Okay, you texted me. Should I read it now, or do you have time for a face-to-face explanation of all the things you find wrong with me?"

He flinched at the loud snap as she extended the carry handle of her Louis Vuitton suitcase and turned to face him.

His heart dropped to the floor at the cold, disdainful look she gave him.

"While you were out on your photo shoots this week, I had enough of sitting around waiting for you to return. I also have had enough of this"—she swept her arm toward the large ocean-view window—"this humidity. I haven't had a decent hair day since we got here. And then there's the sand. I hate sand. I hate the feel of it between my toes, and I especially hate it in the crotch of my bathing suit. And salt should be on the rim of a margarita glass, not on my skin. Cuban cooking gives me heartburn, and half the people here don't speak English, for God's sake. It's like we're in a third-world country, not the United States of America."

Stephanie wheeled her suitcase to the door and delivered the *coup de gras*. "While sitting around the pool, trying to avoid freckles and skin cancer, I met someone who has his own yacht. He speaks English, not Spanglish, and he's invited me to help him take his toy on a shakedown cruise from here to San Francisco. We may even get around to checking out the boat while we're at it."

He opened his mouth to attempt reasoning with Stephanie, but when she held up her hand in a stop gesture, he desisted.

"If you think I don't know about your plan to play a silly game, think again. You received a phone call from someone whose command of English was execrable. He wants you to report to the jai alai stadium, or whatever they call it, for tryouts with the team tomorrow afternoon. He also wanted to know if you brought your baskets along. He called them something else, but a basket was as close as I could picture from his explanation when I told him he needed to speak English or find a translator.

"Gunner, your modeling made you somewhat appealing as a partner, but playing a game no one has ever heard of does not. A professional football player would be acceptable in my estimation, not a man who plays with a basket strapped to his hand. Sorry, not acceptable at all."

He blinked, and Stephanie vanished. If the door slammed, he failed to hear it. His entire system switched into self-defense mode when Stephanie's incandescent anger started to filet his already sensitive skin. Her sudden disappearance from his life had him pondering why such attacks didn't come with a warning sign like a rattle on the end of a snake, or a display of fangs, or frothing at the mouth. Maybe, if she had telegraphed her intention to rip his heart out, he wouldn't be standing in the middle of his luxurious suite with a gaping chest wound. She hadn't even given him the courtesy of administering anesthesia prior to performing his unscheduled open-heart surgery.